About the Author

Sue Fortin was born in Hertfordshire but had a nomadic childhood, moving often with her family, before eventually settling in West Sussex. She is married with four children, all of whom patiently give her the time to write but, when not behind the keyboard, she likes to spend time with them, enjoying both the coast and the South Downs between which they are nestled. Sue is a member of the Crime Writers' Association.

@suefortin1
www.suefortin.co.uk

Also by Sue Fortin

Closing In
The Half Truth
The Girl Who Lied

SISTER, SISTER

SUE FORTIN

A division of HarperCollins*Publishers*
www.harpercollins.co.uk

HarperCollins
PUBLISHERS
Since 1817

Harper*Impulse* an imprint of
HarperCollins*Publishers* Ltd
The News Building
1 London Bridge Street
London SE1 9GF

www.harpercollins.co.uk

A Paperback Original 2017
1

Copyright © Sue Fortin 2017

Sue Fortin asserts the moral right to
be identified as the author of this work

A catalogue record for this book
is available from the British Library

ISBN: 9780008215651

This novel is entirely a work of fiction.
The names, characters and incidents portrayed in it are
the work of the author's imagination. Any resemblance to
actual persons, living or dead, events or localities is
entirely coincidental.

Set in Birka by Palimpsest Book Production Ltd., Falkirk, Stirlingshire

Printed and bound in Great Britain by
Clays Ltd, St Ives plc

FSC
www.fsc.org

MIX
Paper from
responsible sources
FSC™ C007454

FSC™ is a non-profit international organisation established to promote
the responsible management of the world's forests. Products carrying the
FSC label are independently certified to assure consumers that they come
from forests that are managed to meet the social, economic and
ecological needs of present and future generations,
and other controlled sources.

Find out more about HarperCollins and the environment at
www.harpercollins.co.uk/green

I couldn't possibly write a book about sisters
without dedicating it to my own sister, Jacqueline.

Although, I feel I must make it clear,
this story is nothing like our sisterhood!

Chapter 1

Sometimes the coldest places are not in the midst of winter, when your breath puffs white, your feet are numb from the cold and your fingers stiff and frozen. Sometimes the coldest places are in the warmth of your own home, surrounded by your family.

I'm lying in a bed that isn't mine; that much I know. The mattress is firmer for a start; there is no familiar softness that I'm used to. I tentatively stretch out my fingers and can hear the faint rustle of cotton against plastic. A waterproof mattress, I decide.

I can feel the weight of the bedding on top of me. Again, the comforting softness of the fibre-filled duvet is absent. A heavier weight, one less supple, rests over me. I raise my finger and move it against the fabric. More starched cotton. The extra weight, I assume, will be a blanket on top of the sheet. I make a little bet with myself that it is blue. Then, on second thoughts, I hedge my bets. It's blue or green ... possibly white. I have been hedging my bets a lot lately. It will definitely be cellular, though. That, I am certain.

So far I have made a conscious effort not to open my eyes.

On the other side of a closed door I can hear indistinguishable voices of people as they walk by, the sounds growing softer and louder like a lapping tide against the shore.

The faint smell of antiseptic loiters in the air, mixed with the odour of a sweet, sterile environment, confirming my thoughts as to where I am – in hospital.

There's another smell. One I'm very familiar with. It's the scent of his aftershave, which has a fresh aqua zest to it. I bought it for him for our anniversary last year, eight years married. It's an expensive designer one but I didn't mind the cost. I never minded spending money on Luke. It's called *Forever*. Turned out it was a rather ironic name. I'm not sure if I'll be buying him an anniversary present this year. Or any year, now.

'Clare? Clare, can you hear me?' It's Luke's soft voice, close to my ear. 'Are you awake, Clare?'

I don't want to speak to him. I'm not ready. I don't know why, but some inner sense is telling me not to respond. His fingers curl around mine and I feel the pressure of his squeeze. I have a strange urge to snatch my hand away. But I don't. Instead, I lie perfectly still.

I hear the swoosh of the door and cork-soled shoes squeak and squelch across the linoleum floor. 'Mr Tennison?' a quiet voice asks. 'There's a police officer outside. He'd like to speak to you.'

'What, now?'

'He wants to speak to Mrs Tennison too, but I've told him that's not possible just yet.'

Luke's hand slips from mine and I hear the scrape of the chair against the floor. 'Thank you,' says Luke.

I listen as he and the nurse leave the room. Luke can't have closed the door properly as I can hear quite clearly the conversation now taking place.

'DC Phillips,' announces the police officer. 'Sorry to disturb you, Mr Tennison. We were hoping to interview your wife, but the nurse said she's not regained full consciousness yet.'

'No, that's right,' replies Luke. I can hear the protectiveness in his tone and imagine him standing taller, squaring his shoulders. The way he does when he is asserting his authority. The way he does when we argue.

'Maybe you could help us.'

'I'll try.' A hint of irritation accompanies his words now. If you didn't know him, you probably wouldn't notice it. I've heard it a lot recently; more than I care for.

'How would you describe your wife's disposition leading up to yesterday's ... er ... incident?' says Phillips.

Incident? What incident? I try to recall what the detective can be talking about, but draw a blank and am distracted as Luke answers.

'Disposition?' he says.

'Her mood. Was she happy? Sad? Preoccupied? Anxious?'

'Yes, I know what disposition means,' cuts in Luke. This time the irritation in his voice is clear and I imagine him frowning at the detective as if to say *what sort of idiot do you think I am?*

I dredge through my mind to recall just how I have been feeling recently. Sad, angry and frightened all wash up on the shore of my consciousness but I can't pinpoint why.

Luke doesn't answer the detective straight away. He is probably mulling this question over. He will no doubt want to give the right response. If the small ripples of my memory are to be relied upon, a response that I feel I will probably have to counter later.

It's coming back to me now, not exact memories but sensations and not in drips, but in waves. I can feel the anger resurfacing. I wonder if Luke is thinking of how angry I have been; how stubborn I've become? What was it he'd called me during our last argument? Oh yeah, that's it, *fucking nuts*. Will he tell the detective that? And if he does, will he tell the detective what has driven me 'fucking nuts'?

'Clare, she's been under a lot of pressure lately,' he says at last. 'She's had a lot on her plate.'

'In what way?' probes the detective.

'She's had a difficult time adjusting to some changes in her personal life.' Or, as I guess Luke is thinking, *none of your fucking business*.

My mind is racing. What does Luke mean by 'changes in my personal life'? What the hell has happened that has caused me to end up in hospital?

The answer doesn't come immediately, but in those few moments a feeling of foreboding seeps into the room, creeps towards me and wraps itself around my body. I feel cold and goose bumps prick the skin on my arms. I know something bad has happened. I have done something so terrible my mind is trying to block it out. Something that goes against everything I am.

I, Clare Tennison, am a good woman. I am a successful career woman; a partner in Carr, Tennison & Eggar Solicitors.

I am a caring daughter to my mother, Marion. I am a devoted mother to Chloe and Hannah. I am a loving and supportive wife to Luke. I am a school governor, for God's sake. Clare Tennison doesn't do bad things.

So why this fear, coated with guilt? What have I done?

I don't want the next second to come. I try to fight it off, to suspend time, to be ignorant of this knowledge. Living in dread, however awful, is preferable to the alternative – living with the knowledge of what I have done.

Bang!

It's back. I know, with the clarity of looking through highly polished glass, exactly what I have done.

I can see my hands on the wheel, steering the car, as I navigate the lanes back to the house. The pointer on the speedometer darting up and down, the rev-counter needle rising and falling as I change gear and manipulate the vehicle around the narrow lanes. Hedges blur in my peripheral vision and trees whoosh by in a haze, reminding me of a smudged watercolour painting.

It takes a moment before I register her there. Right in front of my path, as over a tonne of metal bears down on her. How have I not seen her? It's broad daylight. It's a clear day. There is no sun ahead to blind me, no rain to fuzz my vision. I have a totally clear view. She appears from nowhere. Stepping right out in front of me. I scream. I hit the brakes. I can hear the squeal of the rubber on tarmac as the tyres bite into the ground. I yank the steering wheel to the left, trying to miss her. It is all too late.

The clear and undeniable memory of the thud makes me

feel sick. I think I'm going to vomit. Instead, I let out a sound from deep within me. It comes up from the pit of my stomach, wrenching my heart out along the way. By the time it escapes my throat, it is a roar of undiluted pain. Too vicious for tears. My body involuntarily curls into the foetal position. The plaster cast prevents me from moving my left arm but my other hand covers my bandaged head, as if I am bracing for an emergency landing on a doomed flight. I feel a line tug at my arm and something rip from my hand.

The next thing I am aware of is the scurrying of people around me. Nurses. The first with soothing, but firm, words telling me to calm down; everything will be all right. A second one with sterner words telling me not to struggle. That I am pulling out the drip. That I will hurt myself. And there is Luke's voice too. Strong yet gentle.

'Hey, hey, Babe,' he is saying, using the pet name I haven't heard him say recently. His tone is like the one he uses with the girls when they are upset, when Chloe has fallen over and cut her knee or like the time when Hannah discovered the tooth fairy wasn't real. 'It's okay. You're okay. Everything is going to be okay. I promise you.'

I want to believe him. I really do, but how can I when I am responsible for such a terrible crime? My body heaves and another sob erupts.

The last thing I remember is the cool sensation of liquid oozing into the back of my hand, smarting as it travels up my arm. I feel my body relax and then everything around me fades away as my mind drifts back to where this nightmare began.

Chapter 2

Six weeks earlier ...

For a moment I think I don't have to get up for work. It feels as if it should be a lazy, summery Sunday. The late September sun is still clinging onto warmer days and a small refreshing breeze billows the gauze curtain every now and then. I always like sleeping with the window open; it gives me a sense of being free.

But as I rouse further into the conscious world, the heavy weight of reality wraps itself around me. I'm anything but free. Particularly this time of year, as we move closer each day to my sister's birthday.

I roll over and cuddle up against a still-sleeping Luke, seeking comfort from just the touch of another human. I check my watch and groan as I realise it's a Monday. I stretch my arm back and switch off the alarm. I don't know why I bothered setting it. I haven't needed it these past few days as sleep has not been a good friend to me.

I think of Mum and how, now we are in the month of September, she looks a little longer at the calendar each day, silently marking time, anxiety levels rising as we stumble towards the twenty-eighth, just another forty-eight hours away. I should be used to this pattern by now. Twenty years on, it's been practically a lifetime for me and yet I never quite anticipate the level of emotion this date evokes. It's almost that, as I've grown older, the absence of my sister has grown bigger, more profound, hurting harder, cutting deeper. I feel my mother's pain and my own.

So many times over the years I've wished Alice was here, and not just because of my mother's own heartbreak but, selfishly, because I have always yearned for the black cloud hanging above us to disappear. As a child, I didn't want to be known as the sister of the girl whose dad took her off to America and never came back or the daughter of the heartbroken mother. I wanted to be Clare Kennedy. I just wanted us to be normal.

I still do.

There's half an hour before I have to begin the military operation of getting the girls moving for school and nursery. I snuggle a little closer to Luke. Sometimes, it's as if he can absorb my sadness and anxiety, soaking it up so my feelings can move freely; no longer repressed.

I feel Luke stir and I tighten my arm across him, hugging him gently. After eight years of marriage and two children, we have never grown bored of each other. Luke rolls over and kisses me.

'Morning, Babe,' he says, without opening his eyes, then rolls back over. 'Night, Babe.'

'Hey, fella, you're not getting away with that,' I whisper in his ear as I run my hand down his body and pull him back towards me.

Luke opens one eye and looks at the clock. 'Jesus, Clare, it's only five-fucking-thirty.'

'Never mind all that ...' I kiss away his protests.

I feel his mouth curve into a smile and he opens his other eye. 'Now, that is cheating.'

He rolls over and swamps me in his arms and for a while I allow myself to forget the challenges of real life.

'And how are we all this morning?' says Mum coming into the kitchen as Luke and I are hurtling around getting breakfast ready and taking it in turns to direct the girls on what needs doing next. Okay, Hannah is rather more capable at seven years old and only needs encouraging, Chloe, however, at just three, needs the more hands-on approach.

We live with my mother, Marion, in the house I grew up in. Initially, we had moved in with her when Luke was a struggling artist and I had just taken my first appointment in chambers straight out of uni. Some would say that Luke still carries the struggling artist hashtag. By that, I actually mean my mother. Although, in her defence, she is very tolerant.

Since then the girls have come along and we have expanded to five of us in one house. Just as well The Old Vicarage, in which we live, is large enough to give Mum a separate living room to us and Luke his own studio in the annexe of the house.

'Seems silly me rattling around in this big house on my own and the house prices around Brighton are ridiculous,'

Mum had said. 'Besides, I'd like the company. I'll be close to the girls as they grow up and you two would have a built-in baby sitter.'

And she was right. All these points made perfect sense and were very pragmatic, but we both knew the real reason why I could never move.

Not after what happened.

And, in truth, I wasn't sure I could, even if my heart wanted to go along with Luke's preferred choice of buying a place of our own, to make memories of our own, my conscience wouldn't allow me. I couldn't leave Mum all alone.

'You can't keep yourself hostage to something that happened in your childhood,' Luke had said one night as we lay in bed, his last-bid attempt to change my mind.

The truth was, though, I could, and I had always known it would be like this. The only way it would change would be if Alice came home.

'Come on, Chloe,' I say, picking her up from the play mat. 'Let's get you to the table. Morning, Mum.' I sit Chloe on the booster seat and push her closer to the table. I take the bowl of Weetabix Luke hands me. He is whistling as he makes a pot of tea.

'Someone's happy this morning,' says Mum, helping herself to a slice of toast. The smile might be there, but the flat tone of her voice is a betrayal.

Luke and I exchange a look across the kitchen.

'It's a beautiful morning, the sun is shining and I have my lovely family around me. You included,' Luke says enthusiastically. He gives Mum his best cheery smile in an effort lift her mood. Mum looks away, her eyes automatically seeking out the calendar on the wall and coming to rest on the date two days ahead.

'I need to go into town today,' she says. 'I've got to pick something up from the jewellers.'

We all know, without Mum having to spell it out, that it will be Alice's birthday present. Never a birthday nor a Christmas has gone by without Mum buying a gift for when Alice comes home. Never *if*, always *when*.

'I'll give you a lift in, if you like,' says Luke. 'We can drop Chloe at nursery and go on straight from there.'

'Oh, would you? That would be kind,' says Mum. This time her smile is warmer.

I like that Luke and Mum have a good relationship. It makes living together so much easier. Most families we know sit down in the evening for their quality time. In the Tennison household, breakfast is our family meal. I quite often don't get home from work until early evening and it's too late for the girls to eat. I appreciate it isn't Luke's ideal arrangement, but he always makes an effort for us all.

'So, Hannah, you have recorder today,' I say in between guiding cereal-laden spoonfuls into Chloe's mouth. 'Luke, you won't forget, will you? I think the music book is still on top of the piano in the sitting room.'

'Er ... yes, all under control,' says Luke. He leans over to Hannah and whispers theatrically, 'Have you got the music book?'

Hannah flicks a glance in my direction and whispers back to Luke. 'No. I thought you had it.'

I pretend not to notice Luke put his finger to his lips and then mutter, 'Leave it with me. I'm on the case.' Hannah gives a giggle and when I look at Luke, he winks at me and then makes a big show of being engrossed in pouring the tea.

'Oh, God, would you look at the time?' I hurriedly shovel another spoon of Weetabix into Chloe's mouth. 'I have the Monday rumble at nine with Tom and Leonard. Come on, Chloe, eat up.'

Luke reaches over and takes the spoon from me. 'Off you go,' he says. 'Don't want to keep the boss waiting.'

'He's not my boss any more,' I say, gulping down the cup of tea Luke has poured, wincing as it burns my throat. 'I'm an equal partner now, remember.'

'Hmm, well, you still act as if Leonard's your boss. And Tom, come to mention it. Make them wait for you for a change.'

Ignoring the comment, I kiss the girls goodbye. 'Have a lovely day, my darlings. Hannah, don't forget to hand in the swimming gala permission form to your teacher. Chloe, be a good girl at nursery. Mummy loves you both very much.'

'Love you too,' says Hannah, blowing kisses as I manoeuvre around the table.

'Uv you too,' repeats Chloe through a mouthful of soggy wheat and milk.

'Don't forget, you're going home with Daisy after school,' I remind Hannah and then to confirm Luke has remembered the details, add, 'Pippa's picking Hannah up and giving her tea. She'll drop her back later.' Pippa is one of the few friends I have in the village. If our daughters hadn't become friends themselves at school, then I probably wouldn't have got to know Pippa. I give Mum a peck on the cheek. 'See you later, Mum.' Then I bend down to kiss Luke. His hand slips around my waist and he holds the kiss for a moment longer than necessary.

'Go get 'em, Babe, at your rumble in the jungle.' He lets me go and shadow boxes Ali style. 'Float like a butterfly, sting like a bee.'

I feel a surge of love for this man. He is my best friend, my lover, my husband, my everything. I give Luke a high-five before I grab my jacket from the back of the chair and head out of the kitchen and down the hall, where my briefcase and sack trolley are waiting, the latter loaded with a pile of files I had brought home for weekend reading. I pause at the door and call back over my shoulder. 'Don't forget ...'

'The recorder!' chorus Hannah and Luke before I can finish.

The drive into Brighton from the village where we live takes about thirty minutes on a good day and today is one of those days. The radio is on and I push thoughts of Alice to one side, singing along to the song currently playing. It fades out and the DJ announces the next song up is their retro record of the week. Within the first few bars, I recognise the song: 'Slipping Through My Fingers' by Abba. In an instant, my heart twists and tears spring to my eyes with such ferocity that for a couple of seconds the road ahead of me is a blur. This song always reminds both Mum and me of the Alice-shaped hole in our lives. The blast of a horn from another car jolts my mind back to the road. My heart lurches again, but this time fuelled by adrenalin as I realise I've run a red light.

'Shit!' I stamp on the brakes to avoid hitting an oncoming car. If my car had tiptoes it would be on them and I'm grateful for my BMW's reliable ABS. I hold my hand up in an apology to the other driver, who thankfully had the foresight to stop too.

I'm no lip-reader but I'm pretty sure he's used every uncomplimentary noun in the urban dictionary to describe me and my driving. I mouth 'sorry' before he puts his car into gear and tears off, squealing his wheels as a final gesture of anger.

A few minutes later I pull up into the car park of Carr, Tennison & Eggar, Solicitors, without any further incident and take a moment to check my make-up in the rear-view mirror. It wouldn't do to go into work with black streaks of sodden mascara down my face.

Feeling composed, I grab my stuff and push open the door to the converted 1930s detached house that are our offices.

'Morning, Nina,' I say to our receptionist as I hold open the door with my hip and yank the sack trolley through.

'Good morning, Clare,' she replies, giving me a second look, which tells me I wasn't successful in disguising the tears. However, she doesn't pass comment. 'Tom and Leonard are already in the conference room,' Nina informs, nodding towards the frosted double doors across the hallway.

I check my watch. It's eight-fifty. They can wait while I lug the files down to my office and repair my make-up.

Sandy, my secretary, is at her desk in a small reception area that leads to my office. 'Morning, Sandy. Nice weekend?'

'Morning, Clare. Yes, very nice, thanks. You?'

'Good, thanks,' I say avoiding eye contact, hoping she won't notice the remains of my make-up. I have a mirror fixed to the inside of the tall filing cupboard and hastily wipe the patches of mascara with a tissue.

'Ah, there you are.' From the mirror, I see Leonard bustling into the office. He pauses and his astute eyes quickly assess me. 'You okay?'

'Yes. Well, I am now.' I wave the mascara wand over my eye lashes.

'Sure?'

'Positive. Was on the receiving end of a bit of Monday-morning road rage.'

'Your fault?'

My hesitation gives me away as I consider whether to be honest or not. Leonard pushes the door behind him and comes over to me. 'Are you sure you're okay? I am aware of the significance of this week.'

I dip my head, feeling embarrassed at not just my lack of concentration but that my feelings are closer to the surface than I care to admit. I look back in the mirror at him with what I hope is confidence as I brush my eyelashes one final time. 'I'm fine. Honest. But thank you,' I smile and Leonard pats my arm in a fatherly gesture.

'Now, come along, we're waiting for you,' he says reverting to his brisk businesslike manner. 'I can't be long. I have that blasted Mrs Freeman coming in.'

'Mrs Freeman?' I try to recall the name from our last Monday rumble as I shove the mascara into my jacket pocket and track Leonard out of the office.

'Yes. Sour-faced old moo she is. Can't believe her husband

put up with her for so long. Must have been bloody good in the sack, that's all I can say. Mind you, you'd want a bag over her head – and one over your own, just in case hers fell off.'

'Leonard, you can't say things like that.' I can't help smiling at Leonard's comment despite my attempt at a reprimand. Leonard is terribly honest, to the point of being rude, but it has provided no end of amusing anecdotes over the years.

In the conference room, Tom is standing at the French doors that open onto the private gardens. He turns as he hears us come in.

'Ah, excellent, you found her.' He smiles over at me and takes his place at the table. 'I've already got you a coffee,' he says. 'Good weekend?'

'Yes, thanks,' I say sitting down. Really I want to say no; it was pretty shit and Mum seems to be struggling more than ever as another birthday looms but I refrain. Tom knows the score. He's been through the whole range of emotions with me over the years. I divert the conversation. 'We missed you at the barbecue. Everything sort itself out in the end?'

'Yeah, sorry about that,' says Tom. 'Isabella decided that she needed Lottie back for some party or something for her gran.'

'Isabella still playing up?' says Leonard, taking his seat at the head of the table.

'From time to time. Usual thing. Money. The latest is a skiing trip to New York she wants to take Lottie on. It's going to cost a bloody fortune and I'm the one having to stump up the cash for it. What happened to a week at the seaside?'

'That's what you get for no prenup,' says Leonard, opening

his notebook in front of him and taking his Mont Blanc fountain pen from his inside pocket. 'How do you think I survived three divorces?'

I exchange an empathetic smile with Tom. Leonard is always banging on about the importance of a prenuptial agreement.

'Lesson learned,' says Tom.

'And you can still get a postnup agreement yourself,' says Leonard, not looking up from his notebook but tapping his pen on the desk in front of me.

'Well, Luke and I have done great so far. I think we'll manage just fine,' I say, feeling slightly prickled at his remark.

'Hmm. Pride before a fall and all that.'

I don't answer Leonard. It is a pointless conversation and one we will never agree on.

Tom looks up and throws me an *are you okay?* look, to which I give a brief nod. Then it's down to business.

Our weekly Monday-morning rumbles, as they are fondly referred to, is the opportunity for each of us to bring the other two up to date with cases we are working on. Leonard is pedantic in his approach to work and sees this exercise as a crucial element to running a tight ship. That way, if any one of us is off work, the other two can easily step in to take up our cases. It's also a nice way to start the week and maintain the family feel of the firm, something that all three of us cherish.

The rumble over and my morning appointment finished, I go down the hallway to see if Tom is free. His secretary is hammering away at the keyboard. She looks up and gives me a brief smile but continues her work. Tom's door is open; an indication he's free. None of us is so pretentious that we need announcing.

'Knock, knock,' I say, as I go in. 'Fancy a coffee?' I raise the two coffee cups I'm holding.

'My favourite words,' says Tom.

Tom and I had gone through university together, graduating at the same time. We had a brief relationship during our student days, but once we graduated we decided it was best left behind the doors of Oxford. We were ambitious, with careers to pursue, but, even so, after parting company we kept in touch and it was me who gave Tom the heads up to the job at the firm a year after I had joined. Both Tom and I were offered partnership at the same time.

I back-heel the door closed behind me and take a cup over to Tom, placing it on his desk. 'So, now we're alone, do you want to tell me what really happened yesterday?' I sit down in the chair opposite him.

'That's what I like about you,' says Tom. 'No preamble. No small talk building up to point of your visit. It's straight for the jugular.'

'And if I did beat around the bush, you'd only say "get to the point".'

'True,' says Tom, nodding. 'Really, though, there's nothing to tell. Isabella going into full jealous-bitch mode once she realised I was taking Lottie to yours. You know … the usual.'

I frown. 'It's pretty pathetic she's still behaving like that. You've been divorced, what, three years now?'

'You know Isabella,' says Tom.

Sadly, I do. Secretly, Tom always blames her Italian blood for her hot head and jealous streak. I'm always grateful for Luke's more laid-back approach to the past between Tom and me.

'Anyway, enough of me. What about you?' says Tom.

I pause, considering for a moment if I should feign innocence and claim I don't know what he's talking about. I dismiss the notion. Tom is all too aware of the significance of the date looming like a black cloud on the horizon. I give a sigh and blow out a breath.

'Tricky week. Mum's mood is dipping by the day. I was hoping the get-together at the weekend would perk her up a bit. She did try, bless her, but I could tell her heart wasn't in it. Leonard was very good, he spent most of the afternoon fussing around her and she seemed to appreciate it.'

'I meant you. I know what your mum's like; it doesn't get any easier for her.' He takes a sip of his coffee before speaking again. 'You, Clare, how are you? Are you sleeping okay? You look pretty tired.'

I give a half-hearted laugh. 'Is that your way of saying I look like shit?'

'Your words, not mine.'

'If you must know, I'm not sleeping that great. This time of year always unsettles me. I'm never sure how I feel or how I should feel. Am I upset for Mum? For Alice? Or for me? Last night I was thinking, do I miss Alice or is she just missing? She's been gone for so long now, her not being here is part of my life.' I look out of the window, pausing for a moment. 'You know we hired another detective firm earlier this year to try to trace her but, as usual, nothing.'

'You wouldn't think it would be so difficult to find someone today,' says Tom. 'A bit different when we were trying to find her.'

'I suppose she could have a different surname. I mean, she's in her early twenties, she could even be married. Perhaps she doesn't want to be found.'

'There is always that. Have you said as much to your mum?'

'It's been mentioned. Mum's not stupid, but she doesn't feel she can let it go until she knows one way or another. It's just so hard to deal with the level of emotion swirling around at this time of year, it frightens me. I don't know how to channel it.'

Tom's phone rings. It's an internal call.

'Hello, Nina. Yes, she's here,' he glances up at me while he listens to the receptionist. I watch his face grow serious. 'Okay, thanks ... Hi, Luke, it's Tom. I'll just pass you over.'

He holds out the receiver to me. Luke never rings me at work. The rule is only in case of an emergency.

I snatch the phone from Tom's hand. 'Luke. What's wrong? Is it the girls?'

'No. The girls are fine,' says Luke, but I can detect the unease in his voice. I brace myself. 'Your mum is okay too,' he says, as if anticipating my unspoken question. 'Nothing bad has happened ...'

'What is it, then?'

'Your mum's had a bit of a shock. You need to come home.'

'A shock? What do you mean?' I look across the desk at Tom, as if he can somehow help.

He gestures to the phone. 'Want me to speak to him?'

I shake my head. Luke is talking again. 'Listen, Babe. Your mum's received a letter.' He pauses and I imagine him shifting uncomfortably on his feet. I can feel the tension through the phone line. 'A letter ... from Alice.'

'Alice?' I gulp for air.

'Yep, Alice.'

'Alice, as in my sister Alice?'

'So it seems.'

'Shit.' I'm already rising to my feet; my legs feel like jelly and I reach out a hand to steady myself against the back of the chair. 'I'll be right there.'

Chapter 3

Dear Marion

    I am sure this letter must come as a total surprise to you, or at least a shock. I've been debating for some time whether I should write and I have started this letter so many times only to scrap it and start again. I mean, what do you say to your mom when you haven't seen her for twenty years? I didn't know if contacting you was the right thing to do, but not contacting you seemed the wrong thing.

    You may wonder why I haven't written to you before, but up until recently, I've not had your contact details and it's not been something I've been able to discuss with my father. It was just something I knew right from an early age I wasn't to ask about. I was so young when I came to America, I only have a few fragmented memories of England, but the ones I do have are precious to me.

    I can remember baking cakes with you, those buttercream ones with multi-coloured sprinkles, and being allowed to lick the bowl afterwards. Being read a bedtime story, my favourite one was about a cat who didn't like fish. I have a strong memory of being pushed on a swing, squealing with delight as I begged to go higher and higher. I wanted to kick the clouds with my feet, which I imagined would be soft and squidgy like marshmallows.

I remember your smile, such a lovely smile. In my mind you laughed a lot and always wore pink lipstick. Not a bright, vivid colour, but a pale pink, which shimmered when you spoke. Sometimes, when I played dressing-up with Clare, you'd let us wear your lipstick. I would make an 'o' shape with my mouth, just as I had seen you do every day.

I've really tried to hang onto these memories, they have always been very special to me. My father didn't like me talking about England and as the time passed and the time apart from England grew, so did the distance in my mind. I don't know when I stopped thinking about my home in England every night, when the days in between those thoughts stretched into weeks and then into months but the memories have always been there, I just stopped visiting them.

I hope you can understand that I haven't ever forgotten you or Clare, I was just so young and my life was being steered in a different direction. I always secretly fantasised that one day I would find you or you would find me and now that I have, I hope so much that we can be in touch.

I don't know if you are aware but my father, Patrick, died last year and your address was given to me by my stepmom, Roma. She said it was the right thing to do, that she had always wanted me to be able to contact you, it's just that my father had prevented this. I don't know what happened between you and my father, as I say, it's always been a taboo subject. But whatever happened, I want you to know that I have always had this sense that I was very loved by you and, ultimately, this is what has convinced me to write to you.

I hope this letter isn't too painful – I'm sorry if it has opened up old wounds.

I would LOVE to hear from you and Clare, even if it's just to have closure for us all, although in my heart, I hope it will be more than that.

Your daughter
Alice
Xx

P.S. It wasn't until my father passed away that I found my birth certificate and realised that my name wasn't Kendrick as I thought, but Kennedy. It seems Dad changed our surname when we came over here and, as I've never had need of a passport before now, I've never been aware of this. It might also explain why you've not found me if you've ever looked for me. x

I run my fingers over the page, the piece of paper that has been touched by my beautiful little sister. The name change explains everything. No wonder we could never find her, we weren't looking for the right person. All along we had been giving the name of Patrick Kennedy to the private investigators. I remember one of them feeling quite confident he would find my father. Although Patrick Kennedy was an American citizen, the PI thought it would be easy to track him down. When he couldn't be found, the investigator had given the excuse that there were lots of Patrick Kennedys in America, given the number of Irish people who had crossed the pond, and that he couldn't identify the one we were looking for. God, I wish we had somehow known about the name change!

Thinking about it now, it makes sense. My father hadn't ever meant to be found. He must have planned it all before he left. I can't mourn his passing. How can I when I think of the pain he has put us through – put Mum through? What he did was unforgiveable.

My father had duped everyone and that was the mark of the man; nasty, spiteful and devoid of empathy. Still, it's no use tearing myself to ribbons about it now. We have a letter from Alice and that is the most amazing thing ever. Whatever he did I don't care about; I only care about the future

I look up at Mum and can see her eyes shining with tears. The lump in my throat grows bigger and in two strides I'm across the room, on my knees in front of her, hugging her. The tears flow as twenty years of anguish pour out of us like a tidal wave.

'Oh, Clare, she's come back to us,' says Mum through her sobs, her mouth pressed into my hair. 'We're going to get her back.'

I'm not sure how long we cling to each other but eventually I pull away. I smile at Mum and she smiles back. She cups my face in her hands and rests her forehead on mine. 'This is all I've ever wanted.'

'I know, Mum. I know,' I whisper. 'She's found us. After all that searching we've done, all those hours, days, months and years of heartache and now she's found us.'

Mum sits back on the sofa and I move myself from the floor to sit next to her. Mum takes the letter from my hand and flattens out the creases caused by our embrace. 'Kendrick,' she says and shakes her head sadly. 'If only we'd known.'

'Let's not focus on that, Mum. We can't change the past,' I say. 'What happens now is what's important.'

'I know and you're right. I just need a little time to digest that. You did note that bit about your father, didn't you?' Her finger points out the line.

'I saw that. He's dead.' I give a shrug. I have no feelings of attachment to the man Alice talks about. All I can remember is being scared of him and of his big booming voice, but I don't know him. I cannot grieve for someone I don't know. I don't remember caring when he left, I just remember caring that Alice had gone. To me, my so-called father has never been alive. Maybe that's why I attached myself so readily to Leonard, who was as close to a father as I was getting.

We spend the rest of the morning discussing how we're going to reply to Alice. We're both keen to let her know how much we have thought about her over the years and how much we have longed to hear from her and how much we love her. Have never stopped loving her.

'I'll draft a reply,' says Mum. 'And then I'll show it to you. You might want to add something yourself.'

'That sounds good. I'll give it some thought.'

Satisfied that Mum is now okay and over the shock, I head back to work. For once my mind can't separate work life from my personal life and throughout the afternoon, I find my thoughts pinging back to Alice and the letter. It's a good job

I have such a competent secretary, as I put the wrong names on a legal document and quoted the wrong settlement figure for a big divorce case. Sandy spotted both mistakes, thankfully.

'It's no wonder you can't concentrate,' says Tom as he walks out to the car park with me at the end of the day. 'I've hardly been able to think about much else myself.'

'Really?'

'Yeah, really. Alice being missing all these years has been such a big part of your life. By default, it's been a big part of my life too.'

I consider this for a moment. I suppose it has. I'd never thought of it that way before. 'Has it defined me?' I ask.

Tom purses his lips before he answers. 'I wouldn't say defined you, but it is part of you. You can't get away from it.'

'Suppose I can't.'

'Hey, you're over-thinking again.' Tom gives me a playful nudge of the shoulder with his. 'How does Luke feel about it all?'

'He was very quiet,' I admit, thinking back to earlier. Luke had pretty much sat in the chair observing. He had made cups of tea and given me a reassuring hug but, on the whole, he hadn't passed comment.

'How much does he know about what happened?'

'Everything. As much as you know. As much as I know. Dad took Alice off for a holiday and never came back. There's not much more to know.' Unexpected tears rush to my eyes and I silently curse myself for not being able to keep my emotions under control. I'm not a crier, or I never used to be.

Tom studies me for a moment and I feel slightly self-conscious under his gaze. He reaches out and draws me into him. The years melt away and it's like being back at university. It feels comfortable and familiar being held by Tom. Reassuring and safe. He drops a kiss on top of my head.

I jerk away, almost head-butting him as I do so. These are the wrong arms to be seeking comfort in. I take a step back. 'Thanks,' I say, not quite able to meet Tom's eyes. I rummage in my bag and hook out my car keys. 'I'd better get home and see what Mum's written. I've been thinking about it this afternoon. I don't want her to get too carried away and scare Alice off.' I'm waffling. Embarrassed by the old feelings that have paid a fleeting visit.

Tom pushes his hands into his trouser pockets. He has a small smile on his face and his eyes are dancing with amusement.

'What?' I say.

He gives a shake of his head and bends down to pick up his briefcase. 'Relax, Clare, it was only a friendly hug.'

'Yeah. I know that,' I say, feeling stupid for overreacting. 'My emotions are a bit all over the place this afternoon.' I give him a hug and a peck on the cheek, just like the sort we usually share. Good friends. Mates. Work colleagues. 'And that's to prove I know it.'

I arrive home and Luke is upstairs bathing the girls. He has a streak of yellow acrylic paint in his hair and a small smudge of blue across his cheek.

'You found a bit of time to get some painting done, then,' I say. 'How's it going?' I kneel beside him and trickle water down Chloe's back as she squirms and giggles in delight.

'Not too bad,' says Luke. 'Couldn't really get into it today. Might give it another go when these two terrors are in bed. Come on, Hannah, time to get out. Here's a towel.'

'Here, hold my hand,' I say, helping Hannah step out of the bath and wrapping a towel around her.

'Out. Out. Me out!' It's Chloe. She always wants to do what Hannah is doing. It reminds me of how Alice used to be. She would follow me around all day, asking to join in with my games or asking me to play with her. Most of the time I would, but I remember sometimes she used to annoy me. I wanted to be left alone. I would go off down to the bottom of the garden and hide from her. As usual, this thought makes me feel guilty. I've spent twenty years feeling remorseful, wishing I hadn't said no to her. Wishing I could somehow make it up to her. And now I have the chance to do just that.

Between us, Luke and I get the girls ready for bed. I sit with Chloe tonight and watch her drift off to sleep as more thoughts of Alice flood my mind. It's as if, by making contact, she has given me permission to revisit those memories.

I can see Alice in the garden. We're having a dolly-and-teddy tea party on a pink-and-white gingham tablecloth. We have picked some blackberries and raspberries from the vegetable patch. We know it's okay to eat those.

Then, for some reason I cannot remember, I pick a couple of mushrooms that have grown in the lawn and put them on the tea plates. When I next look up, Alice is eating one. I tell her off and think no more of it, but after we have finished playing, Alice goes indoors and is very sick.

In the end Mum calls the doctor, who can't explain it. I'm too scared to say anything. Dad will kill me if he finds out. When Mum sees the doctor out, I make Alice promise not to tell anyone about eating the mushrooms. Fortunately, Alice is fine the next day, but I've still never told Mum about the incident.

The bedroom door opens and a chink of light from the landing streaks through. It's Luke.

'You okay, Babe?' he whispers.

Taking one last look at Chloe sleeping peacefully, I get up and follow him through to our bedroom. 'What's Hannah doing?'

'She's downstairs with your mum, having some supper.' He pulls me into a hug. 'How are you feeling?'

'I'm okay. I haven't been able to stop thinking about Alice all day.'

'That's hardly surprising.'

'It's exciting but it's also a bit scary.'

Luke brushes a strand of hair back from my face. 'Don't take this the wrong way, but be careful. Don't go rushing in. I don't want you getting hurt.'

'What do you mean?'

'Well, it's been a long time. You don't know each other as adults. Sometimes these reunions don't always work out the way we expect.'

'You sound very negative about her.' I move from his embrace and begin undressing. I always look forward to getting out of the skirt and blouse of my working day and into my comfy tracky bottoms and T-shirt.

'Not negative, just cautious.' Luke goes to say something else but stops himself.

'What?' I press, pulling my T-shirt over my head. 'What were you going to say?'

'Nothing.'

'Yes you were. I can tell.'

Luke gives a shrug. 'You don't know her agenda.'

'Her agenda? What is that supposed to mean?' He's beginning to annoy me now. Why can't he share in my excitement and be happy for me? He knows what this means to Mum and me, so why the negativity?

'You don't know what Alice has been told about the family breaking up. She might have a totally different take on it all.' He lets out a sigh. 'Look, Clare, I'm glad Alice has been in touch. It's a part of you that has always been in pain, and if her coming back stops that pain, then I'm all for it. All I'm saying is, be careful, take your time and with any luck it will be a smooth ride.'

Luke goes downstairs, leaving me to think over what he has said. A small flicker of doubt begins to dance in my mind. What does Alice know about us? What has she been told? Does she remember anything of us? I think back to the day Alice left.

I was sitting in the living room, helping Alice colour, when I heard the beginnings of what I assumed would be a normal altercation between my parents.

As the argument rumbled on, I became aware my mother's voice had risen, not just in volume but in pitch. I couldn't hear her exact words, but I remember the sound as they were forcibly expelled, as if there wasn't enough room in her throat for them all to come out freely.

My father's voice, on the other hand, was so deep, it boomed through the walls. His voice grew louder. Even from the kitchen, it filled the living room with an ice-like quality. Cold and harsh.

I heard the door to the kitchen being flung open, the handle smashing into the wall. There was a crumbly groove there, from where the door had made similar contact many times before. My father's footsteps thudded down the hall towards the living room. My mother's pitiful crying followed him.

I retreated to the sofa, sinking back in to the depths of the cushions, seeking warmth from the folds of the fabric. I brought my knees up and hugged them tightly, burying my head in my arms. I shivered. I felt the cold.

Alice stayed on the floor, colouring in her princess book, seemingly oblivious to the storm heading our way.

Alice never felt the cold. She was warm. She was loved.

The door to the living room opened and my father strode in. My mother close behind.

I sneaked a look.

Her eyes were pink and wet. She made no attempt to brush away the tears streaking down her face. She didn't register me. She was pleading with my father.

'Patrick, please ...' She pulled on his arm. 'I really don't think this is a good idea. I don't even know where you're going.'

'I told you, to stay with relatives I haven't seen for years.'

'Which is exactly the point I'm trying to make. Why go back after, what, twelve years? It's not like your parents are alive or you have any siblings. Why can't we all go together, please ...?'

He turned to look at her. 'You know why.'

'But this is the ideal opportunity to do something together as a family. Not for you to go off with Alice, abandoning me and Clare.' My mother's voice broke and she wiped her eyes with the back of her hand.

'Enough! Stop being overdramatic, woman. I'm going on holiday and Alice is coming with me. That's all,' he said. His voice, by contrast, measured and hard. And then, as he turned to Alice, the look of contempt and loathing disappeared, replaced by a tender one of love. 'Come on, honey. Pop your coat on, there's a good girl.'

He held out Alice's red duffel coat to her. She hesitated for a moment. I think it was at that point she realised something was wrong.

'Is Mummy coming?' she said. 'Is Clare?'

'Just me and you, sweetheart,' said my father. He gave the coat a little shake. 'Now, please put your coat on.' Obediently, Alice stood up, slipped her arms into the sleeves and turned so he could fasten the toggles.

My mother rushed forwards, gathering Alice in her arms and burying her face in my sister's hair.

She kissed Alice over and over again, stroking her hair, holding her face and looking deep into her eyes.

'I love you, Alice. Mummy loves you so much.'

And then my father was pulling Alice from my mother's grasp.

'That's enough,' he said. 'Don't go upsetting the child.'

All the time, he never looked at me. I didn't want him to. If he saw me, he might want to take me too. I didn't want to go. I wanted to stay with my mother. I wriggled deeper into the cushions, squeezing my knees up tighter.

My father took Alice by the hand, leading her from the room. At the doorway, Alice hesitated. She looked at me and then at our mother.

'Bye, Mummy. Bye, Clare.' Her voice sounded so tiny.

I've often wondered whether she was really saying goodbye or whether she was asking us not to let her go. My mother hurried over to them and grabbed my father's arm.

'Ring me when you get there. Let me know where you're staying. You're back in two weeks, aren't you?'

My father didn't answer but shrugged her hand from his arm. 'Come on, Alice.'

I wanted to stop Alice from going. I wanted to stop him from taking her, but I was too scared to move. He might suddenly notice me. What if he wanted to take me away as well? I didn't even dare to turn my head as I looked out the corner of my eyes and watched Alice disappear.

Free from my paralysis, I launched myself at the window. I could see Alice climbing into the car. My father leaned in and fastened her seat belt. He closed the door before going around to the driver's side. I could see Alice's dark hair through the back window.

Something must have made her turn. She looked back at me, her blue eyes bore into mine. In that second I knew she wasn't coming back.

Alice knew it too.

Chapter 4

I didn't sleep well last night. I had woken up what seemed
like every couple of hours, tossing and turning, images of
Alice flashing through my mind mixed with images of my
father which turned into snakes and spiders. Neither creatures
I particularly like. At one point Luke had rolled over in a
semi-conscious state and stroked my head, mumbling reassuring words and telling me to try to go back to sleep. I
appreciated the gesture despite its ineffectiveness.

I'm already showered, dressed and giving Chloe her breakfast before anyone else surfaces.

'How are you feeling?' says Luke, coming over and dropping
a kiss on my head. 'You were pretty restless in the night.'

'Not great,' I admit. 'Don't say anything to Mum, though.'

'Don't tell Nanny what?' asks Hannah through a mouthful
of toast and jam.

'Don't speak with food in your mouth,' says Luke. 'And
some things aren't meant for little ears.' He gives a playful tug
on Hannah's ear lobe. She smiles through jam-coated teeth.

'That's lovely, darling,' I say and pull a face in her direction.
She laughs and I am pleased the question has been forgotten.

'How did your recorder practice go yesterday?' I ask, just to make doubly sure we are back on safe ground.

'It was okay. We're learning a new song.'

'What's it called?' I wipe Chloe's mouth with the napkin. 'There we go, darling. All gone. Well done.'

Hannah's answer is lost as my attention is snatched away at the sight of my mother coming into the kitchen. The first thing I notice are her eyes. They have been dull and sad and if you looked close enough, you could see pain etched in the back of them, reflecting the pain in her heart and the scars in her memory.

Today, however, there is no dullness, her eyes sparkle like I have never seen them do so before. In fact, I think this is the first time I truly appreciate the phrase. They practically illuminate the room, exuding warmth and happiness.

'Good morning, my darlings,' she says, sitting down at the table. In her hand she holds a piece of paper. 'It's my letter to Alice. Would you like to read it?' The question is just a formality, there being no doubt in her mind that I do want to read it. She passes it over before she even finishes her sentence. 'It's just rough. I'm going to write it out neater this morning. Had you thought about enclosing a small note yourself?'

'I'll write it today. It seems strange that I'm actually going to be writing to her after all the years of imagining it.' Mum and I share a smile, one that is coated with excitement and happiness.

'That's great,' says Mum. She nods at the letter. 'Read it, then.'

My darling daughter Alice
Where do I begin? I can't tell you how happy I am to receive your letter. Happy seems such inadequate word to describe how I feel. I'm truly elated. Thank you so very much for finding me, I've been waiting for you ever since that day you were taken to America. Just waiting. It's like a dream come true.

We, that's Clare and me, have tried to find you. Clare has searched all over social media. She even hired private investigators several times but we didn't know about the change in surname. What happened between your father and me was such a long time ago, I hardly think about it – all I've ever thought is about you. It's a long and complicated story and one probably best saved for another day, when we can talk to each other face to face. Oh, how I long to hold you, my darling beautiful daughter, to hug you, to see you, to hear your voice, to find out all about you. I have no greater wish in my life than to see you, please say you will come and visit. I will pay for your travel and you can stay here, in your home, your own bedroom. Or I could come to America and visit you there. Whatever you want to do, my dearest sweet daughter, just let me know.

There is so much to tell you and so much I want to know about you.

I love you.
Mum xxx

'It's a lovely letter, Mum. But, you know, Alice included her email, why don't you email her? It will be quicker.' I pass the letter back.

'But having something that Alice has touched herself is so precious. I thought she might feel the same about having something real and tangible from me,' says Mum. 'Besides, I hardly use my email account. I'm not even sure I know what my password is any more.'

'We could easily reset it,' I say. Mum looks doubtfully at me. 'Or, I suppose, we could just set up a new email account for you.'

'You could Skype her, Nanny,' pipes up Hannah. I look over at my daughter, who has clearly been taking in much more of the conversation than I realise. Although, I don't know why I'm surprised, she's a bright thing. I smile at Hannah.

'What?' she says. 'We use Skype to speak to Nanny Sheila and Granddad Michael.'

'Is that where you can see each other on the screen?' asks Mum.

'That's right, when we speak to Luke's parents,' I say. Mum pulls a face and I laugh. 'You don't fancy that, then?'

'Oh no, I don't think I'd like that. I'd have to make sure my hair was done and I looked half decent. I could stretch to an email,' says Mum. 'Can't you do it from your account?'

'I suppose so, although Alice might prefer to know she's emailing you direct.' I make a note of Alice's email on my phone and take a last sip of my tea before checking my watch. 'Look, I've got to get to work. We'll talk about it later.'

Mum looks thoughtful and says, 'I was hoping Alice would

enclose a photograph of herself. I'd love to know what she looks like now.'

'Maybe she wanted to test the water first.' It had crossed my mind too, but I hadn't wanted to say anything to Mum. 'Why don't you send her some photos of us when you write back?'

'Yes, I was going to do that. Luke, would you be able to scan them for me?'

'Of course, Marion. Just let me know which ones and I'll do it, no problem,' says Luke.

I kiss him and whisper a thank you in his ear. 'Have a good day, you gorgeous girlies,' I say, giving both Hannah and Chloe another kiss. Some days, leaving them is easier than others. I love my job as a solicitor, it's something I have always wanted to do and something I have worked so hard to achieve. And for the most part, going into work isn't a chore, it's something I revel in. But there are other days when it is incredibly hard to leave my family. I know Hannah and Chloe will be looked after properly and they don't miss out on anything. It's no different to what it would be like if Luke was working in an office and I was at home. But, sometimes I have pangs of guilt about leaving them and moments of self-indulgence when I wish I was the one chivvying them along to brush their teeth or to put their shoes on. I don't resent the roles Luke and I have carved out; it works for us as a family, but I do have secret desires every so often to be the one who works at home.

I did once suggest to Leonard that I worked from home two or three days a week but he made his feelings clear on that idea.

'When you're working, you need to be focused on your work and nothing else,' he said. 'At home it will be too easy to be distracted, no matter what your best intentions are. Not only that, but if something urgent comes up, I want you here, in the office, at the coal face.'

Even when I had protested that I could be at the end of the phone or email, he wouldn't budge. In fact, he had been even more demonstrative, his years in the courtroom coming into play. He had questioned my ability to work with him and whether I would make a suitable partner after all. It wasn't often I was on the receiving end of his sharp tongue, but I definitely came away licking my wounds that day.

I'm still brooding over leaving the girls when I arrive at work. I hurry down to my office, smiling and greeting the receptionist but not breaking my stride. I'm not in the mood for light chit-chat with anyone.

'Hi, Sandy, all okay?'

'Morning, Clare, Yes, everything's fine.'

'I'm going to be working on the McMillan case notes,' I say. 'I need a good couple of hours without any disturbances, so if you could just take messages and I'll deal with everything this afternoon.' I smile at her as I breeze through.

I close the door to my office behind me, knowing this is an unspoken sign to Tom and Leonard not to disturb me. I splay out the files to the McMillan case on my desk and study the papers in front of me.

It's a tough case and Leonard has put me forward to deal with it, saying it would do me good to have some more experience with company law. McMillan is also a drinking pal of

Leonard's and I have a feeling Leonard put me forward to show off in the same way that parents show off their children by getting them to perform a song, a dance or count to ten in French. I'm performing for him so he can bask in the glory of having nurtured my career and so people can pat him on the back and say how well he's done.

Internally, I had baulked at the prospect of representing one of Leonard's acquaintances, especially in company law, which is Tom's forte more than it is mine. Externally, I knew better than to let the enormity of the task show on my face.

McMillan is a well-known local businessman who has political ambition, so any blemish on his character he wants removed by litigation laser treatment. In other words, I'm to make sure not only does he win the case of unlawful dismissal brought about by a former barman at the club he owns, but I'm also to ensure he comes out of it with not a speck of dust or dirt on or around him.

'Don't even think about saying no,' Leonard had said as he had passed over the files. 'You're perfectly capable of dealing with this. The right outcome will do the firm the power of good.'

'No pressure, then?' I had joked with half-hearted enthusiasm.

Leonard had looked me dead in the eye. 'There's every pressure, Clare. Every pressure, so make sure you win.' He had paused in the doorway and turned to me. 'Unless, of course, you don't think you're up to it.'

I hadn't faltered. 'Of course I'm up to it,' I had said. I could read the sub-text. If I wasn't up to the case, then I wasn't up to the job and, therefore, by default I wasn't up to being a partner in the firm.

I work steadily on the case for the next two hours when, despite my instructions that I wasn't to be disturbed, there's a knock on the door and Leonard appears in the doorway.

'Just wanted to make sure you're still alive,' he says coming in and closing the door behind him. 'Sandy said you're working on the McMillan case. How's it going?' He nods towards the papers and law books spread out in front of me.

I sit back in my chair, dropping my pencil onto the desk. 'Not too bad. Difficult, as we expected. It doesn't help that the other party have come up with a witness now.'

'Well, then, we need to come up with a witness too.'

'There isn't one. McMillan isn't the most popular of bosses, as it turns out.'

'Find one.'

'I'll do my best,' I say, aware that there is little conviction in my voice, and instantly regret letting that show. It's not the sort of trait that makes one a convincing lawyer in court.

Leonard hasn't missed it either. 'Don't give me any banal platitudes,' he says. 'Find a witness. I don't need to spell it out to you, do I?

'Of course not.' I rearrange the papers on my desk to avoid eye contact with him. It's no wonder he is one of the best lawyers in town, known for his ruthless streak in the court-room. It can be intimidating just being in the same office as him and that's when he's on your side.

'McMillan is ambitious, not to mention influential,' says Leonard. 'It will do well to keep him sweet. You do know what I'm saying?'

'Yes. Yes, I do.' Of course I do. McMillan puts a lot of business the firm's way. He has negotiated a company law deal for Leonard, which has bolstered Leonard's pension fund, and which was agreed over several glasses of malt at the private club of which they are both members.

'Good. I know you have a lot going on. I spoke to your mother earlier and she brought me up to speed with the news about Alice. But leave all that at home. Compartmentalise your life. It's the best way.'

'I know. That's what I'm trying to do.' It irks me slightly that Mum has already spoken to Leonard about Alice. I know she and Leonard are old friends and he is fully aware of the situation, but it makes it all the more difficult to keep my personal life out of the work place when those two things cross over.

'So, winning the McMillan case – you know it will be a feather in not only the firm's cap, but in yours too.' Leonard turns to leave. 'You're my protégé, Clare, don't fuck up.'

Chapter 5

The girls are already bathed and in their pyjamas when I get home. It's been a long day and Luke is reading Chloe a bedtime story. I feel a little annoyed that he has already started and hasn't waited for me. I love reading to the girls at night. It's probably more for my own benefit, to ease my conscience, my atonement for not being there. Luke knows this and it almost feels like a punishment for being home late.

'Hey, there, precious,' I say in a soft voice as I go into the bedroom.

Chloe immediately extracts herself from the crook of Luke's arm and bounds across the bed. 'Mummy! Mummy!' She launches herself into my arms and I smother her in kisses. 'Daddy read story. Little bunny has lost balloon.' Her face takes on a serious look as she explains to me that the balloon was red and blew away.

'Oh, dear, poor bunny,' I say.

'Come on, Chloe. Settle back down now,' says Luke, pulling back the duvet and patting the mattress.

'I'll finish reading,' I say, slipping my jacket off and dropping it on the end of the bed.

Chloe bounces up and down on the bed. 'Mum-my! Mum-my! Mum-my!' she chants.

Luke gives a sigh and stands up, passes me the book and gives me a peck on the cheek. 'The King is dead. Long live the King.' He gives Chloe a kiss. 'Goodnight, sweetheart. Sleep tight.'

My guilt has now transferred from one of being late home to one of stealing Luke's time with his daughter.

When I go downstairs, Chloe asleep and assured in the knowledge that the bunny found his balloon in the end, Luke and Hannah are in the living room watching television.

'Mum not with us this evening?' I ask, sitting down next to Hannah on the sofa. Luke is sprawled in the armchair, his leg dangling over one of the arms.

'No, she wanted to watch some gardening programme in her own room,' he replies. 'I said you'd probably pop in and say hello later. There's some dinner there if you're hungry. Want me to warm it up for you?'

'No, I had a late lunch,' I say. 'I'll make myself a sandwich or something later. I've been working on the McMillan case today.'

Luke gives me a sympathetic smile and any tension over the bedtime story has evaporated.

'How was your day, Hannah?' I ask, hooking a strand of hair behind her ear.

'It was okay,' she replies, without looking away from the television. She laughs at her programme and, not wanting to interrupt her obvious pleasure, I don't enquire any further. There's obviously nothing to worry about or she would have said. Some days, a cross-examination over the school day isn't necessary, just being aware she is happy is enough.

'Did you scan those photos for Mum?'

'Yep, all done.'

'Thanks, love. Did she say any more about emailing?' I pick up my phone and log onto the email account I created for Mum to use.

Luke shrugs. 'I think she really wants to write a letter.'

'But it will take at least five days to get there.'

'What's the rush? Just let your mum do it the way she wants to. Having a bit of breathing space is probably a good thing.'

Luke is right, of course. There is no rush. The more I think about it now, in the relaxed atmosphere of home, the more I think it's better. We all need to tread with care. We're all entering into a new relationship with people we don't know; all we know is the memory.

I glance over at Luke. His attention has already returned to the TV. Hannah is just as engrossed. 'I'll go and see Mum.'

I make a cup of tea for both myself and Mum and knock on the door to her private sitting room. I balance the tray in one hand, so I can turn the door knob with the other.

'Oh, hello, darling,' she says, as I come in. 'Ooh, cup of tea. You've timed it perfectly, my programme's just finished.'

I place the tray on the small coffee table and take the seat opposite. It's a bright and airy room, the high ceilings giving it a sense of space and grandeur. Mum's furniture wouldn't look out of place in one of those glossy lifestyle magazines, where they interview the Lady of the Manor. It's traditional and elegant. Rather different to our family living room, which is all big squishy sofas and tactile throws and rugs, a bit of a mish-mash but homely.

'Did you write the letter to Alice?' I ask, sitting down in the winged-back armchair, which is covered in a rich burgundy velour.

'Yes, it's there on my desk.' Mum nods towards the Edwardian bureau by the window. 'I've left it open so you can pop your letter in too. Have you done it yet?'

'Not yet. I'll get on with it after I've drunk my tea.'

'Okay, well, make sure you do. I don't want Alice to think we're not replying to her.'

After our tea and chat, I say goodnight to Mum and, taking the letter with me, retreat to our family sitting room. I put Mum's letter on the table, along with my phone.

'What's that?' asks Luke.

'Just the letter from Mum to Alice. I'm going to add mine tonight.' Hannah yawns as her programme comes to an end. 'Come on, I'll take you up. Say goodnight to Dad.'

I hadn't realised how tired I was. One minute I'm sitting in the chair beside Hannah's bed, listening to her tell me about how some boy in her class got his name on the board and then got sent to the head teacher. The next, Luke is gently shaking my arm, whispering to come to bed.

'You fell asleep,' he says, guiding me out of the room and closing Hannah's bedroom door behind him. 'You've had an emotionally exhausting few days. It must be catching up on you.'

'I need to write to Alice first,' I say, following him out onto the landing. 'I'll be up as soon as I've done it.'

I go back downstairs to my study. It's a small room at the front of the house with a small desk, bookcase and shelving. Nothing too fancy. It's a handy space if I need to work on anything in the evenings or weekends, although I try to avoid that whenever possible.

I sit at the desk and take a sheet of writing paper. Despite Leonard's warning about keeping home and work life separate, throughout the day I've been thinking about what to say to Alice.

Dear Alice
Delighted. Overwhelmed. Ecstatic. Euphoric. All these words can't sum up how happy I was when Mum told me you had been in contact. It's unbelievable! I keep pinching myself to check it's not a dream.

I have thought about you so very often. My last memory of you is leaving with Dad, your little face looking out of the car window as it drove off down the drive.

I've never given up hope of finding you again and now you've found us. All this time I've often wondered where you are and what you're doing.

Thank you so much for contacting us. I can't wait to hear from you and to, hopefully, see you again. My darling little sister, you've come back to us.

All my love
Clare
xxx

I keep it simple. There's so much I want to say, but can't put it all down on paper. I want to see her in real life. To hold her and for me, Mum and Alice to all be together again. Luke's warning hovers in the background but I push it aside. We have Alice back and, at the moment, that is all that matters.

I fold the letter in half and, retrieving Mum's letter from the sitting room, I slip mine inside and seal the envelope, leaving it on the side ready to post tomorrow. A warm feeling of happiness stirs inside. I kiss my fingertips and transfer the kiss to Alice's name on the envelope, smiling as I do so.

'You've found us, Alice,' I whisper, before turning the light off and heading up to bed.

The following morning is a scramble. I finally manage to haul myself out of bed on the third alarm. I'm never like this in the mornings.

Breakfast goes by in a blur as I play catch-up, but can't quite make up the time. I'm saying hurried goodbyes and rushing out the door with that feeling that I've forgotten something.

I start the engine and run through my checklist. Phone. Bag. Purse. Briefcase. Yep, I've got all them.

It's not until I reach the office and the postman walks up to the door, pushing his trolley, and takes out the mail, passing it to me, that I suddenly remember.

'Shit,' I say out loud. The postman looks taken aback. 'Sorry, not you. I've just remembered I've forgotten to pick up a letter from home. Bugger.'

I send Luke a quick text message asking him to post Mum's letter to Alice.

'You're looking a bit flustered this morning,' says Tom, as I hand the mail over to the receptionist.

'You know how to make a girl feel better,' I say. 'Why don't you make yourself useful and put the kettle on?'

Tom gives a mock salute, clicks his heels together and marches off towards the kitchen. 'Yes, ma'am.'

The coffee tastes good. I like a cup of tea at home, but at work I tend to thrive on the coffee buzz. 'It always tastes nicer when someone else makes it,' I say gratefully to Luke as we stand in the kitchen. 'Thanks for that.'

'Can't have Mrs Calm-And-Collected Tennison all flustered and dishevelled, can we?'

'Hmm. Feeling the effects of going through the proverbial emotional wringer,' I say. My phone bleeps and I check my messages. It's Luke telling me not to worry, he has it all under control. I put the phone down on the worktop.

'You know you can talk to me, if you need to,' says Tom. His voice is soft and I appreciate his kindness.

'I feel like I've been wishing for this all my life, for Alice to get in touch,' I say, looking down at the dark-brown liquid in my cup and breathing in the aroma of the coffee beans. 'You know when you're a kid and you blow out the candles on your birthday cake and you make a wish? Or at New Year when the clock strikes midnight or when you throw a coin into a magic wishing well? All those times, I've always wished for the same thing, that we would find Alice or she would find us, that someday we'd be together again as a family.' I pause as I take a sip of my coffee to buy some time to blink back the tears.

Tom puts his cup down and rubs the top of my arm with his hand. 'Is it a case of being careful what you wish for?'

'No. Yes. Sort of.' I can feel the strength to keep it together seeping out from me, as if Tom's hand is absorbing all my powers of self-control. 'Now it's happened, I'm ... I'm scared.'

Tom takes the cup from me and rests it next to his. He steps closer and puts both arms around me. 'It's okay to be scared. It's a big life-changing event. You have to try to harness that fear and turn it into a positive emotion.' He rubs his hand up and down my back. 'And, just for the record, this is a hug between friends. Thought I'd clarify that before you jump away from me like you've been electrocuted.'

I laugh into his shirt, grateful the mounting tension has been broken. 'As if I'd do anything like that.'

Tom gives me a squeeze before stepping back, his hands moving to mine. 'Honestly, Clare, I know what all this means to you. I haven't forgotten. How could I?'

I smile and nod. 'I know and I do appreciate you being here.'

'I've always been here for you. I haven't forgotten all those hours we spent huddled round your laptop, trying to trace Alice. And those phone calls! Do you remember the private investigator we hired to organise a search for her?'

I nod and smile at the memory. 'That first one was bloody useless. What a waste of money that was.'

'If only we'd known then that your dad had changed his and Alice's surname.'

'I can't believe that having that one single piece of knowledge would have, potentially, made a difference so much sooner. Looking for Alice Kennedy was a complete waste of time and money,' I sigh. 'Now, if we'd been looking for Alice Kendrick ...'

'Hey, let's not go there. It's not constructive. I'm sorry, I shouldn't have mentioned it.'

'No, it's okay, really. And please don't apologise. You're absolutely right, bemoaning it all won't actually help now. I said as much to Mum. I should start taking my own advice. We mustn't get hung up on the past.'

We stand there for a moment, holding hands, looking at each other. I'm aware of Tom's thumb stroking across my knuckles, a gesture from yesteryear. My last comment was referring to attempts to find Alice, but now I wonder if Tom is reading more into it. I go to speak, but change my mind, aware that I could make a complete arse of myself again. More likely it's me who is reading too much into everything.

Tom keeps his eyes on mine when he speaks. 'I meant what I said, about being here for you. I do understand. I've been down that road with you.' His voice is quiet and low. 'Practically all your life you've had this weight on your shoulders and it's now being lifted; you're bound to need time to adjust. Your world has been turned upside down and it will take a while for you to consolidate everything not just your feelings and emotions but your sense of place in your family. Try to be less uptight. Relax. Let Alice back into your life.'

'You make it sound so easy.' I break eye contact and attempt to withdraw my hands, but Tom tightens his grip.

'Hey, hey. Come on.' He pulls me back into his embrace. 'You just have to take your finger off the control button for a while. I know it's not in your nature, but as I always said, I think you being ordered and controlled as an adult stems from the emotional chaos in your childhood. You have to make an effort to switch that control off and go with the flow a bit more, otherwise you're going to drive yourself mad.'

I laugh and return the hug he gives. 'Thanks. I'll do my best.'

'I mean it, Clare. Remember what happened at Oxford?'

I wince inwardly at the memory. Of course I do. You don't forget having some sort of blackout and not being able to get out of bed for three days. We'd both had a few drinks to drown my sorrows at yet another fruitless report from the private investigator and, for some reason, I had reacted badly to the alcohol. Or that was my theory.

Tom, on the other hand, felt it was down to stress caused by my dogged determination to find my sister. For three days Tom had looked after me as if I was a child. He'd covered for me during lectures and afterwards helped me catch up on the work I'd missed. I certainly wouldn't have been able to pass the exam the following week without his support.

I let out a long breath in an attempt to blow away my anxieties and to show Tom that I'm already trying to relax. I don't want him thinking I'm a basket case.

'That's better,' says Tom. 'As soon as you stop fretting and analysing everything to the nth degree, you'll find it all so much easier to deal with. Trust me, I know these things. Now, come on, we'd better get back before Leonard finds us. He's the last person you want poking his nose into everything.'

'Yeah, come on,' I say, although I'm not entirely sure I agree with Tom about Leonard. I wouldn't go as far as saying he's poking his nose in, although it is true he has always taken an interest in what I'm doing, but I put that down to him being Mum's adviser and long-time family friend. 'Leonard's heart is in the right place, though,' I add in his defence.

Tom opens the kitchen door and turns to look at me, raising an eyebrow as if unconvinced. 'If you say so.'

Chapter 6

It's Saturday and I welcome the weekend with open arms. And an empty bed. I turn over and through bleary eyes inspect Luke's side of the bed. The pillow is as puffed up as when I got in it the night before and the fitted sheet is smooth; not a crease to be seen. He clearly didn't make it to bed last night.

He's having a creative spurt. He's been working on an abstract landscape for a gallery in America. He was commissioned by a client who was visiting the UK last year and saw one of his pieces on display at the Pavilion in Brighton. Luke has been both excited and distracted by it. When I got in from work yesterday, he was already in his studio, having got the girls ready for bed and left them with Mum.

It's still early, not even six o'clock, but my own body clock doesn't appear to be able to factor weekends in. I get up, slip my dressing gown around me and, bare-footed, sneak along the landing, poking my head in at the girls to make sure they're both okay. They're still asleep, although I probably only have half an hour before Chloe will begin to stir.

I avoid the creaky stair, second from the top, and also the one halfway down, level with the spindle that has a small scratch at the bottom from where I'd dropped a toy car down the stairs when I was about six years old. Living all my life in this house, I am fully aware of its quirks and how to avoid detection when nipping up and down the staircase to get midnight snacks or to stay out of Dad's way when he was in one of his moods.

Luke's studio is at the end of the hallway that runs at a right-angle from the main hallway. While it is still very much part of the house, it's far enough away so that he doesn't get bothered by the comings and goings of the rest of the house.

I tap on the door and go in without waiting for him to answer. Sometimes he's so lost in his work that he doesn't always notice me at first. Today is one of those days. His back is to me and he is facing the canvas, brush in one hand, paint palette in the other. He's wearing a pair of slouchy cotton trousers and a white T-shirt. His feet are bare and various splodge marks on his toes give a clear indication as to what colours he has been working with. I dread to think when he last brushed his hair, the untamed curls are all over the place. It could really do with a cut but I usually have to make the appointment and frogmarch him down there. Mum says it's like having another child and I should let him look after himself. Most of the time I let the little remarks go over my head. I like looking after my family. They are everything to me.

I lean back against the wall, admiring my husband as he waves the paint brush back and forth, from palette to canvas and back again. The radio plays quietly in the background. I think it's Strauss, but I'm not sure.

'You'd never make a spy,' says Luke after a few minutes and I hear the amusement in his voice. He continues with the paintbrush, working on an area of sky. It looks perfect to me, but then I don't have a trained eye.

I push myself away from the wall and move behind Luke, slipping my arms around his waist and kissing his shoulder blade. 'Sorry, didn't mean to disturb you. I just woke up feeling a bit lonely. You never made it to bed last night, then?'

Luke turns in my embrace and kisses me. 'Sorry, but I wanted to get on with this. There's been an exciting development.'

'With the painting?' I let go of Luke and look at the canvas and acrylics. I don't really know what I'm looking for.

Luke lets out a small laugh. 'Not with the painting itself.' He puts the palette on the sink over by the window, along with the paint brush. 'I had a phone call in the night. From Teddy Marconi.'

I wrack my brains trying quickly to locate the significance of Teddy Marconi. 'Your American client?'

'You got it. Well, he's only invited me over to his house in Miami.'

'Miami! Wow!' It's not unusual for Luke to meet with clients in their own homes, but usually it's the UK. Luke likes to see where his paintings are going to be displayed; he says it helps him get a sense of what they want. The painting he's working on now is for Marconi's London apartment. When Luke had gone to meet with Marconi in Kensington, I had taken the opportunity to do a bit of sightseeing and we had met up afterwards for a night away in a hotel. It was a very romantic evening, as I remember.

'Yeah, can you believe it?' says Luke.

'So, do I get to go with you again?' I tease. A trip to London and leaving the girls with Mum for the night is one thing, but both of us away to America for at least three nights would be too much to expect of Mum.

'Ah, sorry, Babe, I was just getting to that bit,' says Luke. 'Marconi wants me there next week, Tuesday in fact. He's paying for the flight and everything. Said all I have to do is turn up. So, unless you can get the week off work, I'm flying solo.'

I pull a mock-sad face. 'So you're leaving me behind while you go and have fun in Miami.' I slip my arms around his neck. 'I hope you're going to make this up to me.'

Luke pulls gently at the belt of my dressing gown and slides his hands inside. 'I'm sure I can do that.'

After our little interval, Luke decides that he has probably worked as much as he can for the day. It's not unusual for him to work twenty-four hours solid when the mood takes him. However, he's going to have a snooze for a couple of hours.

'I'll take the girls out for breakfast,' I say. 'Shall we take a walk along the seafront? It's such a nice day for the time of year, would be a shame to waste it. We could get the girls an ice cream?'

'Sounds good to me,' says Luke. 'Come and wake me up at lunchtime.' He yawns and we pad out of the studio together, just as Chloe comes down the stairs.

'Right, we're going out for breakfast,' I say, scooping her up in my arms. 'Let's go and get dressed.'

Upstairs in my bedroom, I dive in the shower quickly while Luke entertains Chloe. I can hear them playing the tickle-monster game. It's a simple game but Chloe loves it and it keeps her entertained until I've got myself dressed.

I hear my mobile ping to tell me I have an email from the charging dock on the bedside table.

My heart gives a double beat as I see the sender's name.

'You all right, Babe?' asks Luke, rolling over onto his front and looking up at me.

'It's an email.'

'And what do you usually do with emails? You read them and reply to them.' Chloe squeals and jumps onto Luke's back. He makes an *umph* sound as she knocks his breath out.

I pick up my phone. I don't know why I'm suddenly apprehensive about looking at the email. I have such a mix of emotions flying around inside me about Alice getting in touch. I suppose it's the reality check now. First there was shock, then happiness and now caution. I wonder if there are stages of emotion for being reunited with a family member, a bit like there are supposed to be stages of grief. I'll Google it later.

'It's Alice. It's come through on the email account I set up for Mum,' I say. 'I'll get her to open it on the computer downstairs.'

'Don't you want to vet it first?' says Luke.

'Why?'

Luke swings his legs off the bed and plants his feet on the floor as Chloe hangs around his neck. 'I don't know. Just in case you have to prepare your Mum for bad news.'

I frown. 'How do you mean?'

'Forget it. It doesn't matter.'

'No, what did you mean?'

Luke stands up, Chloe still hanging on like some sort of circus act. 'In case Alice has changed her mind or something.'

He gives a shrug and unhooks Chloe's arms from his neck. 'Like I said, forget it. I'm sure everything will be okay.'

I pause while I think about what Luke has said. He may have a point. 'Okay, I'll just have a quick look.'

I sit on the bed and tap the email to open it. There's a paperclip icon indicating an attachment and it takes a bit longer for the message to download. Before I can read what Alice has said, I find myself scrolling down to look at the attachment. It has to be a photograph of her, surely. I'm going to finally see what my sister looks like. I close my eyes for a moment, thinking back to the last time I saw her. Her little face looking out at me from the back of a car window.

I open my eyes, expecting to see a young woman. I'm surprised when two faces appear smiling out at me. They look to be sitting on a sofa. It's not a selfie as the shot is too long. Maybe taken with a camera on a timer or maybe someone took their photo. They both have the same dark coffee-coloured hair, which has been curled into big, loose waves and one cut slightly shorter than the other. The two young women look to be the same sort of age; early twenties. I zoom in to have a closer look at their faces, their eyes in particular. I'm looking for those beautiful blue eyes which have haunted me all these years. The picture becomes pixelated and I can't make out their eye colours. I look back at where Alice has signed off and the P.S. underneath her name. *I'm the one on the left.*

'Alice,' I whisper.

'Which one is Alice?' says Luke looking over my shoulder.

'The one on the left.' Chloe, now deposited on the floor, is occupying herself with the shoes from my cupboard. I smile and lean back into Luke. 'Do you think Alice looks like me?'

Luke peers closer. 'It's hard to say. Maybe? The hair's the same and possibly the cheekbones too. Who's the other girl?'

I scan through the letter, skimming across the words. 'It's her friend, Martha.' I go back and read the email properly. 'Oh, shit.'

'What's up?'

'She wants to come over and she's going to bring her friend with her.' I look at Luke. 'Why would she do that?'

'Is it a problem?'

'Well, it would be better if she came alone. But, then again, maybe she's nervous. Maybe she wants someone there who she knows.' I press my lips together in that sympathetic way people do when they want to show someone they know how they're feeling without having to say any words. Usually accompanied by a sorrowful or resigned expression. 'Suppose I'd better tell Mum.'

Mum cries when I open the email on the computer downstairs and show her the picture. She touches the screen, caressing the image of Alice. 'My darling Alice,' she says several times. 'I can't wait to hold her for real.'

'She's bringing her friend,' I say gently. 'Did you read that bit?'

'Yes. It's fine. If that's what she wants, then I don't mind at all. Whatever makes Alice happy.'

I exchange a look over the top of Mum's head with Luke. He gives me the eyes which say to let it go. That's one of the reasons I love Luke. He knows what I'm thinking without me even saying a word. He knows I'm thinking Mum is perhaps being a little more soppy than I expected and he can probably guess that I'm wondering whether I should say anything to her. From the small shake of his head, clearly, Luke thinks not.

'Marion, would you like me to print the email and photo for you?' he says.

'Oh, would you, Luke? That would be wonderful. I mean, it's lovely that emails are so instant, but you can't beat holding a letter in your hand.' Mum smiles gratefully at Luke and then turns to me. 'I'm going to put it with all of Alice's other things.'

'That's a good idea,' I say, knowing she's referring to a small black suitcase, where she has kept Alice's favourite dress, some of her old cuddly toys, like the brown teddy bear who has lost its eyes and the bunny rabbit in the blue jacket like Peter Rabbit, her nightdress with ladybird print, her book about the zoo, anything that provided a connection to her daughter, in fact. There's also a small stash of presents Mum has bought every birthday and Christmas.

Luke prints out the email and photograph and Mum goes off to her room with it. Luke stands behind me and massages my shoulders. 'She's bound to be a bit emotional. It's a lot for her to take in. And you.' He turns me to face him. 'Are you okay, yourself?'

I nod. 'Yeah. If Mum's happy, then I am.'

'That's not what I asked.'

'I am happy. It's just ...' I hesitate, not wishing to sound like I'm put out by my sister coming on the scene and displacing me. Luke says nothing as he waits for me to continue. 'It's just all happening quite fast and I'm not sure about this friend coming, if I'm honest. Seems a bit of an odd thing to do when you're going to meet your family for the first time.'

'It is a little odd, but let's try to relax and go with the flow, eh? Perhaps Alice just wants a bit of moral support.'

'You've changed your tune,' I say.

'I have no control over it,' Luke says. 'Alice is making plans to come over, whether we like it or not. So, we had better get used to it and embrace it, that's all I'm saying. I'm sure everything will be all right.'

'I wish I had your laid-back attitude.'

'Clare, Babe. I know you must be feeling all sorts of things. Christ, I know I am and she's not even my sister, but I've invested the time and emotion in Alice too. Not on your sort of scale, granted, but all those times we've tried to find her, to track her down. The money we've spent ... okay, you've spent, trying to find her. And now, that's all behind us. She's found us. You're getting your sister back, your mum is getting her daughter back, I'm getting a sister-in-law and the kids are getting an aunty. Let's concentrate on the good things.'

'Speaking of the kids,' I say looking up at the ceiling as I hear the sound of feet cross the landing and descend the staircase. 'Sounds like Hannah is up.'

I put on a brave smile as I take the girls out for what is turning into a brunch. Luke is right. I must think of the good things, the positives. My little sister is coming home. Yet, despite this mantra, I can't shake the disquiet that has settled within me.

Chapter 7

The next few weeks pass quickly and I'm surprised at how fast events move. I had anticipated that there would be a gradual exchange of emails and possibly some phone calls before Mum and Alice decided it was time to meet in person. In my mind, it would be at least two or three months but, no, in two more emails, they decide they want to meet sooner rather than later. In person, straight off. No phone calls, no Skype.

'Are you sure you're ready for this?' I ask Mum, the evening before Alice's arrival, as Mum goes into Alice's bedroom to make sure the room is tidy and ready to welcome her. I had suggested to Mum that she redecorate the room, but she had insisted the baby-pink walls and the polka-dot curtains were to remain. She was convinced Alice would remember them. I want Alice to remember them, if only for Mum's sake. I wonder whether I should prime her first, but decide against it. I haven't been involved in the emails. I don't feel quite so connected to Alice yet.

'It looks really nice, Mum,' I say. 'I'm sure Alice will love it, but don't get upset if it takes her a while to remember things. It was a long time ago and she was very young.'

I place a hand on Mum's shoulder and give a gentle squeeze.

'It's okay, love,' says Mum. 'I know it may be a bit difficult, and even upsetting, but I'm prepared for it. I'm not as naive as you may think.'

We go into the guest room across the landing and take a cursory glance at the room. Everything is in place for our additional house guest. Fresh towels are on the end of the bed, a spare dressing gown and some toiletries. 'It looks like a swanky hotel,' I say.

'Do you think it will be okay?'

'Of course. I'd be delighted if I was staying in a room like this.' I check my watch. 'It's late. We'd better get to bed. We have to be at Heathrow for seven-thirty.'

Despite encouraging Mum to get a good night's sleep, I don't sleep well myself and am somewhat relieved when the alarm goes off at four-thirty. Mum is already waiting in the kitchen, obviously suffering the same pre-meeting nerves as I am. We creep quietly out of the house so as not to disturb Luke and the girls. I feel as if I've hardly seen Luke the last couple of weeks. Since his trip to America, he's been pretty much locked away in his studio all day and all night. He came back enthusiastic to get the London commission finished so he could start on the Miami commission.

'How's Luke getting on with his work?' asks Mum.

I focus on the road ahead. 'Really well, thanks,' I say. 'This could be a big break for him. We're talking several thousand pounds. This American client is all over Luke. Loves his work.' I realise I'm rambling slightly. I always feel very defensive about Luke with Mum when it comes to his artwork and money. At the back of my mind, I'm aware that she doesn't totally approve of our set-up. She's behind me having a career, a successful one that preserves my independence, but she's not so keen on me supporting Luke. She once told me that supporting Luke financially was a ransom note. It would keep me tied to him and the girls; that I'd never be able to strike out on my own should I need to.

I know she's thinking of what happened between her and Dad. Mum had been wise when it came to money. She had her own income from her career as a teacher and from the money she had inherited. She had always kept it separate from Dad, she told me, who was wealthy and could support himself. Financially, neither needed the other. Turned out it was just as well. Mum might have been left stranded emotionally but financially she could survive – and survive comfortably.

'That sounds promising,' says Mum, breaking my thoughts. 'It could take some of the pressure off you.'

'I'm not under any pressure.'

'No, but you know what I mean. It will be great if Luke can earn the equivalent to a decent wage.'

'Mum, please. Not now.'

'I'm just saying, you won't have to feel so responsible financially for everyone. It's good to have your own independence, both of you.'

'Like you did. In case something goes wrong. That's what you're saying, aren't you?' I can't help feeling more than a little irritated at the comment and it prickles me into a terse reply. I can feel the static coming off Mum. I sneak a look at her out of the corner of my eye. She's staring straight ahead, but I can see her body is tense.

'Yes. I do, actually,' she says.

'Mum, me and Luke are fine. We've been happily married all this time. We've known each other since we were at school. If something was going to happen, I'm sure it would have by now.'

'But you don't really know that. Sometimes being complacent is the worst thing. You don't see it coming and it blindsides you.'

We drive along in silence for a few minutes. I can feel the weight of Mum's words. I know she is looking out for me. You don't stop being a mum just because your kids are grown up and married with their own family. I know Mum is fond of Luke, but he's not her own flesh and blood so she's bound to be biased. I'll probably be just the same when the girls grow up and get boyfriends. I pick my next words carefully and say them with equal care.

'What happened to make Dad leave?'

Mum has never told me the exact reason why Dad decided to take Alice on holiday on his own. Although, in hindsight, we both realise that to Dad it was never a holiday – it was always going to be for ever.

'Your Dad didn't want to stay with me any more,' replies Mum. 'You know that.'

'But you've never told me why,' I press. Somehow it seems important that I know now. Maybe it's because Alice is coming home. Surely she will want to know.

'It was a long time ago,' says Mum. 'I have no intention of

picking old scars and wounds. I don't want to dwell in the past. We have a future to look forward to with Alice.'

'But she might ask you. What will you tell her?'

'Exactly what I've just told you. Now, please, Clare, I don't want to talk about it any more. It's a corrosive subject and it will eat you away if you allow it.' She pauses and then lets out a small sigh. 'I don't want it to poison you, like it has me. I've never wanted that for either of my girls. All I want is for us to be happy now.'

I let the subject go just like I always do when we get to this point.

The flight from Orlando arrives on time and Mum and I wait patiently at arrivals, scanning the throng of passengers who make their way through the glass doors.

A family of four, a couple in their thirties with their two small children. The mum is carrying the toddler and the dad is pushing the trolley laden with suitcases, a child of about five tags along, holding onto the trolley. A man in a business suit with a small carry-on case in one hand, a briefcase in the other, early-morning stubble grazing his chin. He marches through, not looking for anyone, eyes straight ahead. He's obviously done this journey before, it's not new to him, there's no excitement in being in the UK. I wonder idly if he's American or British.

I see a young woman with dark hair round the corner and for a moment I think it's Alice, but as she comes into view, I see she's with a guy. They have backpacks and are wearing shorts and hoodies. The girl's face lights up and she nudges the boyfriend as she points ahead. I look over and see a middle-aged woman waving back. The passengers file through but still no sign of Alice and Martha.

'They would have emailed if they had missed their flight, wouldn't they?' says Mum.

'Relax, Mum, I'm sure they won't be long now. You know what it's like getting through passport control.'

'Do you think Alice has an American or British passport?'

'I don't know. I suppose it depends whether she took American citizenship or not.'

Mum nods and I can see a look of sadness flick across her face. 'It's the little details that are a painful reminder I don't know my own daughter. I should know things like that.'

'Hey, Mum. Don't be getting yourself all upset, now. We have the next few weeks to find out all these things.' Mum smiles and I can see her making a conscious effort to dismiss the melancholy thought.

I turn my attention back to the arriving passengers. A young woman with long, wavy brunette hair appears and I'm just about to dismiss her and pass my gaze on to the other passengers when something makes me do a double-take. Mum grabs my arm at the same time.

'There!' she says and waves. 'Alice!'

The young woman looks up and looks in our direction. She looks nervous. I smile broadly and wave too. I look beyond her, but she seems to be travelling alone, no sign of her friend. She begins to walk towards us, her stride quickens with every step. She breaks into a small run. Mum leaves my side and is running towards her. The sight of them makes me want to cry. Mum is crying already. They throw their arms around each other and stand there, lost in their own world, oblivious to everything and everyone around them. Mum pulls away, holds Alice's face between her hands, cherishing every feature. She kisses her cheek, lots of times. They look at each other and laugh.

· Then Mum is gesturing towards me and, with her arm around her daughter's shoulder, she brings Alice over to me. I see those beautiful blue eyes; they are even bluer than I remember. I'm momentarily thrown back to the day she left, when those same eyes pleaded with me from the doorway of the living room. I can feel my chest tighten and my throat wants to close. I take a breath of air. I step forward and, within seconds, my darling little sister is holding me and I'm holding her.

'Oh, Alice. You've come home,' I hear myself whispering. All the doubts for the past few weeks seem to wash away with the tears that stream down my face.

Alice squeezes me back hard. 'Hi, Clare. I can't believe I'm actually here. All the years I've thought about you. It was like you and Mom weren't real. And now, it's like my dreams have come to life.'

She has a strong Southern twang and, for some reason, it surprises me. I suppose, in my mind, I expected her to speak just like me. 'Come on, let's get to the car,' I say, wiping my face dry with a tissue Mum has pushed into my hand. She's done the same with Alice. The three of us mop our tears. I pick up Alice's suitcase and then suddenly remember her friend. 'Where's your friend – Martha?' I look back towards the arrival doors. 'I thought she was coming with you.'

Alice waves her hand. 'Oh, yeah, sorry. Last-minute change of plan. She couldn't make it in the end. So, I'm afraid, it's just me.' She grins and gives a shrug. 'Hope that's okay?' The smile disappears and she looks concerned. 'Sorry, I should have let you know, but in all the excitement, I clean forgot.'

Mum slips her arm in Alice's. 'It's okay, darling. No need to apologise. It doesn't make any difference at all. We're just glad you still came.'

'Oh, there was nothing on this earth that was gonna make me miss coming to see you, Mum.' She emphasises the last word, which sounds odd with the American accent, and snuggles her head onto Mum's shoulder. 'It is all right to say "Mum" isn't it?'

Mum kisses the top of Alice's head. 'Of course, my darling. There is nothing that would make me happier.' They walk past me, once again back in their own world. I watch them for a minute, unsure of the odd, uncomfortable feeling that has wriggled inside me. Maybe I'm just not used to hearing anyone else call my own mother 'Mum'. I follow on behind them.

The journey home goes quickly. Mum sits in the front and Alice behind me as I take the wheel. Mum is asking her polite questions, like how was her journey, has she had something to eat, has work been okay about letting her have time off? Safe subjects. Alice answers and asks questions in return. Does Mum drive, does she work, what are her hobbies? More safe subjects.

Mum digs out the computer printout of the photo Alice sent. It's slightly creased and a bit crumpled around the edges. 'Thank you for the photograph,' she says flattening it out on her knee. 'Did you bring any more with you? Any of you growing up over the years?'

I know Mum had asked Alice this in her most recent email. I glance in the rear-view mirror at Alice. She catches my eye and pulls a face that tells me she didn't.

'Oops, sorry,' she says to Mum. 'You know what? I have this awful feeling I left the photo album I made up for you on the table.' She slaps her hand to her forehead. 'Sorry, I'm so dumb at times.'

'That's okay, don't worry,' says Mum. I can tell Mum is disappointed and her upbeat answer is a ruse.

'We can take loads of photos while you're here,' I say. 'We can make our own photo album up.'

'That's a great idea,' says Alice enthusiastically. 'To be honest, I don't have many photos of me as a child.' Again, I look in the rear-view mirror. She looks away, out of the window. 'Dad didn't take many.' Her voice has a sadness to it.

'The girls are looking forward to seeing you,' I say, to divert the downturn in the mood. I spend the last few miles jabbering on about the girls, what they are like, the things they've got up to in the past and how Chloe is the quiet, sensitive one, more cautious in nature and a gentler soul altogether, whereas Hannah is outgoing, fun, adventurous and, at times, rather outspoken.

'I can't wait to meet them. I can't believe I'm an aunt and I have two gorgeous nieces to meet,' says Alice. 'And, of course, your husband, Luke. You're very lucky, you know, to have your family.'

* * *

We drive along the winding lane that leads to the house. The flint wall marking the start of the grounds, running along the edge of the pathless road to the black gates.

'Does it look familiar, at all?' asks Mum. I think she's desperate for Alice to have even the faintest memory from her childhood.

'A little,' says Alice. 'I do remember the black gates. For some reason they stand out in my mind.'

I steer the car through the gates and up the gravel driveway. Luke and the girls must have heard the car as they come out to greet us. Luke has plastered on a smile and looks welcoming enough, although I can tell it's his formal smile. Perhaps he's not as laid back about it after all. Mind you, we are all on tenterhooks. Tiptoeing around certain subjects in the car, analysing every word, facial expression and body language. I'm sure we will all relax once we get to know each other better.

Alice is out of the car and immediately she goes over to the girls and, crouching down, hugs Hannah first. Hannah looks slightly taken aback and I make eye contact with her over Alice's shoulder. I raise my eyebrows and smile broadly, it's an unspoken message Hannah will understand: one I've used before which reads – be polite and say nice things. Hannah obliges and smiles at Alice, who then turns her attentions to Chloe. My younger daughter hides behind Luke.

'Say hello to Alice,' says Luke, but Chloe clings tighter.

'It's okay, she's just shy. There's plenty of time to make friends,' says Alice. She stands up and faces Luke, who holds his hand out to her.

'I'm Luke. Clare's husband. Nice to meet you.'

She shakes Luke's hand. 'Alice Kendrick. The pleasure is all mine.' She gives a small laugh. 'Now we've got the formal English greeting over with, how about a good old American hello?' She lunges forward and gives Luke a hug. 'It's so nice to be here,' she says.

It's Luke's turn to look over at me from Alice's shoulder. He has a *help me* look on his face. I smother a laugh and Mum admonishes me with a tap on the arm. Luke winks at me and removes himself from Alice's embrace.

'Right, let's get inside,' says Mum. 'You must be worn out, darling. Luke, can you bring Alice's bags in, please?'

Mum and Alice head off into the house. Luke gives a tug of his fringe, dipping his head at the two departing women. 'Yes, m'lady.' Mum appears not to hear, thankfully.

'Stop it,' I say, half-heartedly. I go over to Luke and give him a kiss. 'Well, it seems the ice has been broken. How about I give you a good old American hello?' I put my arms around his neck and kiss him again.

'Better not let your mother see you fraternising with the staff,' says Luke, returning the kiss. 'As for the American hello, I'll give you a traditional Tennison hello later.' He gives my backside a playful smack as he sidesteps out of my arms and goes to fetch Alice's bags.

I'm smiling to myself as I turn to go in. As I look up, I see Alice standing at the doorway watching us. I shield my eyes from the early morning sun with one hand and wave to her with the other. She smiles broadly and returns the wave before disappearing inside the house. It's a much more comforting sight than when I last saw her in the doorway. I give my head a small shake and push the sad memory away. The cold days are in the past. The sun is shining and I feel a warmth within me that has been overshadowed for many years but now is finally breaking fee.

Later that evening, when the girls have gone to bed, Hannah being allowed to stay up a bit later than usual because of our guest. Luke tactfully makes his excuses about needing to get some more work done, to leave me, Mum and Alice alone in the living room.

'I'll make us some supper,' says Mum. 'I've got some cheese and crackers. Do you want tea, Clare? Coffee, Alice?'

We both thank Mum and for the first time since Alice arrived, over twelve hours ago, we are on our own.

'So, how long have you guys been married?' asks Alice.

'Oh, erm … must be coming up for eight years now.'

Alice cocks her head. 'Eight? And how old is Hannah?'

'Seven. I was four months pregnant when we got married.' I'm not embarrassed at all by this. It's not exactly shocking news these days. I suppose it's only natural that she's curious about her new family, but all the same, I feel strangely uncomfortable that she might be judging me as she does the maths.

'Oh, I see,' she says and smiles knowingly.

'We would have got married whether I was pregnant or not,' I add hastily, wishing she'd take that look of amusement off her face. 'We'd only just started going out but we always say we knew from about our third date that we wanted to be together. It just felt right.'

'Love at first sight,' says Alice. 'Or was it lust?'

I laugh. 'Too close to call.'

'Did you have a big church wedding?' Alice looks over towards the sideboard and scans the various photographs on my own personal rogue's gallery. They are mostly of the girls with a couple of Mum and one or two of Luke and me. Photographs taken by Luke at birthdays, on walks, on the beach, just snapshots catching everyday events with a naturalness you don't get with posed studio photos. I suppose it's the artistic eye he has, where he can capture those special moments, just one photograph of his can say so much.

'No church wedding,' I say. 'Funnily enough, it was Luke who wanted a white wedding but I didn't want a big fuss. We had a registry office wedding. Very small affair. Family and close friends. We did have a party afterwards, though.' I get up and go over to the sideboard, picking up a silver frame with a picture of Luke and me on our wedding day. Not that you would have guessed. We just look as if we're going to a dinner dance. Luke's wearing a dark-blue suit, pale-blue shirt with a white button-down collar and skinny blue tie and I'm wearing a cream-coloured evening dress with spaghetti-thin straps, a neckline that drapes in delicate folds across my bust. The dress, cut on the bias, reaches the ground. On my wrist I'm wearing a blue corsage to match Luke's tie.

I pass the photo frame to Alice and she studies the picture. 'Luke hasn't changed a bit. Neither have you, actually. And you wouldn't know you were pregnant. There's no trace of a bump there.'

'I was very small. First-time pregnancy and tight stomach muscles. Lucky, I suppose.'

Alice looks me up and down as she hands back the photograph. 'Still very slim now.'

'As are you,' I say, with a smile, replacing the photo frame back on the sideboard. 'It must be genetic.'

'Yeah, I guess it is. Did anyone know you were pregnant when you got married?'

I sit back down, wishing she would drop the cross-examination, but I feel obliged to answer. 'No. We never told anyone. Not even Mum. We waited until after the wedding and then told her.'

'And she was okay about it?'

'She didn't have a lot of choice.' I lower my voice. 'She was more annoyed I hadn't told her straight away. She couldn't understand why we wanted to get married so quickly. Anyway, after all the fuss had died down, she could not have been happier. She adores the girls.'

'Your girls are wonderful, as is your mum, I mean, *our* mum. Luke is pretty awesome too. You have a great family,' says Alice. Her words are tinged with sadness and I immediately feel guilty for the burst of pride her remark brought.

'We're all family now,' I say. 'All of us.'

'Family. All of us. I like that,' she says, as the corners of her mouth tip to a smile. 'Family.'

Chapter 8

'A re you sure you can't take any time off work?' asks Mum
as we sit down on Sunday morning to have breakfast.
Sundays are a much more relaxed affair. There's no set time
for breakfast; we all just get up when we want. The girls have
been up for over an hour and already had their fill of cereal
and toast. They're now in the sitting room, Hannah watching
TV and Chloe amusing herself with her play-kitchen. I'm not
one of those parents who insists they do something structured
and educational every minute of their waking hour.

'I'm sorry, Mum, but I really can't,' I say spreading some
marmalade on my toast. 'I've a big court date coming up next
month. It's really important and I can't take any time off at
all.' I pour a cup of tea. 'We can have a nice day out today,
though. I thought we could all go into Brighton. Show Alice
the sights.'

Mum's disappointed look makes way for a smile. 'That's a
good idea. We could take her to all the places I used to take
you two as children. It may jog her memory. There's the
seafront, the pier, the lanes. We could get fish and chips and
an ice cream. The girls will enjoy it too. Yes, let's do that.'

I smile at Mum and reach over, putting my hand on her arm. 'Mum, you know Alice was very young when she was here – she may not remember anything at all.'

'I know that.' Mum pats my hand.

'I just don't want you to be too disappointed or to be putting pressure on anyone.'

'Ooh, looks like I've timed this just right. Morning all.' Luke comes into the kitchen and, with acrylic-covered fingers, swipes a slice of toast from my plate. Blues, greens and yellows make his hands look as if they're covered in bruises. He's had another night of working on his new commission. He drops a kiss on my head. 'How are you?'

'All good, thanks. How's the painting coming on?' I say as I watch Luke pad over to the kettle.

'Anyone want a cup?' he asks. 'Marion?'

Mum shakes her head. 'No thanks. Put a cup out for Alice, though, I'm sure she'll be up soon.'

'Painting is going great, Babe,' says Luke. He comes to sit down beside me at the table. 'What's on the agenda today?'

'Thought we'd go to Brighton. Show Alice the sights,' I say. 'You coming? Or do you need to get on with your work?'

'No, I'll come. I've had enough for a while. I could do with a break and some fresh sea air. It will be nice to spend some time with you all.'

It's not long before Alice comes down. I can't help raise my eyebrows slightly and exchange a discreet look with Luke. Alice is wearing just an over-sized T-shirt, except, in my opinion, it could do with being a bit more over-sized. Of course, she's got the legs for it. Very American; long and tanned as opposed to my own – long they may be, but as white as two pints of milk. She leans forward to kiss Mum on the cheek and her T-shirt rides up slightly. Luke averts his eyes and makes a big deal out of putting another spoon of sugar in his cup.

'Good morning, everyone,' she says, standing up and running her hand through her hair, dragging it loosely from her face and letting it fall again.

'Good morning, darling,' says Mum. 'Did you sleep all right? Wasn't too hot or too cold? Was the mattress okay for you?'

Alice smiles fondly down at Mum. 'Sure, the bed was fine. I guess the jet lag is starting to catch up on me.'

Mum pulls out the chair beside her. 'Here, sit down. What would you like for breakfast? There's toast, cereal, some pastries. Clare, be a love and make Alice a cup of coffee. It is coffee you want, isn't it?'

Alice smiles and nods. 'That would be awesome. Thanks, Clare. It's really kind of you.'

'No problem,' I say, ignoring the rueful smile on Luke's face as I put down my toast.

'Could I have some toast as well, please?' says Alice. 'I don't suppose you have any peanut butter and jelly,'

'I think there's some jam.' I rummage in the cupboard. 'Here you go.'

Alice picks up the jar and, opening the lid, examines the contents. She screws her nose up. 'I'll take a raincheck.' She looks up at me. 'It's got bits in it.'

It strikes me that Alice is being ever-so-slightly fussy, but

I let it go. 'There's always Marmite,' I say, as I go about making a coffee for her. .

'Marmite?' says Alice.

'Don't even go there,' says Luke. 'We've got jam or marmalade. They're a much safer bet.'

'Maybe, Luke, you could have a look online to see whether we can get the peanut butter and jelly for Alice,' says Mum as I come back with my sister's drink.

'I'm sure we've got something Alice will like,' I say. Luke really doesn't need to go off on a wild-goose chase for Alice's American tastes. He's very obliging towards Mum, but sometimes I think she takes it for granted. I return to the cupboard and start pulling out various jars, the clonk of the glass on the granite work surface representing my irritation. 'Marmalade. Nutella. Honey.' I turn to look at Alice.

'Er, honey will be great,' she says, flicking a glance towards Luke.

'Local honey,' he says, passing the jar over to her. Then, turning, he gives me the eyes, which I return with a shrug and then feel rather embarrassed that my little display of frustration hasn't gone unnoticed by all the adults in the room.

Fortunately, Mum recovers the situation and starts chatting about the day ahead and what we're going to do. I brush my little display of petulance away with the toast crumbs and join in the conversation.

Alice seems happy with the plan and is pleased that we are all going out together. 'Oh, it will be like a proper family outing. Our first real one. One that I can remember, anyway.'

Mum smiles warmly. 'I can't tell you how I've longed for a day like this.'

'Me too,' says Alice.

It's an unusually warm day for mid-October and just a gentle sea breeze behind us as we stroll along Brighton seafront later. Luke is pushing Chloe in her buggy and Hannah is skipping along beside him. I'm walking alongside Mum, with Alice on the other side. The three of us have linked arms.

'Do you remember coming here at all?' Mum asks.

Alice grimaces. 'Not really,' she says.

'What about the pier?' I ask as we get closer. 'We used to go there all the time. We'd get ice cream and run up and down looking through the slats of the pier at the water below.'

'I used to take you down to the amusements at the end of the pier,' says Mum. 'You were a bit small for most of the rides, but Clare used to go on some of them. We'd sit there and watch her.'

'Sorry,' says Alice. 'I guess I was too young to remember.'

We carry on walking towards the pier, taking in the scenery. The pebble beach is empty of the summer holiday-makers and the cool autumnal sun shimmers faintly across the grey incoming tide as it laps gently back and forth.

Hannah comes skipping back to us, while Luke waits for us to catch up. 'Mummy! Mummy! Daddy's going to take me on the big eye,' she says excitedly.

Along from the pier is the Brighton i360. A glass pod, which glides up and down a four-hundred-and-fifty-foot pole, offering a three-hundred-and-sixty-degree view over the city and along the coast. Or so I'm told. I'm not great with heights. I've been on it once with Luke when it first opened, but hated it so much I spent most of the time with my eyes closed.

'Oh, wow! Can I come with you?' says Alice. Hannah looks at me, checking to see what the right answer is.

'That would be nice, wouldn't it? If Alice comes on with you and Daddy?' I say. We've caught up with Luke and, letting go of Mum's arm, I take the buggy from him. 'Did you want to go, Mum?' I ask.

'Why not?' says Mum. 'I keep saying I should go on it.'

I watch the four of them step through the double doors into the glass pod. It reminds me of Stephen Spielberg's *Close Encounters* movie. My family have now been abducted by aliens and when they return they will be different people.

While I wait, I buy an ice cream, which I share with Chloe as we sit on a nearby bench. The sun hangs low in the sky and I angle the buggy so that Chloe is not facing into the breeze. The ride takes about twenty minutes and as the pod slowly descends, I walk over and wait near the doors.

Mum and Hannah emerge first, holding each other's hands. I'm not sure who is helping who down the steps. Hannah sees me and a huge smile spreads across her face. 'It was great, Mum!' she shouts as she negotiates the last of the steps.

Behind them are Luke and Alice. They both look over and smile. By all accounts the ride has been a great success. Alice stumbles slightly on the steps. I give a small gasp – it's the mother in me, I'm sure, as I envisage her falling flat on her face. Luckily, she manages to grab onto Luke to stop herself.

Alice holds onto Luke's arm as they descend the remaining

steps. She's still holding onto him as they walk towards me. I watch as she leans into him, says something and they both laugh again.

I've never been the jealous type. Never had to be, I suppose, but today some strange sort of feeling stirs within my stomach and shoulder-charges my heart. I suddenly have this proprietorial basic instinct surge up within me. I'm not sure why, maybe it's the way Alice looks so at ease with Luke, as if it's the most natural thing in the world for her to be linking arms with him. Whatever it is, I don't like it. Alice looks up and we make eye contact. Outwardly, I can feel my mouth moving into a smile. Inwardly, my face has contorted into something resembling the Incredible Hulk.

Alice returns the smile and drops her hand away from Luke's arm. 'That was just totally awesome, Clare,' she says as they near me. 'I have never been on anything like that before. You should have come.'

'I have done it once before with Luke,' I say. I move the buggy into his path. 'Here, you push.' I tell myself it's because Chloe likes it when Luke pushes her. I slip my arm through Alice's as we walk along the seafront, the wind whipping our hair around our faces.

Alice scoops her hair to one side and gives a shiver. 'Much as I love being here, I do miss the Florida sunshine.'

I laugh. 'By British weather standards, this is good for mid-October. You'll have to get used to it.'

'I should have brought some more suitable clothing.'

'I can lend you a jumper or two,' I say. 'We're pretty much the same size.'

'Like twins,' says Alice.

'When you were little you always wanted to dress up in my clothes,' I say, thinking back. The recent memory of the mushroom incident comes to mind again. 'Do you remember when we had a teddy bear's picnic in the back garden and you were sick all down a pink-and-white-striped t-shirt of mine you were wearing?'

'Yes, I do!' says Alice. 'The T-shirt was more like a dress on me.'

'That's right, we put a belt around the middle. And all the sick got caught in the buckle. It was disgusting.'

'I ate way too much candy that day,' says Alice.

'Candy? No, it was mushrooms. I gave you mushrooms and they made you sick.'

'Oh, really? Sorry, it was a long time ago.'

'You wouldn't eat mushrooms after that and Mum couldn't understand it. She thought it was the berries that had made you sick.' I really want Alice to remember. It's one of my strongest memories from our childhood; a secret we had shared and kept. 'Don't you remember at all?' I persisted. 'And what about now – do you eat mushrooms now?' This time I find myself willing Alice to say she hates mushrooms, at least that will substantiate my memory and even if she doesn't recall the incident, it will give some sort of validation.

'Sorry, but I do like mushrooms. Don't beat yourself up about it, Clare, it obviously didn't cause me any lasting psychological damage. And, just to prove there's no hard feelings, I'll buy you a new T-shirt.' Alice gives a laugh and hugs my arm closer to her, which I know would normally be a natural gesture between sisters, somehow feels awkward – almost too intimate.

We carry on our walk along the pier as I muse over how different people can have the same experience and yet totally different memories. I'd hoped Alice and I would have at least one or two shared memories, something to bond over, to give us a starting block on which to rebuild our sisterhood. While it makes me sad to think we haven't found that yet, and despite what I said to Mum about Alice being too young to remember things, I can't help wondering if there is anything she does remember. Surely there'd be something, wouldn't there?

That evening, when we go up to bed, I clamber in next to Luke and snuggle up to him. 'That was a lovely day,' I say, ignoring the green-eyed monster that was never far away.

Luke wriggles down in the bed and cuddles me. 'It was,' he says. 'Is everything okay, Babe?'

'Yes, of course.'

'Sure?'

'Absolutely.' I'm certain Luke knows I'm not exactly telling the truth. He can read me like a book. He says he can tell as soon as I walk into the room what sort of mood I'm in. To be fair, I can usually tell with him too. I suppose it's because we've known each other for so long.

'You okay with Alice being here?' he asks.

'Yeah. It will be fine. Just feels a bit odd,' I confess.

'How do you mean?'

I blow out a long breath. 'I don't know. A bit awkward, maybe. Not how I thought it would.'

'Which was?'

'More of a connection, I suppose. She's Alice. She's my sister, but the vibe is missing. I can't feel it.'

'Give it time and don't overthink it. You know what you're like,' says Luke. 'It must be strange for her too. Give her a chance.'

I raise my eyebrows at him. 'So, I take it you like her, then?' And there it is, the jealous streak I never knew I had. I can't help myself.

Luke rolls onto his back. 'She's a nice girl,' he says, cocking his head to one side. 'It must run in the family.'

I prop myself up on my elbow. 'Nice?' I say. 'What does "nice" mean? Nice in what way?'

Luke looks out the corner of his eye at me. 'Not jealous, are you?' There's a note of amusement in his voice.

'Me? Jealous? Why would you think that?'

Luke grins and bundles me onto my back, climbing on top of me, his leg astride, and kisses me. 'Don't worry, Babe, you know I have eyes for you and you alone.'

'I'm not jealous.'

'The lady doth protest too much, methinks.' He smothers my reply with kisses.

Chapter 9

'How does a panini and a glass of vino at the wine bar sound?' says Tom, poking his head around the door of my office. Tom has been in court for most of the week and only now, as we head towards the weekend, do we catch up.

'Oh, I don't know,' I say looking at the list of emails still awaiting my attention. It had been a long week. The Monday rumble had been drawn out, Leonard giving me a good grilling about the McMillan case. Sometimes it's as if I'm still an employee rather than a supposedly equal partner. I resisted the urge to say anything, though. It was easier to answer the questions than to get into an argument with him. I'd made that mistake once before, and that was before I even worked for him. It was when I was at university and had taken my eye off the ball and been distracted from my studies by my search for Alice. He had helped a bit at first, but he was adamant that I shouldn't let my grades suffer.

'Come on, you could do with a break,' says Tom. 'It will do you good to get out of the office for an hour. We could just grab a sandwich from the kiosk and sit in the park, if you like? I can tell you how I wiped the floor with the defence this week.' He polishes an imaginary badge of honour on his lapel.

I feel myself relent. It's a nice day and there probably won't be many more chances to get out and enjoy the local park before the weather shifts properly into winter.

'Okay, why not?' I say, standing up and grabbing my bag. 'The park sounds like an excellent suggestion.'

Tom ushers me out of the office, his hand resting between my shoulder blades. 'If we go stealth mode, we can sneak out before Leonard spots us,' he whispers.

I stem the giggle. We're like school kids playing truant.

We both have a bacon and Brie panini and a coffee. The park is quieter than at weekends and we plonk ourselves down on one of the benches that edge the fountain. The white stone basin has recently been sandblasted and the blue-tiled floor cleaned. Brown, yellow and red leaves from the surrounding trees have begun dropping and float in the water like little boats. In the centre is some sort of mermaid and fish statue, the water spouts out of the fish's mouth. When we've been here with the girls, Luke has remarked how hideous the whole thing is. I don't think it's that bad, but then I haven't got the artistic eye he has.

'Congratulations on your win in court,' I say.

'Thanks. Wasn't sure if the witness was going to crack at first, but fortunately I'd done my homework about her reliability and was able to dish the dirt. Once the jury heard how she'd perjured herself in court before, it was game over.'

'I'm glad I won't ever have to come up against you in court. I expect Leonard was pleased.'

'Oh yeah, although he took the credit, of course, and said I'd learned it all from him.'

'That sounds like Leonard,' I say. 'Anyway, how was your weekend? Did you have Lottie?'

'No, next weekend Lottie is with me. I had a pretty quiet couple of days, to be honest.' He leans back and stretches his arm across the back of the bench. 'What about you? How's it going with Alice?'

I knew he was going to ask and it's probably half the reason why he invited me out for lunch. 'Good,' I say. 'It's going well.'

'Is that it? That's all you're going to say? That it's going well?'

I look at him and shrug. 'It's the truth. She seems very nice. Mum is over the bloody moon. Luke and the girls seem to get on well with her too. I don't really know what else to say.'

'You seem very underwhelmed by it. I thought you'd be buzzing with excitement.' He gives my ponytail a gentle tug. 'Come on, Clare. I know you better than that. What's the deal with Alice?'

I rest my head back on his arm and close my eyes for a moment. I'm still having trouble processing my emotions and feelings about Alice. I open my eyes and look at Tom. He gives a sympathetic smile. I let out a sigh. 'Okay. To be honest, I don't know how I feel. No, that's not right.' I sit forward. 'It's very confusing. I feel all sorts of things, but most of all, and don't you dare repeat this.' I pause and wait for Tom to promise. He obliges and makes the Cub Scout promise sign. 'Most of all, I feel like it's a bit of an anticlimax. It's not as exciting as I thought it would be. I feel a bit flat and, if I'm honest, a bit grumpy. I shouldn't feel like this, surely?'

'You've had years of building up to this point; times when you've been excited, enthusiastic, frustrated, sad and resigned to never finding her.' Tom is right. I have experienced all those emotions and many more. 'And now it's actually happened, now you've found Alice, or rather, she's found you, all those emotions have gone and you're left with what? Love? Probably not. You may love the memory of your little sister Alice, but now you're confronted with the real-life, adult Alice. Those two people are poles apart. You probably can't even work out what you're feeling. The euphoric feeling when she first wrote, that's long gone. The fairytale ending has happened. Now you're in for the long, hard slog of trying to build a relationship from scratch. Trying to love someone you don't know.'

'You know what?' I say. 'You actually sound like you know what you're talking about.'

Tom gives another playful yank of my hair. 'Yeah, well, sometimes I do, actually.'

'In my mind I thought, assumed even, that I would have this instant connection with Alice. A bond so strong that twenty years apart wouldn't matter,' I say. 'And now the reality isn't quite as romantic as you see in the films or read in books. The reality is that it's difficult and strained.' I look down at the ground, not wanting to say out loud what I'm thinking, yet at the same time wanting to tell Tom. He seems to understand how I'm feeling. I decide to say it. Talking to

Tom is safe. 'I know this will make me sound like some crazy woman, but last weekend ...' I pause, wondering if I can say it.

'Last weekend?' prompts Tom.

'Last weekend, I even had a few bad thoughts about her and she's only just got here. No, that's not right. Not thoughts, feelings, really.'

'In what way?'

Now I'm regretting starting this part of the conversation, but I know Tom won't be fobbed off. 'Jealous feelings. Just tiny little ones, but they were there all the same. Jealous the way Mum is fussing over her. For example, Alice wanted peanut butter and jelly. I offered her jam, which wasn't good enough, so Mum was all set for sending Luke off to find exactly what Alice wanted. And then there's Luke. On Sunday she went on the i360 with him and when they came off, she was hanging onto him like she owned him. And when Hannah didn't want to hold Alice's hand, you know what? I felt a small ounce of victory wash over me.' Truth be told, I had wanted to high-five Hannah at the time and shout, in very American cheerleader way, *go Hannah, go Hannah!*

Tom laughs. 'Well, this is a first. I do believe it's called jealousy.'

'I know! What the hell's wrong with me?'

'You do trust Luke, don't you?' His voice has taken on a serious tone.

'Of course I trust him,' I say, without hesitation. 'Luke loves me. I know that. He's never once done anything to make me even question his honesty.'

'I know, it's just that men of a certain age can get their heads turned if a pretty young woman starts to take an interest.' He drains the rest of his coffee. 'I've handled plenty of divorce cases where an older man has been flattered by the attentions of a younger woman.'

'Luke wouldn't do that to me, so I don't even know why we're having this conversation.'

'If I recall, you brought it up in the first place. Anyway, you know your husband best. Who am I to say what he is or is not likely to do? We're both probably reading far too much into it. That's what comes of being a solicitor.' He takes the empty panini wrapper from me, scrunching it up with his own and getting up, chucks it into the rubbish bin. 'Everything will be fine. *You'll* be fine, Clare. Give yourself a break. And Alice.' He begins to walk away. 'Come on, we'd better get back before Leonard puts out an APB on us.'

I catch him up and we walk back through the park. 'I think I'm tired. Emotionally. I'll be okay, though. Just a bit of an overreaction on my part.' I drop my empty cup into the next bin we pass. 'Anyway, when do you fancy coming over to meet her?'

Tom pulls a face. 'I don't know. Is it a good idea?'

'Of course it is. Come over on Saturday with Lottie. Hannah would love to see her; they can play in the garden. You can't not meet Alice after all the years of me banging on about her and roping you in to try to trace her. Leonard's coming.'

'Maybe.'

'Absolutely no "maybe" about it,' I say. 'You won't be intruding or anything. I'd like you to come. Really, I would.

Please?' For some reason it's suddenly very important to me that Tom meets Alice.

'Okay,' says Tom with a lack of enthusiasm. 'I'll come.'

'Excellent. Don't let me down.'

'When have I ever let you down?'

Driving home that evening, I make a conscious decision to try to relax a bit more about Alice being here. I need to recapture that initial enthusiasm I felt when she first got in touch. I put my unease down to not only Alice's return, but also the pressure I'm under at work with the McMillan case.

A reminder pings on my phone and I glance down at it and swear. It's that bloody school governors' meeting tonight. I had completely forgotten about it. I can't dip out. I'm part of the sub-committee who have been overseeing the application for new parking restrictions and a build-out into the road to make it safer for the kids to get to school. It will be more hassle not attending and passing on the information than it will to actually attend.

I check my watch. It's not worth going home. I might as well go straight to the school. Hannah's school is in the next village, but due to rural spread of new house-building, the villages of Little Dray, where we live, and Budlington, have almost merged. A small strip of road, about one hundred metres long, is the no-man's-land between the two places. Little Dray's primary school was closed two years ago and the children now all attend Budlington Primary, which has put an increased pressure on the village infrastructure. Traffic flow through the village at school dropping-off and picking-up time has increased considerably. The flock of 4x4 vehicles and MPVs that swarm in and out of Budlington twice a day, when I've been privy to witness it, reminds me of a flock of starlings. They arrive en masse, dipping and diving in unspoken synchronised manoeuvres as they queue to enter the small turnaround in front of the school, drop their children off, or pick them up, and then move on out. The locals living near the school are not very happy, to say the least. I give a sigh and mentally prepare myself for the governors' meeting as I pull up in the school car park. Before I go in, I tap out a quick text message to Luke.

Sorry, school govs meeting. Be home as soon as I can. Xx
A reply comes back just as I'm getting out of the car.

Okay, Babe. See you later. This is accompanied by a sad-face emoji.

If I was of the praying persuasion, I'd run off a quick thank you that I have such an understanding husband and that Luke doesn't highlight the guilt trip I'm already on. Only one more academic year and then I can give up the governor's role. I had taken it on as a favour to the school, really. They needed some legal advice, which I was happy to give for free but, before I knew it, I was more involved than I had anticipated.

As I walk across the car park, I meet with my friend, Pippa Stent. 'Hiya! How are you?' I ask, as we walk together.

'Not so bad. Got a million things to do tonight, as usual. Why do these meetings always fall on the busiest night of the week, when Baz is away and my mother has a new boyfriend to distract her from grandmother babysitting duties?'

'Oh, yes. How is your mum's love life these days?'

Pippa pulls a face. 'Don't ask. Honestly, there should be an age limit on those dating websites. I tell you, the old ones are the worst, I'm sure. Not that I've been on them, of course, but you know. I feel like my mum has turned into a teenager!' We laugh at the thought. 'To be honest, I nearly forgot about tonight.'

'Me too,' I confess. 'Our routine is totally out of the window at the moment.'

'Oh, yeah. How's it going with your visitor? Your sister, I should say, sorry.'

I wave her apology away. 'Good. Yeah, good.'

Pippa stops walking as we get to the main entrance. 'Well, that sounded convincing,' she says, eyeing me suspiciously.

I hesitate, but decide to be honest with my friend. 'It's hard work. It's awkward. It's like you have this total stranger in the house and, yet, you have to behave as if you've known each other all your life.' I look over and notice Michael, one of the other governors, approaching.

Pippa follows my gaze. 'Look, come round for a coffee when you get a moment. We'll chat then.' She gives my arm a reassuring pat and then turns to Michael. 'Hi, Michael, how are you?' The three of us make our way into the school.

The meeting drags on even longer than I thought it would and if it wasn't for the fact that I'm on the parking and speed sub-committee, I would have floored it out of that car park like a F1 driver. Instead, I force myself to make a sedate exit, but once I'm round the corner and out of sight, I drive as fast as I dare from one village to the next. The small stretch of road, which divides Budlington and Little Dray, is narrow and twisty. With no footpath, it's a devil to negotiate as either a driver or a pedestrian. In the dark it's even worse and am relieved as I round the last bend and the streetlights of Little Dray appear. The radar-activated speed sign flashes as I near the village. The digits 30 and the words *slow down* flash alternately. I take heed; it wouldn't do to get a speeding ticket. That would be rather ironic.

I eventually get home and haul myself and my briefcase through the front door. I can hear laughter coming from the kitchen. It sounds like Hannah and I smile, grateful that Luke has let her stay up to see me.

He greets me at the door. 'Hey, there,' he says, coming down the stairs and giving me a kiss. 'Sorry, you've just missed Chloe. She was shattered, so I had to put her to bed.'

The guilt hugs me tighter than Luke. 'It's okay. The meeting went on far longer than usual. I had totally forgotten about it. I'll be glad when I don't have to go any more.'

'Don't beat yourself up, Babe. As long as there's one of us to put her to bed, she doesn't mind.' I put my case down under the coat rack and slip off my jacket. Luke takes it from me and hangs it on the hook. 'I seriously don't think she's going to need counselling as a result of it.'

I smile at his attempt to relieve my guilt. 'Hannah okay?'

'Yeah, she's in the kitchen with your mum and Alice. Look, I was going to get on with some work. You don't mind, do you?'

'No. Fill your boots, but do try to come to bed at some point tonight. It's an awful big bed for one.'

Luke cups my face in his hands. 'Try stopping me.' He kisses me and then, leaving me with a smile, wanders off down the hallway. I hear him stop by the kitchen and say goodnight to Hannah before heading off to his studio. I kick off my shoes and, after giving my mobile one final check for any messages or emails, I switch it off, leaving work firmly behind me. I hear more laughter from Hannah in the kitchen. She has such an infectious laugh. I smile to myself and go down to join the fun.

As I enter the kitchen, I can feel the corners of my mouth sag slightly as the smile I had reserved for Hannah disappears. Hannah is sitting at the breakfast bar, her back to me, with Alice sitting next to her, their heads dipped towards each. They giggle at something I haven't heard.

'Hiya,' I say brightly from the doorway. Neither appear to hear me, their heads remaining bowed, looking at something in Hannah's lap. I spy an array of nail varnishes on the worktop and the smell of acetone hits the back of my throat. Alice looks up as I walk further into the kitchen.

'Hi, Clare. How are you? Good day?'

Hannah turns to look over her shoulder. 'Alice is doing my nails,' she says; her face lights up with excitement for a brief moment and then disappears, to be replaced by one of apprehension. 'I wanted my nails to look pretty, like Alice's.'

'You know how I feel about make-up and nail varnish,' I say, not being able to stop the words from coming out, yet at the same time wanting to kick myself for being such a spoil sport. 'You have school tomorrow. You won't be able to keep it on.'

'Oh, Clare, it's just a bit of nail polish,' says Alice, with a touch of amusement to her voice, in the way you'd tell a child that there were no monsters under the bed.

'It's the school policy,' I say. *God, when did I turn into the fucking head teacher?* 'Hannah, you know that.' I'm aware that I am taking out my annoyance on Hannah, when really I'm angry at Alice. And I know the anger is unjustified. How would Alice know what the school policy was?

Hannah slips her hand away from Alice dejectedly. I look at Alice. 'Have you got some nail-varnish remover? Only, I don't have any – I don't wear the stuff.'

'Yeah, sure. It's right here.' Alice picks up a plastic bottle I hadn't noticed. 'What about if I get up early and take it off for Hannah in the morning? It's such a shame and it's totally my fault. One hundred per cent my fault. I honestly did not realise. Sorry, Clare.' She bites the side of her lip. Hannah looks up from under her lashes, not quite able to meet my gaze head on. I feel a sudden pang of guilt and shame. What harm is it for one night? Hannah should have known better, but the excitement of getting her nails done obviously won out. Christ, she's only seven. I'm the one who should know better.

I smile and go over to Hannah and give her a hug. 'I'm sorry for getting cross,' I say. 'You can keep it on for the night. Either Alice or I will take it off in the morning before you go to school.' I kiss her and instantly am rewarded with a huge smile.

'Sorry, again,' says Alice.

It's at this point I notice what Alice is wearing. It's a pink

T-shirt with the words New York in white letters across the chest. I do a double-take. 'I have a T-shirt just like that,' I say. 'That is such a coincidence.'

I hear a laugh behind me and it's Mum, who must have just come into the kitchen and caught the end of our conversation. Alice laughs and exchanges a knowing smile with Mum, 'Shall I tell her or do you want to?'

'Tell me what?' I look at Mum.

'Oh, Clare, you are funny,' says Mum. 'That T-shirt looks like yours because it is yours.' Mum, Alice and Hannah all laugh together.

'Oh,' is all I can manage to say, finding it hard to join in with the joke. Alice probably thinks I'm a proper misery. First I get all uptight over nail varnish and now I'm failing the see the funny side of T-shirt-gate.

'I spilt something down my top earlier,' explains Alice. 'It was the only pink one I had and we were just about to go out. I didn't want to change my whole outfit. I needed something to go with my white jeans, so Mum said I could borrow yours.' The way she slips the word Mum in, as if it's the most natural thing in the world for her to say, as if she's been saying it all her life, doesn't escape me. 'Look, I'll go change. I shouldn't have borrowed it. Sorry.'

She gets up to leave but Mum steps forward. 'Don't be daft, Alice. There's no need for that. Clare doesn't mind, do you, darling?'

'No, of course, I don't.' I force the words out and attach a fake smile at the end, while acknowledging to myself that Mum and Alice are becoming closer by the day, whereas I'm getting left behind. I feel I'm on the outside of what is fast becoming their little club. 'Hey, isn't that what sisters are supposed to do anyway. You know, share clothes?'

'Sure thing,' says Alice, quickly brightening up and sitting back down. 'Sisters share everything.' I watch as she takes Hannah's hand and sets about finishing the beauty task.

Chapter 10

With the girls tucked up in bed, fast asleep, and Luke working in his studio, Mum, Alice and I settle ourselves in the living room. I bring in a bottle of wine and pour us each of us a glass. I've changed into my slouchy trousers and T-shirt already.

'You look tired,' says Mum. 'Such a shame you couldn't take any time off.'

'Mmm.' There's no point going over old ground, so I opt for a quick acknowledgement and divert the attention onto Alice. 'How are you managing the jet lag?'

'Not too bad. I slept a bit better last night, although I was awake at five a.m. I came down to get a glass of water. I hope I didn't disturb y'all.'

'Not me,' says Mum. 'I don't hear anything in my part of the house. Occasionally, I might hear Luke's studio door open or close when he's working during the night, but other than that, I'm dead to the world.'

'Luke works at night?' Alice looks over at me.

'Sometimes – when the mood takes him. He goes through phases; depends how engrossed in his work he is.'

'Like now,' says Mum. 'I thought I heard him in there the other night.'

'You probably did.' I take a sip of wine. 'It's one of those phases.'

'It doesn't bother you, that's he's in there all night?' asks Alice.

'Not really. He's working,' I reply.

'I wouldn't like it,' says Alice. 'I'd want him right next to me, so I knew exactly where he was.'

We laugh, despite the lack of humour I find in the statement. 'Do you have a boyfriend?' I ask.

Alice shakes her head. 'No. I've had one or two, but nothing serious.' She blinks hard and looks away for a moment.

'You okay, Alice?' asks Mum.

'Yeah, sure. Sorry.' Alice wipes under her eyes with the tip of her finger.

'What is it, darling?' Mum puts her glass of wine down and goes to sit beside Alice on the sofa. I straighten up in my chair, not sure what is about to unfold.

'I never had a proper boyfriend, not one I really loved.' She looks up at me and then Mum. 'Daddy wouldn't let me.'

I can see Mum physically jerk at the mention of Dad. I always knew it would be a tricky topic of conversation and I had hoped we could broach it tonight. Both Mum and I want to know about Alice's childhood, but we had agreed not to rush her on her first couple of nights. Now, it seems Alice herself is willing to talk before we need to ask.

Mum puts a comforting arm around Alice. She glances over at me for what I assume is encouragement. I give a small nod.

'Alice, darling, I didn't want to rush you into talking about your father, but seeing as you've mentioned him, do you want to talk about it? I've always hoped that you were having a happy life and that your father was being good to you. I'm so sorry if that's not the case.'

'No, my Daddy was good to me,' says Alice. 'He loved me; he just wasn't so keen on letting his little girl grow up, I guess. I just assumed all fathers were like that. I expect Luke will be the same with Hannah and Chloe.'

'I think he's already like that,' I say. 'He's always joking with Hannah about no boyfriends until she's thirty.' I smile as I recall Hannah rolling her eyes at the suggestion, but then adding that boys were smelly anyway.

'You know, I wrote to you so many times,' says Mum. 'But I had no address to send them to. I've kept them all in a box upstairs for you with gifts I've bought for you over the years. When your father took you to America, he promised me it was only for a holiday and that he would be back after a couple of weeks.' I can see the pain in Mum's eyes as she speaks; pain heavily coated with guilt. 'I should never have agreed to him taking you. I should have known he wasn't planning on coming back, despite what he said.' Mum dabs at the tears that trickle from her eyes. 'I'm so sorry, Alice.'

'It's okay. Please don't cry. I know it wasn't your fault,' says Alice, softly.

'I love you,' says Mum. 'I always have and never once have I stopped. Your father was a very persuasive man. I was a weak woman.' She holds her hand to Alice's face. 'Please forgive me, my darling.'

Alice rests her hand on top of Mum's. 'There's nothing to forgive. You're my mother.'

I watch as Mum holds Alice tightly and I'm relieved Alice has been so compassionate. The burden of guilt may never lift from Mum, but at least now she has Alice's forgiveness, the load will be lighter.

I top up our glasses with more wine. I think we all need it, Mum especially. She's more composed now and while she remains on the sofa with Alice, I sit back in the chair.

'You're very understanding. Thank you, my darling,' says Mum.

'I've been waiting for this my whole life,' says Alice. 'I don't know what really happened, Daddy never said. He didn't want to talk about it.'

'That first letter you wrote, when you told me the things you remembered, meant so much to me,' says Mum. 'Knowing you had still retained little snippets of your time here was like music to my ears. You hadn't totally forgotten us. It gave me such comfort.'

Alice glances over at me and I detect a fleeting sense of unease. Perhaps it's getting a bit too much for her, but she turns to Mum and smiles warmly. 'And they meant so much to me too.'

Whether Alice is telling her the truth or not, I don't know and, to be honest, I don't really care. All I care about is the sense of relief it is bringing Mum. I know how she has tortured herself over the years about Alice.

'Your stepmother, what was she like?' asks Mum, her voice gentle.

Alice gives a shrug. 'Roma? She was okay, I guess.' Alice looks down at her hands and I sense another shift in her body language.

'Only okay?' asks Mum. Alice shrugs again. 'You can tell us, Alice. Please don't feel you can't. We want to know, don't we, Clare?'

'Well, yeah. If Alice feels she can.' I throw Mum a *do you think this is a good idea?* look. One that Mum either fails to interpret or ignores.

'Tell us, Alice. Please.'

'Okay ... Roma was with my father just for the money. I knew that from a very young age. She would be all nice to me in front of him, but when we were alone, she was horrid. We had our meals before Daddy got home from work. She would serve her son, Nathaniel, a huge, massive portion and, yet, me, I'd get a tiny amount, just enough to feed a sparrow. I didn't get dessert either. Nathaniel did.'

Mum's hand flies to her mouth, a look of horror on her face. 'Oh, Alice, I had no idea.'

'When Daddy wasn't around, she used to beat me with the sole of her sneaker and lock me in my room for hours on end.'

'Didn't you tell your dad?' I ask, aware that I don't acknowledge his paternal relationship to me.

'I did once, but never again,' says Alice. 'He asked Roma and, of course, she denied it. Then the next day, when he went to work, I got the biggest beating I'd ever received.'

'Oh, my God,' cries Mum. 'Oh, Alice.'

'Didn't your dad see the bruises?' I ask, shocked at this awful revelation.

'She was clever,' says Alice, her face contorts into a sneer. 'She never beat me so bad that I had big bruises or anywhere that couldn't be hidden by clothing.'

'Jesus,' is all I manage to say. We all take a simultaneous moment to let this disclosure sink in. I take a gulp of wine and replace my glass on the table. 'How long did all this go on for?'

'Right up until I was sixteen.' Alice once again hangs her head, her hands are clasped together in her lap and she nervously twiddles her fingers.

Maybe it's the solicitor in me, but I have to ask. 'What happened at sixteen to make it stop?'

Alice doesn't answer straight away. 'I ... sorry, I don't know if I can say.'

'It's okay, Alice, you can tell us. We're family,' says Mum. 'I'm your mother, you can tell me anything.'

Alice takes a deep breath and raises her head. Her eyes look over at the sideboard and graze the photographs. She nods to herself and then seems to summon up some inner strength as she takes another breath and sits upright.

I can't help thinking her actions are rather staged and have an air of Hollywood about them.

'Nathaniel was two years older than me. One night he had been to a party and came home drunk. Daddy and Roma were out having dinner, so it was just me alone at home.' She looks from Mum to me. I already know I'm not going to like where I think this story is heading, but I brace myself in the way I do with clients, when they tell me about truly terrible events that have happened to them. 'Without going into detail,

107

he basically … well, you know … took advantage of me. He was bigger and stronger. I couldn't fight him off. He was so drunk, I didn't stand a chance.'

I move to perch on the edge of the coffee table in front of Alice. I take her hands in mine. 'He raped you?' I ask softly. 'Your stepbrother raped you?' I hear a sharp intake of air from Mum, but I keep my eyes locked on Alice. I want her to know that it's okay, that she can tell us the truth. That we won't judge her. She doesn't break eye contact, but nods.

'A bit. He was too drunk.'

'A bit. Whether it's a bit or a lot, it's still rape,' I say, keeping my voice low. 'Did you tell anyone?'

'Roma and Daddy came home. Daddy was putting the car away and Roma came into the house first. She must have heard me crying. I had given up struggling at this point. Anyway, the next thing I knew, she was pulling Nathaniel off me and bundling him into his room. She came back and told me that I was never to speak a word about it. That if I did, I would get more than just a beating.'

'Oh my darling. Oh, that is awful.' Mum's tears begin again. 'I'm so sorry.'

'The next day I told Roma that if she or her son ever laid another finger on me, then I would file a police report.'

'Did you go to the doctor? Did you have evidence?' I don't want to ask Alice in front of Mum if she kept her underwear or bed sheet for DNA from Nathaniel. Alice, however, seems to have no qualms.

'I figured if Monica Lewinsky could keep Bill Clinton's sp …, well, you know …' She screws up her nose and scrunches her shoulders, not needing to elaborate further. 'Anyway, if she can keep Clinton's stuff all those years, then I sure as hell could keep Nathaniel's. In theory, anyway. You should have seen the look on Roma's face when I told her that.'

'Did you have your underwear?' I ask.

'Oh, Clare, you are such a lawyer,' Alice says and grins at me. 'No, but I wasn't gonna let her know that. Anyway, it worked, as neither of them laid a finger on me again. And when Daddy died, she gave me your address. Said she found it in his things, but I think she had kept it all that time and only gave it to me once she realised she wasn't getting her hands on the rest of Daddy's money.'

'You've been through so much. You're so brave. Are you okay? I mean, really okay?' asks Mum.

'Sure. I mean, nothing that a bit of therapy won't sort out. Well, that's what I've been told but, if you wanna know the truth, I think you and Clare and Clare's family are the only therapy I need. Your love is enough to heal all the wounds.'

It's uncharitable of me to think this sounds a bit OTT and clichéd, but then I remind myself that, to all intents and purposes, Alice is American and therapy is far more widely spoken about and accepted over there.

'Anyway, enough of all that,' says Alice. 'It's in the past. This is a new beginning for me. For all of us.' She gives Mum's hand a squeeze and looks at me with a smile, which I return.

I have to admit to being impressed by her resilience. Her ability to push the negativity away so easily is quite outstanding. I've seen it with some clients who have sat in my office or in a police rape suite and had to recount an awful attack they've been subjected to and sometimes there can be a certain amount of detachment. However, I've never seen detachment quite like this. It's almost as if Alice is talking about something much more trivial. I can't help but think if she was one of my clients and this was a courtroom, I would be urging her to show more emotion.

I want to quiz her further, as if I were preparing one of my clients for court and how the defence might try to discredit her, but Mum moves the conversation on far too quickly, asking Alice about school and education, which Alice skims over. I get the feeling she doesn't want to talk about her past too much and, I suppose, who can blame her after everything she's been through? I end up telling Alice more about my childhood and my friends, how I met Luke at school, and so on.

'You must have lots of friends if you've always lived here,' says Alice.

'Maybe not as many as you'd think. Most of the people I went to school with have spread their wings a bit further afield than Little Dray. I'm good friends with one of the mums from Hannah's school, Pippa Stent. Her daughter, Daisy, is friends with Hannah. We're both on the board of governors. I've never really done the whole mums-playground-coffee-circuit thing, mainly because I'm hardly ever there. What with work and everything, Luke knows the other parents better than I do.'

'Don't you miss being a mum?' asks Alice.

Instantly, my hackles rise and I can feel a surge of defensive anger shift inside me. I look Alice straight in the eye when I answer. 'I am a mum. Just because I don't do the school run, it doesn't make me any less of a mother.' I'm not sure whose face I want to slap. Alice's for questioning me as a mother or my own for getting so angry about it. Jesus, Alice is only young, she doesn't have any children and it sounds as though she had a shit role model. What does she know about motherhood?

'I'm sure Alice didn't mean you weren't a good mother,' says Mum. 'She probably just meant the school run, didn't you Alice?'

'Sure, of course. Sorry, Clare, I really didn't mean to offend you.' She bites her lip and both Alice and Mum look at me expectantly.

'Hey, forget it. I'm tired. I didn't mean to snap.' I force a smile. I could do with going up to bed, but if I go now it will look as if I'm flouncing off. And although I'm still pissed off with what Alice said, I don't want to upset Mum or leave with an atmosphere hanging between us all. I'll be the one ending up looking like a bloody idiot.

I fill the next half an hour telling Alice about work and manage to elicit a few laughs with anecdotes about strange clients and the obscure reasons they've sought legal advice.

'The worse was the couple who were having an affair at work and stayed late one night to, how shall we say, cement their relationship.' I sit in the armchair with my feet tucked up underneath me. 'They ended up having sex across the office desk, but in all the excitement, they somehow managed to bundle off the desk and she hit her head on the filing cabinet, which made the boss's golfing trophy topple off and knock her out stone cold. They had to call an ambulance and everything, but the best of it is, she came to see me wanting to sue her workplace for industrial injury due to poor health and safety standards!'

We all laugh at the story and when I'm confident that the equilibrium has been restored, I make my excuses and head up to bed.

Whether it's the revelations of what Alice has been through, the fact that she still has my T-shirt or that she and Hannah seemed as thick as thieves earlier, I don't know, but I find myself waking from a restless sleep. I look at the LCD display of the clock-radio. I've only been asleep two hours. I stretch my hand out across the bed, more to confirm the fact that Luke isn't there than to see whether he is.

I decide to go down and see him. Despite being in a house full of people, I'm feeling lonely. I put it down to a rather traumatic evening and the sadness that I feel for Alice. Although Mum and I had never said it, I'm sure we'd both hoped that Alice had had a good life in America with our father. That she had been loved and cared for.

I think at times it was the only hope that kept Mum going. I dread to think how she would have coped if she had known about the harrowing ordeal Alice had endured. I can't even begin to image how she must have felt. A young girl who had no one to turn to when she needed it most. It was all credit to her that she had come out of it without being affected too badly. Maybe that's why she has been keen to bond with us here so quickly. Now our father is dead and her stepmother out of the picture, she has no one other than her friend. No wonder she wanted to bring Martha over with her. Still, I'm glad she came on her own in the end. I resolve to put any negative feelings I might have been cultivating to one side. Alice needs us.

As I walk down the hallway towards Luke's studio, I'm surprised to hear the soft burr of voices coming from behind the closed door. I can't make out what is being said, but a small giggle punctuates the air. My heart does some sort of double beat and my chest feels as if it's going to burst with the extra air that has filled my lungs. I puff out a long breath and, snatching at the handle, push open the door.

At first I think I'm seeing things, looking at my own reflection. Sitting on a stool in the middle of the room is Alice, still wearing my T-shirt but now her hair is pulled back into a ponytail just like I wear mine to work. Just like it is tonight. Luke has his back to me, facing Alice with a canvas on the easel between them. He turns around and, at least has the decency to look sheepish, but Alice speaks first.

'Oh, hi, Clare.' She smiles at me. 'Are you okay? I thought you had gone to bed.'

'I did, but I couldn't sleep,' I say, surprised at how I appear to be having a civil conversation when what I really want to do is scream at both of them and demand to know what the fuck is going on.

'Me neither,' says Alice, jumping off the stool. 'I think it's the jet lag. I came down to get a glass of water and noticed the light under the door.'

'Alice was just having a look at some of my work,' says Luke.

'Tell Clare the truth,' says Alice, giving Luke a coy smile.

My heart does that funny two-beat thing again. The truth? What is she on about? 'Well?' I look at Luke.

He steps to one side so I can see the canvas he's working on. I don't know why I didn't notice it when I first came in. I was so busy throwing evil looks at the pair of them that I didn't take in anything else. Alice comes and stands beside me, slipping her arm through mine. We both look at the beginnings of a portrait. A portrait of Alice.

'I wanted to surprise you and Mum,' she says. 'I wanted to have a picture done as a present.'

On the canvas I can see an outline of what is clearly Alice's face, made up from abstract colours that will all blend in eventually, to make the perfect composition. It's more than just a couple of hours' work. I've seen enough of Luke's paintings to know that what is in front of me didn't just appear in the last hour. 'How long have you been working on this surprise?' I ask, emphasising the last word.

'Just tonight and last night,' says Luke. He taps the end of the brush against the palm of his hand. There's an awkward silence. I gaze at the canvas, but I'm not taking in the detail. I'm using it as a diversion for the anger I'm trying to tamp down; that green-eyed monster which makes me so angry. 'What do you think?' asks Luke eventually.

What do I think? He so doesn't want to know what I think. 'It's nice,' I say, unable to inject any enthusiasm into the word.

'Erm, I think I'll go to bed now,' says Alice. 'I'm suddenly feeling really tired.' She smiles at Luke in that awkward way when someone is trying to pretend everything is okay, when it clearly isn't. 'Goodnight, Clare.' She pauses, as if she wants to say something but then changes her mind and walks over to the door.

'Yeah, night.' I can't bring myself to say her name. The door closes and I wait until I hear the creak of the stairs and I'm confident she has gone to her room.

'Look, Babe,' says Luke before I can say anything. 'She genuinely came down last night and asked if I would do this as a surprise for you and your Mum.'

'She may have done, but I tell you what, Luke, you're letting a bit of flattery from a young woman go to your head.' The seed that Tom planted earlier somehow has not just taken root but grown into a great big fucking tree without me even realising. Luke looks incredulously at me.

'Are you serious?' he laughs. 'You can't be. Fuck, you are. Oh, come on, Clare, what's got into you? I was just taking the piss the other night about you being jealous, but you really are.'

'What do you expect?' I ask. 'All this cloak and dagger over a flaming portrait. I don't like it.'

'The portrait?'

'No! You two. I don't like you two being all sneaky.' I look at Luke and he has a small smile on his face. 'And I don't like the portrait either, now you come to mention it.' I stick out my bottom lip like a child. Luke's mock look of disappointment is making it difficult to stay cross with him.

He comes over and wraps his arms around me and kisses me, nuzzling my neck. 'Are you saying you don't like it?'

I make a half-hearted attempt to push him away. I want to

be cross with him, but he makes it very difficult. 'No. I don't.'

'Not even this?' He takes his kisses down the side of my neck and moves the shoulder of my dressing gown over, where he kisses my bare skin.

I wriggle free and rearrange my robe. 'That's cheating.' I look over at the canvas. 'I still don't like it.'

'Clare, you're overreacting. Look, I'll wash up and then I'll come up to bed.'

I know sulking is such a childish act, but I can't help it as I retreat out of the room and back up to bed. When Luke comes up some ten minutes later I pretend to be asleep. I'm on my side with my back to him. He gets into bed and leans over and kisses the back of my head.

'Night, Babe. I love you and don't you forget it.' He turns over and pulls the quilt up around his shoulder. It's not long before his breathing slips into the deep rhythm of sleep, leaving me wide awake, battling the green-eyed monster again. How the hell did I become such an irrational and jealous person?

Chapter 11

It's Saturday morning and although I've been really busy with work and helping Mum and Alice prepare for the little get-together we're having this afternoon, I haven't been able to stop replaying Alice's confession in my mind. It's not so much what she said but the way she said it and her body language. I just can't make it all tie in together. And then, in the next thought, I'm chastising myself for being suspicious and reminding myself that Alice has already been through a lot in her life; maybe she has developed a coping mechanism and I've just become far too cynical in my job.

I'm also aware that I may have overreacted slightly about the portrait. I didn't get a chance to apologise yesterday; Luke kept himself shut in his studio for most of the evening and I ended up going to bed alone. He'd come up some time in the night and I vaguely remember cuddling up to him.

When I wake up I can hear him in the shower, so I wait for him to come out and apologise for overreacting.

'Hey, don't worry,' he says generously. 'You've had a tough week emotionally and, I promise you, it was all totally innocent.'

'I love you,' I say, appreciating his forgiving nature. I stop in the bedroom doorway and kiss him.

'I love you too, Mrs Tennison. Now, haven't you got some baking to do for the party?' He gives my backside a tap. 'No soggy bottoms!'

I grin to myself as I go downstairs, feeling a surge of love for Luke.

I spend the next couple of hours with Mum and Alice preparing the buffet food for this afternoon. Luke takes the girls to the park to keep them out from under our feet and when he returns everything is ready and there's an air of happiness about the place.

Mum has only invited a handful of people over to meet Alice. I had warned her about overwhelming Alice. Naturally people are curious to meet her, but I don't want it to turn into a freak show. Mum understood and the guest list extended to Pippa and her family, Leonard, Tom and Lottie and a couple of Mum's friends from the WI.

I'm rather nervous about Tom meeting Alice, for some reason, and I'm not sure why. I suppose it's a bit like taking your boyfriend or girlfriend home for the first time to meet your family. You're never quite sure how it's going to go and what you really want is for everyone to like each other and get on well together.

'Hi, Tom,' I say, opening the door when he finally turns up. 'And, hello, Lottie. How are you?' I give Tom a kiss on the cheek and then bend down to give Lottie a hug. 'Hannah's in the garden on the trampoline if you want to go through, sweetheart.'

'How's it going?' asks Tom as Lottie skips off towards the

rear of the house. He has a bunch of flowers in one hand and a bottle of red in the other.

'Good,' I say. I run my hands down the sides of my trousers, aware my palms are sweaty.

'Not nervous at all, then?' says Tom, nodding at my gesture.

I give a small laugh, which says it all. 'It just feels really strange introducing you to Alice after all this time. I wasn't like this when Luke met her.'

'Deep breaths and relax,' says Tom. He breathes in through his nose and slowly out through his mouth. I do the same. 'That's it. Nothing to be nervous about at all.'

We go through into the kitchen and Tom greets Mum with a kiss and presents her with the bottle of wine. The men get handshakes and Mum's friends get his most charming smile. Finally, it's Alice's turn.

'This is Alice,' I say to Tom. 'Alice this is Tom.'

'Wow, you're really here. Amazing. It's just amazing,' says Tom. He takes a moment to look at her and a small blush rises to Alice's face. Tom steps forward and offers the bunch of flowers to Alice. 'Hello, Alice.' His voice is full of sincerity and he gives her a small peck on the cheek. 'Welcome home.'

'Hello, Tom,' says Alice and accepts the flowers. 'They're beautiful. Thank you, so much. I've never been given flowers before.'

I look on and realise I'm smiling. That's so thoughtful of Tom. I glance at Luke, who looks back and gives a smile and a slight raise of the eyebrows, which I interpret as Luke thinking Tom is being typically smooth and charming. I move over to him, snaking my arm behind him to reach a glass of wine on the counter. 'Flowers, eh? Nice touch.'

'I do far more romantic gestures than flowers,' mutters Luke in my ear. 'I'll show you later.'

'I shall look forward to it,' I reply before side-stepping and going back to Alice. 'I think Mum's just fishing out a vase for the flowers,' I say, nodding in the direction of the utility room, where Mum has just disappeared to. 'You okay?'

'Yeah, I'm fine,' says Alice. 'Tom was just telling me how you went to university together and now work together.'

'Yeah, I can't get rid of him,' I say, winking at Tom. 'He follows me everywhere.'

'She loves it really,' says Tom.

Mum comes over and relieves Alice of the flowers, her face glowing with happiness. It makes me happy to see the sparkle in her eyes. 'Could you get the sausage rolls out of the oven for me, Clare?'

'I'll leave you in Tom's care,' I say and head over to help Mum.

The afternoon goes smoothly and everyone seems relaxed. The children play nicely in the garden.

As I collect empty glasses and used plates, I realise I haven't seen Alice for a while. I scan the kitchen and then the garden but can't see her. Come to think of it, Tom's not about either.

I go out into the garden onto the decking. Around the corner, out of sight from the main party, Tom and Alice are there. They don't notice me at first. They're standing very close together, but something about their body language alerts me. Neither is smiling and Tom appears to be talking quietly to Alice, but I can see no gentleness in his expression.

Alice spots me first and then Tom looks up too. Both smile.

'Everything okay?' I ask coming over.

'Yeah, sure,' says Tom.

'Alice?' I say, looking at my sister.

She hesitates for a moment before speaking. 'I'm fine, honestly. I just needed a bit of air. Sometimes I find crowds a bit overwhelming.'

'I was just making sure she was okay?' says Tom sympathetically.

'Why don't you go into the living room?' I suggest, feeling concern for Alice. 'I'll close the door and make sure you're not disturbed.'

'I don't want to cause a fuss,' says Alice. 'I might just slip quietly up to my room for a while.'

'Of course. Come on, I'll take you.'

Holding Alice's hand, we sweep our way through the kitchen and upstairs to her room. Alice sits on the edge of the bed 'Sorry.'

'Don't be sorry. You have a rest. I'll let Mum know. Everyone should start to go soon. Is there anything I can get you?'

'No. Thanks, Clare.'

I go to give Alice a hug, change my mind and then change it back again. It feels awkward, not least because she's sitting down. As I go back downstairs, I ponder why I find it so difficult feeling genuine warmth towards Alice. I wish it wasn't like this and I hope she hasn't picked up on it, especially if she's feeling a bit out of place.'

Alice spends the rest of the afternoon in her room until everyone has gone. Mum goes up to see her and coaxes her down for some supper.

'I'm just tired,' says Alice. 'I think I'll have an early night.'

'Of course, darling. I'm sorry if it was all too much,' says Mum.

'That's what happens when I leave Tom alone with you,' I joke, in a bid to lighten the mood. Alice smiles but says her goodnights and goes back up to her room.

'She'll be okay in the morning,' says Luke to us both. 'Best leave her to rest now. Mind you, being stuck with Tom for the afternoon is enough to drive anyone to the brink.'

A remark I choose to ignore.

Chapter 12

I can't believe how quickly the past couple of weeks have gone since Alice arrived in our lives. I've had such a swing of emotions, I feel physically tired from battling with it all. Mum, however, seems to be thriving and going from strength to strength.

She was so happy at the little welcome-home party we threw for Alice and I was pleased that everyone turned up. Mum took great pride in showing Alice off; I'm not sure that Alice was quite so enthused but, to her credit, she smiled graciously and made polite conversation. The only thing that seemed a bit odd was when I found her and Tom talking in the garden. I did try to find out from Alice yesterday, but she just laughed it off and mumbled something about Tom boring her with law talk. I didn't buy that and made a mental note to ask Tom today.

I wonder how Alice is dealing with being here. I get the impression she is struggling a bit too as some days she seems more upbeat than others. Perhaps this is the one thing we have in common, the uncertainty of our emotions. I don't say anything to Mum as I don't want to ruin her new-found happiness. She has a lightness in her step and she practically bounces into the room these days. The darkness behind her eyes has disappeared. Even the lines around her eyes don't look so deep. It makes me happy to see her like this. It's been a long time since she has felt any true joy.

It's an inset day at school for Hannah today, so the breakfast table is a little quieter as I haven't woken her. Luke is having the day off to look after her and he's booked Chloe out of nursery too. He's going to take them to the Sea Life Centre in Brighton. Hannah's school project this term is *Under The Sea*, so she's going to take the camera that Luke and I bought her for her birthday. Hannah loves photography. I think she gets it from Luke. He was always taking pictures when he was younger and was never without his camera, but as he got older, he favoured the paintbrush more. Maybe Hannah will take after him and be the creative type, whereas Chloe is quieter, probably more like me. I was a very placid child. I think it comes from always feeling the need to shrink into the shadows, not to be noticed. I've never liked being the centre of attention. As a child, life was easier if my father didn't notice me. I'm glad Luke doesn't have the same relationship with his daughters. It's something we've both worked hard to achieve. I want my girls to be in the warm and not only to be loved but to know they are loved. I want the sun to shine on them every day, even when it's cloudy.

'Penny for your thoughts,' says Luke as he sits Chloe on her booster seat and puts a bowl with chopped-up banana for her on the table. Chloe digs her chubby little fingers in eagerly. She chases a slice of banana around the bowl and squishes it slightly as she traps it in her fist. She shoves it rather awkwardly into her mouth and then sets about repeating the whole process.

'I was just thinking of the girls and how lucky we are to have them,' I say, placing a circular rubber mat under Chloe's bowl to stop it sliding across the table. 'And how lucky it is that you can spend time with them on days like today.'

'I know, it's great that at least one of us can be here for them,' he says. 'I'll get Hannah to take lots of photos to show you this evening. By the end of it, you'll feel like you've been there.' He gives me a grin, as we both know I'll have to sit and look at dozens and dozens of photographs as Hannah happily clicks away at anything and everything. I appreciate he's trying to make me feel better and I resolve to stop feeling sorry for myself and to enjoy just having the time with Hannah this evening, regardless of what we do.

I can't help feeling my mood dip a little as Alice comes into the kitchen. I wish she would put on the dressing gown Mum left her. I then immediately admonish myself for being a prude and sounding like some sort of Victorian maiden aunt. At least today she has a little pair of shorts on under the T-shirt, although I do mean little.

'Hey, guys,' she says. We exchange good mornings and how did you sleep niceties while she faffs around getting herself a coffee and toast. I make the most of Mum not being up yet and telling me to make my sister her breakfast. Alice sits down with us. 'Are you going to work today, Clare?'

'Yes, no rest for the wicked,' I say, ignoring the glance at the kitchen clock Luke gives. Yes, I should be going now, but

I'm hanging out as long as possible, on the pretext I need to help Chloe with her banana but, deep down, I know it's because I don't like Alice being alone with Luke.

'Oh, Clare, I hope you don't mind but I used your laptop last night,' says Alice.

'My laptop?' I reply with surprise.

'Yes. Mum said it would be okay.' She looks uncertain. 'Sorry, is that a problem?'

'Er, no. I just didn't realise Mum knew how to work it,' I say.

'Well, she wasn't sure, but I know my way around a computer so it wasn't a problem.'

'Oh, right. It wasn't locked or anything, then?' I try to recall when I last used it and if I had shut it down properly. It's password-protected and I'm sure Mum doesn't know it. Then, I remember, I'd flicked it on at the weekend. At the party, to be precise. We'd stuck the memory card from Luke's camera in to have a look at some of the photos he had taken. We'd put it on slide-show mode and left it running so everyone could have a look.

'It was just on screensaver,' says Alice. 'It didn't need a password.'

'Yes, I do remember now. We used it at the party,' I say. 'Did you find what you needed?'

'Sure. I just wanted to check my emails, that sort of stuff.'

'Facebook and Twitter, I expect?' says Luke with a rueful smile. He's never one for social media himself, but he uses it for his work. I'm the same. In my job, I don't want people knowing too much about me, although I do keep a low-key

Facebook account, which I set up in case Alice ever tried to find me.

'Oh, I don't do social media,' says Alice.

'Well, that's a first,' says Luke. 'Even Clare and I have accounts.'

Alice's smile drops. 'It was just something Daddy never approved of. I didn't go against his wishes.'

'Was he that bad?' I ask gently. 'That controlling? I knew he was like that with Mum, even though she's never said outright, but I thought maybe he'd be different with you.'

'Why would you think that?' asks Alice.

'Because he chose you,' I say. 'He chose to take you with him to America. Not me.' A heavy silence descends the room.

'Maybe because it was easier to take the younger child,' suggests Alice. 'I suppose a four-year-old would have less memories to cling onto than a nine-year-old.'

It's a logical reason; one that I've thought of before but I've always felt there's been more to it than that.

'Hey, Babe, you're going to be late,' says Luke, breaking my thoughts. He gives me a comforting smile, knowing where my mind must be travelling.

I get up reluctantly. The weight of the conversation clings to me and the thought of the day ahead does nothing to cheer me. I have a Skype call with McMillan to discuss the likelihood of the other party dropping their case and settling out of court. Leonard is putting pressure on me to strike a deal with them so we can avoid all the press reporting. Somehow I don't think it's going to happen. McMillan needs to meet them halfway and he's not in the frame of mind to do that.

Stubborn fool, who thinks he's some bloody mafia Don and totally untouchable.

'What time is your Skype call?' asks Leonard, popping his head around the door to my office, where Tom has just called in to see if I want anything from the deli across the road.

'Not until after lunch.'

'Do you need me to come in on it?'

Part of me wants to say yes, but my professional pride stands in the way. 'No, not just yet. I'll see how I get on with him today.'

'You need to try to convince him to accede to some of the points.' Leonard fixes me with one of his stares. 'Remind him that it will do neither him nor us any favours if we end up with egg on our face over a fucking dismissal that has been blown out of proportion.'

'I take it you don't want me to quote you on that,' I say, in a bid to lighten the mood.

I get Leonard's infamous death stare. 'Just get on with it.'

I know Tom has shot a look my way, but I avoid eye contact as Leonard leaves.

'So, when did you become the henchman?' asks Tom.

'Take no notice of Leonard,' I say. 'He's in a bad mood and throwing his weight around, as he likes to do from time to time. I've known him long enough not to let it bother me.'

'He's not been himself lately,' says Tom.

'How do you mean?'

'More stressed than usual. I went in to speak to him the other day about something and I don't know what he was up to, but he nearly shut his own fingers in the lid of his laptop, he slammed it down so fast and hard when he saw me. And then he shoved a load of papers into a folder and grumbled about not wanting to be disturbed.'

'Really? That's not like him. To be honest, I haven't noticed anything different. He's just the same as always, sugar one minute, arsenic the next.'

'How's things at home with Alice?'

'Funny you should mention Alice,' I say. 'I've been meaning to ask you all week about that conversation you had with her at the party. The one in the garden?'

'What about it?'

'Just wondered what you two were talking about. It looked very serious. Poor old Alice had to go and have a lie-down afterwards.'

'Ah, now that would be telling,' says Tom, with a wink. 'Anyway, I asked you first. Is this you trying to deflect the question?'

We eye each other for an uneasy few seconds, as an under-current of tension ripples between us. I fold first.

'There's nothing to tell, really,' I say. Tom raises his eyebrows and I relent. 'Okay, I'm still adjusting, that's all.'

'How's everyone else getting on with her?' Tom sits down in the chair.

'Good.' What else can I say?

'Leonard seems to be making a fuss of her,' says Tom.

'Really? In what way?'

'Didn't you know? Shit, sorry. I think I may just have put my foot in it.'

'You'll have to tell me now.'

'I saw them having a coffee together, over the road at the deli.'

'When was that?' I'm surprised that Leonard hasn't mentioned it, but even more surprised that Alice herself hasn't said anything.

'Erm, last week. Friday, I think. They didn't see me. I was going to grab a coffee, but they looked so engrossed in their conversation that I detoured to the little café down the road. Didn't like to disturb them.'

'Really? Alice never said she'd met Leonard. Wonder what that was all about?' It seems odd that they would meet up and, not only that, but not to meet at the office either.

'Maybe it was something to do with the trust fund. Which reminds me, I forgot to say, when I went into Leonard and he was all cagey about those files, I'm sure there was a client's account statement with your Mum's name on it amongst those papers.'

'Well, that's easily explained,' I say, feeling the need to put some sort of order and reason behind Leonard's actions. 'He's the trustee for the trust fund; he was probably just checking some figures. Maybe it's even to do with the meeting he had with Alice.' My voice reveals a hint of scepticism on my part. Although this is what I want to believe, I can't help feeling that I'm not seeing the whole picture. It doesn't explain why the meeting was not at the office or why Leonard, according to Tom, was cagey.

'I just thought it was a bit odd,' says Tom.

I sigh and lean back in my chair, tapping my biro on the

edge of the desk. 'I don't know what that's all about, but then, that seems par for the course lately,' I say. 'Maybe it's to do with the trust fund. Now she's back, she'll be entitled to her share. It's due to be paid out sometime next year, March I think. Leonard has all the details.'

'Ah, that's probably it,' says Tom.

'No doubt,' I say, although I'm not sure either of us is entirely convinced. The secrecy around the meeting is nagging at me. Tom, being the sharp-minded solicitor, is probably struggling with the same point. 'I really ought to get on.' I shuffle some papers on my desk, indicating that the conversation has drawn to a close. Tom takes the hint and rises from his seat.

'So, nothing from the deli, then?'

'No. I'm good, thanks.' I don't look up and busy myself with the papers in front of me. After Tom has gone, I sit back in my chair and let out a sigh.

I know it shouldn't bother me and technically it's none of my business, but I'd love to know what Leonard and Alice were discussing. If it was business, I can't see why they wouldn't hold the meeting in Leonard's office. The only reason they'd meet elsewhere would be if they didn't want anyone to know what they were up to. The thought of those two in cahoots both annoys and unsettles me as once again I feel as if I'm on the outside of something, like I've felt from time to time with Mum and Alice.

I glance at the photograph on the windowsill of Luke and the girls, taken on a picnic last summer. Luke is sitting on the ground with Chloe in front of him and Hannah is standing behind, her arms wrapped around his neck, planting a big sloppy kiss on his cheek.

I shake myself from my thoughts. I need to concentrate on work and prepare for this bloody Skype call to McMillan this afternoon. I spend the rest of the day in my office, regularly fending off thoughts of Luke and the girls. The call with McMillan isn't particularly successful. He's an arrogant sod and if I wasn't defending him, I'd relish prosecuting him. How nice would it be to knock him down a peg or two?

I look at my watch and wonder whether Luke and the girls have had a good day at the Sea Life Centre. I'm really missing them today and suddenly, feeling impulsive, I decide to go home early. I just want to be with my family. They can take away my stress. A hug from Luke and a cuddle with the girls can put everything right.

When I pull up in the drive at home forty-five minutes later, I'm pleased to see Luke's car in the carport. I let myself in and call a 'hello' down the hall, but I'm greeted with silence. I poke my head around the living-room door but it's empty, so I track down to the kitchen. The bi-fold doors are open to the conservatory and I can see Luke sitting at the table with Mum and Alice. Even Alice being there can't dampen the feeling of relief and happiness that I'm home. The girls are playing on the climbing frame and swing.

'Hi, everyone!' I say as I join them and slip my arms around Luke's shoulders, kissing the side of his face. 'Hi, you.'

'Well, hello.' Luke returns the kiss and, holding my arms, walks me around the side of the chair and pulls me onto his lap. 'To what do we owe this honour? You're home early.'

'Missed you, that's all,' I say. 'Shit day. Just wanted to be home with you guys.'

'Hello, darling,' says Mum. 'There's tea in the pot; Alice has just made it. You look like you could do with a cuppa.'

I turn around on Luke's knee. 'Thanks, Mum.' Alice is sitting next to Luke and I smile at her. 'Hiya. You okay?'

For the briefest of moments, I don't think Alice is going to return the smile. In fact, the look on her face is practically venomous. Before I can say anything, her mouth moves into a smile, although I can't say the rest of her facial muscles are in on the sentiment. 'Hi, Clare. I'm fine, thanks. Here, I'll pour you a tea.'

'Mummy! Mummy! Chloe comes running in from the garden and I slip off Luke's lap and scoop her up into my arms.

'Hello, sweetie.' I smother her with kisses and blow raspberries under her chin. Chloe giggles and squeezes her arms tightly around my neck. God, this child can lift my mood within seconds. I'm so blessed to have her. 'Have you had a nice day out with Daddy? Where did you go?'

'Sea Life Centre. We saw fish. Big ones. Octa-poos.'

'Octa-poos? Oh, octopus. You saw an octopus? Did he have lots of long wiggly legs?' I set Chloe down on the ground and take the seat on the other side of the table, next to Mum. 'Hey, Hannah!' I wave over at her.

Hannah comes running in and gives me a quick hug and kiss. It wasn't so long ago that she would greet me with the same enthusiasm as her sister. I guess the more reserved greeting is a sign she's growing up.

'Do you want to see my pictures?' she says, grabbing the camera from the table. She fiddles with buttons and holds it in front of me.

'Hannah,' says Luke. 'Let Mummy have her cup of tea first. She's literally just got in from work.'

The look of disappointment that crosses my daughter's face tugs at my heartstrings. 'Why don't I have a look at a few now and then tonight, when Chloe's gone to bed, we can sit down together and go through them all? Just the two of us. You can tell me all about them, then.'

Hannah seems happy with the compromise. I know she likes to have some time alone with me, just as much as I do with her. 'Okay, look this is the octopus. Chloe called it an octa-poos!'

'I know, she just said it to me now.' I laugh with Hannah as we look at the camera. She clicks the button and another image appears. This one is of some sort of eel. 'Ooh, I don't like that. It looks like a snake.' She clicks again. An image, this time of Luke, appears. He's holding Chloe in his arms and they're looking into a tank. 'That's a nice one,' I say, although it's a little dark in there and the flash has reflected off the glass of the tank. Hannah flicks through a couple more photos without stopping, but as she does, one image catches my eye. Something in it is different and stands out from the others. 'Go back a minute,' I say. Hannah clicks back. 'And again.' She clicks back a further frame. And there it is. A pain spikes at my heart as the two faces look back at me. I look up at Alice. There's a small, smug look on her face. No one sees it. They're too busy looking at me.

'Alice went too.' My voice is tight and I can feel my breathing deepen. *Alice went too and no one thought to tell me*!

'So did your mum,' says Luke. He gives me the eyes, which are clearly saying *keep your shit together*.

'But you hate the Sea Life Centre,' I say, turning to Mum. 'You always say it's too dark and dingy, that it makes you feel claustrophobic.'

'I didn't actually go into the centre myself,' says Mum. 'I let Alice and Luke take the girls in. I had a coffee in one of the tearooms across the road. They do lovely scones in there.'

'Here's a picture of a shark,' says Hannah. I can see her look uncertainly from me to Luke and I'm aware that she has picked up on the change in atmosphere. I wonder if Mum has too or whether she's purposefully ignoring it and rattling on about how nice the sodding scone was, to defuse the situation, but all I can think of is Luke and Alice playing happy families, Alice taking my place and Luke seemingly content for her to do so.

'You don't mind do you, Clare?' says Alice. 'I'm sorry. I didn't mean to upset you.'

'Will you stop asking me if I mind and stop apologising?' I push my chair back, astonishing myself at my little outburst as much as I seem to have taken everyone else by surprise.

'Clare! What's got into you?' says Mum, her voice taking on the tone she would use to one of the children when they might have forgotten to say please or thank you, or like the time Hannah said 'shit' once when she dropped a glass of water on the kitchen floor. Her tone that says she is particularly shocked; that's the one I'm getting now.

135

I rest my hands on the table and close my eyes for a moment. This is all getting out of hand. *I'm* getting out of hand. I open my eyes and smile at my family. 'Sorry. I'm sorry, everyone. Alice, please, I didn't mean to snap like that.'

'Hey, it's okay,' says Alice. She exchanges a sympathetic look with Luke, which causes me to take a deep breath to stop my jealousy once again rising to the surface uncontrolled.

'I've had a tough day,' I say, by way of an explanation. It's a pretty poor one, but it's the truth. 'I'll go and freshen up, I think. Get out of these work clothes and then I'll be able to relax properly.' I notice Luke hasn't said anything. I meet his gaze and he raises his eyebrows, giving a tiny shake of his head. He has the look of exasperation. I know my husband well enough to realise I've upset him properly now. Luke is very easy-going; it takes a lot for him to get cross. I think I may have just pushed him over that line.

When I go back down, Luke has disappeared into his studio; a sure sign he's pissed off with me. I find the girls in the living room, sitting on the sofa with Alice. Chloe is one side of her and Hannah the other. I make a Herculean effort to ignore the bubble of jealousy that stirs once again. 'What are we watching?' I say, sitting down on the chair next to the sofa. Chloe mumbles a reply but doesn't take her eyes from the screen.

Something makes me look over at the photographs on the sideboard. Straight away, I notice the glass in my wedding photograph is cracked.

'Oh, no! How did that happen?' I jump up out of my seat. I inspect the shattered glass. There's an impact spot right in the middle and the glass has cracked like a spider's web all around it.

'What's up?' asks Alice. She comes over and looks at the picture. 'Oh, Clare, that's your wedding photo.'

'Do you know how it happened?' I look accusingly at Alice and then around at the girls. 'Hannah. Chloe. Do you know anything about this?'

'Picture broken. Poor picture' says Chloe and turns back to her programme.

Hannah keeps her eyes firmly fixed on the TV. 'Hannah, did you hear me?' When she looks up, I'm not sure what I see. Is it fear? Or is it guilt? 'Do you know how this picture got broken?' She shakes her head. I go over to her. 'Look, I'm not cross about the glass getting broken, it's the fact that no one is owning up. If you tell me the truth, it can all be forgotten about.'

'I didn't do it,' says Hannah.

'Who did? Was it Chloe?' I press. Hannah sticks out her bottom lip and shakes her head. 'Well, someone knows what's happened.' I leave the room to get rid of the glass in the bin.

Mum is in the kitchen washing up. 'Oh, dear, what a shame,' she says when I show her. 'You can easily get another piece of glass, though. Don't get yourself upset about it.'

'That's not the point,' I say. 'I just wish someone had told me.'

'Actually, I didn't want to say anything in front of the girls, but ...'

I look around as Alice comes into the room. 'But what?' I say.

'The girls were already in the living room when I went in and Hannah was over by the photographs,' says Alice, then adds quickly. 'I'm not saying she did it, but she did look, well, you know, kinda guilty.'

'Okay, thanks,' I say, although I don't really mean it. I'm embarrassed that Hannah may have lied to me. I look down at the photograph, now removed from the frame. It has an indent and a crease from whatever pressure was applied. I can't help but feel it might not have been an accident.

Chapter 13

Later that evening, when I put Hannah to bed, she's still a little subdued.

'Shall we look at the other photographs now?' I ask, waving the camera that I had picked up from the kitchen.

'If you want.' She may be in her cute kitty pyjamas and her hair brushed, her skin all clean and her teeth sparkly, looking every inch the seven years she is, but she has an attitude of a grumpy teenager. It's not that she's being rude or bad-tempered, but she's treating me with an indifference, as if she's just putting up with me.

I sit beside her on the bed and switch on the camera, reminding myself not to react adversely to any of the pictures with Luke and Alice in them. I begin to scroll through, asking Hannah questions about each photo and, little by little, the tension eases from her and she talks more enthusiastically the further through the collection we go. Oddly, I don't come across the picture of Luke and Alice in the Sea Life Centre. I was sure it was one of the first ones when Hannah showed me earlier. I don't voice my surprise – I don't want to spoil Hannah's now-upbeat mood.

When we come to the end of the shots, I'm glad I took the time to sit and look through them with her. Luke had warned me there were a lot, but I honestly don't mind as it's lifted Hannah's mood.

I pull the duvet up to her chin and give her a kiss on the forehead. 'Goodnight, darling,' I say. 'I love you very much. You do know that, don't you?'

She smiles. 'I love you to the moon and back.'

'To the moon and back and back again,' I say.

'To the moon and back and back and back again,' replies Hannah. I smile and give her a cuddle.

'Now, go to sleep. You have school in the morning.'

I flick the light off and am about to close the door when Hannah speaks. 'I didn't break the photo frame,' she says. Her little voice comes through crystal clear in the darkness.

I switch the light back on and sit on the edge of the bed. I stroke Hannah's hair and look at her face. 'I know, darling,' I say. 'It's all forgotten about now. Don't be worrying.'

'It was already broken. Alice said not to tell you. That you'd be cross.'

I feel my eyebrows involuntarily rise and although I want to abide by the best mother's handbook and ignore the remark, I can't help grilling my daughter a little further. 'She did, did she? What else did she say?'

Hannah shrugs. 'Nothing. Just said to leave it.'

'Okay, well don't be worrying about it now. It's just a piece of glass that can easily be replaced.' I settle Hannah back down. 'Ooh, I just remembered. I asked Daisy's mummy about her coming for a sleepover and she said yes.'

Hannah's face lights up. 'Yay! Can we paint our nails? What about watching a film?'

'Of course. And popcorn.'

'Thanks, Mum, you're the best.' Hannah snuggles down under her duvet and I'm relieved to be sending her off to sleep with happier thoughts. I just wish it was so easy to lift my own.

When Luke comes up to bed eventually later, I'm sitting up reading a book, or at least pretending I am.

'All right?' He says, going into the en suite. He doesn't close the door and I watch him brush his teeth and splash water over his face. He runs his wet hands through his hair and I can't help feel a surge of love for this man. I hate it when we're on edge with each other. Luke doesn't go in for big showdown arguments; he prefers to let things blow over and then talk about it when everyone is calm and more rational. He strips off down to his boxer shorts and climbs into bed next to me, reaches over and takes the book out of my hands. 'Now, do you want to tell me what's going on up there?' He taps my head gently with his forefinger.

'I don't want us to fall out about all this,' I say.

'Neither do I, Babe. Look, today, that wasn't down to me. Your mum invited herself and Alice along. What could I say?'

I close my eyes briefly. 'I know. It's just … Alice. Oh, God, this sounds so childish but … but it's like she's taking over everything. My entire family.' It sounds so stupid when I say it out loud. In my head, it sounded very plausible, but now I'm starting to doubt myself. Then I remember the look on Hannah's face and this spikes my resilience. I lean over and pick up our wedding photo, now frameless, and hold it out to Luke. 'It's the one that's usually in the living room. I went in this evening and saw the glass was broken.'

Luke takes the photo from me. 'Ah, that's a shame and it's creased too. I can get another printed off, it's not a problem.'

'I know that, but that's not the point. The glass wasn't just cracked like it had been knocked over, it had been crushed. You could see where something had been driven into it. The glass was shattered all around it.'

'It could have fallen and hit something.'

I sit up and take the photograph back. 'No, it couldn't have. Or if it did, I have no idea what would have caused it to damage the actual photograph. No, this was done on purpose. Maliciously.'

Luke lets out a sigh and puts his head back against the headboard. 'Please don't tell me you think Alice did it.'

'She tried to blame Hannah. She said Hannah was playing with the photos, or something, and when I asked Hannah, she said it was already broken, that Alice was in the room first and Alice told her not to say anything.' I look triumphantly at Luke, as if I've solved a major crime ring.

'Either could be telling the truth,' says Luke.

'Are you telling me you believe some stranger over your daughter?'

'Stranger? She's your sister.'

'If that's what she's like, then I'd sooner she wasn't.' I throw the duvet off and get out of bed, grabbing my dressing gown. 'And I don't want you painting her fucking portrait either.'

'So much for not arguing,' mutters Luke as I storm out of

the room, my dressing gown billowing like a sail behind me.

I resist the urge to slam the door as I don't want to wake the children, so I strop across the landing instead and almost bump into none other than Alice. She's leaning back against the banister that looks over the hallway below, her elbows rest on the top rail, one leg is bent, with her foot against a spindle. It's as if she's posing for a photo shoot – a sleazy one.

'Jesus, Alice, you made me jump.'

'Is everything all right, Clare? Only, I heard raised voices.'

I fasten the belt around the dressing gown and wonder how long she's been standing there. 'Yes, I'm fine. Just going to get a glass of water. You okay? Not still suffering with jet lag are you?' I can't keep the little note of sarcasm from my voice.

'Oh, I'm fine, *sister*. Absolutely fine. I mean, why wouldn't I be after such a lovely day with your girls and your husband?' The smile that accompanies her words chills the air.

'You stay away from my family,' I hiss the words as loudly as I dare, without wanting anyone else to hear. Least of all Luke. He thinks I'm a crazy woman as it is.

The smile remains on her face and she pushes herself off the banister, taking a step closer to me. 'Remember, Clare, your family is my family.' Her words are a whisper.

'Don't. Take. Me. On.' I punctuate each word with invisible full stops. 'You'll be sorry.' I have no idea what that threat means, it just came out. I don't wait for a reply and, sidestepping her, I take the stairs, which sweep around to the ground floor. I glance up as I reach the bottom and Alice is now leaning on the rails, looking down at me with that condescending smile still plastered on her face.

I get a glass of water and sip at it slowly in a bid to calm myself. I'm not sure what that was all about upstairs but I feel it was a game-changer moment. Both Alice and I have shown our true colours now.

I don't know why but I feel myself drawn to Luke's studio. I would never normally go into his studio on my own. I've never needed to. It's Luke's workspace. Sure, I go in there when he's there himself, but never on my own. I hesitate, my hand on the door handle, but something drives me on and I ease open the door and step inside, closing it gently behind me. I walk slowly around the room, taking in the paints and canvases I have seen plenty of times before. There's a pot of paint brushes standing on the draining board. The smell of white spirit hangs in the air and I see the bottle next to the brushes without its lid. The red lid is next to it and, instinctively, I replace the cap, turning it tightly before putting the bottle back on the draining board. There are oily rags in a basket next to the sink. They remind me of a kaleidoscope, the different colours merging into each other to form weird and wonderful psychedelic patterns.

As I wander around the studio, I can't help feeling like an intruder.

In the centre of the room is the London commission he's been working on. To my untrained eye, it looks complete and would grace any wall beautifully, but I know, to Luke, there is still much to do. It's all in the detail, he often tells me.

My gaze fixes on a canvas at the back of the studio. It's on an easel but is draped with a white cloth. I know instinctively what the subject is and I can't help myself going over to it and lifting the sheet. And there she is. Alice. My sister. That familiar feeling of jealousy kicks me hard in the stomach. My hand reaches out to the worktop at the side and my fingers curl around something metal. I draw it towards me and look down at my hand. The silver cross-hatched handle fits neatly in my palm. The triangular tip of the Stanley blade pokes out about an inch from the end. Luke never slides the blade away safely. I look back at the picture. 'Bitch,' I mutter, as the jealousy gives a two-footed flying kick inside me.

That night, when I get back into bed, I cuddle up against Luke's back, slipping my arm around his body. He stirs in his sleep and mumbles incoherently before rolling over to face me. His hand slides up my waist and cups my breast.

'Love you, Babe,' he slurs through his unconsciousness.

He takes a deep breath and, sliding his hand down to my hip, pulls me towards him. For a moment I think we might make love, but Luke's breathing deepens and he slips back into sleep. I'm a little disappointed, but considering the time and the fact that I have work tomorrow, it's probably best to get some sleep myself.

In the morning, I wake before the alarm and go about my usual routine. It's all back to normal today for school and nursery. As I take Chloe downstairs, stopping in Hannah's room to wake her, I go back over last night's tête-à-tête with Alice. I'm not sure how it's going to play out now, but I feel slightly regretful, as this is not how I envisaged my relationship with Alice going. I remind myself of the traumatic time she's had, what with her dad passing away and then finding me and Mum and then coming over and meeting us. It must be difficult for her. I should ignore the little transgression of last night. I make up my mind to be more accommodating and less, dare I say, paranoid about her every move and motive behind it.

As if by thinking about her, I've conjured her up. Alice is already in the kitchen, setting the table for breakfast. She's humming to herself, which I recognise as 'Whistle While You Work' from Disney's *Snow White*. She turns and smiles at me as I sit Chloe at the table.

'Morning, Clare. Morning, Chloe. I've just made a fresh pot of tea. Toast?'

I'm taken aback by this cheery greeting. It's as if nothing happened between us last night and I feel a certain amount of relief. Perhaps I've blown it all out of proportion.

'Alice, about last night,' I begin.

'Last night?' she looks confused.

'On the stairs,' I offer, as a memory prompt.

She still looks blank. 'The stairs?'

'Yes. When I came out of my bedroom and you were leaning against the banister.'

She waves a hand at me, as if wafting away a fly. 'Oh, that. Forget it.' She comes over and gives me a hug. 'We were both tired. Now let me make you a cup of tea.' She turns back to the kettle and pours the boiling water into the teapot.

'Thanks,' I say, recalling last night's conversation. There was definitely a sinister tone to it. At least, that's what I recall.

Alice turns to look at me. 'Honestly, Clare, don't sweat it. You're under a lot of pressure. It can do funny things to people, you know. I remember once, my sister was under so much stress trying to put herself through college and bring up a young baby on her own, that one day, when she asked if she could borrow some money from me and I said no because I didn't have any, she totally overreacted. Thought I was holding out on her. She accused me of all sorts. We had a terrible row. It wasn't until a few weeks later, when she had a mental breakdown, that we all realised how much pressure she was under and how it was affecting her. Since then, I've been so much more tolerant. That's the thing with mental illness; you can't see, and you don't always recognise, the signs. I'm much more aware of these things now.'

I sit for a moment trying to take it in. Something is not right. And then it occurs to me. 'Your sister?'

'Aha.'

'Who's your sister?'

Alice has her back to me now so I can't see her face, but I don't miss the tension in her shoulders. Then she turns and flashes me with a smile. 'I mean my stepsister. You know, Roma's daughter. She lived with us for a while.'

'Oh, right. I haven't heard you mention her before.'

'Like I say, she was just living with us for a few months. I never really had any contact with her. She lived up in Georgia.'

'Morning, girls,' Mum says, coming into the room. She smiles broadly and gives Chloe a kiss and rests her hand on my shoulder momentarily. 'Ooh, look, we're being spoiled today, Alice is making breakfast.'

Alice comes over and kisses Mum on the cheek. 'It's the least I can do after y'all looking after me so well.'

I glance over at the calendar and scan the dates. 'You're over halfway through your stay already, just another couple of weeks before you have to go,' I say, without missing the feeling of relief that flicks through me. I catch Mum and Alice exchanging a look between themselves. 'What?'

'About that,' says Mum. 'I've asked Alice to stay. Not to go back to America.'

'You have? When? I didn't realise.' I'm flummoxed. I hadn't seen that coming and I'm supposed to be an unflappable solicitor who is ready for anything.

'I asked Alice yesterday.' Mum puts her arm through Alice's. 'And, she said yes!' Her smile couldn't be any wider. She scrunches up her shoulders as if hugging herself. It reminds me of Hannah when I took her Disneyland Paris and she saw a real-life Cinderella. That's how Mum looks now, thrilled. She has her own Disney princess, Cinderella. I feel like one of the ugly sisters, both inside and out. I can't compete and the jealousy is eating me up inside, but as if on autopilot, I go over to Alice and hug her. 'That's great.'

Hannah comes in and sits at the table, so I'm able to distract myself getting her breakfast ready.

'Is Daddy up?' I ask. I know Luke is not a morning person, but he never misses breakfast.

'He's just walked by,' says Alice, before Hannah can answer. 'I assume he's heading for his studio.'

'I'll take him through a coffee,' I say, deciding there and then, that I'll make up with him properly tonight. We'll go out and have a spontaneous date night. I'll apologise for getting so cross about Alice. Perhaps she's right, the stress of work is getting to me and not only am I overreacting, I'm starting to bloody imagine things too.

Suddenly, Luke appears in the doorway. His face is like thunder and any notion that we might patch things up disappears in a second.

'Clare.' He says it with such controlled anger that it frightens me. 'A word.' He waits to make sure I'm getting up and then disappears back down the hallway.

Mum looks apprehensive. Both the girls have stopped eating. Even Chloe seems to have picked up on his black mood. Only Alice seems disaffected. She smiles at me. I can't work out what sort of smile it is, but I don't have the inclination to analyse it. I need to see what's up with Luke.

The atmosphere in the studio is tense. It feels as though the whole room is being tasered. Luke is at the back of the studio, his back to me. I walk over and stand beside him, taking in what is before me.

The portrait of Alice has been slashed. Not just once, not twice, not even three times. It must have at least a dozen slashes through it. The centre, her face, is in absolute tatters. It is beyond recognition. It looks like one of those door streamers from the seventies that your gran would hang up to stop the flies coming in. A silver-handled Stanley knife sticks out from the top right-hand corner of the canvas frame.

'Jesus Christ,' is all I can manage to say.

'You fucking idiot!' says Luke. 'What the fuck did you do this for?' Now I'm used to Luke spouting the f-word now and again. I'm not averse to it myself, but I have never heard such rage in him before. He grabs my shoulders and spins me to him. His face is an inch from mine. 'You're demented. You've got a screw loose.' He hammers his own head with his finger. 'You're fucking nuts!'

He pushes me away and I stumble backwards. 'I didn't do it,' I say. Even to me, my voice sounds unconvincing and pathetic.

'Bollocks, you didn't! You're a solicitor. Let's look at the evidence, shall we? We had an argument last night. You told me you didn't want me to do this painting. You disappear downstairs. Next thing, I find this. Now you tell me, what does the evidence suggest to you, Mrs Big-Shot-Solicitor-Tennison?'

I resist the urge to say that technically it's all circumstantial. I get the point he's making. 'Luke, I swear to you, I did not do this.' At least, I don't think I did. I can't deny the thought didn't go through my head. What if I had some sort of jealous rage? What if I got the red mist that I've heard some clients refer to, where they actually have no control whatsoever over their actions? I've always been a bit dismissive of those lines of defence, but now I'm not so sure.

Luke picks up the bottle of white spirit. The one I screwed the lid on last night. 'Only you would do this,' he says, almost smacking the lid. He doesn't need to expand. We both know what he's referring to. He chucks the bottle in the sink and then strides over to me and grabs my hand. He turns it over. A smudge of green acrylic paint on my wrist stares accusingly at us. 'You were down here,' he says.

I can feel tears spring to my eyes. I blink them away, not wanting them to betray me. Luke will think they are tears of guilt, when in reality they are tears of fear. What if I did actually vandalise the painting? I think back to last night. I remember coming down here and looking at the painting. I remember vividly the feeling of jealousy it evoked and I remember picking up the Stanley knife. But I still don't remember slashing the canvas. I look at the tattered fabric. That was done by someone in a rage. It's not a calculated act. It's someone in an absolute frenzy. That's how I would describe it in court. And if I were defending, I'd probably go for diminished responsibility. Could it have been me? Did I do that? Am I capable of such an act?

Luke must take my silence and tears as an admission. He bundles me to the door. 'Fuck off to work, Clare. I can't bear to even look at you.'

I stagger down the hallway to the kitchen. Alice is standing in the doorway, a witness to the whole episode. From nowhere, my own rage rears up.

'It was you, wasn't it?' I'm practically shouting. I'm storming towards Alice. 'You did that, didn't you?'

A second before I reach Alice, my mother steps out of the kitchen and stands between us. Alice clings to Mum's shoulders as if she's a human shield. 'Clare, stop it. I don't know what you're talking about. Clare, please stop, you're scaring me.'

'You know exactly what I'm talking about.' I'm screaming the words at her. Mum is pushing me away, she's shouting at me to stop it, to leave Alice alone, but I can't stop. I carry on shouting over my mother at my sister. 'Admit it! Admit that you did it!'

Two hands grab at my shoulders and pull me away. I know, without looking, it's Luke. I'd know his touch anywhere, even amongst all this. I want to cry. I want to turn and bury myself in his chest. I want his arms around me. I want him to tell me it's okay. But I know that's just fantasy.

I'm suddenly aware of Chloe crying. I look past Mum into the kitchen. Hannah is standing there looking terrified. The house has descended into some sort of pub brawl, except no one's drunk.

Luke bundles me down the hallway to the front door. He grabs my jacket and briefcase, snatching the keys from the key cupboard. 'Get the fuck out of here, Clare. Come back when you've calmed down and can apologise to everyone.' He opens the front door and manhandles me out onto the gravel drive.

There's a chill in the early-morning air and it knocks the anger from me. 'I didn't slash your painting,' I say. 'I would never do that.'

'Well, someone did and I doubt very much Alice would do it. She's the one who wanted the painting done in the first place.' Luke's voice is shaking as he fights to control his anger. I get it. I understand his fury. He puts so much of himself into his art, to have it mutilated in such a vicious way is no different to a personal attack of the same ferociousness on Luke himself. His paintings are an extension of him.

'I wouldn't do it. I know how much your paintings mean to you. Please, Luke, you must believe me.'

I'm aware I'm begging. I think Luke is aware of this too. He clasps his hands behind his head and turns in a circle, going to walk away but then changing his mind. He exhales long and deep. He drags a hand down his face and drop his arms to his side. I sense that the explosion of anger has petered out but the flakes still float around us like volcano ash. Any one piece capable of sparking another explosion.

'Clare, go to work. Get your head together. Talk to Leonard, even Tom, if you have to, but talk to someone to get this into perspective. I'm too close to it all, too fucking angry to have this conversation right now.'

'I'm sorry,' I say. My words sound pathetic. I don't even know what I'm saying 'sorry' for.

'We'll talk tonight, when you get back. When we've all calmed down.' He holds my gaze with his for a moment, before turning and taking the steps to the door in one stride. I watch him let himself back in, close the door behind him, leaving me standing on the gravel drive looking at the house. My family all together, on the inside. Me all alone, on the outside.

Chapter 14

'Blimey, you look like you've lost a tenner and found a quid,' says Tom as I get into work.

'Not in the mood,' I say. I want to march straight by and into my office, but it seems my feet have other ideas.

Tom takes my elbow and guides me into the kitchen. 'Coffee,' he says. 'Strong, by the look of it.'

I lean against the worktop, my arms folded, as I watch him make the drinks. He's humming to himself as he does. It reminds me of Alice this morning. I take the coffee from Tom. 'Have I ever forgotten anything? I don't mean just normal, everyday things. Like I might have forgotten where I put my keys or whether I picked up my phone. I mean important things. Like something I've done. Have I ever forgotten something like that?'

Tom tips his head to one side, considering my question for a moment. 'You once forgot to buy me a birthday present. It was my twenty-second birthday, if I remember rightly.'

I want to raise a smile and any other time I would probably find this funny. It's a standing joke that I didn't get Luke a birthday present one year, but that was the time when Luke and I had been on a bender and I'd blacked out, staying in bed for three days, completely missing his birthday. 'No, I'm being serious, Tom. What about sleepwalking? Did I ever do that when we were at Oxford?'

'Not as far as I know. What's up?'

'You sure I never sleepwalked? Remember that time, not long after we had graduated and I said I'd had a really weird dream ... you know, the one that I often have ...'

'What, *that* really weird dream?' says Tom. 'The one where you thought you'd ...' He dabs the air with his fingers, obviously not wanting to say it out loud. He means the dream where I woke up and was convinced I'd had sex the night before, although I couldn't remember who with and I was also convinced I'd taken part in some sort of *Playboy* photoshoot.

'Yeah, that one,' I say, so Tom doesn't have to say it out loud. Somehow it makes me feel so embarrassed it's almost as if it had actually happened.

'Are you feeling okay?' asks Tom. 'Do you think you've been sleepwalking? I mean, all that business with the dream; you weren't very well that week at all. Do you remember?'

'Yeah, headaches, shakes, stress, all that. I think it was my body's way of telling me I was worrying too much. What with exam results and trying to find Alice.'

'Perhaps, it's all getting a bit too much for you again,' says Tom.

It's now that Leonard picks his moment to come into the kitchen. 'Ah, was looking for you two,' he says. He stops and considers us both. 'Okay, what's up?'

Leonard is so perceptive; he somehow knows when something's not right. It's as if he can see exactly what's going on inside my head sometimes. 'Trouble at mill?'

'Yeah, you could say that,' I reply. I give them a very much abridged version of events regarding the day out at the Sea Life Centre and the destruction of Luke's painting. 'I think Luke is more upset that I've destroyed his work rather than the reasons behind it.'

Leonard holds up his hand. 'Stop. You've just incriminated yourself when you've done nothing wrong, or at least there's no proof.'

I check myself. 'Luke is more upset that I *may* have destroyed his work.' I look at my business partners, who are both my friends and confidants. 'I seriously think I might be cracking up.'

'It's bound to be difficult, for everyone,' says Leonard. 'These things rarely pan out like they do in the films. It actually takes a lot of hard work on both sides.'

'What did you both think of Alice at the weekend?'

Tom speaks first. 'She seemed very nice.'

'Jesus, nice! What is it with everyone saying she's nice?'

'Maybe because she is?' says Tom. 'Okay, a less-bland description. She seemed a bit nervous, but she also seemed very happy. Genuinely happy. When I spoke to her, she was very pleasant and couldn't speak highly enough of you and your Mum. And Luke.'

'Exactly. Luke. I swear she has a crush on him.'

'Is it unrequited?' says Tom.

'Unrequited? I should bloody well hope so,' I say, slightly

peeved that Tom might even think Luke is interested in Alice. I'm allowed to think that privately, but somehow I don't like anyone else thinking it. My defensive hackles rise an inch. 'She's just a bit full on, that's all.'

'Sorry, didn't mean to offend you,' says Tom, raising his hands in surrender. 'I was just thinking out loud, you know, being flattered by someone else's attentions, who isn't your wife. I'm sure Luke's not like that at all. He's got too much at stake.'

I shoot Tom a look. I'm not entirely sure what he's implying.

'Sometimes it's best just to apologise and leave it at that,' says Leonard, slapping his hand down on Tom's shoulder. 'I don't think you're helping now.'

'Sorry,' says Tom, with an apologetic expression.

'Forget it.' I wave it away as if it's nothing.

'I thought Alice seemed like a very agreeable young lady, who was perhaps trying a little too hard to be accepted,' says Leonard.

'So, you two don't think she could have wrecked the picture, then. Which means, if it's not her, then it must be me. It's official. Luke's right. I am fucking nuts.' I put the coffee cup down. 'I'd better get on. I've got some court papers to file and some correspondence to deal with for the McMillan case.'

I leave the kitchen, aware that I haven't exactly crowned myself in glory. Having asked for their opinions, I now appear to be sulking because I don't like the answers. *Ain't that the truth?*

And then, as if my day can't get any worse, I can't find the McMillan file. I took it home with me to have a look at some of the previous statements on Sunday afternoon. I think back.

I remember taking it out of the filing cabinet and I'm pretty sure I put it in my briefcase. In the end, I didn't look at it on Sunday. So, where the hell is it? It should be in my case.

I take another look and a surge of panic wells up inside me. I do not lose files. I am organised. I've never lost a file before in my life. I wrack my brains, trying to remember what was in the file. We've no doubt got copies of all correspondence on the digital files, but I'm not sure about originals. Shit, I'd have to reapply for certain legal documents. That won't earn me any Brownie points, and then there's the costs, not to mention the time delay.

I buzz through to Sandy. 'Hi, Sandy, how much of the McMillan file do we have on digital?'

'Probably about eighty per cent. Why, is there a problem?'

I don't want to admit I've lost a file. 'I've left the file at home. Where is the digital file stored?'

'I'll send the link through.'

'Thanks.' I didn't miss the note of surprise in Sandy's voice at my oversight.

The link comes through in less than a minute. I'd be lost without Sandy at times. God help me if she ever decides to look for a new job. I click on the link and open the yellow folder icon. I'm greeted with a blank screen and a message, which reads 'this folder is empty'. That's odd. I return to the link and go through the whole process again, only to receive the same message. I buzz Sandy again.

'I'm getting an empty folder. Is that the right link?'

'Er, it should be. Let me check.' I can hear her tapping at the keyboard. 'Right, here's the file ... open ... oh, that's odd.

Let me try again.' A sinking feeling drags from my chest to my stomach. 'I'm sorry, Clare, I don't know what's wrong. The file's empty. It shouldn't be. I updated it last week.'

'What about the office back-up?'

'It's a weekly back-up. I'll ask Nina. She does that on a Friday.'

I sit patiently and when, some five minutes later, Sandy hasn't got back to me, I get up and go out to find her. She's at Nina's desk. Both look up and I can tell instantly, by the looks on their faces, that it's not good news. 'What's the verdict?' I ask needlessly.

Sandy steps forwards. Nina had to go home early on Friday. She wasn't well.'

'Sorry,' says Nina, her voice barely audible.

'So who's supposed to do the weekly back-up when Nina's not here?' I ask.

Sandy's gaze drops to the ground. 'Either me or one of the other secretaries. It's no one's fixed job.'

'What? It's just left to chance that one of you three will remember?' That doesn't sound like Carr, Tennison & Eggar. We're much more organised than that. 'What about last week's back-up? They're done on a four-weekly rotation aren't they?'

'Oh, God, I'm sorry, Clare, but I didn't update the file last week,' says Sandy.

'How long are we talking since you updated the file? I mean, what weekly back-up will contain the most up-to-date information?' I keep my voice calm. Inside I'm a mix of anger and panic. 'Sandy, how far back are we talking?' The impatience is surfacing.

'Three weeks. I do it at the beginning of each month.'

'Ffffff …' I stop myself from swearing. Or at least I think I do. 'For fuck's sake! What sort of system is that?' I don't want an answer and march back down to my office, yelling over my shoulder. 'The system is shit and needs an overview. We can all stay late tonight to sort it out and get a proper one in place!'

As I slam my office door behind me and slump into my chair, I'm hit with not only the hypocrisy of my rant, but how bloody rude I was too. There's me criticising them, when, if I'd done my job right in the first place, the sodding file wouldn't be missing.

'Shit!' I kick out at the wastepaper bin in frustration.

My door swings open with such force it bounces back from the rubber stopper that prevents it smashing against the wall. I jump and flinch as the memory of my father slamming open doors makes an unwelcome visit. I half expect to see Patrick Kennedy storming in. Instead, it's Leonard. He throws the door behind him and it crashes against the doorframe as the latch clicks into the keep.

'What the fuck is going on, Clare?' He keeps his voice low, but the anger is apparent. 'I could hear you ranting at the girls from my office. Good job I didn't have a client with me. Not sure I can say the same for Tom, though.'

'The back-up system has failed,' I say in my defence. 'The back-up system that isn't actually a system – more hit and miss, if someone can be bothered to do it.'

'That's no excuse for you shouting and swearing, not at your staff, anyway. So unprofessional, not to mention down-right rude.'

I hold up my hands in apology. 'I'm sorry. I'll apologise to Sandy and Nina.' His eyes rest on me without moving. 'It's okay. You can quit with the death stare. I'll apologise right now.' I go to get up.

'Before you do,' says Leonard. 'Can you explain to me what is actually going on?'

'I haven't got a file with me. I left it at home. I wanted the digital copy but it's not up to date. Nina went home early on Friday and no one else thought to back up the week's work. Sandy hasn't updated the digital copy for three weeks. Subsequently, no one has up-to-date records. I have a meeting today and I need the info.'

'What file are we talking about?'

I was hoping he wouldn't ask. 'The McMillan file.'

'When you say you haven't got it with you, where exactly is it?'

I feel like a naughty schoolgirl who has been caught out for not doing their homework. I briefly wonder if I could blame the dog for eating the file. I dismiss the flippant thought. I haven't got a bloody dog anyway. 'It's at home.'

'Can't you nip back and get it, if it's that important?' I now wonder if I can buy a dog this afternoon and post-date the purchase to place the dog at the scene of the alleged crime. 'You do know where the file is, don't you?'

'I thought I put it in my briefcase. Well, I did on Friday, but now it's not there.'

'You had it at home? Where did you read it?'

'That's just it. I didn't. I was too busy in the end.'

'The file's lost. Is that what you're telling me?'

'Possibly. But I need to check at home. Perhaps I did take it out and forgot to put it back. Or put it down without realising. Or put it in Hannah's book bag.'

'What?' Leonard looks incredulous.

'Sorry, that was a joke, that bit,' I say, realising my attempt to defuse the situation isn't going to work. 'Look, I'll postpone the meeting until later in the week. That will give me a chance to find the file.'

'Of course, it would have to be the fucking McMillan file. You couldn't lose some poxy petty divorce file, could you?' I get the death stare again and look down at my desk, feeling truly admonished. 'And don't forget to apologise to Sandy and Nina.'

More door-slamming as Leonard leaves.

I debate whether to call home and ask Mum or Luke to have a look around for the file, but I decide against it. I'm not exactly flavour of the month there. In fact, I'm not flavour of the month here, either. I get up, grab my handbag and shoot out to the delicatessen over the road. I buy cream cakes and deluxe hot chocolates, with all the trimmings, squirty cream, chocolate sprinkles and marshmallows and take my peace offerings to Sandy and Nina, with grovelling apologies for being such a cow.

It's good practice for the grovelling apologies I'll have to make tonight when I go home. My phone pings with a text message. It's Pippa.

Fancy a quick coffee aka a glass of wine? I'm in town. Xx

I smile at the message. I could do with a friendly face. I reply straight away that I'll meet her across the road at the deli in an hour.

Sitting in the window of the deli, some sixty-five minutes

later, my appointment with McMillan successfully postponed, albeit begrudgingly on his part, I start to feel myself relax for the first time today.

'Your text couldn't have come at a better time,' I say, wiping a line through the condensation on the glass of wine with my thumb. 'Honestly, it's been a pig of a day already.' I fill Pippa in on the details, not just the missing file but the hoo-ha at home this morning.

'What's bothering you most? The missing file or Alice?' asks Pippa.

'I don't know,' I reply honestly. 'The file, I can get over. It will be a pain, not to mention embarrassing, having to confess to losing all that info.'

'And Alice? Can you get over her too?'

I stall for time by taking a sip of my wine. 'I wish ...' I look away. 'I wish it was easier with her. Everything has been turned upside down. I can't put my finger on it but it just doesn't feel right. Maybe I'm expecting too much. I'm not naive. I know these things take time, but it's getting worse instead of better. It's like she's come into our lives in a blaze of glory and everyone has fallen in love with her, except me.'

'Ooh, do I detect a note of jealousy?'

'Is it that obvious? Jesus, I've suddenly found my jealous streak, the one I didn't know I had. But it's like ...' I struggle to complete the sentence, knowing it will make me sound so bloody childish.

'It's like she's taking over your life,' supplies Pippa.

'Exactly. Don't I sound pathetic?' It's a statement, not a question.

We finish our wine and Pippa orders us both a coffee. Personally, I could have done with another glass of wine, but knowing we both have to drive home at some point, a coffee will have to do. We sit in silence for a while and I can tell Pippa wants to say something. When the coffees arrive and the waiter disappears, she speaks.

'I saw Alice in the village the other day. Did she tell you?'

'No. I'm surprised you recognised her. I mean, you've only seen her once and that was at the party.'

'Well, here's the thing,' says Pippa. She puts her cup down in the saucer and folds her arms on the table, leaning forwards. 'At first I thought it was you.'

'Me?'

'Yeah, I did think it was funny that you were in the village on a working day but I thought maybe you'd taken the day off work, or something. Anyway, she was across the road, just coming out of the shop, and I was at the bottom of the hill. I called over, but she didn't answer, so I shouted in that rather attractive fish-wife voice I usually reserve for Baz when he's in his shed at the bottom of the garden and no one is about to hear.'

'Why did you think it was me?'

'I'm just coming to that. She had her hair tied back in a ponytail, the way you do. The way you have now. She was wearing a pair of dark-blue jeans, a pair of Converse and, get this, a blue top with white and green fishes on it.'

'A top just like my top,' I say. 'The one I bought when I was with you from that little boutique in The Lanes. The one I wore to the party on Saturday.' I put my coffee cup down and lean towards Pippa. 'She was dressed like me?'

164

'So much so, as I said, that I thought it was you.'

'And you spoke to her.'

'Yeah, I said to her, I thought she was you and she laughed and said something about sisters looking alike, so I shouldn't be surprised.'

'Why would she do that? Dress like me, I mean?'

'Look, Clare. I wasn't going to say anything but, at the same time, as your friend, I feel I can't not say anything. And feel free to ignore me. I mean, what do I know?'

'Skip the disclaimer,' I say. 'Not necessary.'

'There's something about her I don't like. It's a gut feeling, women's intuition, call it what you like, but there's something off about her. A few times at that party I saw her watching you as if she was plotting some sort of revenge attack. She caught me looking at her once and the speed at which her expression changed, I almost thought I was imagining it. She smiled at me so sweetly it made me want to vomit. And you know how much I love sweet things.'

'So I'm not imagining things, then?'

'Nope. And the way she snuggled up to Luke at times, I did actually think it was a good job you couldn't see her. If that had been my Baz, I would have marched straight over to her and donked her on the nose.'

I laugh at Pippa's expression. 'What even is a donk?'

She laughs too. 'That's what Daisy used to say she was going to do to Baz when she was about three and they used to play-fight. Daddy I'm going to donk your nose.'

I smile at the thought, momentarily distracted away from my troubles. I check my watch. 'I need to get back,' I say.

'Thanks for the chat. I really appreciate it.' Outside the deli I give my friend a hug, but before we part company, I can't help myself ask one question. 'Do you think I should be worried about Alice?'

'If you're asking me the question, then you already know the answer,' says Pippa. 'There's something off-kilter with her. You may share the same DNA, but you definitely don't share anything else. Although, I think Alice has other ideas on that score. The next thing you know, she'll be turning up at the office pretending to be you.' Pippa makes a loo-loo sound and twirls her finger at the side of her head before heading off to her car, giving a wave as she turns the corner.

I take a slow walk back to the office, pondering our conversation. By the time, I sit down at my desk, I've made up my mind about what I'm going to do. I get back up again.

'Sandy, I'm going home early. I've a headache and I need to find this file. My diary's empty for the rest of the day. If you take any messages, I'll deal with it all first thing in the morning.'

'Okay, no problem. Hope you feel better.'

'Thanks. And I'm really sorry about earlier.'

I don't bother telling Leonard and Tom I'm going. I'm too embarrassed to face them. I've no doubt Tom will say something about this morning's debacle at some point, but for now, I'd rather not go over it again. I've more important things to do.

I get home some forty minutes later, the traffic a little heavy out of town, but once I'm on the B road to Little Dray, it's a clear run. As I pull into the drive, I'm relieved to see two empty spaces in the carport. Mum and Alice have gone out. I think Mum said something yesterday about them going to Beachy Head. I ignore the suggestions that spring to mind as to what I'd like Alice to do at Beachy Head. Luke will have gone to collect Chloe from the nursery attached to the primary school in Budlington. I have about thirty minutes, tops, alone in the house.

Although I'm pretty certain the house is empty, I call out and do a quick sweep of the ground floor. Upstairs, I call out again and, confident everyone is out, I find myself standing in front of Alice's bedroom door. There is always the possibility that she's in there, resting or watching the TV, or whatever it is she does in there. I step forward and tap on the bedroom door.

'Alice? It's me, Clare. Are you in there?'

I'm met with silence. I place my hand on the doorknob and turn it slowly to the right. The spring inside the brass knob squeaks in protest. It's squeaked for as long as I can remember. As a child, I always knew when Alice got up in the night, the squeak was a dead giveaway. The oak door brushes against the thick carpet as I push it open. I poke my head round into the room. The bed is made, the quilted blue-and-white eiderdown folded neatly down. The curtains are open and the sash window is raised a little, the net curtain flutters gently against the breeze.

I look further into the room at the door opposite. It's the en suite. It used to be a big walk-in wardrobe, but it was converted as part of Dad's renovation programme. He'd had a lot of things brought up to date in the old house, starting with en suites in all the rooms. I have a vague recollection of him and mum arguing one night in the kitchen. Something to do with bed and breakfast. I didn't understand at the time but, looking back, as an adult, I think Dad wanted to open the house up as a B&B, but Mum didn't. It was all academic, as it turned out. Dad was gone a few months later.

The en-suite door is ajar and I walk into the room, giving one more call of Alice's name, just to be doubly certain she's not in the bathroom.

The first thing I do is open the wardrobe. There are quite a few clothes hanging up and it strikes me Alice keeps her wardrobe in the same sort of order that I keep mine in. All the tops together, all the skirts, all the jackets, although Alice's is a depleted version of mine. I reach for the tops and push apart the coat hangers. And there it is, the blue top with the green-and-white fish pattern is hanging up, right in the middle. So, Pippa was right, not that I ever doubted my friend, but it was something I needed to see with my own eyes. I'm then struck by the top hanging next to it. The blue-and-white striped t-shirt with the red piping on the sleeve. I have the exact-same one. I start to rummage through the rest of the clothing. A blue denim skirt, just like the one I wore with the fish- patterned top.

I take a step back from the wardrobe, as if I'm stepping away from the edge of a cliff. My head swims and I take a moment to steady myself as I feel off-balance. I close my eyes for a second and when I open them. I take another, more measured, look at the clothes. They are definitely the same as mine. Are they mine?

I dart out onto the landing and into my room, the next one along in the hallway. I yank open my wardrobe and pull at the garments, shoving the coat hangers apart, looking for the clothes I have just seen in Alice's wardrobe. None of them are there.

'They're my bloody clothes,' I say out loud.

The sound of my own angry voice pulls me up short. I can feel my pulse thumping in my neck and my breathing is coming fast and heavy. I need to get a grip. So what my clothes are in Alice's room? She's just borrowed them, like she did before.

I walk back to Alice's room and go to retrieve them, but pause. Of course, I could play this to my advantage. I rearrange the coat hangers as neatly as I found them and close the wardrobe.

Looking around the room, my attention is suddenly drawn to the dressing table. In particular, the bottle of perfume on the side. It has a sliver top and the bottle is shaped like an hourglass. I know, without even smelling it, that it's the Avon perfume I have on my dressing table. I smell it all the same to be certain. Where the hell did she get another bottle of that? It's like gold dust, having been discontinued a couple of years ago. This will be just more proof.

I sit down on the dressing-table stool and although I know it's wrong, I feel totally justified in looking in the drawers. Her underwear is even laid out neatly in order, the same way as in mine. Somehow, I'm not surprised. I close the drawer and look at my reflection. I think back to the photograph Alice sent me and mum of herself and her friend and how happy we were to have finally been contacted by her.

I notice the bedside table in the mirror and find myself drawn towards it. I've poked around in her dressing table, what's the point in stopping now? I might as well go the whole hog.

I slide open the single drawer of the bedside table. I'm shocked by what I see. A silver photo frame, like the one my wedding photo was in, is lying in the drawer face up. It's not just the frame, though, it's the picture inside. It's of Alice, taken on Brighton seafront, but she's not alone. Standing close next to her, arms around each other, is Luke, both smiling madly at the camera. My mouth dries as I stare at the photograph. My legs feel wobbly and I sink down onto the edge of the bed. My heart pummels my breastbone. I blink slowly and take another look at the picture, in case I'm imagining things.

No, they are still there, smiling back at me. My husband and my sister. Mocking me.

Chapter 15

I can barely wait for everyone to get home. Then I can show Luke and Mum what Alice is really like. I can't help feeling a little guilty, as I know I'm going to cause Mum a lot of pain, but I really think they need to know the truth about Alice, that she's manipulative, deceitful and even a fantasist, if the photo of her and Luke is anything to go by. I can't wait to hear how Alice is going to get out of this one.

Mum and Alice arrive home and, of course, are surprised to see me. Mum comes into the kitchen on her own.

'Where's Alice?' I ask, wasting no time on civilities.

Mum stops and looks at me. She can sense something is up. 'I wasn't expecting to see you here. I hope you've calmed down after this morning.' She places two bags of shopping on the worktop and leaves them there while she checks the post on the table.

'I wasn't feeling too well,' I say. I look back down the hall. 'Is Alice with you?'

'She's just nipped to the bathroom,' says Mum. 'Clare, you still seem very on edge. I don't want any more trouble.'

'Why hasn't she used the downstairs loo?' I ask, noting the

cloakroom door is not closed properly and ignoring Mum's comment

'I've no idea. Does it really matter?'

I hear footsteps on the stairs as Alice trots down. She swings around the newel post and flashes a smile at me.

'Hello, Clare,' she says. She comes into the kitchen. 'You okay? Not at work?'

'Clearly,' I say. 'I've misplaced an important file, so I've popped back to look for it. I don't suppose anyone has seen it, have they?'

'No, sorry, love,' says Mum her tone lightening slightly. 'Have you checked your desk in the study?'

'Yes, but I didn't go in there at the weekend. To be honest, I didn't even take it out of my briefcase.'

'Well, you can't have brought it home, then,' says Alice blithely as she unpacks the shopping. She pops a can of beans in the cupboard as if she's done it a hundred times before. As if it's her kitchen.

'It's not at work, so it must be here,' I say tersely. I catch a glimpse of the expression on Alice's face. Was that a little smile at the corners of her mouth as she turned away? 'Are you sure you haven't seen it, Alice?'

Alice gives a laugh, as if I'm being totally ridiculous. 'Clare, I promise, I haven't seen the file. I don't even know what it looks like. Have you checked everywhere?'

'Of course!' I snap.

'Clare!' Mum gives me a disapproving look. 'Alice is only trying to help. Now make yourself useful and put the kettle on.'

I do as I'm told and by the time I've made tea, Luke has arrived home.

'Mummy!' calls Chloe, running down the hallway. I scoop her up.

'Hello, darling. How was your day at nursery?' I give her several kisses and spin her around in my arms before putting her down. 'Would you like a drink?'

'Juice, pease,' says Chloe, still not quite able to master the word.

I meet Luke's gaze and offer a smile as I try to gauge his mood with me. 'All right?' he says. There's a coldness to his voice and I can't help feeling disappointed as he side-steps me without stopping for a kiss.

'How was your day?' I push on.

'How do you think?' His voice is monotone. 'Yours?'

'Not so good. I've lost a file. Came home early to try to find it,' I say, trying to keep a faint hold on normality.

'Wondered why you were here.'

'I'm going to pick Hannah and Daisy up from Brownies. Pippa asked if one of us could do it,' I say, aware Alice is watching us. I pass Luke a cup of coffee, which he takes and just about manages to say cheers.

'Oh, Alice, I meant to say, Pippa said she saw you in the village the other day,' I make an effort to sound casual as I lean back against the worktop.

'Pippa? Oh, yes, your friend. I did bump into her, that's right,' says Alice.

'The funny thing is, Pippa thought you were me,' I say, forcing a small laugh out. 'She said you had the same top on as mine. You know, the blue one with the green-and-white fish on it?'

Alice looks slightly thrown for a second. I glance at Luke, who is watching the scenario. Mum is too. 'Er, I don't think so,' she says. 'Not the same top.'

'Pippa has an eye for these things. I don't think she would make a mistake like that,' I say. 'Actually, come to think of it, I haven't seen that top for a few days. Look, if you've borrowed it, I really don't mind, you just needed to ask. The same for my blue-and-white stripy T-shirt and denim skirt. Rather than take things, just ask. Although I'd sooner you didn't go into my room when I'm not here. I know Mum lent you my top the other day, but please, if you could ask me first, I'd appreciate that.'

'Clare, I have no idea what you're talking about, I'm sure,' says Alice. She looks at Mum.

'No, I don't either,' says Mum.

'I haven't borrowed any of your clothes,' says Alice.

'Really? So, Pippa is lying?' I say looking Alice straight in the eye. I hold my hand up to Mum as she goes to protest. 'Is Pippa lying?' I ask again.

'I wouldn't say lying, more like mistaken,' says Alice.

'If we were to look in your wardrobe, my clothes wouldn't be hanging in there?'

'Clare, take it easy,' warns Luke, saying more words than he has done so to me for the past day. 'I don't think that's necessary.' He looks apologetically at Alice.

'But I think it is,' I say.

'Be my guest,' says Alice. 'Actually, let's all go up and have a look, shall we? Come on.' She puts her cup down on the worktop and marches upstairs. I follow straight behind her. I think Mum and Luke feel they have no choice but to come as well. I glance back and Luke is lifting Chloe into his arms before following us.

We all stand in front of the wardrobe as if it's some sort of show about to start. Alice makes a big deal of opening the wardrobe door rather theatrically and then stepping back as though she's a magician's assistant.

I pull at the hangers where the tops are. I can't find my fish top at all. I flick through the clothes. No sign of the skirt or the other top. I look in the bottom of the wardrobe, but it's just shoes. I look through the clothes again, but mine are definitely not there. I spin around.

'They were here earlier,' I say.

'You've been going through my things!' says Alice in melo-dramatic tones.

'What have you done with them?' I glare at Alice.

'Clare!' It's a warning word from Luke. He can tell I'm going to blow.

I ignore him and push between my mother and sister and storm over to the bedside table. 'What about this, then?' I yank open the top drawer. There's a packet of tissues, a phone charger and a mobile phone, but no picture. I look underneath, in case I didn't put it back properly. Nothing. 'There was a photo in this drawer. One of Alice and Luke. I saw it.' I spin around and look, once again, at the jury in front of me.

'Clare, I think you need to leave my room,' says Alice.

'You've moved it all, haven't you?' I demand, suddenly

realising what she's done. 'Just now, when you got home. That's why you used the bathroom up here and not the one downstairs.'

'I don't know what's got into you, Clare,' says Mum. She looks at Alice and puts a comforting arm around her. 'I'm sorry, darling. I think Clare is working too hard. It's all getting a bit much for her. Please don't cry, sweetheart. Oh, Alice, come on, darling. Sit down.' She sits Alice down on the edge of the bed.

'Mum! I promise you, my clothes were here. There was a picture in the drawer. I saw it with my own eyes.'

'Luke, take Clare out. She's upsetting her sister.'

Luke picks up Chloe again and looks at me. 'Don't cause a scene,' he says coolly.

I go to protest, but change my mind. Chloe is clinging onto Luke and eyeing me with caution. 'I'm not making this up,' I say, as I leave the room. I march straight into our room and fling open my own wardrobe. I'm not as surprised as I thought I might be when the clothes previously in Alice's wardrobe are now in mine. Luke is in the room. He puts Chloe on the bed and comes over to my wardrobe. He snatches out the two tops and skirt.

'These the ones you're looking for?' He throws them one by one into my arms.

'Luke, they were in her wardrobe. I'm not lying. Why would I?'

Luke takes a step closer to me. He's only a few inches from my face. 'Get a fucking grip.' He says it quiet enough that Chloe doesn't appear to hear, seemingly distracted by the teddy bear on my bed that she must have left there at some point this morning.

I thrust the clothes back at him in my frustration. 'Are you saying I'm lying? Why won't you believe me?'

'You're the solicitor. You work it out,' he says. 'But if you need a clue, it's called evidence.' He drops the clothes onto the floor and once more scoops Chloe up. 'I'm going to sort Chloe out her tea now. I suggest you sort your head out and apologise to your mum and sister.'

'She's no sister to me,' I hiss back at him.

Luke gives a 'for fuck's sake' face and turns to go. He stops in the doorway. For a second I think he's had a change of heart, but he's looking at the bookcase beside the door. He transfers Chloe into his right arm and with his now-free hand reaches out and picks something up from the top of the bookcase. He turns to me. 'Something of yours, I believe.'

I gulp. It's a green envelope file. I don't have to read the black marker pen on the front to know what file it says. It's the McMillan file. I take it from him. 'That wasn't there earlier.'

'Something else to apologise about,' he says. 'I don't know what the hell's got into you lately, Clare, but I don't like it. I don't like you.'

'It's not me, though! It's her! Can't you see what's she's doing? She's putting a wedge between us all.' I don't care that I've raised my voice. I don't care if Alice hears.

Mum comes storming out from Alice's room. She pushes past Luke and stops in front of me. 'Now, you listen to me, young lady.' If it wasn't for the rage on her face, I'd probably find Mum calling me 'young lady' funny. It's what she used to say when I was about ten years old. 'Your sister is sobbing her heart out in there because of you. I never thought I'd say it, but you make me ashamed, Clare Tennison. Ashamed of you. How dare you behave like this to your sister? She's talking about leaving now, going back to America and never coming back.' Mum's voice catches in her throat. She's fighting back the emotion. 'And if she does, I'll never forgive you. Do you hear me? Never.'

Mum has gone out of the room before I can even respond. Her last words have struck my heart like a spear. I look to Luke in my stunned stupor.

Once upon a time, not so long ago, he would have held me in his arms and somehow absorbed any pain, but today he stands still, cold, statuesque. How has it all come to this in such a short space of time? How have I become the outcast of the family?

'Clare what's happening to you?' he says, taking a step closer to me. The anger has gone from his voice. 'I'm worried about you. It's like you're falling apart in front of my eyes, but you won't let me help you.'

'Can't you see what's happening?' I ask. 'Can't you see what Alice is doing to us?'

'She's trying to find her feet back in her family. I thought this was what you wanted. It's obviously difficult for you to have to share your life with her again, especially as you've had us all to yourself up until now, but you've got to get over this jealousy thing. It's like you're constantly analysing Alice, watching her every move and reading far more into it than what's there. You've got to stop it and get a grip of yourself, Babe. It's not a good place to be when you're like this.'

'You're not listening to me,' I snap. 'No one is. You're all taken in by her.'

I push past him and flee down the stairs. I grab my bag and car keys, the McMillan file still in my hand. I jump in the car, throwing the file and my handbag on the passenger seat and floor it out of the driveway, the wheels spinning on the gravel as I do.

At first I don't know where I'm driving, I just know I want to get as far away from the house as possible and the people I love who are hurting me. I start to think of Luke's reaction. He didn't even try to defend me or to see things from my point of view. I can understand Mum's reaction, to a certain extent. She doesn't want to think badly of her daughter. She has been on a lifetime's guilt trip, thinking about how she let Alice go, and now Alice is back she feels she needs to make it up to her. The love she has been harbouring all these years has to come out somewhere. I get that. She loves Alice. But Luke, why does he feel that? It's almost as if he is putting Alice before me.

Suddenly the image of Alice and Luke standing on the seafront rushes to the fore of my mind, swiftly followed by them laughing as they came off the i360, the portrait, them together alone in the studio, Alice in her oversized T-shirt, Luke admiring her legs. The exchange of looks I've caught between them. It all comes rushing, crashing, thumping into my mind. *The bastard! He's fucking her!*

I should be crying. I should be heartbroken, but I'm too angry to feel all that. I'm way past angry, I'm furious. Livid. Incandescent. I'm muttering all sorts of curses at Luke as I drive. All this time I've supported him and his fucking art and this is how he repays me. He's shagging my sister! I thump the steering wheel. Rage settling within me.

It surprises me when I pull up outside Tom's apartment near the seafront in Brighton. I hadn't planned to come here. In fact, I have no idea how I ended up here. I cannot remember making a conscious decision to do so.

What the hell am I doing? I run my hands down my face and then back up across my hair, which, amazingly, is still in the ponytail. I shouldn't be here, but where else can I go? The seafront is a good place. I turn the engine on and put the car into first gear. I'm just about to pull away when the familiar blue BMW pulls in front of me, blocking my path.

I look up and Tom looks back at me. He gets out of the car and comes over to mine. Opening the driver's door, he looks at me and, without saying a word, reaches in, switches off the engine and takes the keys out of the ignition. He leans over and unclips the seat belt, picking up my bag and the file. He gives it a glance, but still doesn't say anything. Then, taking my hand, he guides me out of the car. He locks my car and walks me over to his car, sits me in the passenger seat and then drives into the underground car park.

We end up inside Tom's apartment, still without saying a word, and he pours us both a brandy. We sip in silence and when I'm finished I place my glass on the table. Tom puts his arm around me and holds me to him. I don't resist. I need human comfort. I need kindness. I need love.

Over the next hour, I relay the sequence of events to Tom and drink two more brandies.

'I had no idea it had got like that,' says Tom. 'Alice seemed so, well, so ...'

'Nice,' I supply. 'Yeah, I know. That's what everyone says.'

'And Luke. I'm really surprised at him,' says Tom. 'He should be standing by you, defending you, not making you feel like you've done something wrong.' He pauses for a moment. 'Unless, of course ... No, sorry, ignore me.'

'What were you going to say?'

'It doesn't matter. It's not my place.'

'Tom, you're one of my oldest friends. Of course it's your place.'

'No, leave it, Clare. I don't want to make matters worse. It's not for me to cause trouble between a man and his wife. God knows, I know what that's like.' He's referring to his ex-wife Isabella and the affair that broke up their marriage.

'It's okay. You can say it. You think Luke is having an affair with Alice.'

'Now, I never said that.'

'No, but I know what you were thinking and, it's okay, I've thought that too. The bastard.' I feel the anger surge once more.

'I'm sorry, Clare. It's that bad, huh?'

I feel a tear leak from the corner of my eye, and then another. Before I know it, tears are streaming down my face. Tom cuddles me. He strokes my hair. He rubs my back. His tells me it's okay and to let it out. And I do. For a good ten minutes. Then Tom produces a tissue from his pocket and dabs gently at my eyes, drying my face.

'I'm sorry,' I say. 'I didn't mean to get upset like that.'

'Don't apologise,' says Tom. His voice is soft and I'm suddenly aware of how close we are physically. His head is almost resting on mine. At some point, I don't know when or who instigated it, our lips meet and we engage in more than just a friendly peck. Instantly, I'm back at Oxford, we're twenty-one again and Tom is comforting me when I'm upset that my search for Alice is futile. How ironic that we find ourselves like this again, but because Alice has been found. Or rather, she has found us.

I feel tired from thinking about it all. It hurts too much. It's all so painful and yet, here, in Tom's arms, everything feels familiar and right. It reminds me of those student days when everything was good in the world, when the future ahead was full of excitement and promise. When there were no adult responsibilities. No lost files. No pending court cases. No cheating husband.

Chapter 16

Something inside my head snaps me back into reality. What the hell am I doing? I wriggle out of Tom's embrace. Thank God it hasn't gone any further than a kiss, not that a kiss is okay, but Jesus, what if I'd ended up having sex with him?

'Sorry, Tom,' I say, smoothing my hair back, which has somehow come out of the ponytail. 'I can't. It's not right.'

Tom leans in again and tries to kiss me. I pull even further back. 'No. Seriously, Tom, I mean it.' God, my head feels fuzzy. My limbs and arms are finding it difficult to respond, they're sluggish and tired.

Tom looks at me. 'You sure?'

I nod. 'I'm sure.'

For the briefest of moments, I think I catch a glimpse of anger cross Tom's face, but it's gone in a flash and he offers what I can only describe as a sad smile. 'That's a shame,' he says.

I feel uncomfortable at the closeness of us. I'm now perched on the edge of the sofa and, any closer, Tom would be sitting on my knee. 'Luke's a lucky man,' says Tom. 'He gets to eat his cake and keep it.'

I'm finding it hard to think straight and I massage my temples with my fingertips in a bid to clear my mind. 'Two wrongs don't make a right,' I say. Now that my initial anger with Alice and Tom has subsided, my logical professional brain is kicking in. Well, as much as it can do through this thick fog that is drifting around in my head. I have no proof that Luke has slept with Alice. Earlier I was angry, hurt and jealous. It's amazing how strong those emotions are when they all collide together in one big mess. They're like a jumble of cooked spaghetti; all mixed up, twirling and swirling in a tangle. I much prefer the thought process that goes with uncooked pasta: straight lines, organised and easy to follow.

'I'm not asking you to pack your bags, leave Luke and move in here,' says Tom. 'I'm just offering a safe place of refuge for as long as you like.' He reaches over and picks up my glass of brandy. 'Here, finish your drink and then see how you feel.'

'No, not for me. Sorry. I shouldn't have any more to drink. God knows what's in that stuff, but it's bloody strong. I feel so tired.' My eyes are heavy and I'm sure I could go to sleep right there and then.

'Just sit back for a moment,' says Tom. 'I'll make you a coffee.'

'Thanks, that sounds like a good idea.'

Tom picks up a cushion and as I twist around in the sofa, he places it behind my head. I rest back against it and close my eyes. I feel Tom's hand stroke my forehead. 'No hard feelings?' he says.

'No hard feelings,' I confirm. My words sound as tired as I feel.

The next thing I'm aware of is the blanket pulled up to

my chin and draped over the front of me, tucked in at the shoulders. I open my eyes and it takes a moment to focus. I can't make out where I am. The light is dim but it's not quite dark outside. I look around the room and then, with a sudden clarity, I know exactly where I am. Tom's living room.

A gentle breathing is the next thing I register and I go to move my head, but it hurts too much, so I make do with moving my eyes only to my right. Tom is asleep on the sofa next to me. He is wearing a T-shirt and jogging pants. The events of the last few hours gradually unfold in my mind, rather like a game of pass-the-parcel, each minute gradually unwrapping another layer of memory.

I yank the cover from me and am relieved to see I'm still fully clothed, apart from my jacket, which is hanging over the arm of the sofa and my shoes, which are splayed on the floor, obviously kicked off rather than taken off. There are two brandy glasses on the table. One half-full and the other empty. There's also a cup of coffee, full and stone cold. On the table is a camera, a mobile phone, a scrunched-up tissue and the McMillan file. Then I remember kissing Tom.

I'm filled with a blind panic. I kissed Tom! Not just a peck on the cheek, but a full-on kiss.

Shit!

The next layer of wrapping paper is peeled away and I remember saying no to Tom. To stopping things before they went any further. Thank God for that. Although I can't ignore the guilt that is now hammering at my chest.

I need to get home to try to sort out this mess that has become my life.

I slip my feet into my shoes and stand up, rather wobbly, but I hold onto the back of the sofa for support while I steady myself. I grab my stuff and tiptoe out of the house. Once in my car, I rummage in my handbag for my phone.

When I see the list of messages and missed calls my heart leaps. Three missed calls and a text message from Pippa. Five missed calls, three text messages from Luke and what appear to be three voicemail messages. How the hell did I miss those? The volume has been switched off. I have no recollection of doing that at all. I fumble with the phone, unlocking the screen and scrolling through the messages.

'Shit. Shit. Shit!' I could cry. How has this happened? I hardly dare listen to the voicemail messages. One from Luke and one from Pippa. Oh, God. I totally forgot to get the girls from Brownies. How? What is wrong with me? Talk about self-indulgent. I was so busy worrying about Alice and how it was all affecting me, I didn't give my child and my friend's child a second thought. And now ... shit ... now there's a rather severe voicemail message from Pippa telling me she's at the hospital with Daisy and that she's furious with me and holds me totally responsible.

I slam the phone into the hands-free cradle and hit the dial button for Luke. My hands are shaking as I ram the key into the ignition and tear out of the parking space, heading towards the general hospital in Brighton. It crosses my mind that I had two brandies earlier and nothing to eat. I feel okay, just a little headache coming now. I wish I'd had that coffee. Then I remember a bottle of water in my bag and, with one hand, manage to fish it out, snapping open the sports cap and glugging the water down. It's a bit warm, but I don't care. Luke picks up.

'Clare! Where the fuck have you been? I've been trying to get hold of you. So has Pippa. You were supposed to get the girls. Did you get any of my messages?'

He's angry. No doubt about it but, to be fair, he's been angry with me for a while now. 'Yes. I'm sorry. My phone was on silent. What's happened?'

'Basically, you didn't turn up for the girls after Brownies, so the Brown Owl, or whatever the fuck she's called, phoned home. Alice had to go and get them. She took them to the park on the way back and Daisy had an accident. Fell off the climbing frame or something. Anyway, she's broken her arm and Pippa is up the hospital with her now.'

'Oh, God. I'm sorry. Is Hannah okay?'

'Yes, she's fine.'

'Why did Alice go?'

'She was the only one who could go.' I detect a little apprehension in Luke's voice.

'Why? Where was Mum? Where were you?'

'Your mum went out to her WI meeting and I, err, fell asleep. Alice didn't want to wake me, so she just went straight over to Budlington.'

'She walked?'

'No, she took my car.'

'Can she do that? I didn't think she'd be insured. What if she'd had an accident?'

'For fuck's sake, Clare. You're not the prosecution now. Where were you, anyway?'

'I needed to bit of breathing space. Look, I can't speak now, I'm nearly at the hospital. I'll talk to you later.' I hang up before we can take the conversation further. To tell Luke that I spent the afternoon and evening with Tom won't go down very well. I need to be able to tell him face to face when I can explain it properly, not some hashed phone call while I'm driving and worried about Pippa and Daisy.

To say I'm persona non grata is something of an understatement. As I enter A&E and am advised by the receptionist where I can find Daisy Stent, I've only made it halfway down the line of cubicles when Pippa launches herself at me.

'A bit sodding late to show up now,' she says, not bothering to keep her voice down.

I look apologetically at one of the nurses, who glances over. Pippa's never been one to mix her words. She says exactly what she's thinking. It's something that I love about her and it has caused much amusement in the past. We joke that she has no filter, but today it's not so funny being on the receiving end of her sharp tongue.

'Pippa, I'm so sorry. *Really* sorry. I got held up. My phone was on silent. Sorry.' It sounds pathetic and I am pathetic.

'What the hell happened? Where were you?' Pippa's eyes are burning with anger, but I can also see they are red from crying.

'I had an argument at home. I needed to get out of the house. I'm sorry, Pip, honestly I am. How's Daisy?'

'Broken arm. Baz is in there with her. They're going to put a cast on it in a minute.'

'Is there anything I can do?'

'What? I don't think so. The only thing you had to do was to pick the girls up, but you didn't manage that. Why the hell did Alice get them?'

'She was the only one available.' I don't want to tell Pippa that Luke was asleep. It's bad enough that one of us has failed big time at parenting. I go to offer yet another apology but am cut off by Pippa.

'Look, Clare, we all make mistakes, I know that, but when you're responsible for a child, someone else's child, there's no room for mistakes. I haven't said anything to Baz, but before he got here, Daisy told me that Alice pushed her on purpose.'

'What? Oh, don't be ridiculous. Alice wouldn't do that.'

'You can think what you like, but Daisy doesn't tell lies. Not about things like this, she wouldn't. And I know all that bullshit about parents thinking their child is an angel, I know Daisy's not, but she wouldn't lie about something like that.'

'Maybe she's mistaken,' I suggest, inwardly preparing myself to bat away more of Pippa's wrath. Would Alice intentionally harm a child? It seems a bit much to believe and why would she do it? It just doesn't make sense. And yet, there's a tiny voice at the back of my mind that is challenging my thought process. It wouldn't be the first time Alice has done something different from the perceived norm. Pippa's reply interrupts my thoughts.

'Daisy's not mistaken. I asked Hannah and she just kept saying she doesn't know what happened.'

'Well, perhaps she doesn't know.' The mother in me automatically leapfrogs over my professional brain to the defence of my daughter. 'I'm sure Hannah's not lying.'

'In just the same way as I'm sure Daisy isn't. You ask Hannah and you tell me if she's telling the truth or not.'

'Pippa, that's out of order. Hannah wouldn't lie.' I mentally cross my fingers. I'm sure all children lie at some time. 'Not about something like this.'

'Depends who's applying the pressure,' says Pippa.

'Where are Alice and Hannah, anyway?'

'Gone. I didn't want her hanging around and Hannah was upset.'

'Can I see Daisy?'

'What for? To cross-examine her about the incident? Are you going to get her to swear to tell the truth the whole truth and nothing but the truth?'

'Pippa, please.'

'Look, Clare. Now's not a good time. I need to get back to Daisy. You need to get back to your family and sort out whatever the hell is going on.'

I nod, accepting Pippa's decision. 'Okay, I am sorry, Pippa, you do know that, don't you?'

'I've got to go,' says Pippa.

'Yeah, sure. I'll make it up to the girls when Daisy comes for a sleepover at the weekend. If her arm's okay, that is. Even if she just came for tea. Yeah?'

Pippa looks long and hard at me. 'I don't think that's a good idea right now.'

'Hannah will be devastated,' I say, thinking how much Hannah is looking forward to the sleepover. She has it all planned, a mini make-over, party tea, a movie and popcorn, followed by a sleepover. She's been planning it for weeks.

'I'm not comfortable with Daisy being anywhere near Alice and I'm not even sure Daisy would want to be at yours now, not after this. Don't take it personally, Clare, it's not you it's your sister.'

'But you're punishing Hannah for my mistake.'

'And don't you think Daisy has been punished too? She's got a broken arm. For God's sake, Clare. Stop thinking about yourself all the time. Daisy won't be coming for a sleepover. I don't want her anywhere near your creepy fucking sister. End of.'

Chapter 17

When I arrive home, the reception is just as frosty from everyone as it was at the hospital. The only one pleased to see me is Hannah. She rushes up to me and hugs me. I feel so guilty for not being there to collect her from Brownies. I've let her down and I've let Daisy down. If only I hadn't gone to Tom's and had those brandies, then I wouldn't have fallen asleep and missed it. I still don't know how my phone ended up on silent. I hug Hannah back tightly, drawing on her love. It's the only comfort I'm going to get tonight. Chloe is already fast asleep in bed, so Luke informs me.

I spend the next hour with Hannah, bathing her, washing her hair and getting her ready for bed. I haven't asked her about the incident at the playground yet but as we snuggle up on the sofa together, just me and her, while she has a glass of milk and biscuit before bed, it's Hannah who brings the subject up first.

'Is Daisy going to be okay?' she asks.

I look down at my daughter's worried little face and honestly feel so overcome with emotion that I could cry. 'Yes, she will be. She's broken her arm and the doctors have put a plaster cast on it. You know, like the one nanny had when she fell over last year.'

'What colour is it?'

'I don't know. I didn't see it. I only spoke to Daisy's mummy. Now don't be worrying, Daisy will be fine.' I don't want to upset Hannah even more by telling her what Pippa said about the sleepover. Maybe Pippa will have calmed down by next weekend and will let Daisy come after all. I've already decided to give it a couple of days before I call Pippa and see if we can smooth things over. I don't have many friends and, although that's never been a real problem for me in the past, right now I could do with an ally, especially as Luke seems to have defected.

'Did you see what happened at the park?' I ask Hannah, hoping my voice sounds relaxed.

Hannah circles the rim of the cup with her finger. 'No.'

'What? Nothing at all?'

'No. Daisy fell over. I don't know what happened.'

'You know you can tell me, don't you? Remember how you told me about the photo frame when Alice said not to? Well, it's like that. You can tell me, even if she said you shouldn't.'

'Why does everyone keep asking me what happened? I don't know.' Hannah sticks out her bottom lip. I don't want to upset her even more. I'll try again tomorrow.

'It's okay, sweetheart,' I say. 'Come on, let's go up. I'll tuck you in. You can look at a book for five minutes.'

Alice appears to be keeping out of my way. She's in Mum's sitting room this evening. I know I need to apologise for my outburst earlier, but I'm finding it difficult as I may be sorry for the way I reacted, but I'm not sorry for what happened. Pippa was right, there is something odd about Alice. I think she's playing games, but I just don't know what that game could be or why.

I go into the kitchen to make myself a cup of tea. Luke is waiting for me. He's leaning against the worktop, his arms folded. Even with the scowl on his face, I can't help but think how handsome he looks. The way his hair falls this way and that, his black T-shirt and jeans so casual yet somehow so sexy. I can see why Alice would find him attractive. And then I think of myself and wonder if Luke thinks the same about me or has something changed? Have I lost something? Has he become bored of me? Am I boring? I mean, I go to work, I come home and change into my very casual clothes. Perhaps I've become too mumsy. I can see why Alice would be a much more appealing proposition. It hurts. Deeply.

I take the milk from the fridge and the photograph of Alice and her friend Martha has been put on the door, underneath a magnet that has a sentimental poem about mothers and daughters. I didn't buy it. Alice must have. I look at the photograph and remember how happy Mum and I were when we received it. I slip it out from underneath the magnet. Something's wrong. I can't make up my mind what it is. I look at the photo some more.

'Aren't you going to explain what happened this evening?' says Luke.

I jump. Distracted by the photo, I'd almost forgotten he was there. 'I needed to get out. I didn't know where I was going, but I ended up at Tom's.'

I see the muscles in Luke's neck tense but his face remains impassive. 'Tom? As in Tom Eggar.'

'Yeah, that Tom. I don't know any other Tom.' I want to kick myself for the irritation that creeps into my reply.

'Why?'

'Why did I go there? I don't know. I was upset. As I say, I just found myself there.'

'So, you go off to your ex-boyfriend when you've had a row with your husband. What is that? Some sort of tit for tat?'

'Tit for tat? It can only be that if someone did something in the first place. So I'm assuming there was something with you and Alice, otherwise why would you say that?'

'It's just an expression. I'm just explaining how it's playing out in your head.' He taps the side of his head. 'Your fucked-up head, that is.'

'You're the one with the fucked-up head,' I retort. 'Tom is an old friend and a colleague. That is all.' There's no way I can confess to kissing Tom now.

I look again at the photograph of Alice and Martha, more as a distraction from the argument than anything else. And then I see what has been troubling me about it. I look once again at the two girls in the photo. I peer at their faces. It's too far away to see any detail but the clock in the background I can see clearly. The numbers on the face are in reverse.

I snatch the photograph up and stride out of the kitchen. Luke is calling me. I can hear his bare feet on the tiles following me as I hurry down to Mum's sitting room.

'Clare! Whatever you're doing, stop and think for a minute,' says Luke. He's right behind me, but it's too late, I'm through the door and standing in front of my mum and Alice.

They both look up in surprise. Mum's face folds into a frown and Alice sits back, crossing her arms under her chest. She glances at the photograph and looks a little nervous. I don't know what the implications of what I've seen are, but I know they're important and I want to see what Alice has to say for herself.

'What's wrong, Clare?' asks Mum. 'I hope you've come to apologise.'

'No, I wanted to ask Alice something,' I say. I look at my sister. 'This photograph you sent us, you said you're the one on the left.'

'And?' Alice's eyes dart from the photo to me and then to Mum.

I hold up the photograph so Mum and Alice can see it. 'On the left, that's you here. On the left as you say.'

'Sure.'

'This is definitely you?' I tap at the image of Alice.

'What is this?' demands Mum.

'Clare, are you sure about this?' says Luke, his voice low. I ignore him.

'Okay, we're all happy that this is Alice,' I say, my voice full of mock cheer. 'If that's so, why is the clock in the background reversed?' My eyes never leave Alice. A small flush creeps up her neck. She swallows hard. And then breaks into a smile followed by a laugh.

'Oh, Clare, you are funny,' she says. 'You know what I've done. I've reversed that photo when I scanned it in. How silly of me.'

'But you said in the attached email that you were the one on the left,' I say. 'When, in actual fact, you're really the one on the right, if this photo was flipped.'

'I don't know what you're getting at,' says Mum. 'What does it matter what side Alice is on?'

Alice drops her gaze for a moment and reaches out to hold Mum's hand. 'This is a bit embarrassing,' she says quietly. 'I didn't want to say anything before, it's not something I talk about much.'

'What is it, dear?' says Mum, squeezing Alice's hand.

'I'm dyslexic,' says Alice. 'I get things back to front, letters mostly, but I also have trouble with sequences, you know days of the week, months of the year. I also get my left and right muddled up.'

'That's nothing to be ashamed of,' says Mum. 'I had no idea.'

I feel as if the air has been taken from my lungs. They deflate like a burst balloon. I hear Luke mutter *nice one* from behind me.

Alice looks up at Mum with big, round, sorrowful eyes. 'I didn't want to say, not with Clare being such a successful career woman. It made me feel, I don't know, inferior, I suppose. I didn't want you to think I was stupid. Daddy was always telling me how I would only ever wait on tables because I couldn't get my grades.'

'I thought you were a teacher,' I say. I'm certain that's what she said in one of her emails.

Alice looks up at me. 'Yes. That's right. I am. I proved them all wrong. Just because I'm dyslexic and don't read books, it doesn't mean I'm stupid.'

'But you still get left and right muddled up.' I'm not buying the tears. Big fat crocodile tears, if you ask me. I know she's right about dyslexia and intelligence and normally I wouldn't even imply anything so insulting, but Alice seems to have the knack of bringing out the worst in me.

'Like I said, I just wanted to prove them all wrong. Especially Daddy.' Alice makes a sobbing noise and buries her face in her hands.

'Oh, my darling child,' says Mum and pulls Alice into her arms. Mum looks up at me. 'I think you've done enough damage for one day.'

Pain. I think that's what I see in Mum's face. I've hurt Alice and, by default, I've hurt her. It cuts deep into my heart. I stutter out an apology. 'I'm ... sorry. Mum. Alice.' It's all I can manage. I'm withering inside like the Wicked Witch of the West, but something makes me plough on. Call it tenacity, pig-headedness or it could just be a professional trait I've developed. I don't know, but I can't help myself. The search for the truth is driving me on. I'm totally consumed by it. 'You know, Pippa isn't speaking to me now,' I say, ignoring Mum's look, which intensifies. I try to shut down the hurt this is causing me, rather like I've managed perfectly well to shut down the hurt of my father deserting me. 'She's not letting Daisy come round any more. She says Daisy isn't safe here. What happened today, Alice?'

'Oh, for God's sake, Clare. Can't you just leave it?' It's Luke. 'I'm sorry, Marion. Alice. I don't know what's got into her recently.'

'Don't apologise for me,' I say. 'I'm not accusing anyone of anything, I'm just asking.'

'Bullshit.' Luke shakes his head. 'Come on.' He takes my arm, but I shrug him off.

'I'd like you to leave now,' says Mum. 'If you were a child, I'd be sending you to your room, but you're a grown woman. You need to start acting like it. Now please leave us alone.'

Feeling both humiliated and indignant I do as I'm told. Back in the kitchen Luke sits down at the table, turning his chair inwards, and pulls another round to face him. He nods to the chair and I sit down. He has the air of a man under pressure. He rests his elbows on his knees and puts his hands together, as if in prayer, dipping his head for a moment as if to steel himself. Then he takes my hands in his.

The physical contact from him practically sends a small electric shock through me. I've missed him these last few days. I've missed his touch and I've missed his love.

'Clare, I'm worried about you,' he says. 'You're not yourself lately. You're very ... or rather, you *seem* very tetchy ... almost paranoid.'

I take a sharp snatch of breath. 'Paranoid?'

I want to pull my hands away, but Luke holds onto them. 'Like there's some sort of conspiracy going on with Alice.'

This time I do yank my hands free. 'I can't believe you're saying this.'

'It's only because I care about you. I think you've too much going on at the moment. Maybe you should take some time off work. Have you thought about talking to someone? Not a friend. I mean a professional.'

'A doctor?' I snort at the idea.

'I don't think you're coping,' he says.

I stand up, scraping the chair back across the tiled floor. 'I do not need to see a doctor. There is nothing wrong with me.' I storm out of the kitchen.

My head is killing me and my limbs feel heavy and weak. I wonder if I'm coming down with something. I feel quite rough. What I need is a good night's sleep. I climb into bed and from my bedside drawer fish out a packet of Paracetamol. I pop two from the foil-backed sheet. Hopefully, when I wake up in the morning, my thick head will have cleared and I can start the day fresh.

It feels as if I've only been asleep for an hour or two, but I'm woken by my alarm clock buzzing, sounding like a swarm of bees tapping out Morse code. I'm usually up long before it goes off and had almost forgotten what it sounded like. I reach over and silence the buzzing. It doesn't look as if Luke slept in the bed last night. I sigh as I think back to yesterday and for the umpteenth time wonder how it has all got to this. How my life seems to be unravelling and there's nothing I can do to stop it.

I shower and dress and make my way downstairs. Mum, Alice, Luke and the girls are all there. We exchange muted good mornings and I take my seat at the table. 'School swimming today,' I say to Hannah with a smile, trying to sound cheery for her benefit.

'I've got all her stuff sorted,' says Luke in a tone that says not to interfere and not to enter into any sort of dialogue with him.

The sound of the doorbell ringing and someone hammering on the door-knocker breaks through the uneasy silence that has descended.

'Who on earth can that be at this time in the morning?' says Mum to no one in particular.

'I'll go,' says Luke. We listen to the sound of voices as Luke speaks to whoever it is. Then the door closes and Luke appears in the kitchen, followed by two police officers. One male. One female.

The female officer speaks. 'Mrs Tennison? Clare Tennison?'

'Yes,' I say. A hundred thoughts zoom through my mind as to what they want. This early in the morning can only mean one thing. Bad news. I look at Luke and I don't think I've ever seen such disappointment in his eyes

Chapter 18

I look bewildered at the police officers. I've seen enough police officers in my time to know that this is not a friendly visit. I glance at the children.

Chloe is smiling away. 'Hello, Policeman and Police lady. Ne-nah-ne-nah.' The female officer gives a small smile in my daughter's direction.

I look at Hannah and her eyes are full of fear. She shrinks back in her seat and I'm suddenly protective of her. The poor lamb obviously thinks she's done something wrong. Probably thinking about yesterday and what happened to Daisy.

I stand up. 'Can we go into the living room, please?' I say, giving a little nod in Hannah's direction. Fortunately, the police officers pick up on this subtlety. I smooth Hannah's hair and drop a kiss on her head. 'Don't worry, darling. Mummy just needs to chat to these police officers about work.' Hannah looks unconvinced.

We go into the living room and Luke follows. I hope he's there for moral support rather than to gloat over whatever is going on. His eyes are dark and he stands beside me in front of the bay window. None of us sit.

'What can I help you with?' I say, my professional voice creeping in. 'And what did you say your names were?'

'I'm PC Evans and this is my colleague, PC Doyle,' says the female officer. 'And you are, sir?' She looks towards Luke.

'Luke Tennison. Clare's husband.'

Evans gives a nod of acknowledgment and then turns her attention back to me. 'Can you tell us where you were last night between the hours of eleven-thirty p.m. and six-forty-five this morning?'

'Can you tell me in what connection?' I ask. I'm already a step ahead. They wouldn't be asking me this question if they thought I was some innocent bystander to whatever has happened. I'm clearly a suspect.

'There's been a report of some damage to a vehicle,' says Evans.

'And why are you asking me about it?'

'Clare's a solicitor,' explains Luke.

I watch the two officers exchange a look before Evans carries on. She adjusts her weight from one foot to the other. 'I believe you know a Mrs Pippa Stent of Mulberry House, Church Lane, Little Dray.'

'Yes,' I say, alarm bells ringing a little louder in my head. Has Pippa put in an official complaint about the park incident? I quickly dismiss that notion as it wouldn't warrant this early-morning greeting. Besides, I can't be arrested for forgetting to pick the girls up.

'Mrs Stent's car suffered some damage at some point last night. Intentional damage.'

'And you think I did it?' I snort. 'Why on earth would I do something like that?'

'We understand that you and Mrs Stent had a disagreement yesterday.'

'She reported me? She thinks I did whatever it is that's happened?'

'We have several lines of enquiry and this is just one of them,' says Evans.

'What exactly has happened to Pippa's car?' asks Luke.

'It has suffered a dent to the rear, consistent with the impact of another car reversing into it with a tow bar. There's also graffiti on it.' Evans fixes me with a look that I'd give one of the children if I thought they needed to own up to something.

'What sort of graffiti?' asks Luke.

Evans consults her pocket book, which I'm sure is not necessary but she's playing the part. 'Traitor. Disloyal. Hypocrite.' Evans looks at me and I realise she's waiting for a reaction.

'Quite specific, then. Well, I'm not responsible,' I say.

'The windscreen and door handles were also smeared with dog faeces,' says Evans. 'Do you have a dog, Mrs Tennison?'

'No,' I reply.

'Only, we noticed a pair of shoes on your doorstep with dog faeces on one shoe.'

I look blankly at Luke who looks equally confused. 'I've no idea what you're talking about.'

'So, back to our original question, your whereabouts yesterday evening ...'

I pull a face at the thought. 'I was at home last night. I went to bed just after ten p.m. and I got up this morning at six a.m. when my alarm went off.'

'And you didn't go out at all last night? Can anyone vouch for you? Mr Tennison?'

Luke hesitates a moment too long. 'Yes, Clare was here last night.'

'All night? You know she was here? What time did you go to bed last night, Mr Tennison?'

'Around eleven,' he says.

'And Mrs Tennison was in bed when you went to bed yourself?'

Evans is persistent. She'll go far, she's getting right down to the nitty-gritty details – unfortunately, for me.

'Well, I slept downstairs last night,' confesses Luke. Evans raises her eyebrows, in question. 'I was busy working and I didn't want to disturb my wife. I quite often sleep downstairs. It's not unusual.'

I silently thank Luke for not saying we had an argument. I don't want them to think I go around arguing with everyone every day. Although, currently, that seems to summarise my life.

'May we take a look at your car, Mrs Tennison?' asks PC Doyle, speaking for the first time.

I can't refuse. 'Okay. I'll just get the keys.' We walk out to the hall and I look in the key cupboard. The hook where I usually hang mine is empty. 'That's odd,' I say. 'They're not here.' I scan the other hooks, looking for the small plastic key fob, which has a picture of me, Luke and the girls sitting in a log flume ride at an amusement park we visited last summer. There is no sign of it.

'Your bag?' suggests Luke.

'I never put them in my bag, you know that.'

'Just a suggestion.'

I pick up my bag and rummage through. To my surprise, the keys are in the little side pocket, zipped up. 'I don't understand,' I say. I think back to last night. Had I put them in my bag? Was I distracted enough not to hang them up as I always did? My usual clear head and thought process seems to be deserting me. I can't recall for certain what I did.

Evans gives a sceptical look in my direction. 'Shall we look at the car now?' she says, with the patience of a tired teacher on a Friday afternoon.

As we leave through the front door, I look down at the offending pair of shoes. They're my black work ones with the small one-inch heel and, just as Evans said, dog poo is wedge in the inside of the heel.

'I don't even know what my shoes are doing out here,' I say. 'I'd have known if I had trodden in poo.' Evans looks unconvinced. I don't blame her. I sound like a very unreliable witness. I'm not even sure I believe myself.

We go out to the carport. My car is facing outwards, as I always park it. Evans takes the keys from me and the two officers walk around the car, inspecting it as they do so. They get to the back and after muttering something that I can't hear, they call me over.

The towbar on the back of my car has traces of red paint on it and there is a small dent in the bumper. Pippa's car is red.

'Can you tell us how this happened?' asks Evans.

'I've absolutely no idea,' I say, my empty stomach churning over.

'May we look inside?' Evans presses the unlock button, lifts the boot and, with her torch, shines the beam into the blackness. It's empty. As I would expect. I'm not one for carrying loads of stuff around in the back of my car. Evans bends down and shines the light right into the far corner. A silver aerosol can with a white lid is illuminated. Evans takes a plastic glove from her pocket and, careful to make minimal contact, she retrieves the can. It's the sort of spray paint used on bodyworks for cars. The sort easily available from petrol stations.

'I've never seen that before in my life,' I say, vaguely aware I sound totally unconvincing.

'There's something else,' says Doyle.

This time Evans retrieves a till receipt. 'Looks like it's for this paint. Bought yesterday at the garage on the main road into Brighton. Paid for with cash. At seven p.m.' She looks up at me. 'Can you tell me where you were at this time?'

My mouth dries a little. This isn't looking too good for me. 'I was on my way home from the hospital. I'd been to see Pippa.'

'Ah, Mrs Stent. And this was after you had an argument with her about her daughter's accident?'

I nod. It would be at this point I'd advise anyone to seek legal advice. I realise that the evidence is stacking up against me. It's not exactly overwhelming evidence, although admittedly, we're heading for 'without reasonable doubt' territory. There is nothing solid to place me at the scene or to prove I bought the aerosol and then went to Pippa's. Although the traces on red paint on the towbar of my car aren't exactly in my favour, it doesn't mean I did it.

'We'd like you to come down the station with us for questioning and to make a formal statement,' says Evans.

'Are you arresting me?' I ask

'No, at the moment we're still gathering evidence. You do, of course, have the right to refuse and then I perhaps would consider formally arresting you on the grounds of suspicion of causing criminal damage,' says Evans. 'But, then, you know all that anyway.'

'But I have work,' I say. Leonard will go mad if I don't turn up, especially after taking the afternoon off yesterday. 'Can I come down at lunchtime?'

'No, Mrs Tennison, we would like to you to come now, voluntarily.'

I decide not to oppose. The quicker this is done, the quicker I can get to work.

'I'll ring Leonard,' says Luke, already one step ahead of me.

'And, please don't touch the car,' says Evans. 'We'll be sending someone out to take photos and paint scrapings in case we need forensics to do a paint match.' What she really means is, in case I don't confess to reversing into Pippa's car, covering it in graffiti and, instead, make up some other story as to how I have red paint on my car, a dent and an aerosol can.

I follow Evans and Doyle out to the squad car. I look over at Luke, who gives a shake of his head before turning back to the house. As the car pulls away, I look back to the house and see Alice watching from the living-room window. I'm struck by the memory I have of Alice leaving with my father. I sit back in the seat and concentrate on trying not to cry.

It's three hours before I'm finally allowed to leave the police station. I've made my statement, been interviewed by Evans and Doyle and steadfastly refused to admit to causing the damage to Pippa's car, pointing out that it is circumstantial evidence thus far. Evans says she will look at the CCTV footage from the garage before they go ahead and press any charges.

Luke collects me from the station and I give him a quick résumé of the past three hours.

'Basically they are checking CCTV, checking the aerosol can for fingerprints and taking some paint samples from the tow bar in case they need to run it through forensics for a match on Pippa's car. Oh, and let's not forget the poo sample from my shoe to check for a DNA match with the poo on Pippa's car.'

'Are you serious?'

'Yes. Apart from the DNA bit, but the way that bloody Evans was going on, I wouldn't be surprised. It's hardly a murder.'

Luke lacks any empathy for my black humour. 'They haven't charged you?'

'Not at this point.' We sit in silence. Neither of us knowing what to say. We seem to have run out of words for each other. I call Leonard.

Never one to beat about the bush, Leonard gets straight to the point. 'Clare, what the fuck is going on? I've just had to deal with McMillan out of the blue. You had an appointment with him today. I've had to convince him he's not dealing with some Mickey Mouse outfit.'

'McMillan? I didn't have an appointment with him today, I say. 'It's tomorrow, I'm certain.'

'You rearranged, apparently.'

'Yes, I did, but for tomorrow. Definitely tomorrow.' I run my hand down my face. I feel as if I'm losing my grip on reality. All these things that I think I may or may not have done. None of it is making sense.

'I don't think you're up to the job at the moment,' says Leonard. 'As such, I'm taking over the case. I want you to take some time off work to get whatever is going on at home sorted out.'

'I'm on gardening leave?' I feel indignant. We're equal part-ners and yet he's treating me like I'm an employee. 'I don't think that's up to you to decide.'

'It is when I think you're not in a position to make rational decisions. It won't look good for the company. I've a lot riding on this McMillan case. I gave it to you as I thought I was doing you a favour. Turns out to be an error of judgement on my part.'

'There is nothing wrong with my decision-making,' I retort, hurt by his words.

'Clare,' his voice softens. 'You know how much I care about you. I'm doing this for your own good. It's not an easy deci-sion for me, but I need to do what's best for you and the firm.'

'Please, Leonard,' I find myself pleading like a child who wants to go out even though they've been grounded.

'Trust me, Clare. I've never let you down. This is for the best.' He ends the call and I'm left staring at my phone in disbelief. Another part of my life falling apart.

'You should take advice from the people who care about you,' says Luke as we pull up outside. He cuts the engine and turns in the seat to face me. 'Listen, Clare, I know this whole Alice thing has been difficult for you. No, wait. Hear me out. The memory of Alice and the legacy she left behind; the scar it left on you and your mum has been immense. I know that. And I know how much you wanted to find her. Finding your sister, not just for your mum but for yourself too. So, Alice turning up and not exactly fitting that little slot you carved out for her has been ... challenging.' He brushes a strand of hair away from my eyes.

God I want to sink into him. This small act of tenderness is in danger of reducing me to a whimpering wreck. I fight back the emotion. I swallow hard and it hurts my throat, such is the size of the lump. I stare straight ahead, not daring to look at Luke as I know I will crumble completely. 'I find her difficult. I feel I'm just scratching the surface of what she's really like. I can't seem to warm to her,' I confess.

Luke gives a small sigh of exasperation and he moves his hand away. 'Just because she's your sister, it doesn't mean you automatically love her. You have to give these things time.'

I look at the house I've called home for all my life and think of the love and pain that has coexisted for all that time. I used to think I was safe here, me and Mum. We could shut the gates and shut the world out, but now I realise that's not true. I don't feel safe. I don't feel loved and I don't feel love. It's cold. It's dark. It's dangerous.

In a moment of clarity. I know what I have to do.

Mum and Alice are having lunch in the kitchen when I go in. Mum stops mid-bite of her sandwich and slowly places it on her plate. A small dollop of pickle slides out between the slices of brown bread. Alice takes a sip of her coffee and sits back in her seat.

'I'm so, so sorry, Mum. I want to apologise for my behaviour. And to you too, Alice. It really has been unacceptable; I don't know what's got into me lately.' I drop my head and pause for a moment. 'Please can you forgive me? Both of you?'

'Clare, my darling, of course we can,' says Mum, getting up and giving me a hug. She takes my hand and leads me over to the table. 'Alice?'

'Oh, what? Oh, yes, of course.' She gets up and hugs me too. 'Of course, we forgive you.'

I nod and give a meek smile. 'I think you're right, Alice. About working getting to me. I've not been coping very well.'

Mum pulls out a chair and sits me down. 'Luke, make Clare a cup of tea.'

I don't look at Luke, there's no need, I can feel the weight of his gaze on me. After a second, he does as he's told and goes to make me a cup of tea while Mum tells me how run down I must be, that I'm looking tired and I really must take care of myself. That she and Alice have been very worried about me. In fact, they were only just saying how tense I was and maybe I should go to the doctor.

It takes some effort on my part not to make a retort to that remark. What is it with everyone that they think I'm going mad? I'm not, but I mustn't argue. I don't want to fan the flames.

'Actually, I've been thinking,' I say. 'I do feel as if everything has been a bit overwhelming. I've already spoken to Leonard and I'm taking some time off work.' This time I do catch Luke's eye, but he doesn't betray my version of events. I continue. 'I need a bit of headspace. I thought I'd spend a few days visiting Nadine. You know, Nadine Horricks, who I went to school with? She lives in Cambridgeshire now. She's always said if ever I want to come and visit.'

'Nadine Horricks?' says Luke. 'There's a blast from the past. I didn't know you were that friendly still.'

'We keep in touch, you know that,' I say. Luke makes some sort of noise resembling an acknowledgement, but doesn't comment further.

'I remember Nadine,' says Mum. 'Nice girl. Went on to be a nurse or something, I think.'

'That's right,' I say. 'Anyway, thought I'd go and see her.'

Mum pats my hands. 'That's a good idea, darling. And when you come back, everything will be just fine.'

I take a final sip of my tea. 'In fact, I'll go and email her now.'

I go into the living room and switch on my laptop. Luke comes in and leans against the doorframe.

'What are you up to?' he says.

'Me? Nothing. I'm just emailing Nadine, like I said.'

'That will be Nadine, who I know for a fact you haven't exchanged even a Christmas card with for the last two years.'

'It doesn't matter. She's still my friend.'

'Don't do anything stupid,' warns Luke.

'Of course I won't. I'm just having a few days' break, that's all. I mean, that's what everyone keeps telling me to do. I thought you'd be pleased.' I load up my email account and log onto it. I glance up at Luke, who is still standing in the doorway. 'Don't worry, everything is fine.'

'Hmm,' is all Luke says, before pushing away from the doorframe and leaving the room.

Immediately he's gone, I open a new tab and type in the website for British Airways.

The idea that has been percolating in my mind, consciously since the police turned up and took me away, but probably subconsciously a few days prior to that, has turned into a plan. There are things I need to find out about Alice.

Chapter 19

The first thing I notice when I step off the plane the following weekend at Jacksonville is the unexpected warmth. It may well be the beginning of November, but the Florida sunshine is still hitting at least seventy degrees Fahrenheit during the day and lingering into the evening.

I've pre-booked into a local motel, which is just a short drive away. I check my watch and calculate the time delay. It's around teatime in the UK. I'll get booked in and then give home a ring to speak to the girls before they go to bed. I hate the thought of being apart from them, but I know I have to do this. I can't stay at home and let things carry on as they are. I can't confide in anyone; everyone thinks I'm cracking up and just can't cope with having to share my life with Alice. But little things keep niggling me.

On the flight over, I made a list of all the things that don't add up since Alice has been here: things that have made me suspicious or question her and/or her motives and to question my own sanity.

1. The photograph being reversed.
2. Flirting with Luke.
3. The glass in my wedding photo being shattered.
4. Alice telling me Hannah broke the glass.
5. The slashing of Luke's painting.
6. Alice wearing my clothes.
7. The photograph of Alice and Luke.
8. Daisy's accident.
9. The story about Roma and Nathaniel.
10. Alice with Leonard outside coffee shop???
11. The missing McMillan file and rearranged appointment
    – hacked email account???

And then underneath in capital letters, I wrote the word...

WHY????????
Money? – Inheritance, trust fund??
Love? – Mum? Family?
Revenge? – being taken to America, Mum letting her
go???
Taking over my life???!!!

I'm aware of the number of question marks on the piece of paper.

The motel room is basic, that's all I want and I pay for it using my Visa card. I drop my rucksack onto the bed and take out my phone and call home.

It's Mum who answers.

'Hi, Mum, it's me.'

'Hello Clare,' there's a pause. 'Are you all right, love?' I can hear the concern in her voice.

'I'm fine, Mum, honest. Please don't worry,' I say reassuringly. 'Is Hannah there? And Chloe? I wanted to say goodnight to them.'

'It's only teatime,' says Mum.

I quickly check myself. Mum has no idea I'm on the other side of the Atlantic Ocean and in a totally different time zone. 'I didn't want to call too late and I wanted to catch Chloe before she went off to bed.' Mum seems satisfied with that and I hear her calling to Hannah.

'Hello, darling,' I say.

'Mummy!'

Her voice brings a smile to my face. We have a little chat about the day. How her and Chloe have been painting with Daddy at the kitchen table, which warms me to hear. Then she tells me how she and Alice made cakes this afternoon and how much Daddy loved them, which has the opposite effect.

The image of Alice in domestic harmony with Luke and the girls boots me in the stomach. 'That's nice,' I force the words out. 'Shall I say hello to Chloe now?' I can hear her giggling in the background and I could do with the distraction from Hannah's piece of news. Then I hear Alice's voice.

'Chloe, are you going to say hello to Mummy?'

I want to scream. Why is Alice with my children? Where the fuck is their father?

'Chloe, hello. It's Mummy.'

'Mummy! Mummy! Alice tickling me. We had cakes. Butterfly cakes. Wiv cream.'

217

'Lovely. Were they scrummy? Will you save me a cake?' I force myself to remain upbeat. I can hear Mum's voice in the background telling Chloe to say goodbye and to say 'love you'. Chloe obliges and I'm grateful to Mum for the little prompt. Then she gets Hannah to say the same.

'Love you, Mummy,' she says.

'I love you too. Very much.' Mum comes back on the phone. 'Is Luke there?' I ask, even though as much as I want to speak to him, I don't, in case he asks me awkward questions about Nadine, which will mean I have to tell him more lies.

'He's in his studio,' says Mum. 'He's been moping around today, so I told him to do something creative to cheer himself up. It's not good for the girls; all this bad atmosphere in the house.'

'I know, Mum. I'll be back mid-week and we'll sort things out. I promise.' One way or another, this disharmony must end. I either have to accept Alice in my life or not. I'm unsure what the latter means for me, for my marriage and my family, but at some point, I need to draw a line under it all. We can't carry on as we are.

I'm awake early the next morning, and although the travelling made me tired, it wasn't enough to fully slip into the local time zone. I think I probably managed about five hours' sleep. I cross the road to the local diner and order pancakes with maple syrup for breakfast and a pot of coffee. It reminds me of Luke and me talking about going to America one day. It was a wet Sunday afternoon and we hadn't been married long, Hannah was just a baby and we were trying to plan our first family holiday. America with a six-month-old baby seemed a tad ambitious but we had cuddled up to each other with a glass of wine, making an imaginary list of all the things we wanted to do when we went to America and promising that one day we would actually do it. Pancakes with maple syrup had been high on my list, which had made Luke laugh and he had teased me for a long time afterwards.

I smile at the memory and a wave of sadness drowns the happy thought. I look down at the pancakes and suddenly they don't seem so appealing. Not today, not on my own without Luke or the girls. I push the plate away, pay the bill and leave.

Sitting in the rental car, I take my phone from my bag and look in my saved notes for the postal address of Alice Kendrick and input it into the sat nav. It tells me the location is forty minutes away and I take my time as I drive on the freeway for the first time, paying close attention to the directions, the traffic ahead and the traffic signals, remembering that you can go on a red light if you're making a right turn and nothing is coming. It's a little unnerving, but I manage it. Soon I'm travelling over the bridge that connects Amelia Island to mainland Florida. It's a small island of just thirteen miles in length and a population of less than twelve thousand. It's a popular tourist resort yet, according to the tourist board's website I read earlier, maintains a small friendly town atmosphere.

It's not long before I pull off Jasmine Street and follow directions to a small cul-de-sac, where the sat nav announces I've arrived at my destination. It's a detached bungalow in a road with similar properties, some detached and some semi-detached, but all looking very well kept and modest. Nothing flashy or ostentatious here. Tall trees offer plenty of shade from the blazing sun, which dapples the road with spots of golden light. Long threads of Spanish moss hang from the trees, reminding me of tired party streamers the morning after New Year's Eve celebrations.

Looking at the house, it's hard to tell if there's anyone home. The street is very quiet and there's no sign of life from any of the houses.

I climb the porch steps and knock on the door. I listen intently for any sound of life, but there is none. I haven't come all this way to be put off by an empty house. I take a glance up and down the road, but there still doesn't appear to be anyone about, so I make my way around to the side of the house. There's a gate and when I try the latch, it's unlocked and opens inwards, allowing me access to the back garden. It looks as if it was kept nice and tidy at one point. Perhaps that was Patrick Kennedy's thing – maybe he liked gardening.

I peer through the glass of the back door into the kitchen. Nothing is out of place. There are no cups or plates on the side waiting to be washed up. There's no tea towel flung carelessly on the worktop or fruit sitting in the bowl waiting to be eaten. It looks like a show home. I try the handle to the back door but, unsurprisingly, it is locked. I rattle it all the same, just to be certain. I can't see into any of the other rooms as the blinds are shut.

There are two bins by the side gate. Feeling like some sort of amateur detective, I go over to look inside them. It might give me an indication of how long it's been since someone was here. The first looks like the recycling bin, with a few empty food boxes and drinks cartons lying in the bottom, but as I open the second, the smell that hits me almost makes me want to vomit and the buzz of flies that evacuate the bin makes me squeal, drop the lid and jump back.

There's a piece of bamboo cane propped up against the fence. Picking it up and standing at arm's length from the bin, I flick the lid up. The hum of flies and waft of something rotten assaults me but I'm more prepared this time and with my hand over my nose and mouth, I take a step closer. I peer into the bin from as far away as possible. There must be several full bin bags piled on top of each other, the last one to go in the bin sitting right at the top. White maggots, their colour a stark contrast with the black bin bags, wriggle and squirm their way around the plastic. With the bamboo cane I poke at the bag. It hasn't been tied properly and I manage to flick it open.

I'm not sure what I'm expecting to see in there. Maybe my imagination is running away with me, but I'm relieved when I see food and drinks cartons. On the top is what looks like a piece of rotting meat, which would explain the flies. I flick the bin lid shut, relieved that it was nothing more sinister and then chide myself for an overactive imagination. What did I expect to find in there? A dead body?

Unexpectedly, a face pops up over the fence. A woman who looks to be in her seventies, with her hair neatly combed around her face and a small dash of red lipstick across her mouth, looks at me.

'Are you from environmental health?' she says. 'About time you turned up. I've been calling you for days. That there bin hasn't been emptied for weeks. Downright disgraceful. It would never have happened when Mr Kendrick was alive. It's a health hazard.' She eyes me again and produces a pair of glasses, which she perches on her bony nose. She has another look at me. 'You ain't environmental are you?'

'Er, no. Sorry,' I say. I have already rehearsed my story in case I spoke to any of the neighbours. 'I'm actually a relative of Alice Kendrick. I'm from England and haven't seen her for years. I've come over as a surprise.' I smile broadly. It's pretty near the truth.

'A relative, you say? Of Ali Kendrick? I don't remember her or her father ever talking about a relative in England.'

'Oh, our families lost touch a long time ago,' I say. 'Didn't even realise I had a cousin until recently.'

'Well, you may be on a wild-goose chase. I don't like to disappoint you, but Ali Kendrick isn't here. I haven't seen her for several weeks now. All that business must have been too much for her and she decided to get away for a while.'

'Oh, no. Do you know where she is?' The disappointment and hope are both genuine. By *all that business*, I assume the neighbour is referring to Patrick's death.

'She left me a note to say she was going travelling around Europe. Now, I'm surprised she hasn't gone to England to find you, seeing as you're *long-lost* relatives.'

I can detect the suspicion in her voice as she emphasises the long-lost bit.

'Like I said, our families weren't good at keeping in touch. You don't happen to know where I can find her stepmother do you?'

'Funny how you know she has a stepmother when your two families weren't talking all this time.' The neighbour might be old, but her brain is young and nimble.

'We heard that Patrick had died from his wife's family,' I say, grateful that my brain is able to match hers for agility. 'Her daughter sent me a message via Facebook. You know, the Internet.'

She waves me away with her hand. 'I know what all that is, I'm not stupid.'

'No, of course you're not.'

'Daughter, you say? Well, here's the rub. Roma doesn't have a daughter. Just a son.'

Shit. I'm sure Alice spoke about a stepsister once. I quickly try to remember what the stepbrother was called. 'Nathaniel,' I say. 'Nathaniel sent me a message. Sorry. It's been a long day. I've been travelling for hours. Can't think straight.'

The neighbour appraises me once more. 'Yeah, the kid was called Nathaniel. If you're trying get hold of them, why don't you message him back on Facebook?'

Bloody hell, she's proving quite a match for me. Why wouldn't I do that? From nowhere I manage a fast response. 'We weren't friends on Facebook and I can't find him again. You know, all those privacy settings. You don't happen to have their address or a phone number?'

I get another long, hard look from her before she makes up her mind. 'Wait there.' She disappears and comes back a few minutes later. She waves a piece of paper over the fence. 'That's their address and phone number. You may wanna ring first. She's up in Jacksonville.'

'Okay, thanks,' I say, reaching to take the piece of paper.

She snatches it away. 'First, though, you can do me a favour and put those bins out.'

I suppose I can't complain. It's a fair exchange and I really want that address and phone number.

The neighbour watches while I put the two wheelie bins out and then, once I've done that and she's satisfied that I've fulfilled my part of the bargain, she hands over the slip of paper.

I retreat to the car and drive out of the cul-de-sac, making my way back to Jasmine Street. I'm probably not supposed to pull over and stop, but I do anyway. I'll plead tourist ignorance and use my best English accent, flutter my eyelashes and offer sincere apologies if the police come by.

I call the number on the paper and it's answered on the fourth ring.

'Hello.' The voice is female but that is all I can tell from the one-word answer.

'Hi. Is Roma Kendrick there please?'

'Speaking.'

'Hi, I'm sorry to bother you, but I'm trying to get in touch with Alice Kendrick and I've been given your number. You don't happen to know where she is, do you?'

'Er ... who is this please?'

'I'm Clare Tennison.' I wait for any recognition. There's a silence and now I'm wishing I was speaking face to face. At least that way Roma wouldn't be able to hang up on me, something which, the longer the silence, the more it seems likely.

'I'm sorry. Do I know you?' she says at last. 'And why do you want to get in touch with Alice?'

'No, you don't know me. Before I was Clare Tennison I was Clare Kennedy. My father was Patrick Kennedy, although you will probably have known him as Patrick Kendrick. I'm trying to get in touch with Alice because ... she's ... she's my sister.' I hear the small intake of breath. 'Her sister?'

'Yes. I grew up in England with my mother. We didn't have contact with Alice for a long time.'

'Yes, I know that. Well, I mean I know about Patrick moving over here with his daughter but not about the name-change. Are you sure you have this right?'

'Yes, I'm positive.'

'I'm sorry, you've taken me completely by surprise,' says Roma.

'I expect I have. Sorry.'

'It's okay. Er, how did you get my number?' asks Roma.

'Alice's neighbour gave it to me. An older lady, at number 25.'

'Mrs Karvowski,' says Roma. 'She's quite a character, that one. What did she say about Ali?'

It seems an odd question, but I run with it for now. 'Nothing, really. Just that she hadn't seen her for a few weeks.' I hesitate, wondering whether to add a further explanation and decide there would be no point not telling Roma. 'The neighbour, Mrs Karvowski, said Alice had decided to go travelling. In Europe.'

'Really? Just like that?'

'I got the impression from the neighbour that things had

been getting on top of Alice recently. She hadn't told you that, then?'

'No. She hadn't.'

'Have you seen or spoken to her recently?' I press.

I don't know whether it's the hesitation or the tone of Roma's voice when she replies, but she sounds distant and pensive. 'No. No, I haven't. Not for a while now.'

'Mrs Kendrick, is there any chance we could have a chat in person, you know, face to face? Over a coffee, maybe?' I'm sure I'd be able to gauge Alice's stepmother a lot better if I could see her face to face.

'Oh, I don't know if that's a good idea.'

'Please, Mrs Kendrick. I'd really appreciate it. I won't take up much of your time and I can drive to you.' I look at my watch. 'I could be with you within an hour.' I realise I'm almost bullying her into agreeing, but I'm desperate. I'm sure I can get more information out of her once I have her as a captive audience, so to speak. 'Please …'

'I suppose I could,' she relents. 'Not today, though. Tomorrow?'

'Thank you, I do appreciate that.'

'Meet me in Jacksonville at the coffee shop on Village Walk at one-thirty.'

After the call has finished, I stay sitting in my car, musing over the conversation. I take out the photograph of Alice and Martha. Probably taken in the house I was just at.

If only I could get inside Alice's house, I'm sure I'd find out more about her. Hopefully, Roma will be able to tell me some more tomorrow. I think of Alice's friend, Martha. Now she would surely be able to tell me more about Alice. She'd have a totally different relationship with Alice than Roma would; it will help me to build up a clearer picture in my mind of who my sister really is. The real Alice Kennedy beneath the rather too sweet-and-kind facade currently sitting at home with my family. The little roll of emotion, I recognise now as jealousy, gives a tumble inside me, reminding me of the not-so-admirable quality I've discovered about myself recently.

I think back to Alice's conversation where she mentioned Martha working as a waitress. I'm sure she said the Beach House Diner. It stuck in my mind as it reminded me of where my first Saturday job was; the Beach House Café in Brighton. Thank goodness for the ability to remember little details, always handy with my line of work, I suppose. Thank goodness also for my smartphone as I'm able to tap *Beach House Diner, Amelia Island* into the search engine and in a matter of seconds I've located the diner, got the zip code and programmed the sat nav.

Amelia Island is small and, within a few minutes, I'm pulling up outside the diner. It's blue and yellow, with big, open windows, situated on the corner of what looks like one of the main roads through the town. Big lorries, laden with sixty-foot-long logs trundle past at what seems like two- or three-minute intervals. I assume they are heading to the sawmill I read about on the flight over when I was researching the area.

When I go into the diner, I look around for Martha. I'm looking for someone not dissimilar to Alice, long brown hair, about my height and weight. In fact, I realise I could be looking for either of us, me, Alice or Martha. A small, dark-haired Hispanic-looking young girl comes over.

'Hi, welcome to the Beach House Diner. Table for one, is it?'

'Yes, thank you.' I smile warmly.

'My name is Angelina and I'm your waitress today. Would you like to sit by the window?'

'That will be fine.' I follow Angelina through the diner and scan the area as I go. It's big and must have at least seventy covers. The walls are white and with the big windows, the whole place has a light and airy feel. I sit down at the table and Angelina passes me a menu and runs through the specials. I order a glass of juice and Angelina leaves me to peruse the menu. She comes back a few minutes later with a glass and juice bottle balanced on a circular tray.

'So are you here on vacation?' asks Angelina as she takes the bottle opener from her apron pocket and flips the lid.

'Kind of,' I say, delighted with this opening that I didn't even have to try for. 'I'm actually trying to find a friend of a friend. Last I heard she worked here.' I smile again at Angelina and she looks expectantly. 'Martha Munroe. Does she still work here?'

'Martha? Well, no. She hasn't worked here for about a month.'

'Oh, that's a shame,' I say, hoping I look disappointed. 'You don't know how I can get hold of her, do you?'

'You can't. No one can. She's gone off travelling with her friend.'

'Really? Who's that?' And then seeing Angelina look at me suspiciously, I add, 'I wonder if it might be someone I know.'

'Alice Kendrick. You know her?'

'Is that the girl who Martha lived with?'

'That's right,' says Angelina, and I can almost see her lower her guard again. 'Although, it beats me why Martha would want to go travelling with Alice. Not after what happened between those two girls.'

'Which was?' I prompt when it appears Angelina isn't going to continue.

'I don't know if I really should be talking about them,' says Angelina. 'It's kinda bad to speak behind their backs.'

'But I am a friend of Martha's. Did they have some kind of disagreement?' I'm hedging my bets, but I feel I can't let this opportunity slip by.

'You could say that.'

Chapter 20

I look expectantly at Angelina, willing her to get on with it. She settles herself into the seat opposite me and leans forward, her hands clasped together in front of her.

'Martha has always been such a good friend to Alice, right from the very first time Alice came into the diner. Alice had that look about her, the sort that said how sad and alone she was. Martha spotted it straight away,' says Angelina. 'You know why?'

I shake my head. 'No, go on.'

'Martha had once been just like that, alone and sad. Martha didn't tell everyone but she confided in me about the things she had to endure at home. Her mother was none too good to her; she didn't have a father either. Martha just wasn't loved. She was a burden to her family.'

'And she saw this in Alice?'

'Yep. Martha recognised that in Alice. Martha really felt for that Kendrick girl. She went and talked to her. Each time Alice came in, Martha would always make time for her. Soon they became real good friends.'

'So what happened between them?' I ask.

'The stepmother. She didn't like Martha from the word go. Thought Martha was a bad influence on Alice. She didn't like it that Alice now had a life and was going out and meeting people her own age and all that.' Angelina takes a furtive glance around the diner. 'I can't stop long or I'll get in trouble from my manager.'

'Okay, so just quickly, how come Martha and Alice fell out but still ended up going travelling together?'

'Alice was a quiet girl and totally under the thumb from her dad and stepmom. Martha used to encourage Alice to stick up for herself. After Alice's father died, she asked Martha to move in. Martha was being kicked out of her home and had nowhere to go, Alice was lonely and really relied on Martha's friendship, so it seemed like the perfect solution. Of course, Roma wasn't happy about it. To cut a long story short, Martha and Roma had an argument about Martha's influence on Alice, which then put a strain on Martha and Alice.'

'They fell out over it?'

'Yeah. Martha was all set to move out, said she couldn't live in the same house as Roma.' Angelina is enjoying retelling the events.

'So, what happened next?' Considering Angelina is worried about her boss, she's not exactly rushing herself.

'Well, they argued. Alice begged Martha to stay and rowed with her stepmom, but in the end, it was Alice's house, so evil stepmom didn't have a choice. As it happened, she had to move back to Jacksonville and didn't want Alice anyway.'

'And now the girls have gone travelling?'

'Yeah. Martha left a note on the manager's desk that she

quit. Sent me a text message to say she and Alice were travelling round Europe and that was that. I haven't heard from her since. She never even replied to my messages.'

'That's a bit odd, isn't it?'

Angelina shrugs. 'Kind of, but Martha was like that anyway. You know, quick to move on. She never had any real roots here.' She slides herself out of the bench seat. 'I need to get on now. If you do catch up with Martha, tell her I was asking after her.'

'Sure. Thanks for your time.'

After finishing my drink and leaving the diner, I find myself driving back to the Kendrick's house. I park a little further down the road from Alice's house this time, in the hope that I can avoid detection from Alice's neighbour. I lock the car and walk slowly up to the house. I don't know what has drawn me back here, but I know that the answers lie within. I have to get inside the house somehow.

The bins still stand at the end of the drive and I bypass them, heading straight for the back gate. I have another look at the windows as I go around the property. I can't see any on the latch to let fresh air circulate through. If this were my house and I shared it with someone, I'd probably have a spare key hidden somewhere in case one of us got locked out. Would Alice do the same? It's worth a look.

I go over to the back door and run my hand above the doorframe. Nothing. Too obvious? I lift the doormat and then the plant pot that is beside the back door. I can't identify the plant from the withered stem and dried leaves – it's a long time since there was any life here. I look around the back porch, trying to spot any other potential hiding places.

It's very quiet here in this suburban part of the island. I hear the odd car drive along the road at the back of the property but apart from that, there doesn't seem a lot going on. I catch a small movement from the corner of my eye and a little green lizard, about five inches long from head to tail, scuttles across the decking. He stops at the side of a plant pot and a pink bubble inflates from his throat. It reminds me of the time Mum had bought Hannah some old-fashioned bubble gum. Hannah had been delighted she could blow a massive bubble – that was until it popped and got stuck in her hair. The lizard is much more accomplished at blowing bubbles and does so several times as he watches me with his big goggly eyes, wondering what I'm doing there. I have to admit, I'm beginning to ask myself the same question. What am I hoping to achieve from this madcap adventure? I wanted to find out more about Alice and her life here. Perhaps I should have just taken the time to get to know her properly in person. And then, as per usual, as soon as I have this thought, I'm confronted with some deep-rooted notion that just wouldn't happen. There's some sort of barrier between Alice and me; something is preventing us from getting close. And for some reason, I feel the answer lies here in America. More precisely – in this house.

I take a more careful look around. On the edge of the porch, there's a small garden swing and beside it is a terracotta pot, upturned on top of a terracotta saucer. The pot has been whitewashed and decorated with a few shells. I lift the pot to reveal a little pile of grey ash and several cigarette stubs. The smell of stale nicotine and ash is released into the air. I give the dish a shake and the peak of the ash flattens out to reveal the shiny metal of a silver key.

'Disgusting,' I mutter to myself as I take the saucer round to the flowerbed and tip the ash onto the earth so I can pick out the key.

The key fits into the lock of the back door and as I turn it, I hear the telltale click and feel the resistance disappear as the cogs slide around to open the door. I go in without hesitation. I still don't know what I'm hoping to find in the house. I just know I have to get inside and look around. I close the door gently behind me, slipping the key into the pocket of my trousers.

The kitchen has a breakfast bar, which separates it from the living room, and I'm surprised at how spacious the whole house is; the high ceilings and lack of central walls add to the airy feel. I shiver as I step further into the house. I open the fridge and the smell of rotten food hits me. I pull my head away and, holding my breath, peer inside. Two pieces of chicken look decidedly green at the edges. There is a carton of milk in the fridge door. I give it a little shake and it feels slushy and lumpy. I don't need to smell that to know it's off. Pulling out the vegetable drawer, I see that the salad has started to turn to a pulp and liquid sloshes in the drawer. All pretty disgusting and a sure sign no one has been here for some time. Someone either left in a hurry or left with every intention of coming back, but just never made it.

A creak and groan of an empty house from somewhere

inside makes me jump. I stand still, just to be certain it's not the sound of anyone actually in the place and once my heart returns to a more orderly pace, I let out a small sigh. Creeping around empty houses that I shouldn't be in, is getting to me. I close the fridge door.

Really, what I'd like to do is get the hell out of this house, but I can't. Not until I find whatever it is I'm looking for.

I walk into the living room and immediately notice the clock hanging on the wall. It's the same clock as the one in the picture Alice sent Mum of her and Martha. They must have sat on that very sofa.

Alice on the left and Martha on the right. Or was it? Had the picture been reversed by accident? Was Alice really dyslexic?

I look around the living room. There are a couple of paintings on the wall, one is of the beach, probably local, I assume, and the other is of sunflowers; a prettier version of Van Gough's. I peer at the signature in the bottom right-hand corner. Alice Kendrick.

This is Alice Kennedy's painting. My sister's painting. I touch the canvas, my fingers grazing the signature and, for the first time since I held Alice's original letter in my hand, I feel a connection with her. My sister did this. She painted this picture. My beautiful little sister touched this, she spread the paints across the canvas, she signed her name in the corner. A surge of love swamps my heart and for a moment I think I'm going to cry. I blink away the tears and take my hand away. I can't afford to break down now. Not after everything that's happened.

A photograph on the mantelpiece catches my attention and as I turn to look at it properly, I experience another wave of emotion, this time not love but fear.

A man, probably in his fifties, looks out at me. He has fair hair and it is brushed back from his face. He's wearing a stripy rugby top of pale blue and white and a pair of beige chino shorts. He looks to be standing on the deck of a sailboat, his hand wrapped around the rigging. The sun is shining and the man looks happy and relaxed, as if he's in the middle of sharing a joke with the person on the other side of the camera.

I take a step closer and pick up the frame. I can remember him as clear as day. His memory never once faded with time. This is my father. This is Patrick Kennedy. I haven't seen him for over twenty years and never thought I would, hoped I wouldn't, but now, here he is, smiling out at me. I feel a little sick and take a deep breath, looking away for a moment. The feeling passes and I return my gaze to the photograph. I consciously study my reaction. I'm looking for any flicker of love, any connection, any invisible bond that could never be broken between a father and his daughter. The initial fear has subsided and, unsurprisingly, I feel nothing for this man. Where there should be love, there is just an empty space.

I scan the room for other photographs, but there are none. It's the same for the hallway. There are four doors leading off from the hall and I guess these are the bedrooms and bathroom. I open the door to the first one on the left. It has a double bed that has been stripped. There are no personal items in the room; it looks as though someone has just vacated a holiday home and the room is waiting for the cleaners to come in and make the bed up with fresh linen.

I close the door and take the next room on the left. The single bed is unmade, the duvet cover shoved back. The wardrobe door is slid open and I can see a few items of clothing hanging up; a blue T-shirt, a cardigan and a white blouse. A couple of jumpers are on the shelf above, the arm of one hanging down, as if it's been shoved up there in a hurry. Several empty coat hangers are in the bottom of the wardrobe, along with a pair of trainers. I go over to the bed and perch on the edge, opening the drawer of the bedside table. I have a sense of déjà vu. It was only the other day that I sat on Alice's bed at home in the UK, looking in her bedside table. That time I found the photograph of her and Luke. I wonder what I'll find this time.

I slide the drawer open, but it contains what amounts to rubbish: half a packet of tissues, a hair clip, a pot of red nail varnish and a biro. I open the next drawer. There's a notebook, a small white spiral type. I flip open the cover. The first page has the word 'WORK' written in capital letters across the top of the page and underlined twice. Underneath is a list of dates and times. I assume it's for the diner. I turn the pages, one by one, and most are much the same. I come across a couple of pages with reminders of things to do, or names of people. I bend the edge of the notebook and fan the pages with my thumb so they flick through quickly. They all appear blank. Nothing very interesting or incriminating. I'm just about to throw the book back into the drawer, when I see an official-looking envelope. It's already been opened, so I take a look inside. It's a payslip from the Beach House Diner to Martha Munroe, dated a couple of months ago. I put it to one side and notice a piece of paper. What strikes me is that it looks out of place with the rest of the items in the drawer and, indeed, in the room. It's an A5 sheet of bonded writing paper, the sort you get from a traditional letter-writing pad. I can feel the ridges of the paper between my finger and thumb. I hold the paper up towards the window, where a small stream of light trickles through a gap in the blinds. I can just make out the faint watermark. It's from an expensive pad. On it, written in fountain pen, is a mobile number beginning 07.

It takes a moment for me to realise that this is a UK mobile number, but not one I recognise.

I pull the drawer out further and see another piece of paper, this time the weight is light and there are wide-ruled lines, it looks as if it's from the notebook I've just been looking at. There's also a thin black cardboard box, about the size of a toothpaste box, along with the image of a blue eye. Disposable daily contact lenses. I give the box a little shake but it's empty. I pick up the sheet of paper and turn it over. It's a list. I cast my eye over the items. Passport. Flight tickets. Lenses. Cell phone. Adapter.

A list for travelling abroad. If this is Martha's room, as I think, then she was planning on travelling abroad. Was this her planned trip with Alice?

I wonder where all Martha's possessions are. Has someone been in and gone through her stuff, taking what they wanted?

This room reminds me of my student days. A room where you half live, you bring some of your possessions, but not all of them. A room to stay in, to sleep in, but not a room to call home.

I scoop up the things from the drawer and instead of putting them back, for some reason, I stuff them into my handbag and leave the room.

I take a deep breath before going in to the last room. I know instantly it must be Alice's room. There is a warm ambiance despite its emptiness. The walls are painted white, with one a pale pink. The white Venetian blinds at the window are closed and a piece of pink fabric is draped in a fancy swag across the top of the window frame. There is a white bedframe covered with a pretty pink-and-white eiderdown. It's all very tidy and clean.

The sound of my phone ringing cuts through the silence and it makes me jump. I wriggle it out of my pocket and look at the screen. It's Luke. I check my watch and do a quick calculation of the time in the UK. It must only be six o'clock there. Luke up at that time of the morning just doesn't happen. Immediately I think there must be something wrong. Mum or one of the girls. I swipe the screen to accept the call.

'Luke?'

'Hi.'

'Is everything okay?'

'Clare, relax, everything is fine.'

I breathe a sigh of relief. 'What are you doing up?'

'Couldn't sleep. I've not been to bed.' His voice is quiet and has the sound of someone who is battle-weary.

'Have you been working?'

'Tried to, but not feeling it right now.'

Now I know that's not like Luke at all. Not working and not sleeping, they don't usually go together. 'Is something wrong?' I ask, my own voice soft.

'Fucking hell, you ask the most stupid questions sometimes.' I hear him exhale of long breath of air. 'Of course something is wrong. Us. That's what's wrong. I don't even know how we got to this point in such a short space of time. What the fuck went wrong?'

'I don't know either,' I say, then correct myself. 'Actually, that's not true. I know exactly what went wrong. Alice.' I brace myself for the response.

'You're wrong about Alice,' he says.

'I am not. Trust me.'

'Trust you? What about you trusting me?' says Luke. I can image the look of indignation on his face. 'I've never done anything, ever, to give you any reason not to trust me. I thought we were solid. I really did. I know how I feel about you, it's one hundred per cent. The trouble is, I'm not sure you know how you feel about me.'

'Luke, it's not like that, honest.'

'Of course it is. You've all but accused me of shagging your sister and on top of all that, you've caused fucking mayhem at home between you and your mum. You've even been sodding arrested for vandalising your best mate's car.'

'I didn't do anything to Pippa's car. And besides, I wasn't arrested. I was helping with inquiries.' As soon as the words are out, I want to kick myself for being so pedantic.

'You're splitting hairs. Jesus Christ, what is wrong with you?'

'Look, I may have implied there was something going on with you and Alice and, for that, I am sorry. But I don't trust her.'

'Is there anyone you trust?'

'Can we leave all this until I get back?' I say, trying to defuse the situation. What started off having the potential for being a tender conversation, has ended up in a ruck. 'I don't want to argue with you over the phone. I've come away to clear my head, not fill it up with arguments. It's not productive.'

There's a small silence before Luke replies. 'I don't want to argue either. I'm sorry, I shouldn't have phoned.'

'No, I'm glad you did,' I say. And I genuinely mean it. To hear his voice is the closest thing to a hug I can get right now.

'I'm missing you,' says Luke. 'I've been missing you for days, even when you've been here, I've missed you. Us not being close, it just doesn't feel right. It's torture.'

'I know. Just give me a couple of days.'

'Okay,' he pauses and lets out a small sigh. 'So, how's Nadine anyway? I expect you were up half the night catching up with each other on the past twenty years.' I can hear the injected upbeat to his voice.

'She's fine,' I say in a clipped tone that shuts down the conversation. I close my eyes and wish for forgiveness for my lies.

'I'll let you get on,' says Luke; the dejection is back.

'I'll see you later in the week,' I say. As much as I want to speak to Luke, I don't. The more he asks me about Nadine, the more lies I'm going to have to tell.

'Say hello to her for me,' he says. 'Bye.'

'Yeah, sure. Bye.' There's a small silence. 'Love you,' I say quickly. It's a mere whisper and then the phone line goes dead. I've no idea if Luke heard me or not. I slide the phone from my ear to my forehead and close my eyes as I recover from the painful conversation and ask myself the same question Luke did; how the hell did we even get to this point?

Chapter 21

I prowl the house again, backwards and forwards, from the living room to the bedrooms, as I try to get a feel for Alice and her life here. I find myself drawn back to Alice's room. There is a bookshelf to the right that I didn't pay much attention to before. It's filled with books. I run my finger absently along the spines, looking to see what sort of reading she likes – anything to make me feel close to my sister. One shelf looks like textbooks on childcare and education and, I assume, were to do with her teaching. The rest of the shelves are filled with paperbacks. I pull one out and see it's a thriller. In fact, the whole shelf is filled with thriller-type books. Then the genre seems to change on the next few shelves, where they look more like contemporary women's fiction and romance. Alice is definitely a bookworm, I conclude, and I think back to the recent conversation in Mum's sitting room, where she said she'd overcome her dyslexia, to prove everyone wrong. I'm sure she said something about not reading books.

Something is bothering me about the room, the bookcase in particular. I tap one of the shelves with my fingernail, trying to relax, to allow the thought to break through all the other thoughts that are filling my head. I look around the room and then it strikes me. There are no photographs. I scour the bookshelf and look for anything that might be a photo album, but I see nothing at all. It seems odd that there are no photographs anywhere, other than the one of Patrick Kennedy on the mantelpiece.

A noise behind me makes me jump. I spin round and let out a small scream of surprise. Standing in the doorway is the neighbour, who I now know as Mrs Karvowski.

'Found what you're looking for?' she asks.

'I was ... I ...' I don't know what to say.

'I could call the cops,' she says.

I nod, but somehow I don't think she will. I decide straight-talking is in order. 'I just wanted to feel close to Alice,' I say. 'The thing is, I wasn't quite truthful when I said I was her cousin.'

'I didn't think you were being honest with me.'

'I'm actually her sister. We were separated when we were young children and I haven't seen her since she was four years old.'

'Didn't have you down as cousins,' she says, tipping her head to one side and appraising me.

'I spoke to Roma Kendrick. I'm meeting her tomorrow.'

'She's a good woman,' says Mrs Karvowski. 'You'd think Alice was her own child. You'd never have thought she was her stepmother. She was even good to Alice's friend. Not that she deserved it.'

'Martha?' But Mrs Karvowski is already turning and walking back down to the kitchen.

'Make sure you lock up when you're done and put the key back where you found it.'

After leaving the house, I find myself driving down to the beach and I pull up in a small parking area. With what seems an unconscious decision, I find myself climbing up the wooden steps ahead of me which lead out onto the beach.

The Atlantic breeze whips my hair around my face and I delve inside my handbag, successfully locating one of Hannah's hair bands, which I use to tie my hair back. I slip my shoes off and feel the sandy granules between my toes as I walk down towards the water, coming to a halt as the waves crash in front of me and run up to cover my feet, before racing back out again.

I take a few minutes to let my mind free itself from the tangle of thoughts. I need to stop thinking, just for a while. I breathe in deeply, enjoying the fresh air that fills my lungs. It's certainly a beautiful place and the rhythmic crash and rumble of the waves have a calming effect.

The sound of a little girl laughing brings me back from my empty thoughts. I turn and watch her run along the beach, chasing the family pet, her parents walking hand in hand behind her. It makes me think of Hannah and Chloe and I have a sudden pang of homesickness, coupled with a yearning to get back to not just the UK but to how we were as a family before Alice came home. Somehow, I fear that will never be the same, regardless of what I find out here.

I feel tired and all I want to do is get back to my motel room and get some sleep. Reluctantly, I turn and head back towards my car, leaving the sanctuary of the beach behind me.

Despite my body telling me how tired I am, my brain doesn't want to co-operate. I manage just a couple of hours at a time before I wake and when I try to go back to sleep, thoughts of how my meeting with Roma might go fill my mind.

When morning finally breaks I'm relieved the night is over.

Arriving in Jacksonville, I find the coffee shop in the parade of retail outlets and park outside under a tree.

I realise that I don't actually know what Roma looks like. I stand in the doorway checking the tables for a woman on her own. A tall, well-dressed woman in a blue blouse and white trousers stands up and makes eye contact. She waves me over and I thread my way through the tables.

'Roma Kendrick?' I ask, as I reach the table.

She holds out her hand. 'Clare, I presume.' I shake her hand and she smiles warmly at me. 'Please, Clare, do sit down. Tea or coffee?'

'Coffee, please.'

Roma signals to the waitress, who arrives in a matter of seconds with a coffee pot. Once she's filled my cup and I've added some warm milk from the table, I take a sip and then sit back and look at Roma.

'Thank you for meeting me,' I say.

'I'm not entirely comfortable with us meeting, I must admit. I feel, somehow, I'm going behind Alice's back. I wish she were here too.'

'Yes, so do I,' I say. 'When did you last see her?'

'Quite a few months ago now. We had coffee here, actually. I gave her the address for her mother in England.'

'And she seemed fine then?'

'Yes. She was so happy to have that address. I hadn't been able to give it to her before, not with her father alive. He wouldn't have liked it. Don't get me wrong. Patrick was a good man and loved Alice dearly but he refused to talk about England and Alice's mother. Who I assume is your mother too.'

'Marion. Yes, that's right.'

Roma looks thoughtful as she stirs her coffee with the small silver teaspoon. 'Tell me, why did your mother never contact Alice?' she asks. 'I've always wondered why. I can't imagine a mother just cutting herself off from her own child like that.'

'She tried. She didn't have an address for my father. He would never give it to her. He used to phone from time to time, but those phone calls got less and less frequent. My mother thought for a long time that they would come back. She really believed it was a holiday which just became extended.'

Roma looks thoughtful again. 'So, how do you think I can help? You know I haven't heard from Alice in a while now.'

'Why's that?' I ask, inwardly acknowledging that my questioning is on the pushy side and normally I would tread with greater care, but I am trying to tackle this as I would a legal case. Sometimes that requires a certain amount of direct talking.

'Soon after Patrick died, my mother got ill. I had to move back to Jacksonville to care for her.'

'Alice didn't mind staying behind?'

'No. It was her home; she wanted to stay. I must admit, I wasn't sure about leaving her. It didn't seem right. We used to be very close,' continues Roma as she fiddles with the edge of her napkin. 'I can remember the first time I saw Alice. She was only young and like a little mouse, so quiet and so timid. Those big blue eyes of hers, staring up at me. She looked so sad and so lost, my heart just melted. I knew there would be a whole lot of healing to be done, a heart to mend, and I did manage that to a certain extent, but Alice was such a quiet thing, you never really knew what she was thinking. She had this aura of deep sadness. She never had many friends growing up, until she was older and she became friends with Martha.' The tone in Roma's voice hardens.

'You don't sound like you approve too much of Martha,' I want to keep Roma talking. I still need to find things out.

Roma purses her lips. 'She came with a lot of baggage. And I don't mean the Gucci kind.'

'In what way?' I say.

'She had a tough upbringing, which I know is not that unusual. Lots of kids have it tough. It's just that some come out of it good and some not so good. Martha being the latter. I could see it a mile off and I tried to warn Patrick about her,' explains Roma. 'I didn't like the way Martha ingratiated herself into the family so quickly and so easily. I tried to say something to Alice as well but neither she nor her father could see it. Martha was a very manipulative person. Dangerous, even. She practically imprinted herself on Alice. Almost became her doppelgänger. It was creepy.' She stops and gives a shake of her head.

'You have a son, Nathaniel,' I say.

'How did you know that?'

'From Alice's letter to my mum. Has he not heard from

Alice at all?' I may be stepping on dangerous ground here, but I have to ask the question.

'No. He tried to contact her on social media but she's closed her accounts.'

'She had social media? Like Facebook and Twitter?'

'Well, yeah, I'm pretty sure she did have Facebook. In fact, I'm certain. I remember Nathaniel showing me some pictures of her on it.'

'Has she had Facebook a long time?'

Roma shrugs. 'I don't know. Probably about four years, when she went to college. I don't think she had it before. Like I said, she's a quiet thing, especially when she was younger and didn't have that many friends.'

'It wasn't because she was banned from using it, I mean, her father never said she couldn't have Facebook? You know what some parents are like,' I add, to make light of the question so as not to arouse Roma's suspicion.

'No. It was never banned,' says Roma. 'As I say, Nathaniel had it and Patrick and I treated the children equally. We were, in our eyes, one family, not two blended together.' She reaches over and squeezes my hand. 'I didn't mean to upset you when I said that. I know Alice is your family too.'

'It's okay.' I smile away the comment, to hide the small pang of hurt. I cannot understand why my father was happy to split the family up in such a divisive way. 'Did Patrick ever talk about me?' It's such a difficult question to ask, but somehow I feel I need to know. I need to know if my feelings, or non-feelings, towards him are justified.

I can tell by the look on Roma's face what the answer is. She doesn't need to say a word. Her face is etched with embarrassment and sympathy. She's still holding my hand and when she speaks her voice is gentle. 'He never spoke about England much. When I first met him, he said he had split up from his wife.'

'He didn't say he'd left his other daughter behind?'

Roma looks uncomfortable and averts her gaze. She looks out of the window, her lips pushed together. She takes a deep breath and looks back at me, placing her other hand on top of mine.

'Please tell me,' I say. 'I need to know.'

'I don't wanna upset you, Clare, you seem like a nice young woman.'

'It's okay. I'm pretty tough. I can handle it, whatever it is.' *God, I hope I can.*

Roma hesitates some more but then gives a slight nod, as if she's come to a decision. 'Okay. Patrick said he left his wife and her child.'

I pick over the words. '*Her* child?' Roma nods. 'He didn't acknowledge that I was his child also?'

'You're his child too?' Roma frowns.

'Yes. Patrick Kendrick was my father. My biological father.'

'Oh, honey, I didn't know that. I assumed from what he said, you were his stepdaughter.' Roma sits back and there is a genuine look of shock on her face. 'I thought that was how he came to bring Alice on his own. I mean, why would you bring one daughter and not the other?'

We both look at each other. I have no doubt we are both thinking the same thing. It takes a moment for me to conjure up the words. 'Maybe I'm not really his daughter after all,' I say. It's my turn to slump back in my seat. I don't know how I feel. 'I've always wondered why he never took me. How he could choose between his own flesh and blood, but now it all seems so obvious. It makes sense now. I'm not his child.' I drag my hands down my face, my fingertips cover my mouth as I take in this realisation. It also means that Alice is not my full sister as I had always thought. She is, in fact, my half-sister. I examine this notion. It's easier than thinking about Patrick. I don't feel any differently about Alice, not one bit. She's my sister, full or half. She's always been my little sister.

'Are you okay?' asks Roma. 'Would you like something stronger to drink?'

'No. I'm fine. It's okay. Patrick not being my father makes a lot of sense. It answers a lot of questions. I'm okay with it. Honestly. Although, it does mean I don't actually know who my real father is. I don't know why Mum has never told me. Do I want to know who he is? Wow, it's answered one lot of questions, but has thrown up a load more.'

'It's a shock nevertheless,' says Roma. 'Take your time to get used to the idea. I'm sorry if I've upset you. I may have just gotten hold of the wrong end of the stick ... Maybe I should go now.' She takes a couple of notes from her purse and leaves them on the table. 'My treat.'

'Thank you for coming,' I say. 'Oh, wait ... how did you come to have the address for my mother? The one you gave to Alice after my father died?'

'It was by chance, really. A letter came one day when he was away on business, it was postmarked London, England. It sat on his desk for three days before curiosity got the better of me. I steamed open the envelope and it was a letter from a tracing agent asking him if he was Patrick Kennedy of such and such address. I remember thinking that they must have got him muddled up with someone else because, of course, he was Patrick Kendrick to me. But, for some reason I made a note of that address – don't ask me why but I did. Anyway, Patrick came home and just told me it was a spelling error and not to worry about it, that it was all sorted out now.'

'And you kept the address all that time?'

'Yes. Maybe because Patrick's life in the UK had always been a bit of a mystery and this was the only connection. I don't know why, but it felt important to keep it. To be honest, I forgot about it and then, after Patrick died and I was sorting out our things, I found it. That's when I gave it to Alice. I did say to her I wasn't sure whether it was a wild-goose chase I was sending her on, but it seemed wrong not to give it to her.' Roma stands. 'I really need to go. Please take care of yourself. And if you do get in touch with Alice, tell her I was asking about her and I'd love to hear from her.' Her smile is laced with sadness and I believe her sentiments are genuine. I get to see a lot of liars in my line of work and maybe it's just a gut feeling, but I believe Roma cares about Alice. Roma pauses. 'Oh, one more thing.' She delves into her handbag and produces a brown envelope. 'There are some photos of Alice in there. I thought you might like them.' She places the envelope on the table in front of me. 'Goodbye, Clare.'

'Before you go, can I ask just one more question?'

Roma is standing now but she pauses and nods. 'Do you have any other children? A daughter, perhaps?'

'A daughter? Not if you discount Alice. I just have a son, Nathaniel. Why?'

'I just wondered,' I say.

'Okay, well, goodbye, again.'

I watch the elegant woman leave the coffee shop. She stops at the window and looks in at me for a brief second, before putting on her sunglasses and walking away.

I pick up the envelope and am just psyching myself up to open it when my mobile rings. I flick it on to silent as I look at the screen. It's Luke. Twice in one morning. Now, that is unusual. I can't ignore it – the little voice in the back of my head that warns me it could be an emergency at home with Mum or the girls won't let me.

'Hi,' is all I say.

'Clare. Where the fuck are you?'

'Er ... just out having a coffee. What's up?'

'Where – having a coffee? Where exactly are you?' I can hear the anger in voice, although he's practically hissing the words. 'And don't say at Nadine's.'

'What?' *Oh, God, he's found out.*

'I know you're not at Nadine's. I've got the fucking police here. They want you to go in for further questioning. I found your address book and looked up Nadine because that's where you told me you were. And, guess what? You're not actually there! She's even more surprised than I am. She hasn't heard from you in months!' The hiss has gone and Luke is in full rage mode. This never happens. The last time he flipped like this was when ... ah yes ... was when his portrait of Alice was slashed. 'Clare? Are you still there?'

'Yes. I'm here.'

'Care to share where the fuck *here* is?'

I ignore his question. I don't really want to have to explain myself. Not yet. Not until I know for certain what happened over here. 'What do the police want to question me about?'

'Vandalising Pippa's car.'

'Not that again.'

'They've looked at the CCTV and have you on film going into the garage and coming out a few minutes later with the aerosol can in your hand.'

'That's impossible. I've told you before, I didn't do it.'

'They have evidence, Clare. Didn't you hear me? CCTV evidence.' His tone conveys a mix of anger and exasperation. 'Get your arse back here now.' I can hear voices in the background. Luke speaks again. 'The police want to know where you are and how long you'll be.'

I drum my fingers anxiously on the table. 'I'll be back Wednesday.'

'I don't think they want to wait until then. How about you make it this afternoon.'

'I can't.'

Then I hear the phone being passed over to someone else.

'Mrs Tennison?' says a female voice I recognise as the police officer from the other day. 'This is Police Constable Evans here. We spoke about the damage to Pippa Stent's vehicle.'

'Yes. Hello.'

'As your husband has just explained, we have further evidence to support the accusation that you vandalised Mrs Stent's car and we would like you to come in for further questioning. You may remember, we did say that you should make yourself available for further questioning and someone in your line of work shouldn't really need this spelled out.'

'I know, but I can't come in before Wednesday.' Time to come clean. I can't put it off any longer. 'I'm not in the country and I haven't got a return flight until Tuesday night. I could be with you by mid-morning Wednesday.'

'Mrs Tennison, flying out of the country isn't really acceptable.'

I cut in. 'It's perfectly acceptable. I am not under arrest. I haven't been charged with anything. I haven't been cautioned. You never told me not to leave the country. Technically, I have not done anything wrong.'

'I can't say I'm very happy.'

'That's as may be, but as soon as I'm in the UK, I'll let you know. Now, please hand me back to my husband.'

'What the hell is going on?' It's Luke. 'Where are you?'

'I'm in America,' I say. I carry on talking despite his spluttering disbelief. 'I'll be back Wednesday. We'll talk then.' I end the call. What a nightmare. I think about the new evidence and wonder how the hell they have me on CCTV going into the garage.

I look at the envelope that Roma left still on the table. I'll worry about CCTV later, for now I'm dying to see the photographs. I empty the contents in front of me. Half a dozen photographs spill out. I spread them out with my fingertips.

At first I don't understand what I'm looking at. It takes a moment for me to process the information.

These are all pictures of Martha Munroe. Alice's friend.

The same girl in the picture with her that she first sent Mum.

It seems as though my brain is taking forever to rationalise and order these thoughts but, in reality, it's only a second.

The truth hits me. What I had suspected somewhere in the back of my mind is no longer a nagging doubt. It has morphed into a real-life threat. I feel physically sick and for a moment I can feel my cool legal head melt into a morass of panic and fear.

Chapter 22

I don't know how I make it back to my motel room. I guess I'm on autopilot. I can't think straight; all I can think about is the mess everything seems to be over here. It's hard to take in what I've found out.

I throw my bag onto the bed and sink into the overly soft mattress. I tip the contents out and examine them again.

Photographs from Roma

Copy photo of Alice and Martha together

Travel list

Pay slip

Business card

Contact lens box

I fan the photographs out before me.

I single out a portrait shot of her. She's looking at the camera and smiling. I take the photograph of Alice and Martha together.

They look very similar and, if you didn't know them, it would be easy to muddle them up. Their hair is similar and nothing that a bottle of hair colour or a trip to the hairdressers couldn't sort out. They both have high cheekbones and, from what I can tell, from the photographs Roma has given me, they are of similar build and height. The only giveaway is their eyes.

Alice Kennedy has the most amazing blue eyes. It's something that I remember vividly about her. Everyone who saw her used to comment on how big and blue they were. Blue eyes run in both my mother's family and Patrick Kennedy's family. And there they are, staring right back at me.

I look at the contact lens box on the bed and the blue-eye graphic I realise is not a generic graphic – it's colour-specific. I take a closer look. On the other side, three small boxes are printed, each has one word underneath: blue, brown, green. The square above the word 'blue' is ticked. These aren't normal contact lenses; these are for changing the appearance of eye colour.

A wave of nausea swells in my stomach and for a moment I consider making a dash for the bathroom. I clench my stomach with my hand and, sitting up straight to allow as much oxygen into my lungs as possible, I take deep breaths – in through my nose and release slowly out through my mouth. The sensation passes but my mind is in turmoil.

I push my hands through my hair. I don't know what to do. I stand. I pull at my hair. I stride across the room to the window. It takes just three paces. I stride back to the bed. I want to sit. I want to stand. I pick up the photographs again. I run the scenario through my mind, slowly, very slowly, just to check I haven't made a mistake anywhere. I'm usually very thorough with things like this. I don't usually make mistakes. How I wish that this time I had. I want to be wrong.

I am not.

I shudder and goose bumps prick their way down my spine, then both my arms prickle with fear and I'm engulfed in a fleeting moment of cold air. I shiver and scrunch my shoulders up. My brain formally identifying the terrifying thought. The young woman at home with my family is not who she says she is. She is not Alice. She is Martha and she has taken my sister's identity.

I sink onto the bed and bury my head in the photographs, my arms sweeping them into me. I have no concept of time or space. I can only think of my darling sister and what might have happened to her.

I don't know how long I've been lying on the bed amongst the photographs but at some point the pain has switched to anger. I need to know what exactly has happened to Alice. There is only one person who can answer this – the imposter in my home.

I grab my mobile and call Luke. My fingers fumble with the phone as the adrenalin starts to pump through me. If Martha is capable of taking on Alice's identity, capable of being so cold-hearted and callous to trick, not just me and Luke, but my Mum as well, then she is capable of anything and right now she's with my family. I can't bear to think what this will do to Mum.

While I wait for the call to connect and for Luke to answer his bloody phone, I know I have to detach myself from what I think the worse-case scenario might be. I need to keep a professional head if I'm to get through this and find out the truth. Luke's phone goes to voicemail. I hang up without leaving a message.

It's early evening here in Florida, which, given the five-hour time difference, means it's mid-afternoon in the UK. Luke will probably be picking Hannah up from school. I wait for an hour and then try again, but he still doesn't answer. In desperation, I call the house phone.

Mum answers. 'Hi, Mum,' I say. 'It's me, Clare.'

'Hello.' I can tell from the frosty reception that Mum is not impressed with my transatlantic trip. 'I hope you're ringing to say you're on your way home.'

'Mum, please.' She still has the ability to make me feel like a naughty teenager who is late home from a party. 'I'll be home Wednesday morning. First thing.'

'Whatever possessed you to go to America?'

'I needed to come. There are so many things that don't add up.'

'You're stirring trouble, that's what you're doing. Have you any idea how upset I've been? How upset your sister has been? There's nothing in America that you need to worry about.'

'I met Roma Kendrick,' I say slowly.

'What did you do that for?'

'I wanted to ask her about things. About Dad.'

'Honestly, Clare, I really don't know what you're hoping to find out or prove from this ... this ... carry-on. It's ridiculous.'

'Don't you want to know what she said?' I'm tired and I shouldn't be having this conversation with Mum right now, but I can't help myself. I'm fed up with her avoiding talking about the past.

'No. Actually, I don't.'

'She said Patrick always let her believe he wasn't my father.' The words are out and I can't take them back. I hear Mum gasp.

'She would say that, wouldn't she? What does she know?' Mum's in full recovery mode. 'And even if your father did say that, he would only have been saying it for his own benefit.'

'Why didn't he take me, then? Why take only Alice?'

'Enough! I'm not discussing this fanciful idea any further. Now, was there anything you wanted or did you ring up just to have another argument?'

'I wanted to speak to Luke,' I say, sensing I will get no further on the subject of Patrick tonight.

'Luke's taken the girls for their swimming lessons. Of course, if you were at home you'd know that,' she says, with no sign of the frost thawing. 'Hold on a moment, Alice is saying something.' I hear muffled voices and guess Mum has put her hand over the receiver. She comes back after a moment. 'Alice wants to speak to you. I'll pass you over.'

I try to protest that Alice, or rather Martha, is the last person I want to speak to, but the receiver exchanges hands before I can speak and then I hear Martha.

'Hello, Clare,' she says. 'How are you?'

'I'm fine,' I say. 'Look, I'm quite busy, did you want anything important?' My skin tingles, as if a thousand ants are making their way around my body. I close my eyes and focus my mind, throwing away thoughts of my sister that may betray me.

'Mum says you're in America,' says Martha. I can hear the acoustics change and assume Martha is moving away from the kitchen, or wherever she took the call, to find a more private space, away from Mum. The sound of a door closing confirms this.

'That's right,' I say. I can take this conversation one of two ways. I opt for keeping up the pretence for now. I don't want this all to come to a head in the UK while I'm stuck over here in the States. 'I was going to stay with a friend up in Cambridgeshire, but changed my mind at the last minute.' I keep the facts to a minimum.

'Cool. Where exactly are you? Anywhere near my neighbourhood?' There's a light-hearted tone to her words, but I suspect this is false. Martha is wary.

'No. No. I'm in New York.' I close my eyes and hope Martha doesn't notice how quiet it is. 'I'm in my hotel room at the moment,' I add to counter the lack of background noise of a busy city.

'Is that so?' she says. 'Of course, if you were in Florida, I'd be wondering who you were talking to. Whether you were hanging out at any of the places I used to. Talking to my friends and all.' She gives a little laugh. And I mean little.

I return the laugh. 'Oh yeah, I could, couldn't I? And that wouldn't do at all.'

'No, that wouldn't. But then, you shouldn't believe everything everyone says. You, of all people, should know that,' says Martha. There's an awkward pause and I can feel the tension crackle up and down the line between us. 'Knowledge is a dangerous thing.'

'Knowledge is power,' I say.

'I'm also of the mind that ignorance is bliss,' she retorts, her voice dropping an octave, her words slower as each one is emphasised. 'That way no one gets hurt.'

'That's true. Anyway, I need to get on, got some legal stuff for work to check.'

'Sure, I wouldn't wanna keep you from your work.'

'See you Wednesday.'

'I'll look forward to it. You can tell me all about your trip.'

'Yeah. Sure.' I hang up and close my eyes for a moment, recalling the conversation with all its subtext. It does nothing to settle my already-fragile nerves. I need to get home. I need to protect my family – I'm not entirely sure what from. I can't pin it down to one thing or one word, all I know is that they are surrounded by lies and deceit.

An hour later, my phone rings and I'm sure it is Luke. However, Leonard's name is on the screen.

'Hello, Leonard. Everything all right?' I find myself asking this question more and more often. Every time the phone rings, I think something has happened. I am becoming a nervous wreck.

'No. Everything is not all right. When I said take gardening leave, I meant stay at home with your family. Get to know your sister and sort your marriage out. I didn't mean jet off to America.'

'Hello to you too. Yes, I'm fine. Thanks for asking. Oh, there was something you wanted to chat about, was there?' I can't help myself. Leonard has all the subtlety of a Chieftain tank at times and thinks he can ride straight over me. I swear he forgets I'm a grown woman. An adult. A business partner.

'Didn't realise I had to do the polite chit-chat with you, Clare,' comes the retort, which has the tiniest thread of attrition.

'And while I'm at it, since when did I have to answer to you as to what I choose to do with my spare time? Spare time that I didn't want, I might add. Either I'm working and am accountable for my hours or I'm on gardening leave and can do as I bloody well please.' I feel quite proud of myself for standing up to Leonard.

'Well, that's me told,' he says. I imagine him looking rather startled at the telephone for a moment. 'So, are you okay?'

'Yes, I'm fine, thank you,' I say, the indignation leaving me and experiencing genuine appreciation of the obvious concern in his voice.

'What exactly are you doing in America?'

'I needed to sort a few things out. Please don't worry. I'm flying home tomorrow night. How did you know I was here, anyway?'

'Your mother told me,' he replies. 'She also told me about the new evidence. CCTV footage.'

'It wasn't me.'

'Do you need any help? Legal help or otherwise?'

'No. It's okay. I can sort this out myself, but thank you, anyway.'

'It won't look good for the business if anything comes of this,' says Leonard, his voice taking on a more businesslike approach.

'Nothing will come of it. I didn't do it. Don't worry, I won't sully the reputation of the firm.' I scold myself at my own tetchiness. 'I'm sorry, I'm just a bit tired and on edge, if I'm honest.'

'It's not like you at all. That's why I called, really. Your mum asked me to,' says Leonard softly. 'She's desperate for things to work out well with Alice.'

'I know. All these years, she's just been marking time, going through the motions of life, as she waited for her daughter to come back. The thing is ...' I stop myself short, not wishing to say what I fear out loud. Not yet anyway.

'Don't be quick to judge,' says Leonard. 'It's just as hard for Alice as it is for you. Whatever is it you're hoping to find by poking around over there in America, will only cause a lot of hurt.'

'Has Mum changed her will or anything to do with the trust fund?' I ask, taking the conversation off at a tangent.

'You know I can't divulge any information about your mother's finances. Client confidentiality and all that.'

'But you could tell me, as your business partner. I take it I am still your partner?'

'Yes, of course you are, but there's also conflict of interest. Whatever conversations I have with my client, regardless of the fact she's your mother and how they may affect you are, at this point, strictly confidential. Not even you can be party to them.'

'What about Alice? Has she spoken to you about anything?'

'Alice? No, why would she?'

'I don't just mean professionally, but personally. She's not asked for your advice about anything?' I close my eyes as I think of Tom telling me he'd seen Martha and Leonard at the café. I can't bear the fact that Leonard might be lying to me. 'Even just casually, as a one-off?'

'What's this all about?'

'I'm just asking.'

'You're worrying me, Clare. Stop being so bloody paranoid about everyone and everything. Now, I'm going to end this call before we fall out with each other. I suggest you get a good night's sleep, get yourself on that aircraft tomorrow, get yourself back here and get your life back on track.' With that he hangs up.

I spend the next few minutes staring at the telephone, wondering whether I should call home again and try to speak to Luke. In the end I decide against it.

I head out to the diner opposite the motel. It's a quiet night, from what I can tell, and I sit undisturbed while I eat a burger and chips I don't really want and drink a beer that I do want.

When I came over to Amelia Island just two days ago, I wasn't sure what I would find. I knew there was more to Alice than met the eye, but what I didn't know was the full extent of it. And now I do. Again, I have to banish the thought of might have happened to Alice Kennedy, my sister. I can't let myself go there, not yet.

When I get back to my room, I check my rucksack to make sure I have my passport, tickets and bank card all ready for tomorrow's journey home. I wonder if Luke will call me back. He probably hasn't even looked at his phone. I have to say that about my husband, he's not one for constantly checking social media, uploading pictures of his dinner or pictures of the girls. To Luke a phone is a necessity for communication verbally or via text, nothing more. Still, I wait up just in case he does call. When he doesn't, I put it down to him being busy sorting the girls out for bed. I don't want to acknowledge the notion that he might actually be avoiding me.

When my phone rings just after midnight, I immediately think it must be Luke after all. My heart gives a little flip of relief. At last someone I can talk to, who I trust. I pause. I do trust him, don't I? Another thought to banish. Of course I do. I was just overreacting about Alice or Martha, whatever the hell her name is.

I grapple with the bedside light and snatch at my phone.

Home calling, I'm informed by the screen message. Strange. Why would Luke call on the house phone? I answer it.

'Hello, Luke?'

'It's me.'

I struggle for a second to think who it could be. The voice is lowered to almost a whisper. It's definitely not Luke. 'Mum?' I try the next logical person, although something tells me logic is not applicable here.

'No, it's not your mother.'

'Alice?'

'Who else?'

'Why are you calling me?'

'Listen, Clare, listen carefully.' There's a hardness to her voice I haven't heard before. It puts me on alert. I wait for her to continue. 'I don't know what you're doing in America and I don't know what you think you may or may not have found, but I'm warning you, whatever it is you think you know, you'd be wise to keep it to yourself.'

'What are you talking about?'

'You know exactly what I'm talking about.'

'And why, exactly, would I want to keep it to myself – presuming I know anything?'

'Don't get involved, Clare. You'll regret it.'

'Are you threatening me?'

'Things have gone too far. It's out of my hands now. You need to drop it.'

'Do you really think for one minute that I'm scared of you?' I frantically search my phone for the 'record' app. I quite often record work conversations so I can go back and check the nitty-gritty detail. I have a feeling this is going to be useful.

'It's not me you need to be frightened of.'

'What?' I hit the 'record' button, but it's too late. The line has gone dead. 'Shit.'

I try to ring back but the call doesn't connect. I suspect she's unplugged it from the wall. I check the 'record' app on my phone but all I have managed to get is me saying 'What?'

I rest my head in my hands and try to think clearly. There seems little point in trying to get hold of Luke or Mum. What am I supposed to say? They won't believe me, they'll just defer back to Martha, who will, of course, deny it all and then they'll blame my jealousy or rampant paranoia they've decided I am now suffering from.

I think back over the conversation and grab my notebook and pen as I write it down word for word, or at least as close to that as I can remember. Her final words are the ones that scare me the most. I underline them three times, the pressure of the nib scoring through the paper.

IT'S NOT ME YOU NEED TO BE FRIGHTENED OF.

Chapter 23

I must have dozed off at some point during the night, but I didn't sleep well at all. I awoke several times and checked my phone to see if Luke had called. He hadn't. I'm up and dressed by six this morning. I need to be at the airport by eleven and drop the hire car back. I have a long day ahead with a lay-over in Atlanta of three hours before the transatlantic flight back to the UK.

I keep checking my phone, but by the time I board the international flight from the States, I've given up all hope of Luke calling me.

Even the night-time flight home doesn't grant me sleep. I once again take to pen and paper to try to figure things out.

* Martha is Alice.
* Martha's motive – money? Personality disorder? Wants to be someone else – Alice. Not satisfied with that now, wants everything I have – Mum, Luke, girls. Trying to cut me off from my own life, like she did with Alice.
* Planned in advance NOT opportunist.
* Working with someone – hence threat.

* What has happened to the real Alice? Was Martha involved?

I hate writing the last sentence, but I am somehow managing to keep myself divorced from the emotion attached to the reality. I'll deal with it later. For now, my drive is fuelled by the need to protect my family.

Instead I focus on who Martha could be working with. If it's not her I'm to be scared of, then who is it? It can't be anyone I know. I mean, why would they do this to me? Who hates both Mum and me enough to do this?

I go around in circles, the same questions repeating themselves over and over again, and each time I have no answers. What I need is for Martha to confess. She needs to talk. I can't work this out on my own.

When the plane touches down at Heathrow I'm relieved that the flight is finally over. Once through passport control and customs, I head for the exit and, sitting on a stone bench, try once more to contact home.

It's seven in the morning and the house should be wide awake preparing for the day ahead but, when I try to call no one picks up, it doesn't even go to answerphone.

I try Luke's phone. I hear the call connect and can hear voices in the background for a second before there is a rustling and the noise is muffled.

'Luke? Luke! Are you there? Can you hear me?' I want to cry. The line goes dead and I slam my phone down hard on the concrete seat. Instantly there is the unmistakable sound of the screen cracking. 'Shit!' I inspect the damage. There's a big crack from one corner, stretching out almost to the opposite corner, and I've dented the edge of the casing. Fortunately, it still appears to be working.

The person sitting on one of the seats opposite gives me a 'You didn't want to do that' sort of look. I grab my rucksack and head for the car park, where I left my BMW a few days ago.

As I get inside the car and throw my rucksack onto the passenger seat, my phone bleeps as a text message comes in. I'm grateful I didn't smash the phone down any harder. Expecting it to be Luke, I'm surprised to see it's come through as a number I don't recognise and one that's obviously not in my contacts. I open the message and a picture of Hannah appears on the screen. It's taken from a distance, through the gates of the Old Vicarage. She's just coming out of the front door, dressed in her school uniform, holding Luke's hand, heading towards the carport.

Another message comes through from the same number as before.

Don't do anything stupid. Wouldn't want anyone to have an accident, would you?

A river of ice-cold fear runs through my veins. I fumble with the phone, but somehow manage to hit the call function. The unknown number rings only once. There is silence.

'Who is this?' I demand, my voice shaking. 'Who are you?'

There's a muffled sound of laughter. I can't hear it clearly and there's no way of telling if it's male or female.

'Leave my family alone! Don't you fucking touch them! Do you hear me? Leave. Them. Alone!' I'm aware with each word

271

I say I'm becoming more and more hysterical. I can't help it. It takes another moment before I realise the line is dead. And then, almost immediately, another text message comes through.

I'm being DEADLY serious. Don't involve the police either. You'll regret it if you do.

I grapple with the door handle and hang my head outside of the car. I think I'm going to be sick but I retch instead and only bile comes. I spit it out onto the tarmac, taking a moment to allow the blood to rush to my head and bat away the wave of dizziness. I sit up and look at my phone again.

My hands are shaking as I scroll back through the messages. I want to have imagined it all, but I haven't. It's there in front of me. I stop at the picture of Hannah and Luke, zooming in on the detail. I can't tell when this was taken. It could be any morning. There's nothing in the picture to give any indication if this is today, yesterday or even sometime last week.

I throw the phone onto the seat and shove the keys in the ignition. The engine roars as, heavy-footed, I speed out of the car park, heading for Little Dray. It's going to take a good hour to get there, but if I put my foot down I should be able to make it before the school run.

Fortunately, I'm going in the other direction to most of the rush-hour traffic and I miss the bulk of it as I hammer down the A23 towards home. Soon the countryside I pass slips into the familiar landscape of open fields and undulating hills that I associate with Sussex. I check my watch as the 'Welcome to Little Dray' signpost comes into sight. I ignore the 'please drive carefully through our village' part. I swing off to the left, taking the lane that leads to the house. The hedges smudge into various shades of green as I push the accelerator further down. I check the clock on the dash. It's eight twenty-three. In two minutes' time, Luke will be leaving with Hannah. I press even harder on the accelerator and almost over-cook it on the next bend, the back end of the BMW giving a little step-out. I manage to correct it, avoid skidding off into the ditch and stamp on the brakes, but in doing so also manage to stall the engine.

'Come on!' I shout at the car as I twist the key in the ignition. It starts straight away and, with no thought to anything around me, I rev the engine and wheel-spin away, dust and dirt kicking up behind me from the rear wheels.

I'm nearly there, the flint wall that surrounds the grounds to the house is in sight. I'm vaguely aware of a dark saloon car parked on the side of the verge and at the last minute I swerve to miss it. I hear a crack and as I glance to my left, I see my near-side wing mirror hanging off. I don't care.

I can see the gates and I swing the car round like some sort of stunt man, as miraculously, I slip through without making contact with the flint piers.

I don't see her.

One minute the driveway is clear, the next she has launched herself in front of me. I slam on the brakes so hard I'm practically standing on them. I make eye contact. For a fraction of a second I think she's standing there just waiting for me to hit her, but then I see she's moving. Her arms are outstretched. She's trying to move something out of my way. She looks at me and I see my own abject fear reflected straight back at me. Time stands still until I realise what, or rather who, she is trying to move from the path of the tonne of metal bearing down on them.

I throw the steering wheel to the left to try to avoid them.

Somewhere, someone has screamed. I don't know where or who. Or maybe we all screamed, but then the God-awful thud of impact comes, all other sound being sucked up. Her head makes contact with the windscreen and the glass both splinters out like a spider's web and bulges in towards me at the same time. Another thud. This time the roof.

The car skids, but the speed I'm travelling cannot be countered by the brakes. It hits one of the rocks dotted along the edge of the grass island, the steering wheel is snatched from my grasp and all of a sudden I feel a weightlessness as the car is briefly airborne before flipping onto its side and colliding with a tree, which bounces the vehicle back onto its wheels. The airbag has deployed at some point and my face is cushioned before I'm jolted backwards and the side of my head hits the off-side window.

I'm vaguely aware of screaming and shouting. Voices that are familiar but sound so far away, as if they're calling and yelling from a great distance. I can see figures running towards me. I try to move but I'm trapped by some sort of strap. I can't work out what it is. I'm looking down a black tunnel, which is closing in around me.

'Clare! Clare!'

The tunnel pulses away. I look to the side and I see Luke yanking at the driver's door. 'It's okay, Babe. We're going to get you out of here.'

Before the door comes open, something distracts him and

he looks across the driveway. It's then I hear him roar with pain. He flees from my sight. I hear more shouting but I can't make out what they are saying. The volume and clarity of their voices throbbing in and out.

Then Leonard is next to me. He's talking. His voice is stern. His face is grim. He's tapping my face. He sounds drunk, his words sound slurred. My brain can't understand what he's saying. My vision is blurry and I squint my eyes. I focus hard on his voice and his words become clearer.

'Clare. Unfasten your seat belt. Your seat belt, Clare. Unfasten it.'

He's jabbing inside the car and I move my hand to the side of my seat. I find the buckle and, on the second attempt, I hear a click and the pressure across my stomach and shoulder is released as I slump to one side. The black tunnel is closing around me again. His voice becomes distant. I think I can hear Luke's voice too.

I fight the overwhelming sensation of tiredness. I manage to open my eyes again and see Leonard's concerned face. He's frowning and speaking in such a low voice, I can barely hear him. His words sound harsh, but I can't make them out. Something like: *What have you done? ... Stupid ... Told you.* None of it makes sense.

My head rolls to the side and through half-closed eyes I see steam spiralling up from the bonnet of my car.

I look at Leonard and try to speak but I can't form the words properly. 'Mar,' I gasp. It hurts to breathe. I try again. 'Marth ...'

'Shh, don't speak. Say nothing.' This time Leonard's voice

is clear and it sends a new wave of fear through me.

I hear a child crying. My maternal instinct kicks in, the one that can quell all the chaos around me, dampen all other thoughts and feelings, both physical and mental and zoom in on that one sound. I hear it distinctly. I know instantly it's Chloe. I hear her, but I can't see her.

'Shit.' Leonard jumps up and disappears towards the sound of Chloe. The impact of the car against the tree has left the car at a ninety-degree angle to the drive and now my view is no longer obstructed by Leonard. I can see clearly the horror before me. My brain prioritising what needs my attention the most.

Lying perfectly still, a red stain of blood across her forehead, is Hannah. Luke is kneeling over her. He's yanking off his navy jumper, the one Mum bought him for his birthday, a V-neck from M&S, and covering her little body with it. He's speaking. I can see his mouth moving as he leans over our daughter, but I can't hear any words. All I can hear is me.

'Nooooooo! Please God, no!'

I'm not sure how many ambulances arrive at the house or how many police cars. I'm just aware of the sound of sirens, the wheels scrunching on the gravel drive, radios buzzing and crackling, broken and fractured noises of people talking in firm, professional voices and then soft tones. I ask about Hannah constantly, but I'm told they are attending to her now, that I'm not to worry and that they need to get me to hospital. Then there's the sound of rotor blades and a flurry of activity out of the gateway. I don't know who is airlifted. It isn't me.

They place three orange padded blocks around my head and a strap across my forehead. I'm lifted by several pairs of hands onto an orange stretcher, the straps across my body pulled so tight it's impossible to move. I think there may be a drip in my arm. I can't feel anything, but I can see a bag of fluid hanging up on a clip next to me. I'm asked questions that I don't think I know the answers to.

At some point, Leonard has come back to my side.

'Chloe?' I ask, as the stretcher is lifted.

'She's okay. Your mum is taking her to Pippa's,' he says. Then he lowers his mouth to my ear. 'Don't say anything to anyone. Don't answer any questions until I've spoken with you first.'

I don't have time to ask why, before the stretcher is slid into the back of the ambulance. I close my eyes and the ambulance doors are slammed closed and we begin our journey to Brighton hospital. I'm slightly comforted by the thought that Pippa has taken Chloe. I don't know what this means about our relationship, but at least I know Chloe will be looked after well. I think of Daisy's accident. Pippa thought her daughter would be looked after well too. She thought I was caring for her. How could I be so stupid as to forget to pick the girls up? She's right. I am responsible for what happened, just like I'm responsible for what has happened now.

My head continues to throb and I feel the pull of fatigue. I think of Hannah and try to ask once again what's happened to her, but I'm met with the usual side-step of an answer.

We hit a pothole in the road and the jolt makes me cry out in pain. My left arm is killing me. I can hear myself groaning.

277

'Where's the pain coming from, Clare?' asks the paramedic, who is sitting in the back of the ambulance with me. 'Is it your arm?'

I give a grunt. 'Okay, what I'm going to do, Clare, is give you some more painkiller. Some more morphine. Are you okay with that?'

I give another grunt. Her voice is drifting away from me and I don't think I can fight this tiredness any longer. I just want to go to sleep. And then I think of Hannah. I'm awake again.

'Hannah, where's Hannah? Where's my daughter?' I become more and more agitated with every word and every second that passes. I try to move, but I can't. The paramedic tells me to stay calm. *Calm! How the hell can I stay calm when I don't know what has happened to my daughter?* I scream her name as I'm swamped by dark thoughts and images of her lying motionless on the gravel driveway. And then the blackness comes and takes me away.

Chapter 24

I think the medical staff must have given me a sedative. When I wake, it's dark outside and the room is lit by a small amber glow of a night light. There is the stillness of night in the air. The atmosphere you only get in the dead of the night, when most people are asleep. This time there are no footsteps making their way up and down the corridor, no doors swishing open, no muted bump as the doors close against the architrave and no indistinct conversations.

I sense I'm not alone, though, and turn my head to the right. Luke is sitting in the high-backed hospital chair. He has a blanket pulled up around his shoulders, tucked under his chin, and his head has lolled forwards onto his chest.

Such conflicting emotions rush over me. I want to reach out and have him hold me, but at the same time I want to slap his stubbly face and ask him why he doesn't believe me.

Luke stirs and his eyes open. He sits upright when our gazes meet. 'Clare, hiya, Babe.' He frees his arm from the constraints of the blanket and reaches out to me, squeezing my hand. 'It's the middle of the night. Try to go back to sleep. You need to rest.'

'Hannah. How is Hannah?' I don't care about myself and what my body needs. My mind needs to know if my daughter is okay.

'She's fine. She's on the paediatric ward,' he says.

'The ward?' He definitely said ward and not ICU.

'She has a few cuts and bruises and she banged her head. They're just keeping her in overnight for observation,' he continues. 'She's absolutely fine besides that.'

'Nothing broken? No life-threatening injuries?'

'No. None of those. As I say, a few bumps and bruises.'

'Oh, thank God for that.' A sob of relief fills my throat. I swallow, but can't contain it. I let it out and allow myself the indulgence of tears. 'I thought I'd killed her. No one would tell me anything. And then the police wanting to speak to me ...' The snot and tears have merged into one and Luke takes a wad of tissues from the battered box on the bedside cabinet, pushing some into my hand and wiping my face with the others.

'Routine questions,' he says. And then he looks at me as if he's deciding whether to tell me something. I recognise that look.

'What?'

'Alice isn't so good,' he says, he dips his gaze for a moment. 'She's in ICU. Punctured lung. Several broken bones and a serious head injury. Your mum is with her.'

'Shit.' I'm ashamed by my first thought, that I might not be able to question her about what happened in America, but then I remind myself of what I found out and the shame lifts.

'She's not Alice,' I say. Luke frowns and looks confused. 'That's not my sister in ICU.'

'What are you talking about?'

'That woman who's been pretending to be Alice is actually Alice's friend, Martha Munroe.'

'Honestly, Clare, you must have taken a bigger bang to the head than I thought.'

'I know it sounds bizarre, but I'm nearly one hundred per cent certain.' He gives me an old-fashioned look that clearly says he doubts it very much. 'Where's my bag?'

Luke shrugs. 'I don't know. Still in the car, I expect.'

'Bring it. I need my bag. When you go home later, bring the bag back. It's important. Really important. I can show you what I've found. Then you'll have to believe me.'

'Listen, Leonard said to tell you not to answer any police questions,' says Luke, clearly trying to change the subject. 'I think he wants to speak to you first. What happened? Why were you driving like a lunatic? Didn't you see them?'

I let out an incredulous huff. 'Of course I didn't see them. Not at first. What a stupid question.'

'Why so fast?'

'I was scared.'

'Of?'

'Martha. Alice. Whatever the fuck you want to call her. I was scared what she would do.'

The door opening brings a halt to our conversation and the nurse comes in. 'I thought I heard voices,' she says. 'How are you?' She comes over and unhooks the blood-pressure sleeve from somewhere behind the head of my bed. 'I'll do some checks while I'm here.'

'I'll go down to Hannah,' says Luke, getting up. 'I don't want her to wake up and find herself all alone. I stayed with her until she went to sleep last night.'

'Okay.' I can't begrudge him that. Hannah's needs are greater than mine. 'Tell her I love her,' I say. 'Maybe they'll let me come and see her.'

'Not the state you're in,' says Luke, harshly, and then his face softens. 'We'll see what the doctors say once they've done their rounds in the morning. They're talking about letting her go home, if everything's okay. I'm not sure about you, though.' He looks up at the nurse.

'It's up to the doctor,' she says. 'Sorry.'

'I'll come and see you once I know what's going on,' says Luke. He pauses and I think he's going to kiss me, but he changes his mind and squeezes my hand instead. 'See you later.'

'Don't forget my bag,' I call after him. He acknowledges with a raise of his hand as he walks out the door. I can't help wondering if he's going to call in to see Martha on the way. Does she mean something to him? Do I mean less? I don't know, but there's a void between us, one that neither of us knows how to fill. I'm not sure what's gone missing, but something has.

I spend the next few hours drifting in and out of sleep until the breakfast tray is brought round. I'm not particularly hungry and poke at the cornflakes in the bowl and eat half a banana. I'm more grateful for the cup of tea that follows. I put the TV on and wonder when Luke will come to see me. I'm anxious for news on Hannah and really want to see her, although I'm also aware that seeing me all bandaged up in a hospital bed could be frightening for her. If only I had my phone with me I could at least then make some calls. Pippa would be first on my list, just to check how Chloe is, and secondly, to see if she'll believe me when I say it wasn't me who has vandalised her car.

No doubt the police will be back at some time today to question me about both Pippa's car and the accident. I don't know how I'm going to account for the speed at which I went through the gates to the house. If only I'd slowed down, none of this would have happened.

I think back to events and wonder what Leonard was doing there at that time in the morning. And what were Martha and Hannah doing down by the gates anyway? Then I remember the text messages warning me off. Jesus, did Martha take Hannah down there on purpose to carry out the threat? But then, why would she jump out in front of the car herself and, from what I can remember, she was trying to get Hannah out of the way? I then remember the phone call with Martha. *It's not me you need to be frightened of.*

I catch my breath as a possible scenario plays out in my mind. Martha and Hannah might have been pushed in front of the car. Who would do that? Who would purposefully put a child's life in danger? Attempted murder, nothing short of it.

I need to speak to Martha.

'Clare, darling, you're awake.' My mother strides in through the doors and is hugging me before I even have a chance to say hello. 'How are you? I came down to see you in the night, but you were sleeping. The nurse told me you would be okay.'

'Yeah, I'm fine. Apart from this.' I give a nod towards the cast on my arm. Then I look up at my mother. 'I didn't do it on purpose, Mum. It was an accident. You do believe me, don't you?'

'Of course, I do,' says Mum. I see the pain in her eyes. 'I just can't understand why you were driving like that.'

I think about explaining that I was frightened for everyone's safety. Frightened of what Martha would do, but I stop myself. If Luke doesn't believe me, there's even less chance Mum will. 'I don't know,' I say feebly. 'How's Alice?'

Mum perches on the edge of the bed and holds my hand. 'Not good,' she says. 'She's dosed up with morphine at the moment.'

'She's not unconscious or anything like that?'

'Drifting in and out of a heavy sleep, the doctor says. She hasn't said anything, though when she wakes up it's like she's only half awake. I don't know ...' Mum's voice cracks a fraction. 'I don't know if she even understands what we're saying. She just looks at us and then looks away.'

'It's probably just the morphine,' I say, wanting to comfort my mum. 'What have the doctors said about any long-term prognosis?'

'The brain's a wonderful thing and sometimes just needs a bit of recovery time. They're monitoring her closely.' This time Mum's eyes fill with tears and she dabs at them with a hanky she produces from her sleeve.

'What were Alice and Hannah doing down by the gate?' I ask tentatively.

'I don't know. I thought she was in the living room talking to Leonard.'

'What was he doing there so early?'

'He'd popped over with some forms for me to sign,' says Mum vaguely. 'I think he wanted to catch you before you went into work.'

'He could have just phoned. And why didn't he send the forms home with me? It's all a bit odd, don't you think?'

'No, I don't think, as it happens. Leonard's entitled to come over when he sees fit. He doesn't need security clearance from you. Why don't you ask Leonard yourself when he comes? I'm starting to wonder about your sanity.' Mum stands and strides over to the window. I can see her shoulders heave up and down as she reins in her anger.

'Mum, I need to ask you something.'

She turns and looks at me. 'Don't. Don't ask me anything. I'm not up to it.'

'Mum, please ...'

'Now's not the time.' Mum looks towards the door. 'Oh, there's Leonard. He wants to speak to you.' And then she's striding over to the door and calling Leonard in.

'Hello, Clare. Good to see you awake and sitting up.' He kisses my cheek and I make an effort not to flinch from his contact. Somewhere in the back of my mind the thought is lurking that Leonard was with Martha and Hannah when I drove in. I don't know what this means, but it's unnerving me. 'Tom sends his love. Says he'll come and see you soon.'

'Thanks,' I mutter.

'Now, I've had a word with both the doctor overseeing you

and the police investigating the accident. Basically, I've managed to hold the police off from questioning you for another twenty-four hours. If, for any reason, they do turn up, you know your rights; you're not obliged to say anything without legal representation.'

'I know,' I say impatiently. 'But I *am* my legal representative.'

'No. I'll be that,' says Leonard, waving away my protests. 'You've sustained a head injury. You're in no state to reliably represent yourself.'

'Listen to Leonard, he knows what he's talking about,' says Mum. 'I need to get back to Alice.' She exchanges a look with Leonard that I can't quite decipher and as she gets up, Leonard moves the chair back from her, his hand momentarily touching her elbow as she steps past him. In that second I have an epiphany. I don't know why it has never occurred to me before, but Mum and Leonard are obviously more than just friends.

The next thought hits me right between the eyes.

I watch my mother leave the room, Leonard's gaze following her. He turns and looks at me. Then looks back towards the door as it swings shut.

'How long has it been going on?' I ask.

I'll give Leonard his due, he doesn't try to deny it or make out he doesn't know what I'm talking about. He just sits in the chair. 'A long time,' he says.

'And you never thought to tell me.'

'Your mother didn't want to.'

'Why?'

He eyes me appraisingly and then speaks. 'You know why.'

I shake my head. It hurts to do that. I close my eyes instead.

I run my thoughts through my mind in some sort of order.

'He didn't take me because I wasn't his daughter,' I say finally and look at Leonard, who gives a small dip of his head in confirmation. 'He thought I was, for a long time. I mean, he stayed with Mum and they went on to have Alice. So, it wasn't until after Alice was born that he realised.'

'You should really be speaking to your mother about this.'

'She won't talk about it. So it looks like I'll have to speak to you ... as my father.' There I've said it out loud. It's as if I'm having some sort of out-of-body experience. This is such a weird scenario, but then again, the last few days and weeks have been pretty weird. Leonard looks down at his hands and, for the first time, I see a man who is unsure of himself. I've never seen this trait in him before. 'Didn't you want me? Is that why Mum stayed married to Patrick?'

'No. Don't ever think I didn't want you, Clare,' Leonard says with such force that it makes me jump. 'It was your mother who didn't want to tell him. It was complicated for both of us.' He runs his hands through his hair. 'Your mother should be telling you all this, not me.'

I do a quick maths equation in my head. 'Were you married at the time?'

'Yes. To my first wife. Well, technically married. We were on the brink of divorce.'

'This is actually freaking me out a little.'

'I can imagine.'

'No you can't. You have no idea how I feel.' I surprise myself at the snap in my voice. I'm suddenly overwhelmed with an anger I didn't see coming. 'You've always known. It's not a surprise to you. Although, surprise doesn't even begin to cover it.'

'I'm sorry, Clare. This is not how I wanted you to find out.'

'No, you didn't want me to find out at all. Neither did Mum.' I can't look at him now. 'I'd like you to leave, please.'

Leonard doesn't argue. He stops in the doorway. 'I've always looked out for you. Whatever I've done, I've always done it with your best interests at heart.'

My eyes remain fixed on the grey clouds outside. Only when he leaves, do I let the tears fall.

Chapter 25

It seems an age before Luke returns. I've been trying to take in the latest revelation. In just a matter of weeks, my world has been turned upside down and everything I thought I knew is turning out not to be so.

'I brought your phone charger as well,' says Luke, resting my bag on the end of my bed when he finally turns up.

'Thanks,' I say, grateful for his thoughtfulness. 'How's Hannah?'

'Good. I'll be taking her home soon. The doctor's done his rounds and given her the all clear.'

'Thank God for that.'

'What about you?'

'They want to keep me in for another night but, to be honest, I think I'm okay. I can't see what good one more night will do.'

'Always arguing the toss,' says Luke.

I think it's an unfair comment, but I let it go. 'I'll give Hannah a call later and speak to her. I don't really want her to see me all bandaged up like this. The nurse said they'd put a smaller dressing on my head when I go home.' I touch the bandage. 'I look like some 1940s housewife with this on.'

'Nothing wrong with a bit of 1940s housewife, seamed stockings and all that.' Luke gives a small smile and for a second I see the Luke that I knew and loved before all this … this Alice business started up.

'Luke …' I go to speak, but my voice peters out. I want him to reassure me that this is just a blip, but I change the subject instead. 'What have you said to Hannah about the accident? She does know I didn't do it on purpose, doesn't she?'

'Of course, she bloody does.' The moment has passed and Luke's face returns to its more-favoured frown of late.

'Did she say what happened? Why she and … Ma … I mean, Alice, were down at the gate.'

'She says she was looking for Alice; she'd drawn her a picture of something. Hannah saw her from the upstairs window walking down the drive, so she ran after her.'

'And then what?'

'She's not too sure, to be honest. She got upset when I tried to talk to her in too much detail. I think she must have caught up with Alice just as you came through the gates.'

'Do you think that's true? I mean, do you think she might be too scared to say what happened?'

'Clare, you're doing it again, Babe. You're looking for the angle all the time. No, I don't think she too scared. She's in shock. Witnessing something like that must have been traumatic for her.'

'I can't get the image out of my head,' I say. 'I keep seeing Alice's face, hearing the noise. And now that I know Hannah was there … what could have happened … Oh God, Luke. It doesn't bear thinking about.'

He takes my hand. 'I know, but Hannah is going to be okay. You can't torture yourself about it.' There's a small silence before he speaks again. 'The police want to speak to her.'

'No! Absolutely not.' I snatch my hand away and the tenderness between us dissolves once more. 'I don't want them frightening her.'

'Come off it, Clare. You know the routine. They won't scare her. I've already had this out with that detective anyway. Leonard is going to be there when they speak to her.'

I stiffen at this latest nugget of information. I'm not sure how I feel about Leonard being near my daughter. I refuse to entertain the thought that Leonard's status with Hannah has changed. What a can of worms this all is. Right now, I can't deal with the fact that Leonard is my father. The implications to my children are huge. I don't feel strong enough to go through it all with Luke just yet. I need to get my head around it myself first.

Luke is talking again. 'So, I expect the police will want to speak to you today.'

I shake my head. 'Leonard's managed to put them off for twenty-four hours.'

'Good old Leonard.' I detect a note of sarcasm in Luke's voice, but I ignore it. 'What is it with talking to the police? What are you scared of?'

I eye my bag at the foot of my bed and consider how much to tell Luke. 'It's not so much me,' I say, stretching for the strap of my bag. Luke passes it up. 'It's Hannah. I don't want her involved in all this. I don't want to put her in any danger.'

'In danger? What are you talking about?'

I take my phone from my bag. 'Something's going on. I know you don't believe me about Alice, but I've had some pretty damning text messages. I'll show you.' I ignore the exasperated look Luke gives me and turn my attention to my phone messages. 'That's strange. I can't find them now.' I look back through my messages again, searching for the picture of Luke and Hannah outside the house and the threats that followed. They've disappeared.

'What are you looking for?' asks Luke.

'Have you used my phone at all? Deleted anything? Messages? Photos?'

'Are you for real?'

I go to the call section, where all calls in and out are listed. I'm looking for the one where Martha rang me late the other night. Again, there are no calls from her or any showing the calls I made.

'I don't understand,' I say. 'I had a phone call and text messages warning me off and now they've just disappeared. Has anyone else had access to my phone?'

'First of all you think that Alice isn't your sister, then you think I'm shagging her, then someone's sending you messages and photos that now can't be found, so someone must have tampered with your phone. None of which you have any proof of, I might add.' He paces the room with his hands behind his head. 'You're going mad, I'm telling you.'

'I am not going mad!'

Luke spins on this heel and strides over to the bed, his jaw set hard and a vein in his temple bulges ever so slightly, the way it does when he is really mad at something. He clenches his hands and pushes them onto the mattress as he leans into me, his face inches from mine. I shrink back in the pillow. His eyes narrow and I can hear his breath streaming through his nostrils as he is clearly fighting to keep his cool. 'You need to get yourself sorted out,' he says, his words are ice-cold. 'I don't want you around the kids right now. It's not healthy for them.'

I sit bolt upright, almost head-butting Luke as I do. He doesn't flinch. 'What do you mean?'

'I'm going to take the girls away for a couple of days. Away from all this tension and your crazy ideas.'

'You can't do that!'

'I can. I'm their father and you're not in a good place, mentally, right now. I don't want to do this, but you're leaving me no choice.' He stands up and looks down at me. 'It's just for a few days.'

'No! I won't let you.' I feel panicked and desperate. I feel helpless. 'Where are you going? Have you been planning this all along – you and Alice? Were you always going to leave me? I expect her ending up in hospital has ruined your plans, hasn't it?' The words pour out of me unchecked, but the look on Luke's face stops me in my tracks and the words dry in my mouth. He looks at me for a long second and I see so much on his face in that one moment. There's anger, sadness, exasperation and contempt. He hates me, I'm sure of it.

'I'll tell you what's going to happen.' he says, sadly. 'I'm going to take the girls to my mum and dad's for a few days. You're going get your head straight and sort things out with your mum and, hopefully, your sister. You know, the one currently in intensive care.'

'Don't leave me ... please,' I sound pathetic and I hate myself for it, but I can't bear the thought of being separated from Luke and the girls like this. Memories of Alice being taken away flood back to me. 'Please don't take the girls away.'

Luke's expression softens and this time I see compassion in his eyes. 'I'm not leaving you and I'm not taking the girls away. Not the way you're thinking. I'm not your father. I'll be back in a few days, I promise, and when I am, me and you, we'll sit down and try to work out a way to salvage what's left of our marriage.'

I watch Luke leave, aware that I'm on the brink of tears yet again.

My life is crumbling away around me and only I can put a stop to it. I look down at my phone. I know I didn't imagine those messages, stressed and jet-lagged or not. Someone is conspiring against me. Someone has tampered with my phone and for once I can't blame Martha.

I tip the contents of my bag out onto the bed and check to see if anything is missing. If someone has been to the trouble of deleting messages from my phone, then they may have got rid of other evidence too.

My bed resembles the aftermath of a festival in a park as the contents litter the sheet. Shopping receipts, which were once tucked neatly into my card wallet, mostly for the food and drink I bought in America, a car-hire ticket, my coin purse, a lipstick – my favourite pink one, which reminds me of the colour Mum wears – passport, packet of tissues, the clear-plastic toiletry bag I took on board in my hand luggage, a couple of pens and a map of Amelia Island, along with my notebook. I flick through the pages and all the pages with my notes on regarding Alice have been ripped out. The lens box is also missing. The email printout with the picture of Alice and Martha is crumpled up – once neatly folded it is now looking rather tatty. None of this really matters, compared to the brown envelope of photographs, which is nowhere to be seen. The photographs Roma gave me of Alice have disappeared too.

'Shit.' I can, of course, get some more photographs from Roma, but these were printed ones and somehow felt more real than digital copies. I mustn't let myself get hung up on them, though. I need to stay focused and work out what to do next. I begin to return the items to my bag. I gather up the receipts and sort them so they are all up the same way, slipping them into the pocket of my wallet. I check my bank cards and they are all there. It's only then that I notice the edge of the page I found at Alice's house, the one with what looks like a UK mobile-phone number, tucked between my driving license and Hannah's library ticket.

I had forgotten all about it.

With a new sense of determination, I tap in the number on my phone.

The call is picked up at the other end, but no one speaks.

'Hello?' I say. 'Who am I speaking to?' I can hear their breath and my scalp prickles. I feel a rush of adrenalin coursing to my fingertips. 'It's you, isn't it?' I say, with a bravery I don't feel. 'Speak to me! Stop being a coward.'

A slow *tut, tut tut*, comes down the line, followed by some sort of derogatory snort, before the line goes dead.

'Bastard! I shout at the phone and throw it down onto the bed in frustration.

I know, without a doubt, that the person who sent those threatening text messages is the same person I have just phoned. And now I have their phone number. For a fleeting moment I feel elated because if I can trace this phone number, I'm sure it will lead to whoever is behind what has been happening. And Martha will be able to tell me who it is.

Chapter 26

I pad down the corridor in the fresh clothes that Luke had brought back to the hospital, along with my bag, earlier. Fortunately he had the foresight to bring in a loose-fitting top, which I was able to slide my plastered arm into without too much difficulty. The slouchy gym trousers he bought were pretty easy to put on too, as were the slip-on shoes. He may be cross and disappointed with me, but he was still thoughtful in his choice of clothing.

The nurse at ICU looks up and doesn't seem surprised to see me.

'I've come to see my sister.' The words stick in my throat slightly. 'Alice Kennedy.'

She smiles warmly. 'I had a call from your ward to say you were popping down.'

'How is she?'

'Improving,' says the nurse. 'She's been in and out of consciousness, but she is definitely improving and we're hopeful she can be moved from ICU soon.'

'Oh, that is good news,' I say, and I genuinely mean it. I may be able to get some answers if she's awake.

'You can't stay very long, though. We wouldn't normally encourage other patients to visit someone in ICU, but seeing as you're her sister ...'

I follow the nurse into a private room off the main corridor, which no doubt Mum arranged. The room looks very similar to mine, except there's rather more machinery and equipment here. Martha is connected up to a heart monitor, which bleeps steadily in the background. A cannula is taped to the back of her hand and a line is linked to a clear bag of fluid.

'The IV drip is just for hydration,' explains the nurse. 'And so we can administer pain relief quickly and directly. There's nothing to be scared of. They've put a special sticky plaster over the hole where Alice's lung was punctured by her ribs. She's sustained one broken rib and one cracked rib. It will be painful but it's not life-threatening now.'

'Thank you. That's good to know.'

'Okay, well, I'll leave you alone for a few minutes.'

'Oh, before you go, erm, do you know if her contact lenses were taken out?'

The nurse looks at me with a quizzical expression. 'I wasn't aware Alice had contact lenses in. Let me check the notes.' She picks up the clipboard from the end of the bed. 'It doesn't say anything here. I can't say I've noticed any when I've done routine obs, which include checking for pupil reaction to light.'

'You've checked her eyes? What colour were they?' The nurse hesitates. 'She wears coloured lenses, that's all,' I add quickly.

'Green. I'm pretty sure her eyes are green.'

'Not blue?'

'Nope. I don't think so.'

'Not bright blue. You'd remember if they were really blue, wouldn't you? You could, of course, just have a quick look now. Save you asking a colleague to find out.'

'This isn't regular procedure,' says the nurse. 'But I suppose it won't hurt if I check now.' She takes a small light from her pocket. 'You're sure she wears them?'

'Positive.'

The nurse lifts Martha's right eyelid first and then the other. I try to peer over her shoulder but I can't see properly. 'As I thought. Green. So, we're safe to say no contact lenses in. I'm sure I would have noticed them anyway.'

'Thank you, I just wanted to check. Peace of mind and all that.'

'Okay, well, like I say, just a few minutes.'

I draw the seat up next to the bed and wait for the door to close behind the nurse. I lean forward, supporting myself with my right arm. 'I know you're not Alice,' I whisper into Martha's ear. 'You need to tell me what's going on. Who is in this with you? Who am I in danger from?' Martha's eyelids flicker for a second. Has she heard me? I try again. 'Please Martha, I need to know.'

Martha's arm twitches and her head moves to one side. Her eyelids flicker once more. I say her name again, this time close to her ear. 'Martha, wake up.'

Her eyes ping open and there is a look of confusion and then one of fear on her face. She flinches from me and gives a little moan of pain as she does so. 'Go away.' She wheezes as she speaks, saliva stringing the corners of her mouth together. 'Go away.' She turns her head and closes her eyes.

'Not until I get some answers.' I grab her arm with my right hand and her eyes open. She tries to move her arm away but doesn't have the energy to fight me off. 'Who killed Alice?' I feel a sense of urgency take over me. I don't know how much time I'll have before someone comes in.

'Leave me alone,' says Martha, her speech not so slurred now.

'If you don't tell me, then I'll call the police and tell them who you really are.' It takes all my self-control not to climb up on that bed and shake the living daylights out of her until she talks, broken arm or not. 'For God's sake, Martha!' I thump the bed in frustration.

Martha looks at me with disdain. 'You're just like her.' The sneer in Martha's voice matches her expression. 'You want everything your own way. It's pitiful. Pathetic.'

'What are you talking about?'

Her breathing is more rapid and I hear the pace of the heart monitor pick up. 'Got everything you always wanted, haven't you?'

'Is this about the money?'

Martha lies perfectly still and then, taking a breath, she opens her eyes again. 'Not only have you had everything you've always wanted but you've always been loved. You have no idea what it's like to be rejected. Not to be loved. To have nothing.'

'You have no idea about what I feel or don't feel, but this isn't about me. It's about Alice.' I stand up and loom over her, our faces a mere inch apart. I grab her shoulder with my one

300

good hand, pushing her into the mattress. 'What happened? Where is Alice?'

I'm vaguely aware of the door to the room opening but I can't stop myself as I push Martha's shoulder deeper into the bed, my face now just millimetres from hers.

'Hey! What's going on?' A voice shouts from behind. Two hands pull me from Martha.

Chapter 27

Tom pushes me back into the corner of the room. 'Clare! Clare, stop.' He looks back over his shoulder at Martha, who I haven't taken my eyes from. She looks back at me and I see her acting abilities come into play. She genuinely looks frightened.

'Get her away from me,' she wheezes as she grabs the buzzer to alert the nurse. The ECG needle starts to jump erratically and alarms starting ringing. A nurse rushes in.

Tom lets go of me but holds onto my hand, to make sure I don't go anywhere.

'What happened?' demands the nurse as she tries to calm Martha, whose breathing is coming in small and fast puffs. Her eyes are bulging and she's grappling frantically at the nurse.

Another nurse hurries into the room and, with an expert eye, surveys the scene in front of her.

'Oxygen,' says the first nurse as she simultaneously offers calming words to Martha not to panic.

The medical staff busy themselves with Martha while Tom and I stand helplessly watching from the far side of the room. Tom gives me a questioning look, which I ignore.

I can't so easily ignore the small voice of revenge that is whispering in my ear. If Martha dies now that will be some sort of justice for Alice, for I'm sure something awful has happened her. It will be karma. What goes around comes around. An eye for an eye. All these clichés rush through my mind and for a few seconds I allow myself to enjoy the idea.

'Clare, you okay?' Tom's voice brings me back from my dark thoughts.

I look at him and then back at Martha. 'Yes, I'm fine.'

The nurses have placed an oxygen mask over Martha's mouth and nose. Her breathing is calming down. I don't know what they've done, given her a sedative, perhaps, to lower her heart rate. She seems to be slipping into a sleep.

The nurse looks up at me again. 'Did something happen?'

I shake my head. 'No. She was talking to me about the accident and then got upset.'

I'm not sure if the nurse believes me or not.

'Maybe we should leave now,' says Tom, taking my elbow.

'I think that's a good idea,' says the nurse, clearly unimpressed with me.

Tom guides me from the room. 'I thought for a minute we were going to lose Alice.' He takes my arm again and he walks me down the corridor. 'Come on, you need a coffee.'

We make our way to the rooftop café. It's a blustery day out there and the sky is full of battleship-grey clouds. We sit inside by the window. I'm already fed up being trapped indoors and have a craving for natural light, albeit it stormy.

'The weather doesn't look too good,' says Tom as he puts

303

an Americano down for him and a cappuccino for me. 'I think there's a storm forecast for tonight.'

We lapse into silence while we assess the weather outside and sip our coffees. It's me who speaks first. 'Tom ...'

'Mmm,' He looks up at me.

'Do you trust my judgement?'

'Your judgement? Yeah, of course.'

'You consider me to be of sound mind and all that. You know, not known for rash decisions or jumping to conclusions?'

'Reliable. Dependable. Yep.'

'Thanks for not saying "boring".'

He gives a wry smile. 'I don't think we have to worry about boring. Now, do you want to tell me what's going on?'

I pause while I choose my words. 'You know when someone commits identity theft, they find out the other person's bank details, home address and all that sort of thing?

'Yeah and usually fleece them for every penny.'

'Kind of. But what about identity theft being taken to the extreme? Where it goes further than just remotely taking on someone's financial identity. Where they actually pretend they are that person, in real life, to other people. They go about calling themselves by that assumed name, they take on their history, they even kid themselves that they are that person.'

'As you say, extreme.'

'But possible.'

'Yeah, I suppose it is. That's, of course, if the identity thief didn't come across anyone who knew the victim.'

'No, they'd have to be meeting people for the first time. People who didn't know the victim beforehand.'

Tom drums his fingers on the table and purses his lips. 'What are you trying to say?'

'That's not Alice in there. It's her friend, Martha Munroe. Tom shifts his weight in his seat. His eyes dart around the coffee shop. Anywhere but meeting my gaze. He doesn't believe me and, once again, I've made myself look a fool. 'I'm sorry, I shouldn't have said anything. Ignore me.'

'No, wait,' He looks serious and this time he doesn't avoid eye contact. 'I'm glad you did. You see, Alice told me something and I've been in a dilemma ever since about whether to say anything or not.'

'What did she say? Tell me, Tom. You know that's not Alice, don't you?'

'She came to my house the other night. I know she's not Alice.'

'And you didn't tell me?' I'm indignant that he kept this information to himself.

'She made me promise. She was frightened. She didn't know what to do. Said she'd got herself involved in something that had spiralled out of control and was way out of her depth.'

'Involved in what, exactly?'

'I don't know how to say this.'

'Just say it. Whatever it is, say it.' I brace myself. I'm sure he's going to tell me that Luke knows as well and that she and Luke have been having an affair, that Luke isn't really going to bring the girls back. 'Tell me!'

'A while ago, at work, I was doing an audit on some of the accounts. Routine stuff that we all do from time to time. In fact, I can tell you exactly when it was – it was just before Leonard went to America for that business meeting.'

'The meeting that never amounted to anything,' I say, thinking back.

'Yeah. Well, I don't know what he was doing over there, but I'm pretty sure there was no legitimate business meeting. I think he went to America for another reason.'

'To meet her – Martha?'

'It's possible. And it would make sense.'

'I'm not following you.'

'Right, just hear me out. The other week I was doing a mini audit on the internal accounts and your trust fund was one of them. It was just randomly selected and I had a look at it. I saw some irregularities. Things that didn't add up. I couldn't reconcile them with the file notes Leonard had made either.'

'What sort of irregularities?'

'Money unaccounted for.'

'But he's supposed to be overseeing all that for Mum.' If Tom had told me this yesterday, I would have laughed him out of the room, but after finding out how Leonard has deceived me so easily about Patrick Kennedy and being my father all these years, I actually find it very easy to believe he has been up to no good with the money.

'The business hasn't been doing great. You remember when we became partners we both had to put in quite a large sum of money?'

'I know, but that's normal, isn't it?'

'Leonard has been hiding the true figures from us. Honestly,

Clare, there's so much we didn't know. I have all the details at home.'

'Right, so Leonard has been taking money from the trust fund. What has this to do with that woman in there pretending to be my sister? You said she came to you because she was frightened.'

'That's right. Let's call her by her real name, Martha. She told me that Leonard had got her involved with the deception and that it was all to do with the trust fund and your mum's estate. She didn't know all the details and, to be honest, I'm not sure how it all fits together. I've been trying to find things out, on the quiet, of course, but Leonard's a crafty devil, not to mention clever.' I rub my face with my hand. This is a nightmare. I'm trying to work out what purpose would Leonard have in getting Martha to pretend to be Alice. Maybe he was going to pay her off with some of the trust fund monies? Maybe they were going to split the proceeds. If the firm is struggling or Leonard has some personal debts of his own, I mean, he has been divorced three times, who knows what he owes to who? Maybe he's just desperate for the money. Taking it from the trust fund was a safe bet. Who would know?

'We can't speak here', says Tom. He motions with his eyes towards the glances we are getting from a nearby table.

I lower my voice and lean into him. 'You have to tell the police.'

'No, not yet. We haven't got any proof. I need to know all the details and get it straight in my head before we do anything like that.'

'You say you've got evidence at home?'

'Yeah, on a memory stick.'

'Right, wait here. I'll be back in ten minutes.'

'Where are you going?'

'To get my handbag. It's in my room and then we're going to yours to work this all out. Martha's not going anywhere right now, so we have time.'

'I'll come with you. It will be quicker. Besides, I don't want you wandering around the hospital on your own with a head injury.'

We make our way back to the private ward I'm on, only slowing our pace when we get to the ward corridor, so we don't arouse suspicion. The nurse on the desk looks up and then returns to her paperwork. Once in my room, I grab my handbag and then Tom and I stroll back out again. Fortunately, the nurse's station is empty and we slip out without being noticed.

Out on the landing, Tom presses the button to call the lift. As we wait, I look out of the window and, quite by chance, notice the familiar figure of Leonard walking purposefully towards the hospital with Mum at his side.

'Shit. It's Mum and Leonard. Looks like they're heading this way.'

'We'll take the stairs,' says Tom. He grabs my hand and, checking for the exit signs, we push open the double doors that lead to the staircase.

'I can't go too fast. Every step jolts my arm.' I wince as I clomp onto the next step.

'It's okay, take your time,' says Tom, although I can hear

the urgency in his voice. It's only one flight of stairs to the ground floor and once on level ground, I can quicken my pace. Tom feeds his parking card into the machine, pays the charge and then leads me out to his car.

'What happened to your wing mirror?' I ask as I get in the passenger's side. The glass is missing and there's a big scuff on the casing.

'Caught it on the bloody barrier coming in,' he says getting in beside me. 'I was a bit preoccupied, worrying if you were okay.'

Within a few minutes, we're pulling out of the car park. I glance up at the window to my room and I see Leonard standing there, looking down at us. Tom puts his foot down and, in a flash, we are gone, yet the weight of Leonard's stare bears down on me, filling the car with menace.

'What will Luke say when he finds out you've done a runner?'

'Luke's gone to his parents. He's taken the girls with him.' I rest my head back against the seat, wondering what he told Hannah and reminding myself to call a bit later. The dark clouds look to be settling in for the night and the tops of the trees sway in the strong wind. As we head towards the sea front, the wind feels even stronger, battering the side of the car.

I pull the sun visor down and look at myself in the vanity mirror. 'Can we stop at a shop, please?'

'Sure. What do you need?'

'A clean dressing.' I pick at the tape, which is currently holding my crepe bandage turban together. Eventually, I pick enough to get a good grip between my finger and thumb and manage to prise it away. Then, rather unceremoniously, I unwind the bandage, allowing it to spool like spaghetti in my lap, until it reveals a rectangular dressing of about two by three inches. The middle of the dressing has a dark-red, dried bloodstain.

'Are you sure you should be taking that off?'

'I'll be fine.'

Tom draws the car up outside a mini convenience store and runs in to get a clean dressing for me. He returns a few minutes later with a complete first-aid kit. He shrugs. 'Better safe than sorry. I wasn't sure what you wanted.'

I smile. 'Thanks. No doubt there's something in here that will be useful.'

As we near Tom's apartment, my phone rings. 'It's Leonard,' I say, showing Tom the screen. I go to answer it, but Tom puts his hand over mine.

'Don't give him any clue as to where you are or what you know. We need to work this all out in our heads before we speak to him. You know what he's like. Before we know it, he'll have us convinced we're the insane ones.'

'Good point.' I switch the phone to silent. 'Maybe I should just text to say I'm okay, though. I don't want them to call the police or anything like that.'

'It's up to you.'

I tap out a reply to Leonard saying 'just gone out with Tom for some fresh air', with a reassurance that I'll speak to him later. 'He was going to sit with Hannah today while the police interviewed her about the accident. Maybe I should speak to him. Just in case.'

'No!' The force of Tom's voice startles me. 'Later. You can do that later.'

His eyes fix on the road ahead and I sit back in silence, aware that Tom is rather more anxious about it all than he's letting on. I can see a line of sweat prick above his upper lip. He draws the car into the underground car park and switches off the engine. I can just make out his face in the soft yellow glow from the wall light. He looks at me. 'Sorry. I didn't mean to snap. Just a bit jumpy about Leonard, that's all. Let's get inside. We can talk properly there.'

I exit the car and follow him over to the lift. I've known Tom a long time and his nerves are like steel, so to see him flustered gives me a deep sense of unease.

We enter the lift and, as I rest my hand against my shoulder bag, I feel the vibration of an incoming text message. For some reason I don't want Tom to know.

When we get upstairs to his apartment, I make my excuses to use the loo, taking my bag and the first-aid kit with me. 'I'll just put a new dressing on this cut while I'm at it,' I call back over my shoulder. I make sure I lock the door and then set about running a bowl of water. I take my phone from my bag and check the message. I'm not surprised to see it's from Leonard.

Don't trust him. Phone me. I need to tell you something important.

Chapter 28

'You okay in there?' calls Tom from the other side of the door. I almost drop my phone in panic.

'Yes. Won't be a moment!'

I delete the message and shove the phone back into my bag.

A few minutes later we're sitting in the living room and Tom is handing me a glass of wine. 'Thought you could do with something a bit stronger than a cup of tea.'

'Thanks.' I take the wine. To be honest I'm not really in a wine sort of mood, so I take a sip out of politeness and place it on the table next to me. 'Where's your laptop, then?' I ask, looking around.

'In the spare room. I'll get it all up and running in a moment.' Tom sits on the sofa next to me. 'Are you okay? I mean, really okay?'

'Yeah, sort of. It's all a bit surreal at the moment. I'm not quite sure what I am.' I give a laugh that I don't really mean. 'I can't stop thinking about the accident. It just goes round and round in my head. I keep thinking was there something I could have done to avoid it.'

'You mustn't blame yourself. You didn't do anything wrong.'

'It all happened so fast.'

'You know, I've been thinking about the accident and I hate to be the one to suggest it, but you don't think Leonard had anything to do with it, do you?'

'He wouldn't do anything to hurt Hannah,' I say. 'It was my fault for driving too fast.'

'Let's come at it from a different angle.' Tom looks at me as if there's a significance to what he's just said. I shrug, so he continues. 'What was Leonard doing there? He doesn't usually turn up at breakfast time, does he?'

'No, that's true. Mum said he had some paperwork for her to sign but I think now he might have been there to speak to me before the police did.'

'What if he had guessed you'd discovered the truth about Martha pretending to be Alice? What if he didn't want this information to get out? He might have come to the house to warn Martha. Maybe he wanted to talk to her in private and said to meet him down by the gate ...'

'Knowing that I was on my way,' I finish Tom's sentence and the thought that Leonard is possibly behind the accident makes me feel sick. 'But, how could he have timed it so well?'

'Luck, maybe. You'd already said what flight you'd be back on. It doesn't take a genius to work out timings.'

'This is all conjecture. We've no proof. I still find it hard to think he engineered it all.' I wonder if this is because I don't want to believe it. 'He wouldn't harm Hannah. No way.'

'I'm sure he wouldn't. It could be just unfortunate that Hannah was there.'

I think back to the accident that is never far from my mind, although calling it an accident doesn't seem right now. 'I'm sure Martha tried to push Hannah out of the way. If it hadn't been for her, I can't bear to think what might have happened.' I feel my leg begin to shake at the thought.

Tom rests his hand on my thigh to quell the trembling. 'Sorry, I didn't mean to upset you but I'm just thinking he's tying up loose ends. Martha could have already got rid of Alice for him.'

'She's not a bag of rubbish,' I snap, uncomfortable with the way Tom talks about Alice, as if her fate is a foregone conclusion. One that I'm not prepared to fully consider just yet.

'Sorry, I didn't mean it like that.'

'It's okay. Forget it.' I try to sound gracious. 'We need to speak to Martha again. She's the one who holds the key to everything. She can tell us exactly what happened.'

'I don't think you'll be very welcome there. Leave it with me and I'll speak to her.'

'Okay, thanks.' I take a sip of the wine, which warms and ever so slightly burns my empty stomach. I think about Tom's theory and Leonard being involved. It's hard to accept, but my rational thought process won't let me rule it out. Head over heart wins every time. Despite this, there's something nagging me at the back of my mind, something I can't quite reach and I don't know what it is.

'You know Leonard's always had an evil streak in him,' says Tom. 'He's threatened me in the past. Don't look so surprised.'

'I just feel we're talking about two different people. I know he can be harsh at times but I'd never have said evil.'

'It's different for you, he's a family friend and all that, but there's a side to him you haven't seen. Why do you think he's been divorced three times?' Tom leans forward, resting his arms on his knees. 'I've seen him in action when we went out drinking once. It wasn't long after I'd split up with Isabella and we went to that private members' club.'

'Vanilla Paradise?'

'Yeah, you know it?'

'It's the one McMillan owns and sacked that lad from, who is now claiming unfair dismissal.'

'That makes sense. Well, Leonard was a complete bastard to the staff there and got really out of hand with one of the girls who performed a private dance for him. We had to pay off the girl to stop her calling the police. I'll spare you the details, but Leonard was a complete pig.'

Somehow I feel I should be surprised or shocked, maybe both, but after the events of the past few weeks, nothing shocks me now. 'If he has had something to do with Alice's death, he needs stopping. We can't let him get away with all this. Show me the files before I drink too much wine and can't make head nor tail of it all.'

We go into the second bedroom, which is no more than a box room. I'm not even sure you'd be able to fit a single bed in it. There's just enough room for a desk and a filing cabinet. Tom switches on the laptop and takes a box from the drawer, which contains several memory sticks.

'I don't keep anything important on the hard drive itself. Too easily corrupted,' he explains. Within a few minutes he has logged in and is calling up the files. There are several folders within folders and Tom finally gets to the one he's after.

'Right, here we go. Here's a list of the transactions, the dates, description and amount and over here is a list of where I've tracked the payments to. They criss-cross numerous accounts and are disguised within other transactions, but if you follow this flow chart I made, you can see that ultimately the payment ends up in an off-shore account, which is then linked to Leonard. Have a look.'

I follow the flow chart and look through the various documents Tom has copied into the files as supporting evidence. It's like a spider's web of transactions and, to be honest, company law is not my area of speciality and after a while I lose track and have to take Tom's flow chart as gospel.

'Okay, I'm no expert on this type of law but, if you've got all the evidence to back this up, then what are we waiting for?'

'I've only just put all the pieces of the jigsaw together. I've still got to get some sort of proof that the funds end up back with Leonard. Once I've got that and spoken to Martha, then there's nothing to stop us.'

'Do you think Martha will be able to implicate Leonard? Thinking about it, she did try to warn me someone else was involved. She phoned me when I got back into the UK and I had some threatening text messages. They must have been from Leonard. Do you think you'll be able to persuade Martha to give evidence against Leonard?'

'I don't know. I suppose it depends how deeply she's involved.'

'Martha is the weak link. If we can get to her, then we've got a case.' I sit back in the chair and let out a sigh. 'At least then Mum and Luke will be able to see I wasn't imagining things where Martha was concerned.' I look at Tom. He isn't smiling. In fact, he has an almost sorrowful look on his face. 'What is it?'

'Nothing.'

'There's something you're not telling me. I know that look. What are you holding back?'

Tom shakes his head and looks down at his hands for a moment before sitting up and clicking out of the files and into another set of files marked 'pictures'.

'I didn't want to have to tell you this, but you're one of my oldest friends, you know how much I care about you.' He clicks a folder within the main folder.

'What is it?' I ask again. I have this impending feeling of distress. Tom is about to show me something that I'm going to like least – by far. I brace myself. There can only be one thing.

Tom clicks a picture icon. The screen flickers for a second and is then filled with an image of Luke and Martha in an embrace. Not just an embrace, but a full-on kiss. The picture has been taken at a distance, but there is no mistaking the subject matter. Martha with her hair pulled back in a ponytail, a pink T-shirt, which I have half a suspicion is one of mine, and a pair of jeans. Luke is wearing his surf T-shirt and a pair of jeans. They are on Brighton seafront, the pier in the distance and pebble beach immediately behind them.

'Where did you get this?' I demand, the anger rolling inside me, building up higher and higher. The pressure so tight, I think my chest might burst.

'I took it,' says Tom. 'I followed her for a few days – after you first told me you were suspicious of her. I thought I'd be able to put your mind at rest. But turns out ...' He nods towards the screen.

'I can't believe it. After everything that's happened. Luke was making me feel like I was the jealous one, like I had some sort of problem and was overreacting.' I look at the picture again. I want to smash the screen with my fist. I jump up from the chair and march out to the living room, searching for my handbag, where my phone is.

Tom follows me and before I have a chance to call Luke, he takes the phone from my hand. 'Not now. Leave it for a while. You're angry and upset.'

'Too fucking right I am!'

'Which is exactly why you shouldn't confront him now. Come and sit down. Have some more wine.' Tom coaxes me over to the sofa and places my glass in my hand. 'I'm sorry you had to find out like this, but I thought it was best coming from me.'

I nod and shake my head at the same time, trying to dismiss the image of Luke and Martha kissing. How could he do this to me? 'Oh, God, Tom, what an awful mess everything is,' I say at last. My shoulders sag as the energy seeps out of me. 'I'm tired of all this. I don't know how much more I can take.'

Tom puts his arm around me, careful not to squash my plastered arm. 'It's okay. I'm here for you. Always have been. Always will be.' I rest my head on his shoulder. Even my neck seems to have lost the ability to hold my head up. 'That's it, just relax.'

We stay like that for several minutes as I take comfort in the warmth of his arms. 'You're a good friend,' I mumble into his jumper.

'Have you ever wondered about us?' he says. 'What would have happened between us if you hadn't called it off?'

'Oh, Tom. Let's not go there,' I say softly. 'Too much water under the bridge since then.'

'But have you never wondered?'

I sit up. 'Not for a long time,' I say.

Tom nods thoughtfully. After a moment, he leans forwards and picks up the wine bottle. 'Ah, empty!' He stands up. 'I'll go grab us another from the off-license across the road. Won't be a minute.'

'No, it's okay, Tom. I shouldn't really. I ought to go back. It was silly of me to run away like that. I need to face up to everything. I've got the police interviewing me tomorrow.'

But he isn't listening and is out the door before I've even finished speaking. I pick up my glass and loll back into the sofa, momentarily forgetting about my bad arm. It jars and I jump with the sharpness of the pain, in the process spilling red wine down my top. 'Oh, for goodness sake.'

I go into the kitchen and sponge the stain out as much as I can, resigning myself to the fact that the top is probably ruined. As I leave the kitchen, the screen saver of the laptop in the second bedroom catches my eye, as an image of James Bond marches across the screen and turns to fire his gun. I smile to myself. Typical Tom. He loves his computers and is such a geek at times. I'm sure he'd have made a great spy.

I wander into the room and tap the screen to have another look at the figures and spreadsheets Tom showed me earlier. It's a hollow gesture as I know I still won't be able to make any more sense of them. My head feels a bit fuzzy and I stumble slightly, my thigh knocking the chair, which, in turn, spins around and the arm catches the box of memory sticks. It falls to the floor, spilling the contents across the carpet.

'Bugger!' I kneel and collect them up. As I pick the last one up, the sticky label on the side catches my eye.

Martha Phone Call 0.2

I look at the others and they are labelled with Photos 0.1, 0.2 and 0.3. Work files A-L, Work files M-Z, Personal 0.1, 0.2.

I drop all of them into the box, except for the one marked with Martha's name.

With a shaking hand, I slide the memory stick into the free USB.

I feel sick and I'm not sure if this is from nerves or from the wine.

The laptop gives a whir and the icon for disc drive F pops up. I click on it.

Surprisingly, there's only one file. It's an audio clip, which I recognise from the recorded telephone conversations I have on file at work. I press 'play' as the dizziness strikes me again and I have to sit down.

The first voice is Tom's.

'What the fuck do you think you're doing?'

The next voice is unmistakable. It's Martha.

'Oh, that's a nice way to greet someone.'

'Fuck the niceties, Martha. When I told you to alienate Clare from everyone, I didn't mean to push that fucking kid of Pippa's over. She's got a broken arm, thanks to you.'

'Granted, the broken arm wasn't part of the plan, but really, Tom, you should actually be thanking me because now that bitch Pippa is so pissed at Clare she won't speak to her.'

'That's as maybe, but ease up on the kids.'

'Okay. Is that it?'

'No. Are you okay to stay on the phone for a bit longer?'

'A little while. Marion's gone to one of her coffee mornings but is due back soon. I managed to wriggle out of it, claiming I have a migraine.'

'Where's Luke?'

'In his studio. I'm out in the garden.'

'How are you getting on with him?'

'Luke? He's a nice guy.'

'I need you to do me a favour,' Tom says.

There's a hesitation before Martha answers and her voice is guarded. 'Which is?'

'Get a bit closer to Luke. Make a few waves for him and Clare.'

'I thought that's what I was doing.'

'You need to do more. Clare's got her suspicions about you and the last thing we need is for everyone to start listening to her.' There's an impatience in Tom's voice and a coldness he usually reserves for his ex-wife.

'If I'm her ally, though, then she's more likely to believe me.'

'Leave Clare to me.'

321

Martha gives a laugh. 'Oh, I get it. You want Clare to turn to you. Now, I know you and Clare have history, but I thought that was all puppy love.'

'It's unfinished business and business that doesn't concern you.'

'If you want me to up my game, then I suggest you up your payment.' The laughter has gone from Martha's voice now and is replaced with a steely edge.

'Don't play hardball with me,' says Tom. 'Remember, I know what you did. All it will take is one call to the police in America and it's game over for you.'

'Well, that's where you're wrong,' replies Martha. 'I'm pretty sure the authorities would be interested to learn that you have been swindling money from the trust fund yourself. I think that's called embezzlement.'

'It's not fucking murder, though.'

I give a sharp intake of breath, sitting up in my seat. *Murder? My fears are confirmed.* I miss the next couple of exchanges while I take in what I've just heard. Aware that Tom could be back any minute I force myself back to the recording and take the mouse to slide the cursor back a few seconds and listen to that part of the conversation again.

'It's not fucking murder, though.'

'It was an accident!' Martha's voice is indignant but angry too.

Me, I feel numb. I'm trying hard to take in what is being said. My own head is throbbing and the nauseous feeling won't go away. Tom is talking again and I make another effort to focus.

'You pushed her. She hit her head. Fatally. You didn't call the emergency services.' Tom emphasises each point, as I've seen him do so many times in the courtroom. I imagine him strolling back and forth in front of the witness box, marking each point off on his fingers. 'You hid the body. You went home to bed. Even when you woke the next morning, you did nothing.'

'Shut up! Just shut up!' Martha hisses.

'At worst, this could be premeditated murder, at best manslaughter,' Tom continues, ignoring her. 'Then there's concealing a crime and/or evidence, withholding evidence, perverting the course of justice ... do I need to go on?'

'If I go down, so do you.'

'You'll go down for life, I, on the other hand, could be out in a few years. I might even get a suspended sentence. My life will go on. Yours, well, that's not looking so good.'

'You're bluffing.'

'I can assure you, I'm not. I even know where to tell the authorities to look for the body. The woods near the bridge to Talbot Island. It won't take them long to find her.' Tom has an air of confidence about him. 'Ever heard the expression 'loose lips sink ships'? Well, I have this whole conversation recorded. And our previous one.'

'Bastard.'

'I've been called worse.'

There's an uneasy silence between the two and I can hear Martha's breathing deepen as she fights to control it. Not unlike what I'm doing myself right now. She speaks again after a few seconds.

'So, you want me to make trouble between Clare and Luke? Is that it?'

'Yeah, that's it.'

'What if he's not interested?'

'A good-looking girl like you? I'm sure you can turn Luke's head.'

'Why do I get the impression this is not necessarily because you care about Clare?'

'You're very perceptive,' says Tom. 'I must congratulate you. Put it this way, love and hate are very close friends. If this little part of the plan doesn't work out, then it's okay, I have a Plan B.'

'You're one sick bastard.'

'I just like winning.'

'I've gotta go. Marion's car has just pulled up on the drive.'

'Don't let me down, Martha, and if you do really well I might actually give you that pay rise after all.'

I hear the line go dead, but Tom hasn't cancelled the recording yet as I hear him mutter to himself. 'Silly fucking bitch.' Then the recording ends.

I hold my head in my hand. I can hardly believe what I've just heard. If anyone was to give me all this information, then I would say that they were completely crazy. That I trust Tom implicitly. That I've been friends with him for years and he would never betray me.

The sound of a car horn tooting and the engine revving somewhere out on the street knocks me from my thoughts and I suddenly think of Tom. He'll be back any minute now.

My heart is racing as I snatch the memory stick from the

USB port. I go to put it in the box with the others, but change my mind. This is evidence. I shove it into the pocket of my trousers. Then I remember Tom saying that he had recorded his previous conversation with Martha. There was only one recording on this memory stick, which means there must be another. I search the box, but I can't see one annotated in the same way.

The sound of the front door opening and Tom whistling as he comes in causes me to nearly drop the bloody box again. I shove it back on the side and hurriedly stand up.

'Clare! You okay? I've got the wine!'

I dart out of the small bedroom and into the bathroom next door, my shaking hand only just managing to slide the lock across.

His voice is getting closer. He's come through the living room and into the hallway.

'Just a minute,' I call as I flush the chain for effect and, looking in the mirror check I don't look too flustered, I take a deep, steadying breath as I push down on the handle and pull the door open. I fix a smile. 'Just needed the loo,' I say, aware there's a small tremor in my voice.

'Thought you'd done a runner,' he says with a wink and then waves two bottles of red wine he's holding in each hand. 'Buy one, get one free. It would have been rude not to.'

'Naturally,' I say, as I follow him back to the living room.

'Where's your glass?' says Tom as he opens the first bottle.

It's then I remember that I've left it in the small bedroom when I was listening to the recording. 'Erm ... Oh, err, the bedroom,' I say, aware that I'm stumbling over my words. 'I had it in my hand when I went to use the bathroom. I just shoved it on the desk on my way through.' I stand. 'I'll get it.'

'No, it's okay. Sit there. I'll get it,' insists Tom.

He returns a few seconds later with two wine glasses hooked between his fingers. 'New bottle, new glass, I always say.'

I don't actually remember Tom ever saying that, but I don't argue as I watch him set the glasses down and open the wine. 'Just a small glass for me,' I say. 'I shouldn't really be drinking.'

Despite this, Tom pours a full glass and hands it to me. 'Did you have another look at those files?' His question catches me by surprise. He doesn't look up as he pours himself a glass.

'I thought about it, but decided I really wouldn't understand them. You're the numbers man, not me.' I'm aware of an undercurrent passing between us, one that wasn't there before. I take a small sip of wine as we both pretend everything is normal. All I want to do is get out of here.

'Cheers,' says Tom, raising his glass.

'Cheers,' I respond with a faux smile.

Tom tugs his tie loose and unbuttons his collar. 'Think I'll get out of this shirt and tie.' He comes back into the room a few minutes later wearing a grey T-shirt. I can smell the fresh dash of aftershave he's applied. 'There, that's better. You not drinking your wine?'

'No. My head's hurting a bit, actually.'

'Come on, it will do you good.' He slides the glass I had abandoned on the table towards me.

'No, really, I'm fine.'

And then, out of nowhere, I remember what was bugging me earlier when Tom spoke about the accident. It seemed irrelevant at the time, so much so I must have totally forgotten about it. The thought has finally filtered through and popped to the fore of my brain with the force of an uppercut from a heavyweight boxer. It literally throws me off balance and I close my eyes for a second as I feel my body sway to the left and then back to the centre.

'You okay?' asks Tom. 'You look like you've seen a ghost.'

Chapter 29

'You were at the accident, weren't you?'

Tom places his glass on the table. 'What makes you say that?' His voice is low and I sense a menace in the air.

'I saw your car parked up in the lane. I'd forgotten all about it, what with everything else. It's been bugging me that I was missing something important and then it came to me, just now. Like when you're trying to think of someone's name and it's on the tip of your tongue, but you can't for the life of you get it. And then you can be lying in bed that night or in the supermarket a few days later and, out of nowhere, it pops into your mind.' I pause and look at Tom. 'That's what's just popped into my mind. I smashed your wing mirror as I went by. Your car was there. But you've never said. You've been keeping that a secret. Why would you do that?' The sarcasm is creeping into my voice, mixing with the anger that is surfacing.

'Clare, stop. You don't know what you're saying.' It's a warning, not borne out of concern for me, but of fear for himself.

I ignore him. 'The only reason you didn't want anyone to know you were there would be because you have something to hide.' I go to stand up, but my legs are wobbly and I almost stumble. 'That party we had at the house, when we thought we were welcoming Alice home. You and her were in the garden together. You knew then, didn't you? You knew she was Martha. What were you talking about?'

'Sit down, you've had too much to drink.'

The second attempt sees me standing, but my head is swimming. 'What did you put in my drink?'

'Why would I put anything in your drink?'

My legs are not co-operating with my brain but I make it to the kitchen. I grab a cup from the tree mug and switch on the cold tap so hard that the water bounces back up from the sink and sprays across the work surface; I somehow manage to fill the cup. I fling open the cupboard doors until I find the one with the food in. My one good hand fumbles with the tins and packets, knocking them over. A tin of beans hits the worktop. Finally, I find what I'm looking for. Grabbing the salt pot, I flick the lid and pour it straight into the glass of water. I need to make myself sick. Whatever I've ingested needs to come out – and quick.

I raise the cup to my mouth, but it's taken from me. 'You don't need that,' says Tom, tipping the contents down the sink. 'It doesn't have to be like this, you know.'

'What are you talking about?' I hold onto the worktop to steady myself.

'We could make a good team together,' he says. 'You must know how I feel about you.'

I frown. 'We're friends, Tom. Old friends. Friends since we were at school together.'

'We've been more than friends, though, and we can again.'

I shake my head. 'That was at university. It was nothing serious. We both know that. We've always said so.'

Tom slams the cup down so hard on the work surface that the handle comes off in his hand. He chucks it into the sink. 'You said so. I didn't.'

'But, Tom, we went on and fell in love with different people. You married Isabella and I married Luke. We, me and you, we just had a student fling.' I rub my face with my hand. Everything is totally fucked up.

'Every time I saw you two together, you looked more and more in love. And it just reminded me how much *not* in love I was with Isabella.'

'What are you hoping to achieve by all this?'

'Do you have any idea how much maintenance I have to pay Isabella? I have to pay for that bloody great big house she lives in. Can't be a modest two-up two-down, can it? No, it has to be a big fuck-off house in the most expensive part of Brighton. And then there's all the things she needs for Lottie: the private riding lessons, the one-to-one swimming lessons, stage school on a Saturday, French lessons with a private tutor. I could go on and on. And on top of that, I have to live myself, pay for this place, my car, my own lifestyle.'

'I don't understand. What has any of this got to do with me?'

'Luke's cheated on you with Martha. I showed you the evidence. Leave him and we can be together.'

I laugh. 'It doesn't work like that. It's not quite that simple. What about Martha? And Alice?'

'What about them?'

I look into Tom's eyes and all I see is a blank space. He's totally removed from his actions. He has no sense of empathy for what's happened to me.

And that is the thing that frightens me the most. I need to get out of here. I don't trust Tom and what he's capable of. My eyes give me away as I glance at the door. Tom doesn't miss this and blocks my exit route. I don't wait to find out what he's going to do next. I grab a tin of beans that had fallen out of the cupboard earlier and with all the strength I can muster, I smash it into the side of his head.

He looks at me. Unmoving. A trickle of blood comes out of his nose. He raises his fingers to his lip, dabbing at the blood, before inspecting his red-stained fingers. I'm trapped against the worktop. I'm not sure if Tom is swaying or if I am. And then he falls to the floor. I let out a cry and then there's a silence in the room.

Dear God, I think I've killed him.

The need to get as far away from him as possible is almost overwhelming but I know my body is beginning to shut down. Whatever Tom put in my drink is taking its toll. I grab the broken cup and once again fill it with water and salt. I force myself to drink it. To gulp it down. It's disgusting and my throat wants to close, to spit it back out, but I refuse to give in. And then, my stomach convulses and I'm throwing up. It looks like blood as the red-wine vomit splatters the sink. I repeat the process with some more water and salt and my stomach burns as I throw up for a second time.

I remember being told when the girls were little that if

they were ever to ingest any bleach or something like that, to give them milk to line their stomach and stop it being absorbed into the bloodstream. I have no idea if this is right or not, but I snatch open the fridge and grab a plastic bottle of green-top milk from the door. I gulp down as much of the milk as I can, not wanting to cause myself to throw up any more.

I step over Tom and, as I do so, he groans and puts out his hand. I scream as his fingertips touch my ankle and I stumble out into the hallway. I look back through the doorway and Tom is pulling himself up onto all fours. He lifts his head and our eyes lock. For a moment, I'm static. Unable to think. Unable to move.

He shakes his head, like a dog who has got hold of a toy in its jaws, and putting one hand up on the breakfast-bar stool, hauls himself to his feet. He rubs the side of his head. 'That wasn't a very nice thing to do,' he says.

The sound of his voice snaps me out of the trance I'm in. My survival instinct kicks in and I'm racing down the hallway, through the living room and out onto the landing before I can even think straight. I hammer at the button to call the lift, but looking up at the numbers I can see that the lift is on the ground floor.

'Clare! Wait!' Tom is out on the landing, his hand to his head, his other holding onto the doorframe. 'Don't go. We need to talk. We can sort this out.'

'No, Tom, it's too late.' I'm too scared to cry but I know my heart is breaking inside. I turn and push open the door to the emergency exit. Momentum carries me through and I'm on a small metal fire escape on the outside of the building.

My body crashes into the rail, tipping me forwards. I scream. I think I'm going to fall, but I manage to hold on tight to the rail with my one good hand. I push myself back to safety.

Rain is lashing at my face, made stronger by the fierce wind of the storm. My hand skims across the water that is sitting on the handrails as I thunder down the steps, the fresh air bringing a new sense of awareness to me. My feet work fast as I try to put as much distance as I can between myself and Tom. I'm on the second floor when I hear the crash of the fire-escape door above me. I hear Tom call my name, but the words are whipped away by the wind and then I feel the vibration of his feet on the rungs and the dull thud of his steps as he too belts down the staircase.

I reach the path below and for a moment I'm not sure which way to go. I'm in an alleyway at the rear of the property. I've lost my sense of direction. To my left is blackness, to my right the glow of the street lighting calls me. I'm running down the alleyway, trying to keep my plastered arm as close to my body as possible to avoid jolting it so much. The pain is shooting up my forearm and through my shoulder, but I ignore it. All I can think about is getting away.

As I reach the end of the alleyway and burst out onto the street, I don't wait to look behind me. The street is empty, the storm keeping everyone inside where it's dry and safe. I don't think I'm going to be able to outrun Tom. He's a fitness fanatic and running is his thing. I need to hide from him. I run to the end of the street, pausing for only a second to look behind me. The dark, shadowy figure of Tom looms after me.

I can see the seafront ahead and I charge that way. My

hair slashes at my face where it has come loose from the ponytail and the strength of the wind coming in off the sea almost knocks me off my feet. I hurtle along the path, my foot slipping on a wet drain cover, which almost has me tumbling down into the gutter. A car blasts its horn as it drives past.

I wave my arm frantically. 'Stop! Stop!' It carries on, the red tail-lights disappearing out of sight.

And then I feel a hand clamp down on my shoulder. I spin away. The pain shooting through my broken arm makes me scream. I hurtle across the road, not looking to see if anything is coming. Another blast of a car horn and the screech of tyres, but somehow I find myself on the other side of the road and running down the promenade.

The bright lights of the pier lie before me. If I can get there, surely someone will help me. I keep running, cradling my broken arm in the other. I can feel my pace slowing as I become more and more tired. The pier looms bigger and brighter; it's my beacon of hope. Somehow I reach it and I burst through one of the entrance archways and out onto the boardwalk.

The place is deserted. I'm not sure of the time, but it's dark and I guess some of the attractions have closed for the night. The fairground rides at the end of the pier are still open, though. I can see the lights and hear the music.

I'm about halfway before I hear running footsteps behind me. I turn and Tom is just a few metres away, determination etched on his face. I look around frantically for someone, but there is no one. I can hear myself crying as I know I'm not going to get away – and then he has me. His hand claws at my arm. I scream with pain and he bundles me into the white lattice railings of the pier.

'Get off of me!' I yell. I try to fight him off but he's too strong. 'Oh, God, Tom. Stop, please.' I'm resorting to begging. I just want this whole nightmare to end. I feel the energy seep away from me and Tom lets go of my arm.

'You should never have gone poking around,' says Tom. 'I don't want to hurt you, Clare, and there is still a way out of this.'

'If it was money you wanted why didn't you just ask? I could have helped you.'

'And what a lovely gesture that would have been. Clare Tennison giving not only her husband handouts but her ex-boyfriend too.' Tom is almost snarling. 'I do have some pride, you know.' His rapid mood swings frighten me.

'So you and Martha hatched a plan to get the trust fund money and split it between you?'

'You're quite good at all this, but then that's why you're such a good solicitor.' He takes a step closer.

'How did you know she was Martha and not Alice?'

'At the party. I'd gone up to use the bathroom because someone was in the downstairs toilet and her bedroom door was open. She was on her hands and knees looking for something. I thought it was an earring. I went to help her, but she was really quite rude, demanding I leave,' says Tom. 'She wouldn't look at me and then I saw the contact lens box. She made the mistake of looking up at the box and then at me. I saw it straight away.'

'Her eyes?'

'Yeah. Well, one of them. She'd lost a contact lens and was

trying to find it. When she looked up, she had one blue eye and one green eye. It was game over for her.'

'And that's what you two were talking about in the garden later?'

'That's right. She took a bit of persuading but she had no choice,' says Tom. He smiles at me. 'What do you think happened next?'

Jesus, he's loving this. He has that smug little look on his face, the one he always has when he thinks he's been particularly clever.

'I don't know. I'm not as smart as you,' I say, going for the flattery angle.

Tom sighs and looks up to the dark sky in an exaggerated look of despair. 'I had things I needed to repay. Not just the financial kind. I needed to repay you.'

'Me?'

'For our Oxford days. For loving Luke. For having the life with him that I wanted to have with you.'

'I had no idea you felt like this,' I say, genuinely shocked by the intensity of his words and emotions.

'Of course you didn't, you never fucking asked. I tried to tell you, but you always rejected me and made me feel this small.' He holds up his finger and thumb millimetres apart. 'Even tonight, when you have no one to turn to, you still turn away from me.'

He rests his hands on the railings and looks out over the water. 'Course, this could all come down to Leonard. He has, after all, been cooking the books of the trust fund and creaming money out of it for his own needs.'

'But it's not Leonard, is it?' I feel such a fool to have been taken in for a while with all the crap Tom told me. 'Those files, they're such fiction. You've made them all up. You knew I wouldn't be able to understand them just at a glance like that. You knew I'd take your word for it.'

'I'll be honest with you, Clare. You and the money were two separate issues, which happened to dovetail quite nicely in the end.'

'And you really think I want anything to do with you after all this? You can't get away with it.'

'I'll give it a damn good try. Like I said, I have it pretty much covered.' He pushes himself up from the side rail and takes a step closer to me.

'Leave me alone.'

'It can be good between us. You do know that, don't you?'

'Over my dead body.'

'Tut, tut, you really shouldn't say things like that.'

I go to walk away, to call his bluff, but he grabs me, pinching my broken arm at the top, which makes me squeal in pain. 'You're hurting me.'

'Not as much as you've hurt me.' He releases his grip a fraction. 'Why you stay with Luke, I don't know. He's a free-loader. Sponging off you while he ponces around painting fucking pictures. What sort of job is that? You deserve better than him. He can't be trusted. I showed you that photo of him and Martha. What more do I have to do?'

'I don't care. I love him. I don't love you.' And it's true. Whatever has happened between Luke and Martha pales into insignificance after everything else that has happened. I love my husband and we're strong enough to sort things out. I won't let my family be broken, not without putting up a fight.

'How can you say that? He's treated you like shit recently.'

'He's my husband. He's the father of my children. I love him.'

Tom throws his head back and lets out a wild laugh, which catches on the wind and bounces off the kiosks and windbreaks behind us. Tom eventually quells his laughter and looks at me. The smile on his face has no warmth to it. 'He's the father of your children and that makes what he's done all right?'

'Yes. Yes, it does,' I say defiantly.

'Oh dear, Clare, it looks like it's going to have to be Plan B,' says Tom. He cocks his head to one side and looks at me with pity. 'Remember that day, not long after we had graduated and I came over to see you. Your mum told me you were upset about not being able to find Alice?'

I think back. 'Vaguely.'

'We went to The Crow's Nest for a drink?'

I do remember it now. I'd had quite a lot to drink, as it happened. It had taken me a couple of days to get over it. I think I'd almost given myself alcohol poisoning. Mum had been furious that I'd got myself into such a state. Later that week, when it was Nadine's birthday, I had still felt hungover and we'd gone to the pub with a load of other friends and that was the night I bumped into Luke. It was the first time I'd seen him in years. I wasn't drinking that night and Luke was the designated driver with his mates, so we spent the night chatting and consoling each other about having to be sober with a load of drunk friends.

'Yes, I remember,' I say to Tom.

'And you know that dream we always joke about, the one where you were in a *Playboy* photoshoot?'

I can feel the world around me grinding to a halt. The lights dim and the music of the funfair all but disappears. 'Yes,' I say.

Tom takes his phone from his pocket and taps at the screen. A picture appears and he turns it so I can see it properly.

Chapter 30

I gasp at what I see on the phone. I try to snatch it from Tom's hand, but he pulls it away too quickly. Over Tom's shoulder I see a figure hurrying along the boardwalk towards us. I can't see clearly who it is, but it looks familiar. I think it's Leonard. I can't let Leonard see what Tom has on his phone.

Tom is distracted and turns to see what I'm looking at. I seize the moment. In one fluid movement I take a step closer to him and knee him right in the balls. He yells in pain, doubles up, clutching his groin. I grab his mobile with my one good hand and wrestle it from his grasp. I stagger back and shove the phone into my trouser pocket.

Tom isn't deterred by my attack and, fuelled by what's at stake, he lunges for me, pushing me against the iron bar. The bar is pressing against my spine and the weight of Tom's body against me is making it hard to breathe. I try to lift my knee to once again make contact with his groin, but I can't. Tom pushes harder against me and I feel my feet losing contact with the ground.

He's shouting at me to give him the phone. He's holding

my right arm with one hand, while using his other to try to find which pocket I've put the phone in. As his weight transfers slightly to the right, I try to squirm away to the left, but he forces me back. My feet come completely off the ground and I tip even further backwards. I can hear running feet and Leonard shouting. Shards of rain pummel my face and I feel myself slipping. The centre of gravity shifts and the night sky above me slides away.

Tom is still on top of me as I feel my body roll over the railing. I can see the dark water below, the white tips of the waves crashing over and roaring as they slam into the rushing water beneath. It takes forever to fall. At some point I lose contact with Tom. His hand slips from my wrist.

At first I think I've missed the water completely and hit the shoreline, such is the force and pressure against me. But then I carry on falling, but slower this time, as water rushes up my nose and into my ears. I keep my mouth closed. It's silent under the water. I can feel myself being dragged down. It's a high tide; the water is deeper than normal. It's quiet and peaceful and I want to stay here. Away from all the madness in the world above me. Down here no one can harm me.

An image of Luke and the girls flashes before me and in that instant I know I must survive. I can't give myself up to the English Channel like this. I start to kick my legs wildly and draw myself up with my one good arm. The plaster cast hinders my progress. I can't make out which way I'm supposed to go. Which way is up? I squint open my eyes and am surprised by how much I can see in front of me. It's not as dark and black as I imagined. My instinct is to look up and

I can see the lights of the pier shimmering way above me. They look like little fairy lights on a Christmas tree.

I push upwards. My lungs are burning and my body wants me to take a breath. My mind knows I can't. Not here, not in all this water. Just a few more meters. The urge to breathe is overwhelming me. My lungs are on fire. I'm nearly there.

I burst out of the water and gasp frantically for air, only to be pounded by a breaking wave, which takes me back under. I fight my way back to the surface. I'm more prepared for the next wave and manage to hold my breath. I can hear shouting from above and then a splash. I look beyond the crest of the next wave and I see something floating in the water. It's a lifebelt. I make clumsy overarm movements with my right arm. My left arm is heavy, the plaster sodden with water. Another wave breaks and this time taking me with it. I'm dragged towards the life ring and with the tips of my fingers managed to grasp the rope. I pull it towards me. I'm so out of breath. I'm panting, trying to take oxygen on board, refilling my lungs. I can't get the life ring over my head. My plastered arm is getting in the way. I cling onto it and feel the tide take me closer to shore. If I can hold on, someone will rescue me. I just need to hold on. Just a bit longer.

I can feel myself slipping. My eyes are heavy and my arm is so tired. In fact, my whole body and mind are tired and cold. The deep water below beckons me. I could just float away, back into the depths, where it's quiet and calm. I remind myself of all the reasons to stay alive and my body fights back again.

With each wave that tosses me forwards, the shoreline gets

closer and closer. And then there are figures wading into the water. I hear the splashing and sloshing of the legs as they try to get to me as quickly as possible. I reach down with my feet and I can just about touch the bottom. I'm safe. I'm not going to die.

Two pairs of arms drag me to the shore. Blue lights pulsate up above on the seafront. The uniformed officers drag me onto the beach. One speaks rapidly into his radio, calling for assistance, summoning an ambulance. The other sits me on the shingles, grabs the jacket he must have discarded before wading in, and wraps it around my shoulders.

'You all right, love? What happened?' I look up at the pier. My body is shaking violently from the cold and shock. 'You came over the side, did you? Was there anyone else with you?'

Was there anyone else with me? I look out to sea, scanning the waves as they crash onto the beach. I look back and I see Leonard careering down the stones towards me.

'Clare! Jesus Christ. Are you okay?'

'Do you know this lady, sir?'

'Yes.' Leonard arrives and sits down next to me, putting his arms around me. 'She's my daughter.'

I look up at Leonard but don't say anything. It seems odd him saying 'daughter', but I let it go. I can deal with it later.

'Were you with her when she fell? Is there anyone else in the water?' asks the police officer.

'I was on the pier but further away. I didn't see what happened. One minute she was there. The next, she was gone. I threw the life ring in.'

'What's your name?' the police officer asks me.

'Clare Tennison.'

'Okay, Clare, this is very important. Was there anyone with you? Did anyone else go into the water?'

I look from the police officer to Leonard and back again. Tom can't swim. I should be telling them that he's out there. Drowning. If I tell them and they rescue him, he could ruin everything. If I don't tell them, then all his secrets go to the seabed with him. Can I do that? Can I let another human drown?

'She was on her own,' says Leonard before I can speak.

'Okay, you're certain?'

'Yes. Absolutely.'

'No!' I cry out. 'No. I wasn't alone. Tom is in the water. He can't swim.'

The police officer has a right to look surprised. 'I thought you said she was alone.'

'I didn't see anyone else,' says Leonard.

The police officer calls to his colleague and together they wade into the water, their torch beams scanning the waves. One speaks urgently into his radio. I can't hear what they're saying.

'Tom can't swim,' I repeat looking at the officers.

'Probably a good thing,' says Leonard.

They break the news to me the next morning. Tom's body was recovered from the water at first light. The weather conditions were too poor the night before to carry out a full search-and-rescue operation. They tell me he probably drowned within the first few minutes of entering the water.

I cry for Tom. My friend of many years. I cry for the years we spent together and the good times we had. How we made it through university together and then worked together. He was one of my best friends. I don't cry for the Tom who deceived me. The Tom who has stolen money from the trust fund and the Tom who tried to blame Leonard.

'I've had my suspicions about him for a while now,' says Leonard, as he sits beside me in my hospital room. I've been taken back to the same room. Luke is on his way back from his parents with the girls, although I've asked him not to bring them to the hospital.

'Why didn't you do anything if you thought he was up to something?' I ask. 'Maybe it didn't have to get to this point.'

'Proof. I couldn't prove anything. You know Tom's a whiz on the old computer. He has set it all up to look like I'm the one who's crooked. After everything I've done for that boy. I never thought he'd turn on me like that.'

'He must have had his reasons.'

'Gambling debts, a messy divorce, maintenance payments. All the classic things.'

'I wish he'd come to me and told me. I would have helped him. I would have given him the bloody money. He didn't need to steal it.'

'Trouble with Tom, he thought he was far too clever to get caught,' says Leonard.

'He needed help. Not just the financial kind.'

'Clare, there's something I want to ask you.'

I have a good idea what it is and I suppose I owe it to Leonard to tell the truth, but I also have a loyalty to Luke.

No one needs to know what happened between Tom and me on the pier last night. I change the subject quickly. 'I hope Luke gets here soon. He left a message with the nurse to say he was dropping the girls off with Pippa and then coming straight over. I don't want the girls to see me in hospital. I want to see them at home tonight. If they ever let me out of this bloody place. What about Mum? Hadn't you better get back to her?'

'Her friend from the WI is with her. The doctor came and gave your mum a sedative.'

'I should be there with her. If it wasn't for the bloody police coming to interview me, I'd go home but I don't want them turning up at the house, not with everything that's gone on. It will be too much for Mum.'

'Are you sure you don't want me to stay for the police interview?' says Leonard. 'They've got rather a lot to talk to you about.'

'I'll be fine. It's Martha they should be talking to. Is she still not saying anything?'

Leonard shakes his head. 'She won't say a word. Even when I told her Tom was dead. She just turned away and looked at the wall.'

'What's going to happen to her now?'

'It will need to be dealt with in America. She's not actually committed any crime here, apart from entering the country on false documentation. So, I assume, deported back to the USA, where she'll be arrested for the murder of Alice and then she'll face a trial. The conversation you found on the memory stick in Tom's apartment will be a crucial piece of evidence.'

'They still have the death penalty in Florida,' I say, picking at the edge of my new plaster cast.

'If she gets herself a good defence attorney, I suspect they'll enter a plea of manslaughter. I don't think she'll face the death penalty for that.'

'Despite what she's done, I don't wish that on her,' I say, looking up at Leonard. 'All I want is to find where Martha buried Alice.'

For the first time I allow myself to cry as an overwhelming sense of loss engulfs me. I accept the comforting embrace of Leonard and sob quietly into his shoulder. I'm conscious that this small act is the start of a new connection between myself and Leonard but I can't think about the future yet, not when I still have so much of the past the contend with.

Leonard has only been gone for about twenty minutes before the police and Luke turn up, practically at the same time.

'Hi,' says Luke. 'I met these in the corridor. Sorry, it's not the customary bunch of flowers husbands are supposed to bring their wives.'

My heart does a little flip of joy. In that one sentence, I know that Luke and I are going to be all right. I smile at him. 'Don't worry, all is forgiven.'

He offers a smile in return and comes over to me, kissing the top of my head and perching on the bed next to me. He picks up my hand in his and turns to the police officer. 'What did you want to speak to my wife about?'

'A couple of things, actually,' says PC Evans. 'First of all,

Mrs Pippa Stent is dropping the charges about the damage to her car.'

'Okay, thank you. That's good.'

'Yes, we couldn't identify clearly from the CCTV footage who bought the paint from the garage. They were wearing a baseball cap and Mrs Stent is convinced it wasn't you after all. She said she thought it might be your ... er ... Miss Munroe but under the circumstances it's not in our interest to pursue the matter further.'

'Pippa's cool with everything,' Luke says. 'I spoke to her today. She'll call by in a couple of days to see you.'

'We need to take some information regarding the accident at the house but, as I understand it, that will be part of a new investigation, so my colleagues in CID will be discussing that with you at a later date.'

'Is that it?'

'Yes, we'll be in touch soon but if, in the meantime, you could stay in the UK, that would be much appreciated by our colleagues in CID.'

'Of course.'

'Thank you. We'll be off now, then.' Evans and Doyle depart, leaving Luke and I alone.

'I'm so glad to see you,' I say. The relief that Luke is here envelops me.

'I came as soon as Leonard phoned,' says Luke. 'He's told me everything. I'm so sorry for not believing you about Alice, I mean Martha.'

'How has Mum taken it?' I ask. 'I think Leonard was playing it down.'

'I'll be honest,' says Luke. 'Not great.'

'I need to get home and see her. And the girls. Are they okay?'

'They're going to stay with Pippa for the night. I know you're desperate to see them, but what with your mum being so upset, I don't think it's the best place for them right now.'

I can't argue with that. 'Okay. But I'm seeing them tomorrow, no matter what.' I look down at our hands still entwined. 'Luke, there's something I need to ask you.'

I hear him sigh. 'This sounds ominous.'

'I believe you that you didn't sleep with Martha and I'm sorry for accusing you of that.'

'But? I can feel a but coming on.'

'Tom showed me a photograph of you and Martha. You were on the seafront. Arms around each other. Kissing.'

Luke looks genuinely confused. 'I promise you, Clare, I have never kissed Martha. Never. I don't even know where Tom would get a photograph from.'

'It's okay. I believe you. I just needed to check.'

'So what about the photo? I'd actually quite like to see it myself.'

'It's on Tom's laptop. I think it's probably photoshopped. I just needed to hear you say it.'

'Photoshopped? Tom always liked messing around with computers and cameras, I wouldn't be at all surprised. Why was he showing you that anyway?'

'Just causing trouble. Forget about it. He can't hurt us any more.' I'm not sure if I'm trying to convince myself as much as I am Luke. I give Luke a kiss and luxuriate in his response. It seems such a long time since we've kissed like this.

'Mmmm, I think we need to get you home, Mrs Tennison,' says Luke. He grins at me.

God, I've missed him. I'm so glad he's back.

Luke helps me dress in yet another set of clean clothes he brought me and after waiting for what seems an age to be discharged, we finally make our way out of the ward.

'Before we go, I want to see Martha,' I say.

'I'm not so sure that's a good idea,' says Luke. 'Why don't you wait for the dust to settle for a few days?'

'No. I need to see her. I want to know exactly where Alice is.' I can't bring myself to say Alice's body, although inwardly I acknowledge that is what we are dealing with now. 'We need to find her as soon as possible.'

Luke strokes my hair and looks into my eyes. 'The police can find that out. You don't have to.'

I place my hand over his and offer a small smile of gratitude for his thoughtfulness. 'I know they can, but I need something to focus on, to keep me positive. I'm scared if I stop now, I'm going to cave in. I can't rest until Alice is at rest.'

We take the lift up to the next floor and head round to the ward Martha has been moved onto, having come off the critical list last night. As we turn the corner onto the ward corridor, there is an obvious sense of urgency about the place. A nurse is dashing into a room on the left and as the door swings shut, I get a glimpse of several members of staff already in there. The sound of assured, yet urgent, voices hum from inside the room. Another nurse hurries out and grabs a trolley with what looks like a defibrillator on it.

I look at the whiteboard behind the desk which has a list of which patients are in which room. I scan the names. Kendrick, Alice – Room 3. I look now at the door numbers. My feet take me forwards, Luke holds my arm. The emergency is happening in Room 3.

I shake Luke's hand from me and I'm at the door, pushing it open. A male nurse is performing CPR on Martha. She's lying on the floor, a white cotton sheet beside her. It's been made into a noose.

I scream out her name. A male nurse spins round and is bundling me out of the door into Luke's arms. 'You can't come in,' he's saying. 'Stay out!' The door slams shut and Luke catches me as my knees buckle from under me. There are some visitor seats in a small communal area by the nurses' station. Luke takes me over and sits me down.

'She's tried to hang herself,' I say in disbelief. 'Why?'

Of all the things I thought she was capable of, suicide was not one of them. I thought Martha was the sort of person who always looked out for herself, without much care for anyone else, no compassion and no remorse. It looks as though I got that wrong.

Chapter 31

It took the American authorities nearly a week to find Alice, and then another four days to confirm her identity through DNA testing. The grave, as the officer referred to the shallow trough in the ground where Alice was found, was in the middle of a particularly dense part of the area, several metres away from the trail. Walkers, tourists, horse riders and beach-goers had all passed within a stone's throw of Alice, but not one had noticed her. It makes me sad and guilty that I was so close to her and never knew it.

So, now I am back in Florida again with Luke, Mum and Leonard to give Alice a proper burial.

We had thought about bringing Alice's body home to England but in the end had decided that, much as it pained us, America was her home and, no matter what we thought about Patrick Kennedy, he was Alice's father and it was only fitting that she should be buried next to him.

Leonard's relationship with Mum is out in the open now. I really don't know why they didn't tell me in the first place. I wouldn't have minded. I'm gradually coming to terms with the idea that Leonard is my father. It feels quite surreal when

I think too hard about it, so I let the notion wash over me from time to time and I try not to question it too much. It's difficult – it's not in my nature to let things go, but I'm trying to take a new approach to things. I'm trying for a more Luke-like approach to life. It's hard to break old habits, but I'm starting to let go, I've even cut down my working hours to three days a week now.

Leonard has taken on a new assistant and the business is just Carr & Tennison, Solicitors.

Luke is also making some changes. At the beginning of the next academic term, he's going to be teaching evening classes – art, of course. He says he wants to make a more regular financial contribution to the family. I like the new balance we have and the girls, Hannah in particular, are always so excited when it's my turn to take them to school and nursery. I'm sure the novelty will wear off soon for them, but for now I'm making the most of it. I've even taken up an invite of coffee with one of the other mums, who Pippa introduced me to. Mine and Pippa's friendship is back on track after our little blip and I value her company more than ever now.

It's an unusually chilly day in Florida and I look down at the coffin as the pastor says some words of comfort. Mum stands next to me and I hear her crying softly. I wish I could take away her pain.

Roma and Nathaniel have come to pay their respects. I was worried how Mum and Roma would be in each other's company, but all my fears were unfounded. They were united in grief for a young woman who was a daughter to them both. They spent some time together yesterday, talking about Alice. Roma was so good sharing her memories of Alice with Mum and although I know it pained Mum at times, I'm certain it has brought her some comfort and will continue to do so in the future. Roma gave Mum some family video footage of Alice taken over the years and an envelope with some more photographs in to replace the ones I had lost, which I now think Tom took from my car immediately after the accident.

'Thank you so much for coming,' I say to Roma before she leaves. 'And for taking the time to speak to Mum yesterday. It means a lot.'

Roma hugs me. 'You remind me of Alice,' she says, looking at me. 'Not just in your looks, but in your nature too. Alice would have been so proud to have you as her sister. She loved you very much.'

I choke back the tears. 'Thank you. And I always loved her too.'

I return to the car with Luke, leaving Mum and Leonard to follow in their own time.

'You okay?' asks Luke, putting his arm around me.

I rest my head on his shoulder. 'Yeah. I will be.' I look out the window of the car at the newly dug grave where Alice is buried. How I wish it could have been different. I remember when Alice first got in touch with us and I questioned whether I had ever actually missed her. I still don't know if I did, but I know with an unflinching certainty that I miss her now and will do for the rest of my life.

The door to the car opens and I look round as Mum and

Leonard climb in. Luke asks the driver to take us back to the hotel.

'We found you in the end, my darling Alice,' says Mum, looking at the grave as the car pulls away.

I don't think I've ever been more glad to see our home than I am when we pull up this morning. I managed to sleep on the flight but Mum is tired and goes straight to her room.

'I'll get off to the office,' says Leonard. 'I'll see you over the weekend, no doubt.'

I step forward and give Leonard a hug. 'Thanks for everything,' I say. 'For looking after Mum. It means a lot.'

'You don't have to thank me. It's what I do. I look after people.' He smiles. 'You included.'

I nod and give a half-smile. 'Thank you.'

'You know it's Tom's funeral tomorrow,' he says.

I nod again. 'I'm not going. Part of me feels bad. I feel I'm mourning for the person I thought I knew and yet when I think of the person he really was, I can't summon up the same emotion.'

'It's all still very raw. It will settle down eventually. It will leave a scar, but one that you can live with.'

I walk out to the drive with Leonard, my arm tucked in his. 'I know. I have a few scars already. One more to add to the collection,' I say to try to make light of the moment.

We stop at Leonard's car. 'Clare, there's something I've been meaning to ask you.

'Right,' I say slowly. 'You'd better ask, then.'

'That night on the pier with Tom. What did he say to you?'

'He didn't say anything,' I reply steadily.

'He didn't show you anything on his phone?'

'No. He didn't.'

Leonard appraises me through his beady eyes. 'I suppose if his phone was ever found, it would be damaged by the salt water by now.'

'Yeah. I guess so.'

There's a small silence as Leonard seems to be deciding whether to say something or not. In the end, I guess he decides against it. 'Right, well, I'd better get on.'

'Bye, Leonard.'

As soon as Leonard's car turns out of the gate and I hear the engine power away down the lane, I go straight indoors and up to my bedroom. I turn the lock on the door and go over to my wardrobe. I keep all my shoes in the bottom, neatly paired up on shoe rails. At the back stand my boots. I delve my hand into the long knee-high black-patent boots, which I rarely wear these days but can't quite bring myself to part with. From the toe of the boot, I pull out a black smartphone. Tom's phone, which I had stuffed in my pocket just before we went into the water.

Leonard's comment about Tom's phone has unnerved me. What if the salt water hasn't damaged it enough and the image he showed me is still there? I take the phone into the en suite, along with a pair of stilettos. I take the sim card out and with my nail scissors I cut it into three pieces, wrapping each piece individually in tissue paper and flushing them down the toilet. Then I wrap the phone in a towel to deaden the noise and smash the heel of my stiletto down on the screen. I hear the glass crack. I repeat this several times before I unfold the towel. The phone is smashed to smithereens.

I wrap what's left of the phone in the hand towel and put it into my gym bag, making a mental note to gradually dispose of the pieces over the next few days in various different bins around Brighton.

I go back downstairs and Luke is sitting at the computer. 'Just thought I'd check my emails while I had five minutes.'

'Good idea. I dread to think how many I've got. I've had my phone switched off the whole time we've been away.' I turn my phone on and after a minute it pings into life.

'Do you want a cup of tea?' asks Luke. 'The computer's on the go-slow.'

'Yeah, sure. I've missed a good British cup of tea.' I click on the emails. 'Forty-eight emails and I bet they're all junk,' I say, as I begin to quickly scroll through, looking out for any important ones.

I almost miss it as I whizz through the names, but then I see it. Two emails from Tom Eggar. I drop my phone as if it's burnt my fingers. 'Shit!'

'You okay? It's not broken is it?'

I grab my phone up from the floor. 'No. It's fine.' I tap on the first email entitled Plan B.

Hi Clare

I set this up while you were in America. I knew you had sussed out what Martha and I were up to. If you're reading this, then I guess you didn't want to come in on Plan A and I'm possibly in jail, which I sincerely hope not, or I've disappeared off the face of the earth where no one will find me or the money.

So, why am I emailing you? Well, Clare, this is Plan B aka REVENGE. Had you decided to accept my offer, then I would have cancelled this scheduled email.

Of course, I will never get the satisfaction of witnessing the effects of Plan B, but imagine me sitting on a beach somewhere hot with a nice cool beer, wondering how the hell you're going to explain this one to Luke.

Enjoy the rest of your life!

Tom

Frantically, I go to the next email from Tom and the subject heading makes me feel sick.

More than one cuckoo in the nest

The picture that Tom showed me that night on the pier slowly downloads on to the screen of my phone.

It's of me lying on a double bed stark naked. The photo is taken from the foot of the bed and I'm on my back, looking at the camera with half-opened eyes. I have one hand curled up, holding my hair away from my neck and the other resting on the inside of my thigh. It was taken the night Tom and I went drinking at The Crow's Nest.

All these years, I had no idea that he had taken these photos. I wonder now if it was more than just alcohol that had rendered me so useless.

I read the message.

There's a date, a week before I met Luke at the pub, the night Tom took me out drinking, with the words *Who's the daddy?* Underneath is Hannah's name and date of birth. It doesn't take a genius to work it out.

'That's odd,' says Luke, his voice somehow penetrating my thoughts. 'I've got an email from Tom.'

'Don't open it!' I shout. I race across the kitchen. 'It's a virus,' I say. 'Delete it. Don't even open it, it will corrupt your computer and all your files.' I grab the mouse, almost pushing Luke over.

'All right, calm down,' says Luke. 'How do you know it's a virus?'

'What else can it be?' I delete the email and then go to recently deleted files and delete it from there too. 'His account must have been hacked. I mean, he's dead, right? It's not like he can speak to us from the grave.'

Luke makes the tea and I repeat the procedure on my phone. Tom must have been able to set some sort of time delay on his emails, like a newsletter or something. I'll have to go through all his files and make sure everything has been deleted and then destroy the hard drive of his laptop, despite what he said about never storing anything on there, I'm not taking any chances. After that, I'll destroy all the memory sticks. I'm just glad we didn't hand anything over to the police. After I had been plucked from the sea, Leonard had the foresight to go to Tom's flat and grab the memory sticks and laptop. He wanted to keep the whole business of Tom stealing money out of the equation. We played it down and put Tom's death down to an accident. The police seemed happy with that.

I sit down next to Luke and smile. He doesn't ever have to know or doubt whether he's Hannah's father or not. I don't know for sure and I have no intention of going down the DNA-testing route. What good will it do? Luke is Hannah's father, biological or not. It doesn't matter.

'Love you,' I say.

Luke leans over and kisses me. 'Love you too, Babe.'

I hold onto his arms, squeezing them tight around me as I close my eyes in a bid to banish the image of the photograph from my mind and all that it represents.

Sometimes the darkest places are not in the pitch black of the night, when the moon is clouded over. Or when you close your eyes and track the sparks of colour dancing behind your eyelids. Sometimes the darkest places are when your eyes are wide open. When the sun shines brightly and the dust motes float in the beams of light.

Acknowledgements

As always, a big thank you to all the team at HarperImpulse, who have worked so hard in getting this book to publication.

Gratitude to my agent for continuing support and advice.

Much love and thanks to my family for their never-ending cheerleading!

Author Note

Dear Reader

Thank you so much for taking the time to read *Sister, Sister* and I do hope you enjoyed it.

I've always been fascinated by the family dynamics and not only how diverse they are today but also the diversity within each unit. Coming from a family of four children and having four children myself, I have experienced and witnessed how just one person can change the dynamics simply by walking into the room. Everyone may have been brought up by the same parents and to all intents and purposes received the same upbringing, yet their own personalities and sense of what's right and what's wrong can't help but come through. This can manifest itself in some sort of unseen undercurrent that can change the rhythm of the room, whether it be for the better or worse.

I wanted to bring this element into the story of Clare and Alice and show how Alice/Martha's arrival changed Clare's sense of her own being and position within the family and how this impacted on her relationship with her husband and mother.

I also wanted to look at preconceived ideas, or in the case of Clare and Marion, the fairytale ending they thought they would have once Alice came home. Clare, in particular, had a hard time matching her expectations with the reality of the situation and the rawness of her own emotions which surfaced. Of course, Clare had good reason to feel a sense of disparity but if Alice had really come home, would she automatically feel the love she expected she would? Marion was blinded to any uncertainties she might have had because she so wanted Alice home, not least to relieve her own guilt for letting her daughter go in the first place.

Some of these questions I have used as prompts in the book club question section.

Turning to the setting, Brighton is very local to me and is a city of great diversity, having a very cosmopolitan feel to it. There's an amazing buzz about the place and has earned it the nickname 'London by the Sea' and, yet, it still retains its English seaside town feel with ease.

Brighton is a major tourist city and when I started writing *Sister, Sister*, I used one of its then famous landmarks, the

Brighton Eye in the book. However, when it came to editing the book several months later, the Brighton Eye had been removed and replaced with the Brighton i360. Fortunately, the i360 worked just as well as the previous attraction so it didn't interfere with the plot.

I really enjoyed using Brighton as a setting and have used it in my previous books. I have no doubt it will appear in future books too!

As I say, thank you for taking the time to read *Sister, Sister*, do feel free to contact me through my website or social media, it's great hearing from readers. If you did enjoy the book, perhaps you would consider leaving a review, it doesn't have to be any more than a sentence or two, but they really are invaluable and very much appreciated.

Finally, if you are reading this book as part of a book club choice, there are some questions which you may like to consider.

Thanks so much, again!

Sue

x

Book Club Questions

1. Why was Marion so eager to accept Alice into the family? What emotions and thoughts affected her decision?

2. Is the bond between a mother and daughter/sister and sister strong enough to withstand a separation of twenty years?

3. If a stranger came into your life purporting to be your long-lost sister, how would you react?

4. Clare was a successful career woman, while Luke was the stay-at-home parent. Do you think it makes a difference to the child who their prime-carer is?

5. Do you think mothers experience more guilt towards their children when they work full-time than the father does?

6. Do you think grand-parents make as good carers for their grandchildren as the parents do? Does the child really mind who looks after them, as long as they are cared for and loved?

7. Do you think Clare was right not to tell Luke about the final email from Tom and the consequences? Is this fair to Luke and, indeed, to Hannah?

8. In the end, do you think Martha was sorry for her deception?

9. How do you think Marion and Clare will feel going forwards knowing they will never be reunited with Alice?